AND THEN THERE
WAS BILLY

Brandi

Baby, you are just as amazing as you say I am. You'll do great things, & if you need anything I've got ya, promise, here's to many more....

much ♡ always
Xavier
Neal

AND THEN THERE WAS BILLY

A Novel

Xavier Neal

iUniverse, Inc.
New York Lincoln Shanghai

And then there was Billy

iUniverse books may be ordered through booksellers or by contacting:

iUniverse
2021 Pine Lake Road, Suite 100
Lincoln, NE 68512
www.iuniverse.com
1-800-Authors (1-800-288-4677)

This is a work of fiction. All of the characters, names, incidents, organizations, and dialogue in this novel are either the products of the author's imagination or are used fictitiously.

ISBN-13: 978-0-595-40818-4 (pbk)
ISBN-13: 978-0-595-85181-2 (ebk)
ISBN-10: 0-595-40818-4 (pbk)
ISBN-10: 0-595-85181-9 (ebk)

Printed in the United States of America

Thank you to God, my family, Billy's family, my friends, those who said I couldn't, and last but not least Billy.

PART I

VACATION

CHAPTER 1

The Start

I have the urge to act like a kid again and bother my parents with the 'are we there yet' question. They'd probably just turn around, tell me to shut up, and that I need to go back to sleep. I guess when you're sixteen you shouldn't ask questions like that. After all you're not supposed to care about the concept of time or your surroundings, just clothes, music, or the opposite sex. It's written in the big book of rules teenagers need to live by in order to survive. A book parents try to read but don't understand, and a book teens understand but don't try to read.

Smiling to myself I look over at Mia who looks like an angel until I see the river of drool flowing its way towards one of my favorite feather pillows. Ew. I damn sure don't plan on sleeping with that thing now that her slobber has stained it. Do you understand how gross it is to have someone's spit on your pillow, just staining your pillowcase, before seeping its way through to the actual pillow, where the smell will stay even after the spit is gone? Maybe I'll just give it to her. Slouching down I look out the back Suburban window. I never thought I'd see so many rusty, discolored cars, some with duct tape windows, others with cracked windshields, rolling on dubs. Now I can understand if your car is at least clean and has all of its windows, but these cars look like they're just about to collapse. Dubs are meant to be placed on clean, good-looking cars, not scrap metal. Only in Ft. Worth, Texas can you see things like this on a daily basis.

Checking the time I grit my teeth. Fifteen minutes until five, fifteen minutes until we're there, fifteen minutes until my living nightmare begins. Now you may think I'm being over dramatic, but trust me I'm not. This is where Satan left his spawns to prey on the happiness of your average human. I always thought I was a good person, but somewhere down the line God decided, hm, Kie's life doesn't have enough problems, so let's send her to hell on earth. You think maybe I'm overreacting. Overreacting? This place ruined my childhood.

"Can I hang out with you?" I ask pushing up my falling light green glasses wishing not to get my eight year old hopes up. Not really getting an answer, but a disgusting, disgraceful look I slouch.

One of them snatches the basketball in the front lawn chair next to me, "No nerd. Now go play with yo' dolls or some'n."

"You don't have to be so mean about it," I stand up defending myself. I may be a girl, a flimsy girl, even a bit of a nerdy girl, but I still know how to look after myself.

"What are you gonna do 'bout it? Cry?" the other boy taunts from the yard in front of us.

"Shut up," I yell to him balling up my fists like I'm actually going to do something.

The one in front of me jumps to defend his friend. "Don't talk to him that way," he pushes my shoulder back.

Gasping I push back, appalled that he would ever push a girl especially that hard. Before I know it, the two of us are in the middle of the yard rolling around. One minute he's got me in a head lock, the next I'm pulling on the miniature fro sprouting from his head. This hostility continues until he rolls over my glasses that have leapt from my face. I'm dead.

You would wonder in the back of my mind wouldn't I at least give it another try now that I'm all grown up and mature. Acing a geometry exam, butt naked, in the middle of the parking lot, with my entire school watching, would by far be easier.

Our car comes to a screeching halt as we pass by our stop. Bad directions, breaks screeching, parents about to yell at each other, oh yea, its vacation time alright.

Mia groans as she begins to lift her head off of my pillow. Glancing at me, she asks with her eyebrows what just happened. Poor girl, she doesn't know what she's got herself into with my family. Soon enough she'll be rethinking about if she ever wants to go anywhere with us again.

I just shake my head and wipe my lips off, giving her the sign to do the same. There's no way I'd let her embarrass herself in front of the people we're about to see. Folding my blanket, I listen to my parents argue as my dad puts the car in reverse.

Entering the neighborhood I've never felt safe in, I clutch my blanket tighter. I can remember when my grandmother was alive. She used to tell us stories about how Big Mama, her best friend, helped raise my mother and her siblings. The tales usually rambled on and I found myself sleeping with my eyes closed around intermission between the third and fourth story.

She's lived in this neighborhood since my mom was a kid and apparently has been raising children, sometimes her own, sometimes not. This place has never been a safe part of town, but one thing is for sure, in this crime capital and poverty, her house is the sanctuary every one's looking for.

The house is just as dirty as it has always been. With mud stains plastered all over it, it makes you question has it ever been cleaned once in its time of existence, while the cracks from head to toe make you wonder who is watching you from the inside. They're so big they look like peepholes. This house doesn't even deserve to be called white, or a house for that matter. It needs to be called a heap of materials to make a shelter that's neglected from all sorts of care.

Turning his slightly hairy fifty year old knuckles white, he begins to mumble profanity underneath his breath. "Learn to tell someone before they pass by the place," my dad says continuing in reverse.

My mother, the last person you really want to snap at, lifts her claws as if to reach for my father's slightly chunky chocolate neck. Her finger nails are like cat claws, they're pretty sharp, not fake, and usually in attack mode. She resists the urge to dig them into him. "I did tell you! Long before we got up here!"

Jerking it into park, my father blows up like a bomb whose designator had been delayed for a moment. "You did not!" He rips the keys out the ignition. "Do I need to explain to you the definition of the word long?"

I try not to laugh, but it's hard. Every time he drives this exact argument happens. I could recite word for word what is coming next. 'Whatever Darryl, I told you within enough time for you to prevent our family from getting whiplash.' My mother will say this in approximately five seconds.

"Whatever Darryl! I told you within enough time for you to prevent our family from whiplash!" My mother's dark brown face is now in my step-father's. Being forty two and that temperamental you think it would be due to menopause, but my mother's just naturally that aggressive.

Must they do that so loud? This might be embarrassing for quite a few teen-agers, but Mia knows my parents fight like pit bulls. It's sad because she finds it just as funny as I do. See normal teenagers would be scared their parents constant fighting would lead to divorce or separation. In my house, it just means everything is all right. Worrying will begin when they become lovey-dovey.

I grab my pillow from behind me before looking at Mia whose attention is on something outside. Oh no. I hope its not ... I know it is. Them. Guys. Ugh. She's watching the game of basketball in the next yard on their court. Not really their court since Big Mama owns both houses, but you know what I'm saying. Her tongue is barely sticking out to the side, like its going to make its way across but never moves. I know that means she's attracted to one or more of them. God help me.

"You never told me there were going to be hot boys here," she looks back at me.

Looking on the ground for my flip-flops I reply to the preposterous comment, "Why would I lie to you like that?"

"Excuse me, but uh have you looked outside?" She points out the window.

It's not have I looked outside, but do I *want* to look out there? I'm only going to see the same juvenile delinquents that harassed me when I was younger, except of course now their older with deeper voices. I don't doubt that their maturity level is the same.

I shake my head, "No thanks. Do you know what kind of STDs and other types of highly contagious diseases those *things* carry?" Pausing I take a quick glance at them. "Just by looking you could catch one." Hopping out of the car I pull down my jean shorts. "I'm telling you Mia trouble is their first and last name."

"Yeah well if troubles their first and last name it's my middle 'cause I know I wouldn't mind gettin' in between a couple of them," she smirks getting out behind me.

"Did you have to go there?" I laugh and shake my head tossing my backpack strap over my shoulder.

"Yo Billy," the one with braids stops the game to point. "Check out the hun-nies," he cocks his head to the side while cradling the ball under his arm.

"I think they could use a lil' help," Billy says while grazing his bottom lip with his tongue. "Let's go DK."

"Hey the yummy ones are headed our way," she mumbles putting on her purple backpack while fixing her hair.

"Do you ladies need some help?" Billy's eyes quickly but not slyly process my measurements.

Gross. Now it's one thing to check me out, but to do it while I'm giving you the evil eye isn't bright. It wouldn't be a surprise if his stupid actions were a result of smoking too much weed.

"Yeah a little would be good," Mia smiles at DK and opens the back of the Suburban.

Rolling my eyes, I turn the corner of the Suburban. I don't need a 'big muscle man' to help me. I am fine and dandy alone. Reaching for my bags I feel a hand touch my lower back.

"Here let me get that," Billy removes his hand after my quick wicked glare at it. Trying to hide his fear with a crooked smile, he reaches for my bags.

He better watch himself because my wrath is not a pretty thing, and believe me in the end it'll leave you for dead.

Approaching the run down house, my attention focuses on the dirt and random strands of brown grass that they call a yard. I see a younger version of myself crying causing me to tense up as I remember all the evil they use to cast from right there. As the wire gate swings behind me closing loudly, I step up onto the porch to follow them into the house.

You can tell by that gleam in her eye that she's more than glad we get to walk behind them. Really, must she stare at their behinds as we go? With baggy jersey shorts not much can be seen through them, not that I'm looking or anything.

"Thanks," Mia wets her lips, pouts them, and then returns them to their normal form.

Goodness. What is it about these types of guys that makes her find them so irresistible? Maybe it's the way their pants sag off their hips revealing the days color choice of boxers, or maybe it's the way their shirts cling to them after a hard day of ball. Who knows, it could just be the way they look at you with that cocked head, half smile, and beautiful eyes.

After traveling down the dark narrow hallway passing a bathroom, as well as two other rooms, one in which my parents will be in, we arrive in our back room that's one of the nicer ones in this roach motel.

"Wha's yo name anyway?" Billy asks me politely. I figured that much. I'm sure if he remembered I would have been carrying my own bags like I wanted.

"Kie," I answer slipping out of my backpack strap. Satan's first born sure is forgetful of the people's lives he manages to ruin.

I can tell the name hasn't quite registered in what's left of his baked brain. He's more than likely scanning names of girls he's messed around with from out of town. It's not like they tend to stay *here*. "Kie … sounds familiar."

"Sure it does. I use to try to always hang out with you when we were young. You were always asking me was I gonna cry when you picked on me." I refresh his memory walking away to the king size bed. It's not like he cares. The only thing floating through his overcooked mind is 'can I bone her?'

"The skinny, nerdy girl who wore the really thick green glasses all the time?" his eyebrows dart forward as I flop onto the middle of the bed.

"Yeah," I answer as Mia sits next to me still staring at DK with that smirk on her face. I'm about ready to pull that tongue out of her mouth and smack her with it. Whatever it takes to bring her back to reality.

"Fo' real?" he continues to ponder over the thought as he licks his lips and rubs his hands together.

What's he gloating about? Something tells me that I don't want to know, "You can go now. I'm sure some poor defenseless girl is just waiting for the two of you to deflower her."

Grunting a laugh he nods at me getting one last good look. Better take it because if his eyes continue to stay pasted on me they won't be in his head much longer. "A'ight. We'll see you later. DK," he strolls out of the room, leaning to one side like his equilibrium is off.

Rolling my eyes I let them land on grinning Mia. She's happy about either the fact she plans to hook up with him and can't wait or that he wants her and she finds it funny. "What?"

"What do you mean what? What?" She questions back folding her arms across her chest.

"I know that twisted mind of yours is coming up with something and I wanna know what it is."

"Nothing," she plays innocent revealing her acting skills, which have room for much needed improvement.

"Come on Mia. Be real."

Her fingers comb through her long brown hair, "Nothing. I'm just thinking about how much fun it would be to hang out with them while we're here."

"If by hang out with them you mean not, than yes," I nod and slide down to a laying position.

"Aw come on Kie, so they ruined your childhood memories, get over it. They're hot and want us, so let's at least have some fun with them," she pleads pulling all of her hair into a bun.

Does she realize what she's asking me to do? It's not something simple like brain surgery or rocket science. My best friend is asking me to let the wounds of my most sensitive years heal like you heat up leftovers in a microwave. She's got another thing coming if she supposes I'm going to just disregard my pain and go for this wacky plan of hers.

A few hours later we're doing the same thing we do when we're home. Nothing. Just singing along to the radio, which is mediocre for us. We're always singing along because it's great practice. This summer is all about the singing, the dancing, and the preparation needed for the spring contest we're going to enter. Andrea, Natalie, me, and Mia are the group. We don't really have a name yet or the money for it, but we're on our way. All summer is devoted to gathering enough cash to showcase our talent to the world. We're going to be big. Big!

I move my head to the beat of the song as I turn the page in a fashion magazine. I don't understand these people who have millions of dollars and want to spend it on things that look like someone just cut and glued fabrics together to make one big mess.

There's a sudden knock at the door before it's cracked open, "Yo can we holla at the two of you fo' a minute?" Oh yay, the man with a penis for a brain. I wonder what *lame* excuse the two of them came up with this time to try to talk to us. There are always two of them, so where is his intellectually challenged wanna be twin?

"Sure," Mia calls him in. Billy follows in behind him staring directly at me with a smirk frozen on his face. Is his face permanently stuck in that cocky open position?

They stand there staring at us. Why is time moving, but their mouths' still aren't?

"Did you come in for a reason or just to gawk over Mia's low cut shirt?" I look at DK whose eyes are caught in the act. Her shirt does have a plunging neckline, but you try living in Texas. You can fry an egg on the sidewalk Christmas morning and then go swimming that afternoon. It's like there are two seasons here, hot and hotter.

"I came," he turns his head with attitude at me, "to ask you two ladies if you wanted to go to the club tonight."

He just had to tempt her didn't he? Her dark brown eyes are going to get all big, her jaw's going to fall, and she'll turn to me with that look that says she wants to go. If I didn't know any better I would say he knew she'd want to go to the club rather than being stuck in this house playing solitaire while listening to the radio DJs make asses of themselves. Sure I want to go out, but with thug and thugalicous? No. No. No.

"Well ..." Mia slowly turns towards me, grin growing with her eyes that are just screaming please, "Can you two give us a sec? I need to talk to Kie about something." She crawls off the bed. Wait, what? Talk to me about what? I bet we're going to argue.

"Sure." The two of them walk out so fast turtles could do laps around them. Closing the door after their exit, Mia turns around eyes darted, lips clinched, and arms crossed. Man your battle station.

"Are you going to be uncompromising?" She leans against the door. I simply nod. "Is it really that unbelievably awful to be around them?"

"Yes," I bluntly remark. Someone doesn't understand the concept of hatred.

Her missiles are loading up, she aims, and she fires, "Why Kie? All I wanna do is go out and have a bit of fun rather than playing stupid radio games!" She blows up. I make a crashing sound under my breath as I hit the headboard with my head. Usually she'll just try the easy approach, by making it seem more fun than it could possibly be and I give in because well you know, I'm a good friend. Maybe she knows the nice approach isn't strong enough for this. "Is that so wrong?"

"Yes."

"It is not, and you know it. Damn it Kie! I'm not trying to make you miserable, but I just wanna have some fun. Come on Kie ..." she whines coming towards me. Talk about annoying me into saying yes.

"No," I cock my head to the left and open the magazine once more.

"Look," she snatches my magazine away. Whoa, enemy on home front. "I don't care what you want. We are going out. You're going to suck it up, and deal with it. Now stop being lazy and go look through your bag for something to wear," she tosses the magazine inches in front of my feet.

Damn. I'm all out of ammunition. The aggression in her eyes is telling me she's serious. Attempting to reload, I get stopped by the finger. You know the pointed index finger that possesses some strange type of power to shut people up.

"Not another word," she reinforces. "Get your stubborn, whiny ass up and go get dressed."

I may have lost the battle, but believe me the war will be mine. Besides, she'll owe me because that's what best friends do. We come to a medium. "Alright."

Confused Mia stutters to answer, "What?"

"Alright." What else does she want me to say? We can have a hot foursome as soon as we get back?

She shakes her head, "Ok, Kie this isn't funny. Toying with my emotions is totally not cool."

I laugh at her. She's really trippin' now. "I'm not messin' with you."

"Ahhh!!!" She squeals clapping. "You actually gave in!" I hesitantly nod as she throws her arms around me. "Hey DK!"

"Yeah?" He opens the door, his beady eyes checking out Mia once more. Can we say slime ball?

"We're up for it. You drivin'?" Does he have to drive? Wouldn't it be safer to walk through oncoming traffic, at night, on the highway? Heaven forbids I trust someone who had to take the test six or seven times to get their license.

"Yeah me or Billy will drive," he nods. Oh you or the retard that doesn't seem like he can talk, even better. This night is just shaping up beautifully. Death should be calling any minute now.

"When we leavin'?" She drops her arm from around me. Good I feel less crowded now.

"Can you be ready in about an hour?" His tongue grazes his lips slowly before pulling it back in. I wish that thing would stay in its possibly gold tainted cage. With a nod from Mia he continues, "A'ight then. See you pretty girls soon." He turns around closing the door behind him.

We both start in our bags. She's got a dazed look of enchantment on her face. I hope she just doesn't fall for his off the wall horrible charm. There's no way I could handle it if she began to like him or even worse fell in love with him. I couldn't deal with anyone falling in love with either of them. Only something tragic could come from it.

After I informed my mother what was going on, not like she could disagree with me, being nearly drunk and all, Mia and I came back in the room and put on our favorite CD. I have to admit that getting ready to go out is always fun, especially to the right music. Every girl has that one CD that gets her all pumped up to go and dance. A couple of times we've gotten so pumped up while dancing around the room we got too tired to go out.

Mia is curling her extremely long brown hair. No matter what she does with it, it looks absolutely beautiful. From the minute she wakes up, even after a hard day of nothing but sweating, it still manages to look great. Some people think because her hair is so long that she's got extensions, but she doesn't. It flows from years of careful growing and envy. Every girl has wished to have that Barbie like hair, pretty and perfect. It just so happens she got that lucky. She use to tell me stories about girls who tried to cut if off while she was sleeping because jealousy got the better of them. I'd never snip away the thick locks I've spent years braiding, twisting, and curling. They're my friend as much as she is.

"Kie, how does my hair look in the back?" She asks fluffing it out some. Anyone who spends over an hour washing, combing, and brushing their hair deserves it that long.

"Cute and all curled," I smile curling my hair inward to shape my face. I'm going for the plain and simple, cute thing. My hair isn't nearly as long as hers. See my hair stops a little above the middle of my back. People think its weave too, but it took years and years for me to grow this.

"Good," she pushes a few loose strands behind her ears. "So how do I look?" She steps away from the dresser where the mirror does us no good. The mirror leans forward, which is creepy because I always think it's going to fall.

"Like you're about to break some poor boy's heart," I glance at her outfit up and down. It's quite funny how Mia is shaped. Most guys just want that Jennifer Lopez look in a Hispanic girlfriend. You know small boobs and a "huge" behind. Well Mia's got a chest a tad bigger and a butt that even Jennifer Lopez would envy her for. I'm talking about junk in the trunk, but not like us black girls. Some say she's got a couple of black genes in her.

She never goes wrong with what she wears. Take tonight's outfit. Tight, low rise, pocket-less, light wash blue jeans, with a sleeveless black shirt that has three slits down the front but stops just in time to see her belly button that has a few sparkles around it, which she learned from me. Always lookin' hot. Lucky.

"If I'm lucky," she mumbles before bending over to grab some money out of her purse. "You know I may break some poor boy's heart, but you girl ... you look like you're ready to chain some guy up, make him your love slave, and then leave him to starve," she laughs flopping on the bed to put on her shoes.

I let out an airy giggle. As nice as it was supposed to sound, it still came out a bit messed up. "Uh ... thanks?" I laugh again turning off my curling iron.

"You look irresistible," she fastens the side of her black heel shoes that have just one strap before the toes and one around the ankle. "I'm sure Billy won't be able to resist himself."

"And why would I want Billy's attention?" I pull up on my black tube top.

She stands up and pulls her hair back to one side while watching me put on my strappy shoes that look just like hers, but with a little more heel since I'm shorter. "Because it's obvious that you like the fact he's attracted to you. So what better way to keep his attention than by wearing those tight, low rise, black pants, with that sparkly belt and tube top? Come on Kie. You're outfit screams seduction."

"Whatever you say," I smile getting up off the squeaky bed. When you flop onto it you can just feel the mattress go down to the ground like it's never going to pop back up again. It fits right in with everything else in this house.

Knock. Knock. Oh yay, the jackass and his friend are here. Let the party begin. I stand back up as Mia goes to answer the pealing beaten to death door.

"Come on Kie," Mia calls me from the door now smirking widely. Oh no. DK is probably standing in front of her looking at her like she's a piece of Thanksgiving turkey that he's just ready to carve.

"One sec, let me get my cash and ID," I bend over pulling them out of my purse that's sprawled out across the floor next to Mia's. The room seriously looks like someone went on a violent rampage searching for something.

I wonder if the guys actually pulled up their pants, ironed their shirts and went for the gentlemen look. Yeah right. I stop once more looking around to see if I am missing something. My phone. Should I bring it even though I don't want to?

"Mia, ask dickhead and his sidekick do either of them have a cell phone," I stare at mine still debating.

"They both do," she turns around pressing her lips together with raised eyebrows. There's the 'he looks fine …' look. Brace yourself Kie not to care how good Billy may look. No matter how attractive he might appear I will restrain myself from flirting even the least bit.

I walk over to the door where Mia is waiting. "Let's roll," I hit the light not letting either of them get a glance at me. I shut the door behind me before stopping in front of the door on my right.

My parents are staying in the room exactly next to me, but it's ok because they can't hear me since our walls don't touch each others. They don't listen in on my conversations or go through my stuff, so it's not like it matters. They trust me, so it's no big deal. I lean against the door with my ear pressed tightly. It's quiet, a little too quiet. If my parents aren't arguing it's not a good sign. If I'm lucky my mom is passed out from the welcome back card game that was accompanied by lots of beers while my dad is worn out from the drive. I knock twice and wait for any sound or movement.

"Mom … I'm out. Be back around two or three." No response. Must be sleeping. "Big Mama," I call down the hall screaming into DK's ear. My bad, did I hurt him? "Leave the front door unlocked for us ok?"

Big Mama shuffles her seventy year old feet our way while humming a gospel hymn. "Ok sweetie. You girls stay out of trouble and you boys be nice to them, ya hear?"

"Yes Big Mama," I smile at her as I wait for her to get to the door behind us. "We'll be good."

"All right now," she says with her country accent that she's always had. She's just so adorable. I'll make sure to spend time with her within the next few days. "Billy you watch out for them, ya hear?"

"Yes Big Mama," he goes out the door behind DK. No one ever disagrees with Big Mama. The little old lady may be sweet, but she knows how to lay the smack down when it's time.

I smile and follow out behind them letting Big Mama close the door. This night can't be all that bad can it? I mean something good has to come out of it. You know the saying, go in with your head up and come out that way. Might as well try it.

"How old are you two girls anyway?" DK asks making his way around the cars that are crowding the driveway.

"Sixteen going on seventeen," Mia answers. Yeah we'll let her answer all the questions given by him.

"We got a couple of young ones here," DK elbows Billy making him chuckle a little cute laugh. A bit low, kind of childish but still the way a guy should laugh.

"We're what two, three years behind you, even though the evidence of that isn't apparent right now," I smirk as DK hits the alarm on his black Mercedes four door that's sitting on dubs. Good god. How on earth did a chump like that get this car? Probably stole it.

I see DK turn around and give me a bit of a glare. As hard as he keeps trying to be nice to me, I just can't help but be as rude as possible to him. Any guy who treats women like Kleenex damn sure doesn't deserve any respect.

"Kie, be nice," she gets shotgun as Billy walks around the car to get in the back with me. Yuck. Did I ask for him to invade my space?

"Trying," I answer with a bit of an attitude as I get in.

"Well try harder," she raises her voice. What does she want me to do; jump in his lap and say take me baby. I really want to grip my hands firmly around his neck and squeeze until his ego pops along with his misshaped oval head.

"Ok," I nod. When she turns back around, I roll my eyes. You may like him dear, but if he isn't careful I'm going to knee him in the balls and make his jaw click.

As the two of them make small talk in the front I stare out the window. I need to know my surroundings and where this fool is taking me. Damn sure wouldn't want to end up somewhere where it was just us. I could guarantee you that I'd come out of that situation with a new car.

Tree … tree … light pole, tree, light pole … bush, light pole, where are we headed? I've never seen so many trees and random light poles a day in my life. I always thought that you drove down the highway to clubs, with other cars, but I guess they're avoiding the public eye for some criminal reason.

Now I'm just listening to the radio, keeping myself calm when I glance out the corner of my eye to see Billy staring at my chest. Ew. Can you believe that? Does he not understand the fact I didn't enjoy him checking me out earlier, and I damn sure don't like it now. An occasional look I could handle, but this boy is nonstop staring. The kind that makes me want to walk out the house in long baggy jeans and a huge t-shirt. I shift my weight around and cross my legs. Ok, so I look good, not to sound conceited, but that's no reason to continue gawking. He's probably coming up with perverted things in his mind that he'd love to do to me. News Flash: You Will Never Get The Chance To Fulfill Your Fantasies. Finally he looks away. Good. I hope we're almost there because I'm sick of listening to Mia pretend to be interested in what DK's dumb ass has to say.

At last we're here. Here being a tall dark building with almost no lights surrounding it. Great, it's an old warehouse with a parking lot forever long with predictable trashy cars. I should have known better than to think it would be downtown with the rest of the clubs. No, no, the club they take us to just has to be right next to a dark alley where some poor vulnerable girl can get hurt or raped. Spiffy place isn't it?

"How did you get this car?" Mia asked as he puts it in park. Good question. Here's a better question though; why the hell is he parking way back here?

"When I signed my record deal this was part of it," he winks at her.

Now Mia is interested, "You have a record deal?"

"Yeah I got signed a few months ago," he nods. "Why does that turn you on in some way? Ya know, to date a rapper?"

Did he have a giant bowl of himself for breakfast? Everything is either a dating tactic or flattery to himself. How desperate do you have to be to say something like that to try to pick up a girl? Really, now have some self respect jackass.

"A. I'm not dating you. B. 'Dating' a rapper in general doesn't turn me on. Dating a fine, sexy guy with real talent does," she taps his chest a little.

Dismissed. Way to go Mia. Finally she shuts him down. That's my girl.

"Oh well, you can have yo' shot at datin' a rapper before he hits it big baby. Ya know, hook up wit' him before you can't even get to him," DK unlocks the doors. I laugh under my breath.

"I would, but I need a real man to handle me. Not some little boy whose ego is bigger than anything he has to offer," she glances down at his crotch, licks her lips, and looks back up.

DK licks his lips and smiles. Mia is now back to herself. If the two of them keep this up, this night will be more entertaining than I thought.

I get out of the car and stand along side Mia who is ruffling her hair. Ooh she is feeling feisty now. Mia is totally prepared to take these Fort Worth boys by storm.

"Ready Kie?" She asks me pressing her lips together.

"Of course," I smile widely. I can't help it. That fight in the car just made my night.

"What are you smiling about?" She asks following behind DK.

"Nothing," I shrug. "Just glad we're about to have some fun." So I lied. Forgive me. If I told her the real reason I was smiling she'd give me some kind of smart remark, and then that could lead to a mini argument that I don't want.

"We'll I'm glad. It's nice to see you smile. I think this is the first time since we've been here you have," she nudges me in the side.

Continuing to cross the parking lot I mutter, "Mmhm." The boy might as well have parked in outer space. He's got me walking miles to get into a warehouse full of horny people who have decided tonight is the night they want to grind on someone while they're full of liquor. How many different ways can I thank him for this wonderful pleasure? Let me count with my knee in his balls.

"How's it hangin' Big J?" DK greets the bouncer slapping hands with a quick one-arm embrace.

My eyes rise to the six foot three, bald, black body guard. He's so big I wonder does he eat the people thrown out the club or the ones who try to sneak in. Damn if I lived here I wouldn't come with him patrolling over the line like they were snacks waiting to be eaten. His snug fitting black shirt and jeans makes me wonder, does he believe that black is really slimming?

"Jus' checkin' out all these fine females," he sucks his teeth at a few of the skanky girls in line. Surprise, surprise.

Rubbing his chin with his hand DK glances too, "Righ', righ'."

"Speakin' of fine ladies …" he sucks his bottom lip in as he gazes over Mia and me, "who are these two hunnies you brought?" The bouncer is looking at us like we're the objects of his next dessert conquest. I'm a bowl of milk chocolate and Mia's butter pecan. As he continues looking at us like he's in search of a spoon, I move behind Billy hoping that will stop all the drool coming out of his mouth.

"Kie and Mia," DK points to us when our names leave his filthy mouth. "They're here on vacation. Ya know, I thought we'd try and show 'em a good time." He pauses as the bouncer nods. "So can you hook us up, ya know, let us in?"

Debating for a second as if he's deciding for syrup, sprinkles, or both, he makes his decision, "Yeah sure, ya know you my main man." The bouncer opens the thick steel metal door letting us through. So he has a connection to a club, big deal. Connections are no big deal any more; no matter how much he thinks it makes him look better.

"Thanks," DK says to him as we pass by. Our asses are now huge donuts to the giant. He should really spend less time eating and more time in the gym because all that food is really showing. All that skin pouring over his jeans and breaking his shirt really can make a person change their mind on wanting to go in.

We walk in to be greeted by a live porn show. Ok, I'm over exaggerating a tad. My eyes roam the room analyzing the sorts of people in here. On the dance floor I see too many girls with their asses hanging out of a mini skirt or short shorts along with so much cleavage I wonder why they came in anything more than a bra. Guys on the floor are making me feel like there's only one team in the NBA. Their saggy jeans do nothing more than prove it really is a challenge for them to pull up their pants.

The girls sitting at tables have their heads arched towards the floor like they're detectives. They even have clothing that's sleek, like their trying not to be noticed. Shuddering them off, I scan the crowd of gathered guys in various places that resemble the ones on the dance floor.

Other than the people I like the scenery. The multicolor lights that are dancing around the place emphasize the music that's blaring loudly. Hip-hop is strictly what I'm into when it comes to dancing. Sure I'll let an R&B song slide here and there, but when it comes to the best I like those beats that go hard. This club hits my taste pretty well. As shocking as it is that they pinpointed that right about me, I have no confidence whatsoever anything else will be on cue.

"Hey Kie," Mia leans over talking in my ear as we follow them up the stairs. "I see this fine guy over there eyeing me ..." she points to him. That's smart. Point to the guy. Did she think about what if this guy rolls up on her and looks like Jason gone through a blender seventeen times?

"I see him," I nod. It looks like the bar is going to be my date for the night.

"Yum," she giggles flipping her hair out.

Laughing a little as the rapper with no talent and his loyal pal stop at the bar, I pretend to agree.

"What it do?" DK greets the bartender sitting down at the edge of the slightly curved wooden bar.

"Ya know, gettin' these females drunk," he laughs tossing the cup towel over his shoulder. He's younger than the bouncer, but not that much older than the people in the club. The marker sized, light skinned brother looks like DK's type, which really makes me not want to socialize let alone order from him. Besides anyone who is proud of putting females in a vulnerable state deserves the same treatment as all other people I disgust.

"Yeah," DK laughs as he sits on the barstool. "Think you can hook us up tonight Jay?"

He looks around suspiciously as if a cop is seated somewhere near. "You got the cash?"

DK nods. I'm sorry I must be confused. Why does he need cash if he's getting a hook up?

"How many?" he says under his breath while cleaning out a shot glass.

"Four tonight. We've got youngns." A motion is made towards us.

Mia and I impatiently wait to comprehend what's going on. Checking once more before silently answering yes he puts the shot glass down in front of DK who slips a twenty in it.

"What the hell is that about?" Mia leans over to whisper in Billy's ear.

"You've got to be twenty-one to drink and none of us are. We pay the bartender a little extra, and he lets us drink without carding us." He answers loudly enough for me to hear too. She nods before he says something else, "Yo I'm gonna go holla at some of my boys. I be back," Billy smiles strolling off. Great, one down now the other one.

"I'm going to go talk to that boy eyeing me," Mia nudges me in the side. Wait don't leave me with Satan's child.

"Alright, I'll be here," I sit down on the barstool one away from DK. Just how hard is it to pay more than five dollars for decent cologne and to shower away that musty smell?

A few minutes later the realization kicks in that Mia's gone, DK's talking, and Billy's probably pushing up on some girls. What's there for me to do? Even in the club I have nothing to do. How pathetic is this?

"Hey can I get a drink over here?" I call to the bartender waving at him a little.

"Just one sec," he says to me as he continues to flirt with a chicken head. Rolling my eyes about the girl I shake my head. It isn't enough they create problems in relationships and madness in the streets, but they have to come into clubs and start mess up in here too. It's a damn shame. Just one sec? Yeah try just one hour.

"Ya know this place doesn't serve juice boxes," DK laughs turning towards me. Jokes are not his strong point.

"You must have ordered the keg with a straw. You know they throw in a free blow up doll with that. It'll be the only action you see all night." If he hasn't realized yet he's not messing with some uptight bimbo who has no idea how to deal with him in his little quirks.

He smirks and nods. "Who shoved a library book up your ass?" He tilts his head to the side perking up his voice.

"The same person who lied and told you that you have a big dick," I say shrugging my shoulders pretending to be excited about something. When I do that, it tends to piss people off more than just being a smart aleck. His eyes are squinted, his lips sucked in, and his weight is slowly being shifted like he's about to get real serious.

"Watch yourself," he threatens me with his 'scary' finger.

"Or what? You're going to send one of your ex, one night, love struck, future groupies to come get me?" I rest my elbow on the bar and then my chin on my balled up fist.

He growls. He actually growled at me. What is he again? Oh yeah I forgot he's a dog, and that's what they do. Growl, bark, hump, roll over, eat, poop, and drool, all the skills he's mastered. He gets up, still upset, and moves back towards the stairs.

Laughing I turn back around to face the bar. Wow, someone can dish it, but not take it. It's really not hard to get that this is no longer a man's game. Anything he throws at me, I can handle.

"Excuse me," I call politely to the bartender who has seemed to forget that I want a drink. I patiently wait for him to stop flirting with that girl and come to me. I swear if I keep waiting like this I'll never get a drink. Why is it these guys with huge egos don't understand normal conversation and questions? It sounds ironic, but I'm not in the mood to be rude to a stranger. "Excuse me," I call to him again. This time he puts up the one finger. Stupid universal finger. All right if it's a bitch he wants that's what he'll get. "Yo, idiot with a cock for a brain."

He pauses to look at me unhappily. In fact if I didn't know any better *he* looks annoyed.

"Oh I'm sorry was that rude?" I mock his attitude with my tone of voice.

"What can I get you?" He asks me like nothing's wrong, pretending I haven't been calling him for the past 5 minutes; like I'm just another girl he'll flirt with and promise a free drink to. Fool please.

"A sex on the beach," I answer with a huge smile.

"I think I can take care of that order myself," Billy smiles plopping down next to me. Must he sit so close? I forgot DK is allergic to girls who speak their minds. What makes Billy be gone?

"Nope," I snap and look back at the bartender.

"Have that drink for you in a sec," whatever he says. It'll be another twenty minutes before it gets here and by that time I won't want it. The male species is so irritating.

Billy's smiling and staring at me again. I'm sick of this boy watching and grinning at me all the time. I need to know why he is, and what he's thinking. "What's with you? Why do you keep staring at me and smiling? I mean do I have something on me that I need to brush off, or are you just that mesmerized by my features that you can't stop thinking about me in bed for two minutes?" Harsh? Yes. I think he needs something to break that grin and those eyes from my poor body that's feeling violated.

"Damn," Billy shakes his head. "What's with *you*? You've got a serious attitude problem. Ya know not *every* guy from the hood is a broke dog that only has sex on the brain. In fact a good portion of us do try to better ourselves. So next time you open yo' mouth to stereotype all of us, think about *that*." The fact his eyes didn't tear away makes me feel like he isn't just trying to be a smart ass.

"*You're* one to talk about stereotyping. You don't think I know that's what you and DK have done to me since I was a kid? So what I'm from a good school around a bunch of rich people, and so what I pronounce most of my words correctly and don't add extra Rs into what I'm saying. You think I'm some stuck up rich girl who doesn't understand what its like not to have money," I argue back snatching my drink from the bartender. Before I even get the chance to slip the bartender the money Billy hands it to him.

Shaking his head, "I love how you tell me what I'm thinkin' all the time when you have absolutely no clue." Billy looks off into the distance behind the bar for a moment I guess to gather the few thoughts he has. "Look Kie, I know I was wrong for treatin' you like shit when you were younger, but I've grown up," and quite nicely may I add. "And if you wanna have fun while you're here, loosen up and quit biting off everybody's head for speaking to you."

My tongue slides across my slightly glossed lips as I try to look elsewhere. He has no idea what he's talking about. Having fun isn't my concern. Making sure I leave here with the same self respect I came with is. But what if he's right? The past is the past and he has grown up or so he claims. Something makes me want to at least try. I mean for Mia of course. I should try to show her a good time while I'm here.

"By the way," Oh no there's more? "I've been starin' and smilin' at you tryin' to figure out how to say I think your beautiful without makin' a complete ass of myself," he adjusts his sleeveless black shirt. We don't all fall for that beautiful crap, but I'll let him get away with it this time. After all being called beautiful isn't a terrible thing.

"Thank you," I smile at him. "For the drink too." I cross my legs and lean back towards the bar. Sure hope he doesn't think he's broken down my force field of hate. It's just temporarily out of service that's all.

"You're welcome," he ruins my wish of him not smiling any more. His clean white smile implies that he knows how to take care of at least one thing on his body. The one dimple on his left cheek, the opposite of the cheek I have mine own on, is pretty cute too. He's still doing it. Jerk. "Kie I know you still hate me a lot … but is there any way I could get you to dance?"

I put my half finished drink down and turn my head towards him. I do want to dance, and there aren't any remotely respectable guys in here. I still feel like this is all some sort of a sick twisted game him and DK have set up to mess with me. Then again I don't know if they're smart enough to pull that off. I give them too much credit sometimes.

"Please?" his face forms to that hopeful yet questioning one. Aw. Damn you Mia. It's your fault for letting me have a heart.

"All right," I sigh and nod.

"Fo' real?" Billy tries not to smile. Fighting the desperation to roll my eyes and tell him no I've changed my mind is getting harder.

With a very well rehearsed fake smile, "Yeah. I guess it can't kill me to try and be nice to you. So let's dance."

He laughs and nods as he gets up. "My pleasure," he sticks his hand out. I take it and follow behind him down the stairs to the dance area. I wonder where Mia's happy behind is. She's more than likely drunk. It's a vacation, and she's just trying to enjoy it, so I can't hate on her for having more fun than me.

Billy pulls me a little closer behind him as we make our way around people on the dance floor. Oh no, wouldn't want him to loose me. I agreed because I do want to dance, but I don't think I want to dance this bad. We stop a few feet in front of Mia who's dancing with a different guy than I saw her with when she first left me. This one is dark like that nasty Hershey's dark chocolate. Ooh and he's short. They barely make eye contact. He doesn't even look older than us. Oh and now she's waving at me. I wave back as I feel Billy pull me a little into him. Here we go.

Billy is waving his hands in the air like guys always do. He's one of those guys that just kind of bounce their heads to the music while moving their hands in different directions. That's not dancing, that's pretending. I don't intend on faking anything.

I slowly circle my hips towards his, and the next thing I know BOOM they've met. He asked me to dance and then when I do he's confused. I keep moving my hips around until he joins in. Great now we're pelvis to pelvis, just grinding slow and hard. He's got that look in his eye like he's thinking something that no girl ever wants to know. I feel him slip one of his hands onto my lower back. I swear I will kill him if his hand even grazes my butt.

As we continue dancing this way, the DJ mixes it with another song, and slowly I twist myself around to where my back is facing him. I don't know if this is exactly the best thing because well lets face it; he's a guy and a black one at that. So it's not your normal excited that he has an ass against his crotch, it's a higher excitement as he pictures hitting it from behind.

Is he afraid I'm going to drop kick his ass if he puts his arms around me? Only if he over steps my boundaries of course. I take Billy's hands and wrap them around my lower midriff. He'll survive through the sparkles. I can tell he feels more comfortable because the grip around my waist just got tighter. My arms wrap themselves around his neck as he snuggles his face next to mine continuing to smile. I smile back enjoying myself.

We continue to make this moment hotter and more turned on than it already is. I can feel his 'friend'. Sad that a little touching in the area wakes him up. I snicker inside as I move my hands from his neck to place them on top of his. The DJ has changed songs again, yet this one's a bit mellower. I hear him mixing another beat with the current meaning he's going to switch songs once more. When he finally does, I move Billy's hands and slip them into mine allowing me to finally drop it like it's hot. If you don't get it, don't worry about it.

I keep a bit of a distance between us while I wobble a little giving him the chance he's wanted all night to look at me from behind without having to worry about getting cussed out or smacked. When I turn to face him I have a look of seduction in my eyes. You know girls get real intense when they're dancing and know a guy is totally into them. We get a sick joy from toying with their hopes. I smile and lick my lips at Billy while just twisting my hips a little as he caresses my body.

The DJ is getting ready to switch songs again. I roll my body towards his just a little, turn with a roll around so my back is to him before I drop it, it being my butt of course, and bring it up real slow making sure its strictly ass to crotch. The bulge in his pants tells me he liked that move. I hold back my giggles. Mia's doing the same thing I am with another guy she secretly hopes can handle her. I pray she doesn't end up going to DK's cocky stuck on himself behind.

Suddenly there's slow music playing. To dance with Billy or to not dance with Billy, that is the question. I turn around and make sure I make eye contact with him before I slip my arms around his neck. Wouldn't want him to think I couldn't look him in the eye after being all freaky with him on the dance floor. He slides his arms around my lower back. Hey buddy the same rules apply. You touch my ass you die.

"Damn girl I didn't know you had it like that," he moistens his lips into a grin. Could he live without his own salvia plastered on his lips?

"Yeah well you don't know a lot about me," I answer trying to leave the attitude out of my voice, but it's hard.

"Obviously," he glances at my body up and down and smiles again. Perv.

I didn't know he had a nice body, at least from what I can see. He's got on this black sleeveless shirt that stops a little after the top of his jeans, which are nicely fitted on his hips and baggy, the rest of the way down. I didn't know he owned a belt. I could check on the cool to make sure that's the reason his pants are up so well, but I won't. He's got a pair of shell top Adidas on that have the black stripes. My eyes roll themselves back up towards his eyes. The silver chain around his neck goes along with the diamond studs he has in each of his ears. No braids. Now there's something different. He looks good with a fade; it balances out his whole look that he's got going for him. It's sort of a Ginuwine, young R&B thing. I can't front. Billy looks good. Good enough to almost date. Only if he didn't talk and have DK for a best friend; I'm sure it would work. What am I talking about dating this crazy boy for?

By the way by Billy is leaning in towards me. I think he's going to try to kiss me on the sly. Oh no. I need a big red flag that says 'no'. "Thanks for giving me a second chance," now he's all up in my personal bubble.

Boy could use a tic-tac. I hope he has more to his game plan other than corny lines. "I guess you deserve it. Everyone does."

"Even DK?" we continue slowly swaying back and fourth. He was really looking to make me laugh with that one.

I give him what he wants. I laugh. "Hell no." I smile with him. "There are exceptions to every rule, and he's this one." I damn sure don't plan on giving that two-timing, playgirl wanna be, sleazy, twisted, scum another chance.

"Well good to know I'm worth another shot," he says smoothly. Yeah you're worth another shot, but I'm sure if I aim this time my fist will reach your face.

"Yeah," I nod. There he goes. Lips moving in, eyes closed, tongue anxious. NO. I remove one hand from around him and place it in front of his face firmly blocking him, "I don't think so."

Billy lets up slightly leaning backwards.

"Sorry Romeo, but it ain't happenin'," I pull away from him.

"My bad," he looks perplexed. "I just thought—

"You thought wrong," I walk off from him. I'm not stupid. All that nice talk was to see if I would give in to his cheap over done ways.

"Kie," he calls from somewhere behind me. Yeah this isn't a movie so that's not going to stop me. Trying again he calls out, "Wait." Wait? Wait for what? I danced with the baboon. He should be happy and let me be. Too bad that's not how reality works. We all know he'll do one of two things, stay there and feel stupid while he beats himself up over it before running to apologize and try again or stay there and feel stupid while he beats himself up over it before running to apologize and try again. Wow, look at those options. Wonder what he'll do.

Less than five minutes later here he is sitting next to me again, apologizing. To think in the two hours we've been here I haven't even finished a single drink. Yeah we danced a really long time. Hm, maybe that's why he felt so close and comfortable like he had to kiss me … no it definitely had the be the happy camper in his pants that told him to.

"I'm sorry," he grovels again.

"It's ok," I nod and blow him off. "Yo Jay. Drink."

"Kie, I—

"I get it Billy. You didn't mean to cross the line with me, all is forgiven. Now you can go back and play with the chicken heads that you know so well," I say in a motherly voice.

"Kie—

A stern look shuts him up. Sighing he gets up and strolls off. Thank goodness.

"Yeah," the bartender answers me too late.

"I'll take a rum and coke," I tell him. He promptly walks off to actually make it. I scan down the bar that has no other girls on it. It must be time for them to find someone else to bum drinks off of.

"Here you go," he hands it to me. As I reach in my pocket to get my money someone sits down and hands him the money for it. I swear I am so sick and tired of Billy trying to say he's sorry in different ways.

"Look Billy—" I look up to see some other older man. He's bald, with scruffy facial hair. He's got a beer gut that he tried horribly to hide in a pair of too tight black jeans with a shirt to match. Well that makes me want to throw up.

"Excuse me?" He questions in that deep booming bass voice. Creepy.

"Oh, I'm sorry," I apologize to the man. "I thought you were my friend … I mean I thought you were this guy I know," I shake my head. Friend my ass. "Thanks for the drink. You didn't have too," I say. Didn't have too at all. I would rather go thirsty than take a drink from your disturbing ass ever again.

"No problem. It's a surprise a lovely young lady like you don't have men flocking to her." What's creepier than an old dude telling you how lovely you are? How about an old dude with his hand on your thigh? Swallows.

"It's no big deal," I remove his hand. Ew. Ew. Ew.

"It's a very big deal," he scoots closer to me. He has just invaded my personal space. Time to move out of this uncomfortable position. "You have to be the sexiest thing in here tonight, so how about we go some place alone to talk?"

What the hell? Oh my gosh! A creepy old dude is hitting me on, and he wants me to go some place to talk with him. Yeah right, more like take me somewhere and rape me. Does he think I'm that stupid? I know better than to leave strange places with strange older men who hit on me.

"Um," I am so disgusted that I can't drink anymore. "No thank you," I smile politely. Don't piss off older men who look like stalkers or psychos one knife away from being killers.

"Are you sure?" he moves in closer to me. Cringing on the inside, I move away from him slowly scooting my body to the opposite side. I just want to smack him and scream for help, but I'm in a club. What good is that going to do?

"I really don't want to," I stand my ground. If I move away I'm showing weakness and fear yet if I stay I'm in an even more vulnerable position. What kind of sick middle aged freak hits on jailbait?

"I think you do," he places his hand on my thigh this time gripping it.

Panic time. I take slow deep breaths. Right about now my mind has frozen solid. I want to scream, but my voice can't. I want to smack the hell out of him, but my hand won't move. Worst of all, I just want to leave, but can't because of the incredible force he's placing on my leg. I swallow hard. That's going to leave a bruise. They tell you in school not to panic, just handle the situation in a calm manner. Good to know that they tell us straight bull shit.

"Let go," I say firmly in a powerful tone, but that only makes him squeeze tighter. In the same approach I plead, "Please." He leans over and whispers something dirty in my ear. How much more uncomfortable can I get? A 30-year-old guy won't stop gripping my leg.

"I bet you'd like that huh," he grins as I grip my drink. See I've always been taught not to throw things when you're angry, but no one ever said not to when you're scared, or you're going to be a victim of some sort.

I pick up the glass and toss the drink in his face causing him to remove his hand, allowing me to get up and start for my escape when he grabs my arm. Ok Kie, don't panic. Why is no one ever here when *I* need help?

His grip is now the tightest it's been, "You're gonna pay for that."

I feel my stomach twist up into knots, and my heart must be going ninety a sec. Gasping for air, I feel my whole body ringing the warning alarm that now would be a good time to prepare myself for a worst case scenario.

"Hey baby," Billy slowly comes towards me seeing me struggle for my arm. Even in the time of danger this boy moves slowly. He asks the abusive man trying to kidnap me, "What's goin' on?" Out of all the dumb questions to ask, he picks that one.

"Ya know, tryin' to leave with this hunnie," he finally loosens his grip and winks at me.

"You tryin' to leave wit' my girl?" Billy peals the guys hand off my arm. Ouch. Definite bruise.

"Oh this yo ho'?" he steps to Billy.

Damn I didn't mean to start a cockfight. I just needed a little rescuing from a future criminal on the 'America's Most Wanted' list. By the way is it really called for him to pretend to be my boyfriend? Is it the only way he can live out his fantasies?

"She ain't no ho', but she's mine. So why don't you step off," Billy mans up. Well at least he's not shorter than the guy. Billy's somewhere close to six foot so height won't be a threat.

"Or what," he tilts his head to the side the way DK does when he gets an attitude. The flabby man doesn't look like he can do anything, but sit on Billy to try to stop him.

"I think you know," Billy never breaks eye contact. It's better than just an action; it's a bond, a signature, a promise.

Backing down after one hard look he mumbles, "Ain't want that trick no way," before strolling off.

A deep sigh escapes me as Billy turns to me. "You ok?" Wasting no time I throw my arms around his neck and hug him tightly. "I gotcha," with my eyes closed I feel him slowly hug back. Doubt I'd ever admit it out loud, but I owe him big.

I whisper in his ear, "Thank you."

"Any time," he whispers back. Holding me for a second I feel him reassure me that yes indeed everything is going to be all right. I don't know why he did that for me. As rude as I was to him, and just plain spiteful, it's a surprise he just didn't let him take me. I guess he has more of a heart than I give him props for. "Wanna go home?"

"Yeah, most def," I nod and pull away from him.

"All right," he gives me a gorgeous closed mouth smile. "Let's find Mia and DK so we can bounce," we stroll off holding hands. Taking out his cell phone, he flips it open to call DK. I guess that's the easy, lazy way to find him.

"Yeah," DK answers the phone laughing as he clinks beers with a group of girls.

"Let's go," Billy maneuvers us to the stairs.

Taking another swig of beer DK questions, "Now?"

"Yeah," he says pulling me closer to him as we go through the crowd of people. "Find Mia first. Meet us by the door."

"On it," DK closes his phone before hesitating to remove a few girls' hands from him.

'Billy, I'm sorry for being rude even though you deserved it, but thank you for saving my ass,' is what I want to say, but being good old Kie, I say nothing. Not a damn thing.

"Why ya'll ready to go so soon," Mia slurs with her bad mixed drink breath poisoning the limited clean air I'm inhaling.

I respond quickly, "I'll explain later."

"Well I wanna know now," DK demands pretty wasted himself. I wish they wouldn't mix their drinks at least for their breaths sake.

Gently pulling me out the door still holding my hand he pauses, "Later D." Better not get used to holding my hand.

"Fine," they groan and laugh in unison.

"We said fine together," Mia giggles. "How crazy!"

"Yeah," he chuckles back tossing his arm around her shoulder for balance.

"Yo DK," he holds his free hand out, "keys."

"No problem playa," he whips them out. Wagging a finger at him he hiccups, "Now you drive safely."

"That shouldn't be a problem since I'm not liquored up like the two of you," Billy glances behind us to make sure that they don't stumble off.

DK nearly trips over his own two feet, "And why not? The drinks were off the chain tonight."

"On the real though," Mia agrees as we come up to his car.

"I bet," Billy unlocks the doors. "Can you two get in ok?"

"We're fine, F-I-N-E," Mia's words form a giant one. Everyone loves when their best friend gets drunk.

A few minutes later we're all in the car. As for all awake, that's another story. DK and Mia have checked out for the evening. They're peacefully sleeping against their windows even though we haven't left the parking lot yet. Billy pulls out still not saying anything. Maybe I should say something. Maybe not. I think I should. No. Ok.

Turning down the radio, I murmur, "You're right."

"'Bout?" he asks looking into his rearview to check for approaching vehicles.

"The thing about all guys from the hood aren't dogs," a smile creeps across his face.

"If I'm not mistaken that sounds like an apology," he quickly glances at me and then back at the few cars on the road.

"Something like that. So, are you trying to better yourself? Or were you just speaking in general terms?"

Finally creeping his way onto the highway, which we never ventured to on the way here, he answers with a shrug, "General."

That's what I thought. No hopes, no dreams, no ambition. Looks can't get him everywhere in life. "Do you have a job?"

"No," he says straight up. No job means no ties, no ties means no responsibility, no responsibility means no commitment, and no commitment means he's closer to being a dog.

"Why not?"

"There's no need," he shrugs accelerating.

"You have to live don't you?"

"I live with DK. He pays for jus' about everything, so I figure why the hell waste time on some'n like a job?" spoken like a true broke male.

If that isn't the biggest load of crap I've heard come out of this boy yet. Waste time? A need for your own personal spending cash is a waste of time? "How do you make cash to pay for clothes and stuff like that?"

Without eye contact, maybe because he feels guilty for what he does, he steady looks at the traffic, "DK and I sell stuff." Oh 'stuff'. Stuff implies millions of things. For all I know the boy could be selling old tires and buckets of sand, but I'm not that naïve. I know that by stuff he means drugs, more than likely weed, and or bootleg things.

"Don't you think you should get a *real* job?" I say pushing the loose strands of hair out of my face.

"Why? 'Cause that's what all the guys *you know* do?" Hey now, I've been nice, and he's trying to take a stab at me. He better watch himself before I pull out the big guns.

"No. You should get a job because you can't sponge off of that forever," I point to sleeping DK. "You never know. He might not make it far, or he might not even make it period. He's got a deal, big whoop. Do you know how many deals fail, or how many CDs get put out, but no one listens to them? You gotta learn to take care of yourself." So I gave him a bit of a speech. "Man up to life." Maybe it'll get through to him, and he'll realize it's time to get a job. "Ya feel me?"

"Yeah," Billy nods with a hurt look. Geez, even when I'm nice to the boy he still gets his feelings hurt. Suck it up.

With an apologetic smile I say, "Just tryin' to look out for you a bit. I wouldn't want everything to come crashing down on you leaving you with little or nothing."

"Well don't worry about that. I'm always welcomed at Big Mama's," he laughs. Ain't that the truth? Every child is. Most of the ones who get left there to be raised by Big Mama have parents who have run away, are in prison, or have passed on. It's like an orphanage with a great food and freedom of expression.

I giggle a little with him, "Right, right."

"Ya know, you've got a great smile goin' for you. You should do it more often." Oh no. Here we go again with those lame compliments. Come on buddy; that line has been used more often than the trashy cheerleaders at my school.

"Give me a reason to, and I will," more clever than thank you. Besides I love negotiating. You're nice to me, and I'll smile. Seems fair right?

After looking at me with his glowing, hazel, 'fall for me' eyes he remarks, "Be careful. I just might." He winks at me. I stare into his breath taking eyes admiring the never ending glow around them that could hypnotize even the least unwilling girl to become his girlfriend.

"Yeah ok," I sarcastically remark as we approach the last main road before Big Mama's neighborhood.

There's a few minutes where neither us say anything. It's not exactly awkward, but not a walk in the park if you catch my drift. I wonder what he's thinking. No I don't. I'm afraid to know. I mean what if it's about me? What if it's something bad, like how incredibly bitchy I've been to him? It could be good though, like how I've warmed up to him. Maybe he's thinking about me naked again. Remind me again why I care. Oh that's right. I don't.

As we pull up to the house I can tell he's going to say something. Maybe I should get to him first before he does; that way I can save him some humiliation if that's the case. He parks on the side of the street where they did earlier. Billy turns off the car and just stares at the wheel for a second. Talk about uncomfortable.

"Kie," he starts. Oh no, no, no. I'm talking, not him.

"Wait, before you say anything let me talk. I know I was pretty harsh to you earlier. I didn't mean to come off so strong, and I'm sorry from brushing you off before when you tried to apologize. I guess I'm just so use to fighting you that being nice instead is very difficult," I smile politely getting the same reaction from him. "But I do owe you for helping me out of that situation. If you hadn't have been there I don't know what would have happened."

"I'm jus' glad I was," his eyes find me. "It may sound like a load of bullshit, but I do care if some'n happens to you, especially if you're out with me when it does."

I smile, "I believe you, and the fact you care says a lot." When in doubt go with your conscious. I lean over and kiss Billy on the cheek. He's so nervous as it happens that his Adam's apple plunges down deep and pops back as my lips come off his warm soft cheek. I find his nice light chocolate skin, almost perfect. Just a tad darker than mine. I smile warmly once more. Mia would have a heart attack witnessing that. "Friends?"

"Friends," he nods with a relieved sigh. I have a feeling he was hoping for something more, but reality check. We're not exactly each others type, and on top of that we live in two different cities four hours away from each other. I could do the quick week fling thing, but that brings us back to point number one. We're not each other's type.

I pick up the pen off the floor hoping it works. After all this is DK's car. It's a surprise the thing starts. "Call me tomorrow afternoon, and we can hang out," I jot my cell phone number on his hand.

"I'll make sure I call befo' we show up. Give you two girls a chance to rest and ya know ..." slowly he nods. "I will definitely call you though."

"Well ... um ... have a good night. Drive home safely," I open the door. Have good night? Drive home safely? Oh my gosh Kie, what's wrong with you? I sound like I'm clueless. I know how to say goodbye to guys, and that was totally not it. What was I thinking?

I open Mia's door for her. I shake her, and that's all it takes to get her up. It's weird how when she's drunk she'll wake up instantly to go to a bed, but when she's sober she could careless. I help her out as she mumbles and moans incoherent things. She'll be fine in the morning and have millions of questions to ask me about the car ride home, my club experience, and why we left early. I can deal with them in the morning, but not now. Definitely not now.

I wave through the open window, "See you tomorrow Billy."

"Bye," his grin is wide watching us go to the door. I assume to make sure we get in ok.

As strange as this sounds I think we might actually become pretty good friends. I know that I change my mind quite quickly, but what do you want from me? I'm sixteen. You expect me to feel the same thing about a person for like forever? I don't think so. Especially after he saves me from great danger and grinds with me. Yeah I admit it; I enjoyed grinding on him. He's fine, and I'm a girl. What do you expect? There's probably more to this situation, but it's too late to over think all these feelings. I'm tired and leading Mia down the unlit hall is a task. I'm sure everything will be gravy in the morning.

CHAPTER 2

Foul Play

I can feel Mia tossing and flopping around trying to get comfortable again. Must she move so much while I'm trying to sleep? I can feel a spring trying to pierce my leg. I wish I could blame that on keeping me up last night, but unfortunately I had Billy on my mind. I just don't get it. No matter how hard I try to hate him, I can't. The boy is quite persistent. It's like rejection motivates him to try harder. I don't know why he wants someone with nothing to offer him other than a smart mouth or a punch in the face.

"Kie," Mia slightly groans and sits up ruffling her hair.

"What?" I roll over to the middle to face her.

"You awake?"

I give her a blank look. Am I awake? My eyes are open, I answered you when you called my name, and I just rolled over. I can tell someone's brain hasn't quite started to function yet. "No. I'm sleep talking," sarcasm is the best in the morning.

"Well wake up, and tell me why we left so early last night," she yawns pulling all of her hair into a bun with the ponytail holder she had around her wrist from last night.

I groan and close my eyes. I don't feel like explaining everything that happened. She's going to start asking me questions, making accusations, but worst of all gloat because she was 'right'.

"Kie," my name leaves her lips again this time more awake than before.

Since it doesn't seem to be clear enough to her that I'm avoiding the subject, I roll over pulling a pillow over my head.

"Come on," she rips the pillow off and hits my butt with it. With another hit, this time on my back, she whines, "Tell me." Must she be so violent?

I fold my arms behind my head after rolling onto my back, "We left because it was getting late."

"Don't lie. I remember we left for a specific reason." Oh that she remembers all liquored up, but how disgusting DK is she forgets. "What happened? Did you get hurt? Did Billy get into a fight? Did he piss you off?" Millions and millions of questions are rushing out of her mouth along with specs of spit. Her head should be throbbing leaving her incapable of asking this many questions yet due to her scientifically shocking alcohol resistance, at such a young age, last night has no consequences on her body.

I shift my head her direction to at least try to divert the subject I ask, "Do you even have a headache? Are you the least bit tired?"

"Nah I'm cool. It's a little after noon, so you know I'm reenergized," she smirks and rolls up the sleeves on the gray shirt I helped her slip into last night. "Now back to last night ..."

My eyes shut again, "Last night was last night. Past tense."

Pulling the blanket over her feet she gripes, "You said you would explain it to me. It's one of the only things I remember from last night."

"What else do you remember?" I hope she doesn't say me kissing Billy on the cheek. She was asleep for that, but then again she could have been faking it. It wouldn't be the first time. What if she remembers the hand holding that went on? Oh I would never hear the end of that one. Then of course there was the dancing ... God, the dancing. She was staring right as us while we gettin' our freak on. I knew better than to dance where she could see. Damn you Kie! Learn to go with you instincts.

"I had some of the best drinks I've had in awhile," please say nothing else, "and you humping on Billy." Damn it.

"What?" I ask innocently. Yeah that's it. Play innocent. I'm sure that'll work.

"I saw you put that thang on him. Mmhm, work that magic," she nods. "I knew you would."

"I have no idea what you're talking about," I lie.

"Sure you do!" She squeals gleefully. "You dropped it like it was hot a few times, and you rolled your hips with him looking too scared to touch you." Why do I get this feeling like she selected specific events to remember just so she could prove me wrong about this whole Billy situation? See what kind of friends I have.

Rolling my eyes I plea, "All right, all right. You didn't have to put it like that. I danced with the boy. Yes. Guilty as charged."

"I knew it! You enjoyed it too! Don't front," she points her finger at me.

Cringing, I put the pillow over my head again this time to muffle out the sound of my laughter. I can't believe she's busting me out like this. Giggling with me, she removes the pillow from my face.

"Just a little," I'm smiling now. Oh I give up. I did like it. In fact, it was the most fun I've had in awhile.

She squeals clapping her hands together. What's she so excited about? It's not *that* big of a deal. "I knew you liked him!"

"Hey now," I rise up. Shaking my head I insist, "Don't get ahead of yourself. We're cool and all, but not like that." Like the boy? Maybe if I was some hoochie without any hopes and dreams like him, but since we don't share a common ground like that I'm going to stand firm at no.

She raises her eyebrows, "If you don't now, you will soon enough." Excuse her. How does she know? I could bet her big bucks that she's wrong about this. "Back on topic, why'd we leave early?"

I continue to hesitate to tell her the story. She'll get all excited, and then throw the Billy thing in my face again. Here goes nothing. Beginning from the moment Billy approached me at the bar, I take her on a whirlwind recap of my night up until the very moment we met back up.

"Whoa," she says mesmerized in an airy tone. I know she's amazed and going to ask what happened next, but I'll let this part settle in for a second. Mia begins to bounce up and down on the bed, "Aww!"

"Aww?" I question rolling up the sleeves on my baggy white t-shirt I'm wearing.

"He rescued you?" She pushes me softly. "I would have thought he would have left your ass high and dry."

With a half smile I look down, "You and me both."

"See, he's not completely the asshole you figured he was," Mia smiles proudly. "So what happened on the way home? You guys make out or what?"

Make out? I mean a quick kiss on the cheek is ok; a soft kiss on the lips wouldn't be horrible, but his tongue in my mouth? My stomach clenches causing me to feel nausea. So I guess my gag reflex is working. I'm pretty sure his tongue has been in a few too many girls' mouths for me to handle. "Gross. I thanked him with a kiss on the cheek."

"The cheek? You're worse than I thought Kie," she shakes her head.

"Huh?" I'm confused. Hey it wasn't like I just left him completely un-thanked.

"Kie you kiss people like Lloyd on the cheek for buying you lunch when you don't have lunch money. When a guy saves you from being a victim, you kiss him on the lips, 'mind you length is not important."

"I'm sorry I didn't know there were rules of etiquette to follow when a guy rescues you. I mean if I would've known …" I drift off. I doubt I'd even do it then. "I still wouldn't have."

The corners of her mouth peak before she snaps, "Don't lie. You know you want to kiss him just as bad as he does you."

"No." For real though, I don't think of those soft, pout lips on mine. I really don't.

"Sure," she does a fake nod. "Did you two talk?"

"Nothing worth repeating." Billy growing up and getting a job isn't any-thing important to anyone else.

"I bet," she mumbles. "Did you tell him to come by today?"

"I gave him my cell number to call," I begin to look around the messy floor wondering where it is. As my eyes continue to wander around the room I get the vibe that she's staring at me. "What?"

With a shrug she sighs, "I'm just thinking about what kind of trouble we're going to get into today." Why don't I believe her? My money is on thoughts about me and Billy. How do our names keep ending up together like that?

"Who knows what we're going to do today. So Ms. All Up in My Biz, any-thing happen to you? Meet a hot guy? Get free drinks?" My voice quickly becomes high pitched, "Play fetch with a dog named DK?"

Mia flops back onto the drool pillow, snuggles under the sheets again, and answers, "Plenty, yes, and we danced once."

"You danced with that?" I scrunch my face in disgust.

"Yeah. I've had better," she glances at the clock again.

"Haven't we all?" I grab a ponytail holder from the nightstand on my side of the bed.

"Ain't that the truth," she rolls her eyes. "DK could be worth something with a little work. Just gotta whip him right ya know?"

"That dog has a lot to learn. Besides the fact he's not potty trained, his bark needs some work. Oh and he could definitely use a muzzle," I laugh with Mia. It would do the world great justice for him to never utter another word, but since we can't take away his ability to speak muffling will just have do.

"Does Billy need much work?" I knew she would bring him into this. All Billy needs is a girl with her head on straight. On the other hand, DK needs a girl with a bitch button that's easily switched on to teach him the ways of civilized people.

With a quick smirk I remark, "Don't know. Don't care."

Someone's phone begins to ring. My guess is it's Mia's. Guys are always calling her cell. When she turns it off for a few hours she ends up with like fifteen missed calls and thirty-two messages. I don't know what she does to those poor boys to get them whipped so quickly, but she needs to stop before she meets her match.

She points to my phone that's flashing multicolored lights, "Kie, that's your phone."

I nearly break my neck grabbing it. Unknown number. It's a little early for it to be Billy, right? In a high pitch polite tone I answer, "Hello."

"Is Kie there?" I recognize the voice on the other end of the phone.

"Speaking," I answer to Billy who sounds wide-awake.

"Is that him?" Mia mouths excited as I move towards my suitcase to have a bit of privacy. I nod as I listen to his voice.

"Hey," Billy sits down on a bench in the lobby of a five-star hotel.

Slowly I begin to fold the clothes I threw around last night in desperation, "Aren't you supposed to be sleeping?"

"You would think that," he says smiling watching guests walk by, "but actually I had a job interview to attend."

There's silence on my end of the phone. Did he just say J-O-B? I didn't know this boy could pronounce the word let alone get one.

Laughing sarcastically, "That's righ' oh silent one. A job interview." Good thing his nickname is not funny.

I struggle to break through my overwhelming shock to say, "What made you want to get a job?"

"I don't know," he tries not to smile. "I guess some'n someone said to me."

"Oh, and what was that?" I smirk cockily. Wow, talk about being easily swayed. You mention one thing and all of sudden he's ready to be whoever you want him to.

"You can't depend on someone else fo'eva."

That he takes to mind. "Where did you have an interview?"

"A hotel," he nods winking at the front desk.

"As what a bell boy?"

"Naw. I'll work the front desk most of the time. Ya know, givin' people their keys and takin' reservations. I only have to be a bell boy if they're short-handed."

"So did u get the job?"

He gloats, "Of course."

Life has no guarantees especially regarding jobs. "What do you mean of course?"

"The job was offered to me awhile back 'cause my boy owed me one. He told me it was always open if I needed it, so well ..."

"Oh," should've known. It would have taken too much effort for him to pick up the newspaper and search for something the normal way. This loser lives off of other people. What would happen if he just tried to survive on his own? "So you called to tell me you got a job, or something else?"

"You told me to call you 'bout hangin' out this afternoon ..."

I was just being polite. I didn't really think he'd call. "Yeah."

"I was thinkin' we could hang out after I go to my other job interview."

"You have another one?" Overachiever.

Checking his watch Billy responds, "Yeah. I'm tryin' to be a bartender at club Caliente weeknights and the occasional weekend. I can always use extra cash."

"Right," sure extra cash is great, but it's good to remember that money isn't everything.

"You wanna hook up when I'm done?"

Not really. I twirl a strand of hair around my finger, "It's kind of early. I mean I just got up."

"Well, I have to stop there, have lunch, and pick up DK, which will take a few hours," he explains to me *his* schedule like I'm supposed to fit myself into it. Come on now ...

"I guess that's ok."

"Is that a yes?"

As much I just wanna scream 'NO!' into the phone, I don't. I just roll my eyes and look at Mia who's glaring at me. She's telepathically telling me to agree while indicating with her tapping fingernails there will be punishment if I don't go along with it. Great ... "Yes."

"A'ight," Billy gets up excited. "I'll see you then."

"Bye," I hang up my phone. A club is one thing, but an afternoon of just them? That's like DK handing me the knife to kill him with. Maybe I'm over analyzing the situation. Let me take a step back and give an overview to the thought of possibly having fun with Billy. Can fun blossom from the hatred soil our friendship, if we must call it that, is planted in? Probably not.

Around four we're not doing anything except telling my mom and Big Mama about last night. Now this conversation is a *long* one. Everything we say reminds them of a time from their adolescents. They've told us six different stories in forty-five minutes with Mia hanging on to their every word. Too bad by the look on my face she knows I've heard them all at least twice.

It's just like a guy to do this. He'll tell you 'I'll be there in a few hours', but what he really means is 'I'll be there when I remember that's where I'm supposed to be'. It's simple when you think about it. Say what you do, and do what you say. A girl wants her man to be on time, not that I'm calling Billy my man; I'm just saying he should still keep his word. A few hours? Try an eternity. I don't mean to sound like I'm desperate for him to be here, but my nerves are just on end with annoyance.

"So he rescued her," Mia's hand gestures over-exaggerate the situation. She demanded to tell the story because I would've left out everything that didn't have to do with strictly being harassed.

"Kie I am so glad Billy was there for you. You really should be grateful for that," my mom nods blowing out smoke from her cigarette.

Nodding Big Mama looks away from her day-time soap opera, "Good Kid. Billy is the type of boy you need to be around."

"True," my mom agrees letting the cigarette sit between her lips. Suddenly a different glaze appears in her eyes and she remarks, "I think you should thank him. You owe him something."

I wait to hear Twilight Zone music. No? Nothing? My own mother is sitting here telling me I owe him something, and we're not in a parallel universe? The kiss on the cheek was enough. And what the hell is Big Mama talking about? Good kid my ass. Friends are a reflection of you, and well DK's a jackass ... enough said.

"Naw she doesn't owe me anything. Her thank you was enough," Billy casually turns the corner, strolling through the kitchen to reach us. Oh, *now* he appears. Go figure when someone starts to talk about his ass he shows up.

Nonchalantly my mom puts out her cig, "You should hang out with them while they're here." Trying not to keep my eyes from shifting to an evil state, I notice Mia restraining her laughter. I cannot believe my own mother is against me. Did I miss the memo that said 'My Misery Equals Everyone Else's Happiness'?

"Sounds good to me," his hands slip into his jean pockets as he posts himself up against the outer kitchen wall.

I give him a fierce look. Lucky for him life's going his way and not mine. We all know if it was up to me he'd be six million feet away posing next to an Egyptian pyramid.

"Ooh good," Big Mama squeals in a gleeful grandmother tone. If she wasn't the sweetest old lady to ever walk the face of the earth, I'd suggest committing her. Adjusting her faded pink bathrobe while grabbing the remote I assume to change channels she sighs, "Go ahead, and start now."

Nodding in agreement Billy smirks, "Good idea." Do the darted eyes and frown on my face mean nothing?

"Yeah," Mia exclaims. Ganging up on me with everyone else and taking advantage of the situation, makes her an evil friend. Evil.

"Great," I slowly force the muscles in my mouth to form a smile. Swallowing hard, I get off the green leather couch.

Waving, Big Mama props her feet up and turns back to her soaps, "Have fun."

"Be good," my mom giggles under her breath winking at Big Mama.

Biting my tongue, I nod and start to the kitchen. Trying to focus my attention on other things, I observe the changes they've made in here since I last visited. The fridge directly to my left from the living room entrance finally appears to be clean on the outside with pictures of her kids, grandkids, and god children. Sadly, the walls are now an off-yellow color to match the house's yellow stained grout. Pictures of African artwork are slanted, barely hanging on their nails. All the counter tops are wooden, to match the square wooden table that's smashed in the corner of the rectangular room. On the counter tops there's spilled sugar, flower, and bread crumbs. My favorite thing has to be where the stove is located because it's right as you exit to the other side of the house. It's to the left of the counters when facing them, which makes it really easy to smell whatever's on the stove, which at this moment happens to be bacon grease and biscuits from breakfast.

I turn out and start down the hall towards our room. Why do I feel like Billy and Mia are gloating about their conspiring plan finally working? Though I don't blame them for being insanely happy about my misery because I know if it was reversed, and I was the one creating the mayhem by getting what I wanted, I'd gloat too.

As I head over to my suitcase I hear Mia mumble, "Kie."

"What?" I growl as I start to put my hair in a bun.

She shoves a piece of gum in her mouth, "Don't be pissed."

"Why would I be pissed?" I say in a sarcastically perky tone. "My best friend, mother, and grandmother-like person, all want me to hook up with a guy who is too manipulative for his own good."

After checking to see if my shoes are tied tight, we quickly head towards the front door where we assume they're waiting outside.

Snickering she rolls her eyes. "Can you look at the bigger picture here? They want us to have fun, and they want *you* to give Billy the chance to be your friend like he deserves." Tossing me the pack of tic-tacs she continues, "For once in your life stop being stubborn, and take a chance on something new."

Without removing one, I toss the tic-tacs back as she opens the front door letting the two of us out. Hey I'm not so pig-headed that I believe only I'm right twenty-four seven. In fact I try new things for other people all the time. Well sometimes. Ok, once in awhile. Mm, for sure at least once.

The sun wastes no time pouring out its heat rays onto us. It would be one thing if it was just hot, but it's so dry I feel like I'm in the Arabian Desert rather than supposedly one of the cooler parts of Texas. Is it the burnt patches on the grass, in both yards, that tells my mother this is an aesthetic place to vacation?

I see Billy and DK sitting on top of a silver two-door convertible Benz. Ok now a record company may shovel out one nice car if they're feeling confident or desperate in his case, but two just doesn't happen.

"Whose car?" Mia asks stopping in front of them after checking out the rims that keep spinning when you stop. Rapper complex anyone?

Billy proudly strokes his chin, "Mine." I catch him shooting me a glance.

"What?" The two of us say in unison. How did he get it? Rob a celebrity? Break into an impound lot?

"Yup," Billy nods tapping the trunk as if congratulating it.

"How?" I quickly remark with obvious doubt on his ownership being legit.

"When my mom died I took the insurance money along with what we had left in the bank and bought my baby," he grins at it. I don't remember being told his mom passed away or that he was left any sum of money. Wow, the things he should mention he doesn't.

Mia beats me to the question, "And where does it reside?"

"A parkin' garage. Usually I jus' roll around in DK's car, but I wanted to take my own car while I ran errands," he focuses his attention on me as DK lights up a cigarette.

"Don't trust it out in the open?" Mia chuckles what sounds like an innocent flirtation laugh while she slips her hands into her back pockets. Did she change her mind on which boy she would like?

"Yeah," he shakes his head at DK who offers him a puff.

"So you took a good amount of money and blew it on a car with some nice rims?" He hates my attitude. Good, because he's a genuine moron. Seriously. He could have taken the money, bought a decent a car, and got his own apartment on the better side of town. He could have given himself the gift of life and a chance to live the right way, but what does he do? The typical thug thing. Such a shame.

"Hell yeah," he ignores my tone as DK blows smoke towards me. Did I ask for a gust of his disgusting lung diseased air? I don't think so.

Mia starts coughing and fanning herself. Pointing towards the road she sighs, "Excuse me, but blow your nasty smoke that way."

After nodding in agreement to Mia's comment I snap my head back to Billy, "Are you really that brainless?"

Billy slides his hands into his gym shorts pockets, "What?"

"You have the chance to make a difference in your life, yet you blow it on a car?" I lick my lips. Yeah I know what you're thinking, but just be thankful I'm not constantly doing it like Mr. Lick and Slurp or Mr. Drool and Smear.

He merely stares at me vacantly. Good thing I've had enough blank looks from him to last a lifetime.

Turning towards her I say, "Moving on. Mia ... ball?"

She hesitates, which isn't a good sign, and points across the road to the field, "I had my hopes set on riding the horses." Oh yes, the lovely horses that also belong to this family.

Besides owning the property next to her where the basketball court is, Big Mama owns the land across the street to have a place to keep the horses. She also owns the house we're staying in, the one beside her where her youngest son and his family reside, as well as the acres of land behind them. I'm not real good with measurements, but I know it's a giant open field with cows, chickens, and more horses. Isn't it amazing how much property she owns in such a cheap part of the city?

"I don't feel like riding anything," I roll down the elastic part of my black sweat pants so that they hang below my belly button. As much as I wish it were flat to fit America's standards of perfection, it's not. However it helps insinuate my curves. Good to know Billy's eyes are stuck on my stomach now like my own.

Whining in a fierce tone, "But Kie …"

"No," I tug at my shirt.

"I'll ride with you," DK blows out more smoke, this time towards the road. Oh look, the dog can follow commands. Maybe he thinks if he does what she says he'll get a treat like normal puppies in training.

"What?" Mia's attention diverts to him. With eyes raised, head tilted down, and mouth opened slightly, she gives off her typical 'yeah right' vibe. I know she won't go for it. Although, lately, she's been surprising me with things she likes to do. Let me correct my previous thought; I hope she doesn't go for it.

Blowing out smoke one last time, DK tosses his cigarette on the ground, hops off the trunk, and sly puts it out. "They can play ball, and I'll ride."

"What makes you think he wants to play ball?" I snap. What kind of friend just suggests their friend is willing to do something without being courteous by actually checking? Oh wait, mine.

"'cause he mentioned it earlier," he shoots Billy a look. Liar! You just want to spend time with Mia alone to convince her to make me suffer through more days with the two of you. I've got news buddy. You're not slick.

"Right," I nod sarcastically.

"I did," Billy jumps aboard the lying train.

"I like this," Mia smiles. "You and Billy can play ball while DK and I go ride the horses. Everybody wins!"

Sure, everybody but me. You win because you get to force me to spend time with Billy while you ride your damn horses. Billy wins because he gets to drool and awe over me. DK wins because he gets your attention. Oh, and I win an afternoon of annoyance. Fan-fucking-tastic.

In unison Billy and DK quickly agree, "Yeah." Talk about the world conspiring against you.

"Ok then," Mia squeals at me bright eyed. I open my mouth to respond, but she stops me with a 'don't be stubborn' look. This is punishment of the cruelest and most unusual kind for a crime I didn't even know I committed.

Strolling across the street with Mia next to him, I hear DK mutter out something that resembles a pick up line, "So have you ever ridden before?"

Great. Just great. It's me, basketball, and him.

"You wanna play a lil' one on one?" His mouth comes to a short simple grin. Why do I feel like that was a sexual innuendo?

"Sure." I mean basketball, but if he tries anything else, he'll be playing one on one with my knee in his balls.

"A'ight then," he nods sticking his key in the trunk lock. Sure hope he's getting a basketball and not a blanket preparing the best way to present the idea of sex to me.

I see him struggle with the key to pop it open. Peeking around to see him grab his basketball I fall into a quick debate of judgment. This says one of two things about him. He's either very athletic and his sport of choice is basketball like many young black males or he had a game plan about us playing basketball. My ruling is choice number one. But now that I think about it, it's a bit too suspicious for him to carry one around in a car he hardly drives. Maybe they planned this whole thing. Would he really stoop that low?

Billy pulls it out and gently tosses it to me, "Here."

I hope he doesn't think he has to go easy on me just because I'm a girl. That girls can't play ball crap is way over done. We can play ball better than a lot of guys. Sure they've got tricks but let's be honest. When it comes down to the fundamentals of the game girls take the cake leaving them with the crumbs.

Dribbling the ball up the driveway and I go in for a lay up. Swish. That's the sound I like to hear. Of course I'm trying to show off to prove my point. As I turn around chuckling, I see Billy walking towards me shirtless.

Instantly I find myself doing a double take of his muscular, luscious, brown, bare skin. The boy has abs for days, just stacked. I bite the side of my bottom lip struggling to fill my lungs back up with air. Now I know his personality spells out in fine print just why the male species disgusts me, but his body is the epitome of everything that makes me forget why personality matters.

His perfection is sculpted from that smile of his to those rock hard abs I could iron a shirt on. At least now I realize it's not his charm or wit that keeps the girls coming back for more. Can I have a second helping of that chocolate deluxe brownie?

Clearing my throat, I try to slide my glued eyes away from his chest, but come on. A good-looking brotha', I mean more appealing than ice cream on the hottest day of the summer, strolls over to you, and you don't drool a little? Puh-lease.

Politely he takes the basketball from my loose grip, "What?" Like he doesn't know what. He's like my own Hershey's chocolate bar that I would love to melt in my mouth. Whoa, I didn't mean that last part … completely.

"Why are you shirtless?" I struggle to lead my eyes back to his.

"'cause I don't wanna get my nice shirt all sweaty," he replies. Nice shirt? I think for a second about what shirt he had on before he graced me with that ripped body. Whatever. My brain's not functioning right to figure that out. Billy cradles the ball under one arm, "Does it bother you that I don't have it on?"

Bother me? No. Turn me on? Yes. I would love to ride you all day long like the horse outside of Wal-Mart. I giggle inside. If liking him weren't against everything I've taught myself to hate, and if I lacked the morals I've become so proud of, I picture one on one being what he was implying earlier. Good thing he doesn't know the dirty things I'm thinking right now. "No. I was just asking," I shrug it off until I see him flex his arm when he shoots the ball.

I feel my jaw become unhinged a second time. His arm is like KA-POW! You can see the shape of his muscles without the veins. In my opinion, if the veins show it means he doesn't have enough meat on his bones, but from the looks of it, that doesn't seem to be an issue.

"A'ight then," he rebounds his own ball.

Damn. His ass looks good in those shorts that hold his hips while sagging just enough to see his boxers. I wouldn't mind him backing that formed not framed, thang up on me. Geez Kie. Get a hold of yourself.

Billy asks, "You want first ball?" I snicker under my breath. That's not what he meant.

"Yeah sure," I catch the ball trying to put on my game face.

It's an intense game for the first thirty or forty-five minutes. We're working so hard covering every angle and position that it's really wearing me out. I almost think sex would have taken less energy. He's trying to prove that he's a 'real man' who can handle himself while I'm trying to prove my feminist thesis. No injuries are at risk, just pride, which in true perspective tends to last longer than any minor scrapes or bruises. Everyone knows a damaged ego can haunt you for a lifetime.

Billy's got the ball, and it's thirty-six to thirty eight. He's down by a basket. I don't want to loose. In fact, I hate to loose. Even if girls don't show it all time, we care about our egos just as much if not more than guys do.

"Oh can I make the shot," Billy bounces the ball in one spot. What I would do to help him miss this shot with a swift kick in his shin.

Scratching more of my exposed stomach I huff, "If you don't, that's game." I made the discovering conclusion that the more of my skin he sees the more distracted he becomes. I swear it's like he's never seen a girl's stomach.

He dribbles it between his legs grinning widely, "That's just it. I will."

"Yeah we'll see," I smile back sarcastically at him. A solution is cooking up in my mind. I sure hope he can't smell trouble.

Billy nods and starts towards the basket. Because the desperation to win is so overwhelming it pushes me over the edge to hop on his back playfully before he shoots. He sees me grasping the opportunity forcing him to catch me before I hurt his back. I'm not like a whale, but I know that I definitely have a bit of weight on me. Although if anyone jumps on anyone else's back unexpectedly, it can seriously damage them. Watching the ball bounce into the grass I giggle wrapping my arms around his neck. He can't do anything but start to laugh with me.

"That's not fair," his head tries to face me.

Leaning over his shoulder to look into his glowing eyes I argue, "Is too."

"Is not," the grip around my legs tightens in a flirty way.

"We never said that wasn't allowed," I pat his head a little. "Therefore it's fair."

"Oh it's like that?" I hope you're not getting comfortable with me being here. It was a temporary spur of the moment thing not a well thought out plan to get close to you pal.

"Yeah. It's like that," I continue to giggle. "So that means you loose." The giggle transforms into a full fledge laugh when Billy joins me.

"Which means you win," he licks his lips to a smile. Most guys wouldn't say that with a smile, but I think he wanted me to win. Something I figured out is when a guy *let's* you win he likes you. It works that way because he's willing to push his pride aside and put you first. But since it's Billy my guess is he's using this as another tactic to get into my pants.

"That's right I win," I throw my arms up in the air, and he twirls me around. Screaming at the sky, "Yay!" I let him spin me around a couple of more times while continuing to laugh.

He insists on giving me a victory ride to the porch where we'll sit to wait for DK and Mia. Instead of being my knight and shinning armor he's the horse the prince will have me join him on. I must admit I do think it's cute how he's carrying me.

Is giving into his slight charm such a horrible idea? I mean I'm being his friend right now and seem to be living. What's the worse that could happen if friendly making out occurred? Wait. Reality check. Who knows where this boy has been, and what kind of germs are lingering around in his mouth. It sucks it's written in dark red lipstick all across him what a womanizer he is.

As I take my seat on the porch step Billy says he's going to go get us a couple bottles of water from inside. Good thing he's so concerned with trying to impress me otherwise I would have had to haul my lazy ass to get it.

My head twirls around to the two white pillars, the faded red plastic chairs beside the door, the dusty concrete I'm sitting in, and finally the grass that's desperately trying to grow in front of me. Homey isn't it?

Moments later, after I've managed to fan myself slightly cool, he returns with dripping ice-cold bottles.

"Here ya go," he politely hands it to me. Plopping himself down beside me he quickly twists the lid off of his as I struggle with mine. "Need some help?"

"No," my battle progresses. I see how it is. Be polite enough to get me water but rude enough to give me the water bottle with the world's hardest lid. Thanks.

"You sure?"

"I'm fine," I use every bit of my wrist muscle. It doesn't budge an inch.

Watching me, he puts his own bottle down just waiting for me to take him up on his offer. Once I reach the point of frustration he's been waiting for, I hand it to him. With one clean twist it pops open. I warmed it for him.

"Thanks," I mumble under my breath before letting the ice water soothe my dry throat.

He nods.

The awkward silence we've become a bit accustom to arrives again. We listen to the sound of each other breathing and swallowing. Exhilarating.

Billy breaks through it head first. "Can I ask you some'n?"

I lean back on my elbows stretching my legs out in a desperate attempt to get comfortable, "Go ahead."

Billy uses all the courage in him to belt out, "Are you attracted to me?"

My mind hits the panic button making my heart race. Talk about being caught off guard. How do I *safely* answer that question? I know it's clear his body does it for me by the puddle of drool I created the second I saw him without his shirt on, oh and last night when he was looking very decent for the club, but personality wise? Can I say I find him only physically attractive without looking like a total tramp? "Possibly."

Billy softens his smile. "Possibly," he nods. "It's better than a no."

Wasting no time to return the question I cock my head his direction, "Are you attracted to me?" I look back as he leans forward trying to hide his face. Trying to stop grinning, he takes another sip of his water. Tick. Tock.

"Am I attracted to you?" he repeats the question to buy himself time. "… Am I attracted to you?"

"Come on," I demand for his honest answer, not that I couldn't draw the conclusion myself from the thing that was growing against my thigh last night.

Leaning back on his elbows too his eyes glance over my body that's drenched in sweat. God I hope he's not thinking what it would be like to make me sweat another way. "Hell yeah."

I smirk a little. Who doesn't like knowing someone thinks there hot? "Mmhm …"

"So …" he scoots a little closer. "You *possibly* are attracted to me, and I'm *definitely* attracted to you," he catches his eyes with mine. "The question is what do we do about it?"

Shaking my head I sit up, "Nothing."

"Nothing?" He pops up like me. His voice quickly fills with disappointment, "Nothing at all?"

"Look Billy," I stand up and dust off my butt that now has dirt on it. "Hell's fire may have been put to rest, but that doesn't mean I want to date you. Let's be real for moment ok? You manipulate, use, and play women. And if that's not a clear sign to you that I, of all people, am not into you, then I don't know what it is."

"Basically you think I'm a dog?" he sounds offended.

"Playa is a better word."

"Who told you I was a playa?" He stands up trying to look guilt free. What? He's just misunderstood? Who's he trying to fool?

"I don't have to be told. Look at you. You hang around niggas like DK who demoralize women. Everyone knows that if your friend treats women like shit so do you," I lean against the white pillar next to me.

"You're wrong," he walks down the couple of steps to stand in front of me.

I laugh sarcastically. "Let me guess your longest relationship was what 3 months?" Any low random number I choose will prove my point.

"So? What if it is 3 months?" Damn I didn't think I'd get it straight on point, "That doesn't make me a playa. That makes me not very good at relationships …"

"Ooo even better … not just a guy who can't commit to one girl, but one who's not very good at relationships in general." Folding my arms across my chest I sarcastically say, "The more and more you talk, the more and more I want you." There goes his chance at friendship.

"Look Ms. Judgmental, just because I don't have long lastin' relationships doesn't make me a playa. What makes you think it's all my fault? How come the girl can't have fucked up issues with her shit?" He says in an aggressive tone. I think I awoke the beast within. At least now I can get something real out of him and not this fake image he's pretending to be to get me to fall for him.

"If by her shit, you mean afraid you're cheating on her, because you ARE, then sure it's her fault," I nod with a smile. He's glaring at me the way DK does. The word bitch is probably popping up repeatedly in his head right about now.

"Hey," he points a finger at me. Oh no, now he means business. "I only cheated once. The other times girls like you wit' this complex that every guy cheats because his best friend does, jus' assumed I was," Billy jumps all over me. "You don't know shit about me, so don't think you can sit back and give me some bullshit psycho analysis." I roll my eyes at his pathetic attempt to defend himself with the textbook line that 'I don't know anything about him'. "But since we talkin' 'bout relationships, where's yo' boyfriend?"

I sit back down on the step. "I don't have one." His messed up ways are one thing, but mine are a whole other I don't feel like getting into.

Mimicking my actions and tone of voice he says, "Why's that? Does the constant judging and chewin' people out scare guys away?" No one told him to get an attitude with me. He doesn't have to cock his head to the side like that because he thinks he's right about something or hitting a soft spot with me.

"Go figure a girl with determination and her own opinions would turn guys off."

"I don't think that's the turn off," he says matter of factly like he's speaking from personal experience. Billy slides down next to me, now using a tone with care. "Ya know guys like girls who know what they're about, who can handle themselves, and who can make choices. It's actually really sexy," his compliments towards me might erase a few of his bad marks on his slate. "But even a girl who has all those features is still a turn off if all she does is jump down a guy's throat, judge him before she knows him, and worst of all, assumes all he wants is sex from her." My attention is off in the distance. "Take it from me Kie. Guys know it's a front when you behave like you do. You may not like guys getting' to know what's under the aggressive attitude and smart mouth, but if you keep doin' what you do ... a real man who's right for you will never get the chance he deserves." His eyes fall out towards the road where mine are.

Whatever. Like his life isn't messed up. "Since we're being real about relationships let's strike your weak spot shall we?" I turn my head towards him sharply. "We both know it's not about the girls thinking you're cheating all the time. It's about that word that haunts every man 'til his grave. You've had commitment problems ever since your mom died, which leaves you just as inaccessible to people as I am. I hide mine with attitude, but you choose to never get attached to anyone for a significant amount of time. Looks like we're two of a kind. So why don't you look into the mirror and recite what you said to me to yourself."

Now we're both upset. Misery really does love company. We both just stare at the burnt patches of grass in the familiar silence. I wonder where Mia is. See what her and her plotting gets me? It gets me overheated and very, *very* unhappy.

"Kie," I hear Billy manage to let my name slip out of his mouth.

For some reason I answer, "What?"

"I meant what I said about you. Someone deserves a chance. No matter how hard you push me ..." he moves a little closer to me and shakes his head slightly smiling. "I'm not goin' anywhere." I wish he would. I wish I could push him off a cliff. There has to be at least 40,000 other women who want him, but he wants me. Why?

I just nod with raised eyebrows. That's my way of saying 'whatever' without having to say it.

He turns back around towards the car pulling into the driveway. I wonder who that could be. Could it possibly be someone else to join the party of emotional bashing? I sure hope so. I grit my teeth.

I see a girl with long braids get out of her red Honda Civic. Chicken head alert. She removes her sunglass and squeezes them into her tiny jean pockets. Where the hell are the rest of her shorts? She looks like she's in her underwear, or those shorts you aren't supposed to leave the house in because their strictly to walk around privately in. What's the need to submit the whole world to your ass that's falling out? Good god, look at her shirt. Her sad excuse for boobs are trying their best to escape her baby T that stops right underneath them. She looks like hooker Christy accessories not included.

Opening the gate and strolling in wearing stilettos she says, "Billy, I knew I'd find you here." Ooo she wrong. She's got on a red shirt and pink heels. Girl needs to quit playing around with fashion like that.

"How?" He questions unhappily. I can't help but laugh a little at his sudden change of elocution.

"I called DK earlier. He said ya'll would be here lata," she stops, shifts her body weight and pops her butt out to one side. That's attractive.

It's girls like this that make me wonder why some girls are still single. These tricks can get men, but the ones who have something more than five-inch fake nails working for them can't. Another puzzle I can't quite put together with any other answer beside the obvious. It's all about sex.

Billy uncomfortably shifts his weight, "He did?"

"Yeah. Ya know I've called you 'bout fo', five times," she flips her braids to the back.

"I know," his nervous fidgeting continues. "And I told you we were done Chanté."

"But baby I thought since you weren't feelin' on nobody else that maybe me and you could …" she pushes her lips together to make a smacking noise.

My gag reflexes scrunch together. I think I'm gonna be sick. To think the things she's thinking makes me want to request a vomit bag and have someone gouge out my eyes so the nasty picture of them in bed is permanently removed.

"No," he says straight up. Wow a word I didn't think he came out of guys like him.

She shifts her weight to the other side as she twirls her gum around her finger attempting to be sexy, "Come on B, you know you miss me puttin' it down on you, doin' that twisty little thang you like." Great. Now my ears have to me removed.

"Look Chanté it was good while it lasted, but I need more than jus' sex. I need to be able to talk to my girl … other than dirty," he grins to himself making me roll my eyes.

That's why you don't give project girls good sex. You give it to them, and they'll never leave your ass alone. He lives here, and he doesn't know that? Talk about not being the brightest crayon.

In a high pitch tone she whines, "You can have that wit' me too."

Enough is enough. Kie to the rescue! "No he can't."

She pops her head at me with the attitude chicken heads are known for. "Excuse me?"

"He can't have that with you," I pop my head back in retaliation. I can't believe I am about to do this for this boy. "He's with me now."

Billy's eyes are popping out of his head. His jaw has dropped and hit the floor now. That's right. I'm doing *him* a favor. He better remember this too. I'm about to mess with a chicken head over her ex man, and they tend to get violent.

"You?" She says like I'm beneath her.

Pretending to be proud I remark back, "Yeah."

"Billy?" She turns and looks at him. He's still staring at me in amazement. I think he's having a harder time believing it that I am.

With the shocked look still on his face he faces her, "Yeah."

"Are you datin' this propa' pop princess wanna be?" with a flick of her nail she eyes the competition.

It's going to be international diva when I enter the game so that statement needs to be fixed. As for proper, just because my sentences make since in most English classrooms there's no reason to hate. I would say that to her if I thought it would do the trick, but I know it won't. Here comes the loud rude approach. "Look you half dressed, stripper reject, with a bad weave," I stand up in her face. Billy raises himself up to be by my side. "You better watch who you talkin' to like you crazy."

"Oh no you didn't heifer," Chanté waves her finger in front of my face.

"I did. Now you and every other fake part on you need to get your ass in your car and bounce because Billy's my man," I point a finger in her face. Talk about taking acting to a whole new level. "It's too late for yo' bitch ass."

"Bitch? Who you callin' a bitch?" She is about to touch me when Billy grabs her arm to hold her back.

Like I'm actually going to throw down I yell, "You! You crazy ho." I will if I have to, but from the looks of it, Billy won't let that happen.

Trying to break away for me she screams, "Bitch you betta' be lucky his ass got me." He's laughing. I'm glad he finds it humorous to watch me fight over him. Well I hope he don't get use to it, because this will not become a constant thing.

I cock my ass out towards the coast mocking her, "No you better be."

She struggles in his arms. After enough is enough Billy grabs her attention, "Hey! Go home."

Gently he leads her back towards her car while continuing the restraint, "Billy—

"Chanté please leave me and my girlfriend alone," he shines up his own acting skills. Hm. He said that a little too proudly. I hope these past ten minutes haven't made him forget he's back on my bad side.

"Fine!" she yells in his face opening her car door. "You want that trick pretendin' to be black, take her!"

As she starts up the car I scream, "Fuck you."

"No, fuck you," she waves her middle finger in the air before she backs up into the street.

"That's right! Get yo' bitch ass up out of here," I try to keep my angry face until she's completely out of sight. Once she's gone I bust out laughing.

That was like a whole new breed of fun. I'm laughing as hard as Billy is. He rushes over to lift me into the air for a hug. Enjoying his sweet embrace and the smell of his cologne I loose myself. His hold tightens for the next couple of moments.

"Thank you," he draws his bare chest body away from mine with a giant smile. Gently Billy puts me down, "Girl you were amazin'. For a minute I almos' thought you were a chicken head." I feel a playful nudge in my side. His smile makes little butterflies in my tummy.

"Yeah well we're even. You saved my life, and I saved yours." I remove my arms from around his neck. We all know every girl has that bit of crazy in her that a good man, not to call him one, can drag out of her under the right circumstances. "Actually I just saved you from a stalker, but caused you a possible window bashing," a flirty laugh escapes me as I fold my hands behind my back.

Of course he flirts back with a similar laugh. "I ain't worried about that," he glances at it. Nodding he agrees, "But we're even. Mos' def'."

To hate him or not to hate him that is the question. Sure he doesn't have great luck with girls, and sure his best friend is the world's biggest jackass, but he is very irresistible at moments.

"What are you two doing?" Mia comes back grinning widely.

"Chillin'," Billy answers slowly pulling his eyes away from me.

"Why are you shirtless?" she asks him as I look behind her to see DK covered in mud.

"Why's he muddy?" I point to DK who doesn't look like he had fun.

"I didn't wanna get my shirt all sweaty," he scratches his arm and starts to laugh at DK. "What happened to you nigga?"

DK points to Mia who's still smiling now with crossed arms right next to me. We all turn and look at Mia waiting for her to say something.

She shrugs innocently, "What?"

"Why's that all muddy?" I ask referring to DK.

"Oh," she plays naive. "We were horseback riding and stopped to let the horses have a little something to drink back in the woods by some pond when DK tried to put the moves on me. So I pushed him, and well he landed in the mud."

Billy and I both start laughing together like we have all day.

"Say wha'," Billy cups his mouth somewhat.

"Damn," I shake my head letting my laugh fade into a snicker.

"Can we go now?" DK looks at his khakis and wife beater that are drenched in mud.

He gets up still chuckling, "Yeah. Don't sit yo' ass on my seats either. Get a towel from the trunk." Billy tosses him the keys.

Mia opens the screen door and sneers, "Be careful."

"Thanks," DK nods at her with the same smirk.

"Kie," she calls to me in anger.

In the same tone DK groans, "Billy."

First they want us together, and now they don't? Why are they indecisive? It's ironic the second I actually want to hang with him they don't want me to. Gotta love life.

"In a minute," we say at the same time with our heads turned in opposite directions.

Mia goes in the house, and DK disappears in the front seat. I turn back around at the same time he does.

"I guess since their funs over so is ours," he smiles taking my hands into his. Good choice of action to continue the innocent flirting.

"Yeah," I smile and look at our hands. They don't look so bad together. In fact, his soft hand touching mine feels good. Hold on. Don't get too ahead of yourself Kie.

"How about tomorrow night I pick the two of you up and take you to our crib? Watch a couple of movies or some'n?" His fingers gently slip away to softly rub the back of mine. "They should be cooled off by then."

I look down at our fingers and slowly pull my eyes up to his making a well needed pit stop at his chest. "I—

"Before you shut me down like I know you will," he moves his body closer to mine. Oh boy not again with a kiss. I don't want to kiss you. "Remember what I said earlier."

I divert my attention up to the sky. Now if I say no he'll swoop in there and convince my mother or Big Mama to make us go. Basically I'm going to have go regardless of how I feel. I might as well erase the middleman. "Sure."

"A'ight then. 'round seven?" his attempt to give me a choice is not the least bid amusing or reassuring I'm making the right choice.

Again I smile, "Sounds good." Wow. I think if he asked me to do anything followed by that smile of his … I would.

"I'll call before I come," he leans in towards me.

Casually tilting a bit back, I make the point clear that it's ok to flirt, but we're not to the point of kissing yet, "You do that."

"Thanks again," his pre-moistened lips softly imprint themselves on my cheek. "Clean start tomorrow?"

In the kind tone I've been using, I reply my not too well thought out answer, "Yeah."

"Good. I think tomorrow will be a lot betta' than today," he smiles widely.

"Better be, or I won't be spending any more time with you and your retarded twin." I giggle as I point to DK whose wiping mud off of his face.

Billy merely smiles, "Dido."

"NOW!" Mia and DK yell together.

"Tomorrow," his fingers leave mine.

I wave with my index finger, "Tomorrow."

"Bye," Billy jogs off to his car where DK looks frustrated with the towels.

I'm having a total mind spasm. It's going around in circles fighting about what to do. Why's it so difficult to do what I know I want to? Why can't I just do what my heart says? Because I can't hear it over the fighting in my mind. Maybe I'll take a risk for once. Pull instead of push. It sure would please a lot of people … maybe even me.

Mia tosses her hands up in the air as she storms down the hall towards our bedroom. "Can you believe him?"

As I stroll by, my mom calls from her room, "Did you have fun?"

I trot back and peek my head in. "A lot. We're going to hang out again tomorrow."

"Good," she smiles and I remove myself.

"He had the nerve to try and kiss me," she sprawls out across the bed. "Oh and try to put his hands—

I close the door behind me and pull off my shoes. "Mia, you know he's wanted you since we've been here. Plus you're feeding the boy mixed signals, so what do you expect?"

"What? Are you on his side now?" She freaks out. "I mean are you saying I deserved to get attacked?

I laugh. "Oh now you got attacked?" For someone who was so sure she wanted to be around these guys she's being ungrateful for my sacrificing. "You wanted to go horseback riding, and he volunteered to go with you. I forfeited my afternoon to spend time with them like you kept asking me too. So don't even try to be all pissed about the fact DK had the chance to make the move he's been dying to."

Mia rolls over and looks at me spitefully, "Yeah well I was wrong for that. We don't have to spend any more time with that thing and his friend." She lays her head down to give herself a well deserved rest.

"Actually ..." I mumble moving towards my bag. "We do."

"What? Why?" She whines sitting up Indian style.

Letting my hair down I grin, "Billy asked, and I figured since you're all about fun and hanging out with them you wouldn't mind."

"Very funny bitcharella." Mia cups her hands together, "Well great then. It's going to be so much fun." Always ungrateful. Even when she gets what she wants.

"I sense hostility," I battle the tangles with my brush.

She gets up to grab her backpack, "You may sense it now, but you will see it tomorrow by far if he tries my patients again ..."

"Where are you going?"

"I smell like scum," she grabs her toiletries and pajamas, "oh yeah and horse. A nice hot shower followed by comfort binging will make it all better."

"Ok," I smile and keep brushing my hair when she stops at the door.

"I don't know what you and Billy did, but I do know you can't stop smiling. Keep it up," Mia gloats her way out of the room.

After her exit I return to debating. A movie can't be *that* bad. Nothing *drastic* can come out of it right? I know I said that about today and yesterday and was wrong ... but how can you go wrong with rented movies? Sometimes I wonder if I over react and over think every situation. I wonder if I over analyze him. Hm. There's something about Billy I don't understand. How on earth does he manage to keep me thinking about him when he's not around? Does he want me to keep debating if he's a good guy or not? By making me debate, he's making me think of him even more. By making me think of him more he thinks I'm going to find more things I like about him. For that train of thought I have to give him a couple points. Billy thirty-eight. Kie thirty-eight. I guess I didn't exactly win did I?

CHAPTER 3

Shots Anyone?

"What about this?" Mia holds up a red sleeveless shirt.

"I don't know," I shrug brushing my hair. This girl has held up at least six different shirts in the past ten minutes which all look relatively similar. She wants to look hot, but not too hot to where DK makes a move. You know for a girl who doesn't seem to care what he thinks she's spending an awful lot of time trying to pick something to please him.

"You have to know!" She screeches, throwing down the shirt into the pile with the others that have seemed to attack me while I'm sitting on the edge of the bed. "What says I'm sexy, but you can't have me?"

Watching her pout, I brush the other side of my hair, "The red one was fine."

"Really?" A hopeful look appears in her eyes.

"But so are the other five shirts that are trying to eat me alive," I push them towards her. What the big deal? He knows her clothes can cling on for dear life or look so loose they could fall off. His chance for viewing the best of both worlds has already passed so again what's the huff about?

"Grr," she growls at me running her hands through her hair for the second time in three minutes, a clear sign of frustration.

"Look," I turn and switch sides of hair once more, "DK is going to want you despite what you wear. You could walk out in a ballerina leotard with a grass skirt and slippers. The boy is still going to want you. He's attracted to a little more than what is on the outside," I roll my eyes in my own disbelief, "surprisingly enough." You would think a prick like him would be shallower than I'm giving him credit for.

She smiles a little at me and tilts her head. "That's great Kie," her voice sounds sincere, "but I still don't have anything to wear!" Mia tosses her hands my direction. "All your pep talk did was confuse me even more."

Now brushing the back of my hair, I laugh under my breath at the fact I could send her out in a pair of green socks, a black halter-top and a purple mini skirt with no questions asked. I guess it's time to be a good friend and dress her. "Wear the red shirt that defines the word dream in gold with those black tight pants you've been obsessing over. As for shoes, the cute red two strap sandals."

"Thanks," she smiles finally loosing the bitterness in her expression. Quickly pulling her up pants she asks, "Aren't you a little nervous?"

"About?" I squeeze into my favorite pair of light low-rise jeans. Even though it may appear like the only type of pants I own are low rise, the truth of the matter is I'm the most universal of my pants out of my friends.

"Tonight." We button our pants at the same time.

"What about tonight?" Why would I be nervous? It's not like we're walking down a dark alley, and I'm afraid of being mugged or something.

"Billy ..." Oh yeah like now it all makes sense.

"Now put it all together," I tell her as I change my shirt. My sleeveless white shirt clings to my chest and then a few centimeters under my boobs it splits into an outward V. It reveals my belly button, which is a bit sparkly. See. Nothing special.

Pulling her hair into a high ponytail she leaves two strands to shape her face, "You and Billy are feelin' each other, and tonight he might make a move."

"Ew. No. We are just friends," I brush her off and return to primping.

"Sure," she tightens her ponytail before plopping to the floor to put on her make up.

With my white bandanna in one hand I grab my brush. "We are. Nothing more."

"Kie be real with me. Do you like Billy?" She's asked me this question fourteen million times, and to her disappointment my answer hasn't changed.

"For the last time no. I'll keep you posted if my answer changes," I wrap my bandana to make a headband leaving two strands similar to Mia's around my face.

"Too bad."

"Why's that too bad?"

Wiping away excess eye shadow she nonchalantly says, "Because I know for a fact he likes you."

I plant myself next to her grabbing my own eye shadow from my bag, "How do you know for a fact that he likes me?"

Dusting her face with powder to hide blemishes she's afraid she has Mia gloats, "Well before DK tried to pull a fast one and ended up with a mouthful of mud, we were talking about the two of you. He mentioned to me how Billy couldn't stop going on about you."

He's been talking about me? Gossiping? What is he a girl? They're supposed to sit around and scratch themselves while watching sports on TV. What's happening to the world? Dear god, are we going to be sitting around on our asses, scratching ourselves, and yelling at the TV while they gather in the kitchen and talk about whose sleeping with who? For the sake of all that is good in this world, I hope not.

"What did he say about me?" I dust my own powder across my face getting rid of the same bumps. We usually wear just a little make up on our eyes and face. A good rule for any makeup user is less is more.

"Nothing really. I didn't pump DK for info. He just rambled something about Billy attempting to change to suit your better liking," she smiles proudly before glossing her lips.

Following her actions I gloss my lips, "Well all I said was stop sponging off of DK's no good ass."

"Anyway, the boy must like you if he's changing a few things in his life to try to be with you."

"Whatever you say," I stand up grabbing my belt off the bed.

Mia stands up to plop down on the bed, "Did you not hear me? He's changing certain things in his life to *try* to be with your crazy ass. He knows it's not guaranteed, and he's trying to better himself to fit your ridiculously high standard of what a guy should be. Doesn't that say something to you?"

It says he's easily swayed. Ok seriously though. How likely did it seem that he was just going to change who he was because I voiced my opinion as always. Could he really be doing what Mia's saying? Am I just being a bitch to him? He sets him self up hoping that I'll give him a chance, and I just beat him senseless with my judgments and attitude. I'm such a bad person.

She buckles her other shoe, "Earth to Kie. You haven't said anything for a good three minutes. Are you even listening to me?"

"Yeah. I was just letting it process."

"Right," she slips her lip-gloss in her pocket. "And you came up with?"

"That this discussion is not leading down the path of anything I like," I stand up to face her.

With her hands on her hips I know what this means. Head biting action is ready to commence, "Well get over it. You nit pick every half decent guy who comes your way. Go figure you blow off the first guy who'll do whatever it takes to be with you."

What's with everyone shredding me apart? Why does everyone have to yank out my flaws, toss them down on the table, and say look at them Kie. Fix them. Am I not entitled to be afraid of heartbreak? That shit hurts. I made a choice a long time ago not to get mixed up with it again. It's like I took cupid, tied the bastard up, and shoved him in my closet.

"Are you done now?" I try to get by, but Mia pushes me back on the bed.

"No. Not until I get through to that over opinionated mind of yours," she thumps me on the head. Ouch. "I'm not saying you have to marry the boy, but give him a chance. Got it?"

If she likes the boy so much, why doesn't she date him? "Got it," her eye contact is overpowering me. I've seen Mia be belligerent, but this takes it to an entirely new level.

"Alright then. Let's go see if they're here," she starts out of the room.

I lag for a second to think it all over again while I search for my phone. Whatever happens to me tonight, I just pray I make it out alive.

"Mom," I say closing the door to our room behind me. "Mom," I knock at the door. "Mom," I open it to see her cuddled on my step dad. Ew. Why on earth are they cuddling? What is it about this place that makes everyone want to be in love? This isn't freakin' Paris people. It's the ghetto side of Ft. Worth, Texas. Has everyone forgotten that but me?

"Yeah," she lifts her head off his chest. Cringing I scratch my arm. Seeing them happy is like a rash.

I lean against the door, "We're leaving. I've got my cell."

"Where are you going?" My father holds my mother closer to him.

"To hang out at Billy and DK's apartment."

"Is it safe?"

"Yeah dad I'll be fine," I force a smile on my face.

"He's here," Mia yells down the hall.

"Well I would like to meet this young man," he clears his throat.

As I hear Mia' voice call to me again I rush, "Next time we go out dad. I gotta go."

"You have fun," she snuggles in his grip. "Be careful, and call me later to let me know when you'll be home."

"Will do," I nod and shut the door. As I stroll down the hallway I shudder off the image of them. At least I don't have to talk to Big Mama about leaving with Billy. I wouldn't want her to start with the 'you should go for him' thing again. That lecture from Mia was enough, to hear it again would send me into cardiac arrest.

Big Mama scoots her feet across the wooden kitchen floor and calls out, "Kie." Damn. I spoke too soon.

"Yes," I stroll towards her.

Once she finally meets with me she asks, "Are you going to Billy's?"

I smile leaning against the frame that leads to the living room by the front door, "Yes. We'll be back later."

"You remember what I said," she wipes her hands on her housecoat.

"I will," a sigh escapes me as I force myself to smile politely.

"Good boy," Big Mama smiles putting one hand on her aching back. Her country accent peeks out, "Great person like you."

Hesitating I nod, "I know Big Mama. I'll make sure I have some fun."

"If anything happens, you come straight home. Ya hear me?" She wags her finger at me. I love her almost more than my real grandma. God rest her soul.

Sneaking up behind me, Billy wraps his strong, warm arm around my side, "Don't worry I won't let anything happen to her."

"You better not," she gives him a similar finger threaten. "I'll take my switch to you."

He tosses his head back in slight laughter. "Aw come on Big Mama, not the switch. I'll take good care of her. I promise," Billy looks down at me and smiles. There he goes again smiling.

Big Mama touches his arm slightly, "All right baby. You be careful."

Leaning down he kisses her on the cheek, "I will. You go back and sit on the couch."

"Mmhm," she strolls off humming.

I remove his arm and turn around to face him. When doesn't he look good? Somehow his pants always sag off of him just right. A pair of light washed jeans is tonight's prime example of this. Then there's how his shirt sticks to his arms, not in that gross muscle shirt way though, and hugs his chest. It's black and says FUBU in gold cursive. To top the ensemble off, he's got on a backwards black baseball cap. See what I mean. Hot.

"Funny how you magically pop up when we start talking about you," I step back as he leans against the doorframe.

Billy grins proudly, "What can I say? I've got great timing." Cocky bastard.

"And a great wardrobe," I lick my lips. "You look good."

He grins to himself rubbing his chin, "If my ears didn't deceive me, I think I just heard you compliment me."

"And if I did?" I tug the bottom of his shirt. Billy looks down at my hand. Did I mention that I'm usually a big flirt?

Slightly confused he touches his bottom lip with his tongue, "Are you hitting on me?"

"And if I am?" I move my body into his slightly letting our chests touch.

He nervously chuckles as the stutters come running out of his mouth proving he's not ready for a girl like me. Yet. "Uh …"

After I believe I've let him suffer enough I pull away, "You wish."

Billy clears his throat as if to regain his dignity, "Very funny."

Following behind me out the door I hear Billy mutter, "You look pretty cute yourself." His eyes glance down to my butt as we head through the gate towards his car.

"Me or my ass?" I wink.

"Oh so they get counted separately?" Ha-ha. That joke wasn't exactly funny, but it still made me smirk. Billy speeds up around me, "Wait, wait."

"What?" I stop to look at him. Do I have a bug on me? Geez I hope it's not a bee or anything else that stings. Man I really hope it isn't a spider either. I hate them because they crawl. Just the thought is giving me the shivers.

Billy opens the passenger door for me, "Your door."

"Thank you," I smile as I climb in. Thank God it wasn't a bug.

"No problem," he winks and shuts the door.

"He opened the door for you with his own free will?" Mia speed talks trying to get the question out before he gets in the car.

I casually nod.

Billy gets in, smiles, and fastens his seatbelt. His mouth is always in an upright position when I see him, which is something that simply fascinates me.

As we pull off down the road I decide to investigate the cause of his muscle spasm, "What are you smiling about?"

"Can't a brotha' jus' be happy?" he gently taps the gas petal.

"No," I answer playfully.

"Damn."

Gently touching his arm with my index finger I lean over, "So why are you smiling?"

With the same flirty grin he leans back, "Because I get to see you."

We stare into each other's eyes for a brief moment at the stop sign. Billy slides himself back over and presses down on the gas once again. Talk about an over used textbook line.

"I'm sure that's it," I feel Mia nudge my seat.

Easing into traffic he continues spouting his textbook lines, "It's hard not to smile when I see yo' beautiful face."

Did he buy How to Get a Girl to fall in Love with You for Dummies? I swear every line he spits can be found in chapter two: How to compliment her while sounding like the corniest guys in history. Heaven forbids he uses anything original. I don't respond; I merely smile for him to enjoy. There's no reason to push the flirting into overdrive.

"Besides you've got a great smile that makes me smile. You jus' don't show it enough," he compliments me again. Tactic number eighty three, compliment her to death. I hide my smile with my hand. "Don't be tryin' to hide it," he pulls my hand off of my mouth at our first stoplight. "Let me enjoy it."

Shaking my head I continue grinning. This flattery is going to go to my head. I glance at Mia in the review mirror to see her teeth are showing, her cheekbones are high, and her rightness meter going up. Great, when we get home I'm going to get the 'I told you so' lecture.

There's silence in the car now. Music is playing just loud enough to compliment a conversation if we were having one. At least their stations play music rather than commercials.

Finally getting her turn to speak Mia leans between the seats, "So where's DK?"

Switching lanes, Billy continues to cruise down the highway, "He went to get the movies."

"Well isn't that nice," Mia plops back in her seat to look out the window.

I bet he's renting movies that can be considered mediocre porn.

Mia mumbles in an unpredicted annoyed tone, "Turn up the radio please."

I reach for the knob to turn it up so you can hear the bass. It's loud enough to really feel the vibes, but not to the point where you feel like you're in a vibrating chair.

She sings bouncing around in her seat. I'm glad she's entertaining herself.

Billy pulls off the highway and up to the stop light twenty minutes from the last one. He leans his head against the headrest and starts smiling at me. I do the same thing he does giving the so-called grin he loves.

"You're beautiful," he mouths. See if that wasn't the worst pickup line behind 'you've got beautiful eyes' maybe I could enjoy it. He broke out the big guns and didn't even have to. Maybe he doesn't mean for it to sound as corny as it does. I'll just let this one go and say thank you.

"Thank you," I mouth back at him seeing him close his small open mouth smile to just a simple one. Billy places his hand on top of mine letting our fingers lock together. How did I miss that this is where all the compliments were leading?

When the light turns green his hand doesn't move. Do I let it stay, or do I make it move? I guess I enjoy flirting with him, but that hasn't erased the fact I know what sort of person he is. There's no harm in just holding hands with him right? Out of the corner of my eye I see Billy smiling the widest I've seen yet. As I face forward I feel his grip tighten reassuring me that this is ok.

Fifteen minutes later we're parked outside these old rundown apartments. They're brown, well faded brown, have broken windows, at least one on every building, and rust clinging onto the railing as well as the stairs. Now I have been taught never judge a book by its cover, but this place looks like it wouldn't be anything worth my wild to read. I should give it a chance though. I mean it can't possibly be that awful. Oh my gosh is that car on fire?

"We're here," he turns off the car. If only he was kidding.

Undoing her seatbelt Mia asks, "Downstairs or upstairs?"

"Down," he points to the apartment in front of us where a bright light is shinning through.

Well at least I won't be afraid that I'll break the stairs when I walk up them. I can't imagine having to live here. What I don't get is how these people have their cars rolling around on dubs, but they live in a place like this. Does that make any sense to you? Instead of putting your car on twenties use it to get your ass up out of the ghetto, unless of course you just love living here. Maybe they enjoy living here so much that they don't want to move to a nicer neighborhood. Not the best thing in my opinion, but whatever makes them happy.

Billy takes the keys out the ignition and unlocks the doors. He waits politely for me to reach the front of the car where he takes my hand leading me to their door with Mia following behind us. As he twists his key in the door my eyes focus on the 4A that's falling off. Is it just too much trouble to fix it? I mean it's not like I'm asking him to repaint the faded blue door, which I might add makes me question who came up with the color scheme for this building.

When we walk in we're greeted by a surprisingly clean and very well decorated apartment. He lays his keys in a bowl on a cute little glass table that's within the first few feet of when you walk in. I walk along side Billy as I admire the open living room we're welcomed to.

My attention diverts to the knock off paintings of abstract art leaving the slightly stained sky blue carpet out of judgment range. Once you're actually in the room there's a wooden dinning room table with a glass table behind it leaned against the wall. The glass table has flowers in a vase, and we all know they're only to impress females. Across from the dinning room table is a mini bar that comes out just a little like an L leaving the living room still wide open to walk into the kitchen. The living room has a black leather couch and a leather recliner both cocked to side aimed towards the thirty-six inch TV. It has a mantle piece above with pictures of DK, Billy, and some unidentifiable people. Near their couch is a glass coffee table that happens to have magazines of some sort on it. So far it's much better than I thought it would be.

Letting go of my hand Billy heads down the hallway, which is a right when you first walk in. "Yo DK." I'm going to assume their bedrooms are that way because I have no intention of finding out.

"Yeah," DK pops up in the mini bar with shot glasses, limes, a saltshaker, and tequila.

Turning around he acts surprised, "Oh there you are."

Ignoring Billy's comment he slides his way to us, "Well, well, well, if it isn't the finest bitches from Austin to ever step foot in this part of town." DK plops his materials for our 'evening of fun' on the table.

"Finest, only, same thing," Mia mumbles strolling over to the table. Snickering under my breath I watch as she points, "So what's all this about?"

DK scratches his bare sculpted arm, which is clearly a sad attempt to draw Mia's attention to it, "Shots."

"I see that," she says raising her voice to a perky tone. "Why?"

"I thought it would be a nice way to relax everyone. A way to get ova' the pas' while lookin' on to a very bright future," he winks at Mia.

"Here, here," Billy cheers taking his place next to DK.

I have this gut feeling that after she made him eat mud that he got home, got cleaned up, and got laid. That would explain the unusually cheerful vibe he's giving us. Isn't it amazing the effect sex has on certain people?

Mia sarcastically raises her eyebrows, "Right."

"I mean you don't have to," DK takes the childish approach to get Mia to drink. "If it's too intense fo' you then …"

"Oh I can handle it," her eyes shift up and down glancing him over.

With a devilish smirk DK leans towards her, "Do it then."

"I'll do shots if Kie does," Mia leans against the table.

Did she have to say that? Why does everything really have to rely on me? It's not enough pressure trying to make myself look available without looking desperate, but now I have to drink or the whole night's fun is ruined? Anyone ever heard of this thing called fairness?

"Well in that case looks like you won't be drinkin' anything but caffeine free coke," DK's pathetic joke gets no chuckles. A glare from me, a sarcastic look from Billy, and a sneer from Mia, but no one laughs.

"D," Billy moves next to me on the other end of the table.

He apologizes in a fake tone, "Sorry." Bastard.

"I'll do it," I say proudly. Yeah I don't know why I will get drunk in a strange house with people I hardly like, but it sounds like fun.

Looking heartfelt Billy objects, "Kie you know you don't have to." What he really means is 'you have to so that we don't break out into fights with each other'. I'm very good with reading in between the lines.

Shrugging, "It's all right. I'm up for it." What's the worse that could happen?

"Say wha'?" DK looks at me.

With attitude I repeat myself, "I said I'm up for it."

Moving back to the table he mutters, "Surprise, surprise."

"I think tonight will be full of those," Mia strolls over to be by my side.

"Well then, let's get this thang started," he pops off the lid to the tequila bottle and pours some into two of the glasses. The next thing we know we're all standing at the table with shot glasses filled with tequila. "Mia, you gon' let me do a body shot off of you?"

She glances at me with a strange smirk. Dog's have fleas. If she wants to get them then she can go ahead.

Pulling her hair to one side she hops up onto the table, "Only where skin is showing."

DK jumps on his first opportunity to touch Mia with permission, "Fine by me."

Mia leans back on her palms so DK's attention will fall onto her chest as he determines where he's going to put the salt.

Scanning her body for the sexiest skin he can find he decides on the tad bit of midriff, unfortunately for her, "Found it." Lifting up the end of her shirt, he sprinkles salt underneath her belly button. After the lime is secured in her mouth, Mia watches as he slowly lick the salt off.

I feel like I'm having a panic attack. It's not like having to watch him lick her isn't enough, but I have to listen to the sound of him sucking limejuice. My stomach cringes so tightly I have to put a hand on it to hold back vomit. What did I get myself into?

"Mmm," DK wipes his lips off. "Good."

Mia raises her eyebrows as if intrigued, "I've been licked better."

Billy and I laugh together. Out of all the things she could have said …

"Billy you gon' take a straight shot, or will you be givin' some girl pleasure wit' yo' tongue?" he nudges him in the side.

Rolling my eyes, I hop on the table next to Mia. Pleasure with his tongue? We aren't about to engage in oral sex. It's just a little licking and sucking, which I guess does sound sexual.

"If Kie don't mind," his hopeful expression is pathetic.

"Same rules apply," I take a similar stance to Mia's.

She smiles at me as to try to comfort me. Does she think I'm nervous? You know, despite what everyone likes to believe, I know how to have a good time. Just because I'm not one of those girls who go to parties just to get drunk and felt up by some guy so they can have credit in their social cliques, I'm automatically classified as being uptight.

"All right," he takes the salt. Stuffing the lime slice in my mouth, I let my mind wonder over the possibilities of how he can get around the rules like he's praying too.

Billy takes my hand and lightly puts a few grains on my inner wrist. I glance at Mia who's probably swooning about the spot he picked. In one clean sweep, it's gone. With a deep sigh I feel my temperature rise. Afterwards he uses his mouth to slip the lime out of mine.

Licking his slips he mutters, "Tasty."

What do I say now? Do you ever feel like saying 'please insert comeback here'?

DK questions while refilling the glasses, "Now shots off of us?"

"Yeah," Mia hops down. Correct me if I'm wrong, but once you lick a guy you've been flirting with, you leave the impression that you want him. Sad thing is I don't know if I want that impression there or not.

She hits my thigh making me pop up, "Yeah." I bet I sounded like the worse possible echo right there.

Geez they're like kids in a candy store. This has to be the best treat they've gotten all day.

"Lick me anywhere baby," DK opens his body up to her.

Seductively she wraps her fingers around a shot glass, "I bet you'd like that."

"I'd really love it if you licked my—" Mia shoves the lime in his mouth. I would have shoved it down his throat personally. Giggling she hands me a lime. Poor Billy looks like he's a bit uneasy with having me lick him.

Making the objection like a considerate young man should, Billy whispers, "ya know you don't have to righ'?"

DK quickly removes the lime from his mouth, "Will you just shut the hell up, and let her lick you?"

With a snigger I nod, "I have to agree with him this time."

I place the lime in his mouth and smirk at him reassuringly. Out of the corner of my eye I notice the devious grin on Mia's face. Aw man. Can this really get any dirtier than licking them?

Mia leans over and whispers in my ear, "Let's lick them on their lower abs at the same time."

Oh why not? I've been dreaming about those rock hard muscles since I saw them.

DK whines with the lime in his mouth, "Hey no secret plots."

"Shut up before I decide not to lick you at all," she threatens.

I laugh and shake my head at the two of them. Maybe DK likes her because he has to fight to be in control, or maybe the idea of her not being putty in his hand turns him on.

Lowering her voice she bites her bottom lip, "Both of you lean back." The two of them do as instructed.

Synchronized, Mia and I lift up their shirts. When I lift up Billy's I see this beautiful gold light shine and hear music play. It's just so incredible. I don't know how a guy can have abs that look like they came from god himself. Hell I don't need salt to lick them; I would just do it for fun. We sprinkle a little on their lower abs knowing their attention is rooted on us.

"One," her eyes meet DK's.

"On your mark," I look into Billy's.

She lowers her mouth towards his abs, "Two."

"Get ready to lick," I lower myself as well.

"Three." Our tongues attack their stomachs. It's like licking salt off a rock, a very hot rock, in temperature and appearance. We grab our shot glasses, drink, and suck the lime out of their mouths. Well, at least I do. Mia get that out of your mouth! You don't know where that's been. When she's ready, she pulls her lips off of his not revealing a lime, which I thought was the point.

Mia slowly removes the lime from her mouth and tosses it onto the napkin where mine is. She licks the juice, or at least what I hope is juice, off of her lips.

"What the fuck was that?" DK asks half excited, half confused.

She giggles at his reaction before she wipes the juice from around her lips, "A body shot."

"That was not a body shot! That thing you did wit' yo' tongue in my mouth … I thought you weren't supposed to kiss in body shots." Why is he suddenly a nervous wreck? Wow it's like he's never been kissed before. "Don't get me wrong girl. It's not that I didn't wanna be kissin' you. I jus' thought …" DK sounds like such a little girl right now.

"You can't kiss me," she taps his chest, "but when I do a body shot, I can kiss you."

Yanking down his shirt DK grunts, "I didn't know those were the rules."

With a wink she replies, "I make the rules."

"Let a nigga know that's how you play baby," he grabs the tequila bottle and shot glasses.

Flirting vibes are bouncing off the walls in this house. Welcome to the house of love. Did I say the house of love? I meant the house of unwanted, uncontrollable urges referred to as lust.

Handing a glass to Billy he whispers, "Our turn."

"Same rules," Mia points a finger.

"Yeah," I agree looking at Billy who has just grabbed a lime.

"All right," DK hands Mia a lime.

Billy grabs me by my belt loops and pulls me closer to him. He tilts my head to the side a little allowing him to sprinkle salt on my collarbone. Placing the lime into my mouth indicating he's ready, he leans over as I close my eyes. His hot tongue pushes against my soft skin. The next thing I know I feel really warm, and my heart is beating a little faster. As his tongue pushes against my skin again, I whimper out a moan. My hands grip the table when Billy's tongue presses against my collarbone one last time. He lets his lips linger for a moment before he sucks the lime away from me. It slips from my grip to his. Removing the lime from his mouth, he tosses it in the pile with the others.

After swallowing he licks his lips, "Good."

I feel my words trapped in my throat, "Very." How on earth do I manage to resist him? I should get a prize for being the strongest woman on earth. Anyone who can resist him deserves that prize. I may not being doing it well, but I'm doing it.

Billy smiles widely at me. We glance at Mia who's obviously letting the liquor take control of her inhibitions. See. This is exactly why we shouldn't have alcohol.

"Our turn," Mia slithers out from DK's grip letting him pour two more shots.

I rub the top of Billy's hand, which happens to be resting on my thigh, "How many are we doing?"

"Three," she answers handing me a glass. "It's just enough for a nice buzz while we watch some movies."

I nod and look back at Billy. As you could probably guess we handle our buzzes differently. To Mia a buzz just means you're welcome to talk to her if you weren't before, lucky DK. Me on other hand, I get a little friendlier than expected. I feel a need to cuddle or take a nap, depending on the environment.

Before sticking the lime in his own mouth Billy politely asks, "Having fun?"

"Of course she is," Mia nudges me in the side preparing to pour salt on DK. I wish he was a slug.

I nod hesitantly. Excitement is one shot, fun is two shots, and uncertainty is three.

Tilting Billy's head to the side I sprinkle a little on his jawbone line. I put the salt down and glance at Mia who nods letting me know it's time for our tongues to assail. Slowly I drag my tongue up his jawbone line. No. No. I mean S-L-O-W. I make sure to circle each area with my tongue before moving on to the next. Billy's body trembles as he shuts his eyes. He grips my thighs as I reach to the middle of the salt line. As I finish up I press my lips gently on the spot I licked last. I take the shot, suck the lime out of his mouth, and smile innocently.

Tossing the lime aside I look at Mia, "Fun."

"Yup."

As Billy's eyes open I try to meet them with mine. I have to say it's pretty hard to keep my eyes on his and not his friend that's trying to join the party.

"That's was …" Billy manages to say in an airy tone. "Whoa …"

"Good?" Mia asks DK while he struggles to bring himself into reality.

Rubbing the back of his neck he mumbles, "If only you knew."

We each go for another round as planned. There's something about hormonal teenagers, alcohol, and being alone that doesn't add up. You know, if adults were to be judging this situation they would begin to place bets on how long until sex occurs. I can't blame them though. There's so much raw sexual magnetism in here I don't know how *I'm* controlling myself.

After finishing their last shots the boys begin the clean up. DK makes his way into the kitchen with the bottle and limes while Billy grabs the glasses.

"Throw me a water bottle," Billy says putting the shot glasses on the bar. DK slides the liquor on the counter and tosses him a water bottle.

"Thanks," he strolls around the couch and picks up the top movie out of the bag. "What do we have first on our list?" Billy reads the side of the box, "101 Things to Do about Charlie."

Mia quickly squeals, "I love this movie!" She plops down in the recliner and proceeds by tossing her legs over one of the arms.

"Good to know," Billy nods turning on the TV. Slipping the DVD in he turns to ask me, "Do you like this movie too?"

Sliding myself onto the couch I agree, "Yeah." I feel like I'm in a oversized freezer. Aren't you supposed to have your house hot to make girls want to take their clothes off; not cold to make them want to layer it on? That would be DK's way of thinking. Maybe he figures if he freezes us to death we'll be forced to cuddle with them for body heat. I have to give the sneaky bastard credit for his creative methods of getting girls to do what he wants. Rubbing my arms I struggle to keep warm.

Like a moron he questions, "Cold?" Who rubs their arms when they're not cold?

"Just a little."

"How 'bout a blanket?"

"Sure," I smile politely.

Billy takes a few steps down the hall to arrive at their coat closet where he grabs a dark green cotton blanket.

Plopping down next to me, he covers us both, "Here ya go." I didn't know we were sharing. Although with the way this night has been going I could have guessed it.

DK turns off the lamps and slinks himself down on the floor next to the recliner where Mia has made herself comfortable. Sometimes his plan of attack is too obvious for his own good.

I snuggle beside Billy letting him wrap his arm around my waist as our fingers intertwine. The smell of his cologne is sending me into a trance. Why is it he has to smell like paradise? It's like being on an island having no worries and all the romance you could dream of with a hot native.

You know, I've never lived like this before. I've never just been in the moment or done things that are just about the now. Long-term plans are always on my plate, but I'm dying to know what it feels like to lock your inhabitations in the closet for the night. Then again what if this is the moment that determines where Billy and I go from here? I'm not saying I want more, but on the other side of this argument I'm not saying I want less. To be blatantly honest here, I don't know what I really want. Place the blame on my sixteen year old hormones that warp my capability to make the right decisions.

There are moments I can feel his lips on mine with his hands tracing my curves, and then there are moments where I know he can't do anything for me I can't do for myself, so to speak. He *just* jumped on the ball to straighten his own life, so why should I think that he would be capable of doing anything else besides messing mine up?

Around twelve thirty we're starting the third movie. Mmm, I love his strong arms cradling me, his face nuzzling against mine, and his warm breath sending chills down my spine. I wonder if he's getting lost in his feelings like me. With a deep breath I let my eyes fall on Mia who's smacking down on the popcorn she demanded DK make. I'm sure she could get him to do anything she wanted right now. Speaking of which, where is DK?

"Billy you want some Kool-Aid?" DK pops up behind the couch with two glasses in his hand.

Shaking his head he answers, "Naw I'm straight."

"You sure?" he leans forward letting the extra class of juice spill out onto the blanket and me.

Jumping up instantly I yelp, "My shirt!" It continues dripping deeper until it's between my boobs. Now that's not the type of juice that belongs there.

"My couch!" DK yells at me like it's my fault.

Mia, Billy, and I divert our attention from the stain that's setting on my shirt to DK who has to be the most inconsiderate person alive.

DK hesitantly apologizes, "Sorry."

I glare back down at one of my favorite shirts that now has a bright red spot to accompany it. Great. It looks like I was shot. Not only was it a very expensive shirt, on sale nonetheless, but it looked so sexy on me. A perfectly drool worthy shirt gone to hell with red stains that won't come out all because of that clumsy jackass.

"It's a bit cold," I mummer out feeling the air create more shivers.

"Come on Kie. You can wear one of my shirts," Billy takes my hand leading me towards his room.

DK yells as we turn into the first door on the right, "Sorry." The door is already open, so I just follow in his room where he wastes no time turning the light on. At least he knows not to try anything slick.

"Nice room," I give it a wince over. It turns out that his window is the one closest to the parking lot. His king sized bed, which is pushed up against it, has a navy blue comforter and pillows to match. Talk about lady presentable.

Sliding his closet door open to reveal a surprisingly tidy scene he mumbles, "Thanks."

His dress shirts are gathered together on the left descending in color from darkest to lightest. Next are his nicer every day shirts, collars first, ones without next, also descending in color. After those are his jerseys. To no one's surprise they are separated by teams. Finally there is stack of undershirts divided on three different shelves. A bit anal retentive are we?

"Looks tidy," I attempt small talk as he begins to decipher through his shirts. My attention wonders down to the bottom of his closet where his shoes mirror the organization of the clothes. My view isn't exactly clear, but I'm pretty sure they descend from dress shoes, to basketball shoes, to flat top shoes. Is it ok that it frightens me his room is neater than mine?

"I try," Billy smirks reaching for a white wife beater. "This should work righ'?"

I nod at the simple shirt. He tosses it to me and plops down on his bed like he's going to watch me change.

"Uh ... excuse me," I fold my arms. "I need to change."

"Go ahead," he leans back on his bed. "I won't look."

"Like I'm really falling for that."

Tossing his hands up he surrenders, "Fine."

"Thank you," I shut the door behind him.

My eyes begin around his room again as I pull my shirt off. On the night-stand next to his bed I check the time on his digital alarm clock only to realize it's nearly one. Next to the clock there's a little wooden brown box that I can't help but wonder what's in it. Giving in to curiosity I sneak a peak. Condoms. He keeps his condoms in a decorative box on the side of his bed. Shaking my head I toss my shirt into his hamper that's in the right corner of the room.

As I adjust my bra my eyes find themselves attracted to his wooden six drawer dresser beside the door. After slipping the shirt on I maneuver my way to it and begin to browse through the CDs. Does it surprise anyone that there are only rap and R&B CDs?

Next to the CDs is a wooden box similar to the one of his nightstand. Nosily, I tilt the lid up a tad to reveal a small stash of weed. Once again I shake my head as I notice a picture with a circular locket draped over the side of it on the corner of the dresser. Lifting the wooden frame into my hands I make sure to be careful with the vintage looking necklace.

Billy creaks open the door to catch me staring at the picture of the woman. "What are you doin'?"

"Looking at this picture," I say as he comes all the way in closing the door behind him. "She's really pretty."

Scratching the back of his neck he hums, "Mm."

For some reason I can't draw my attention away from her. "Who is she?"

"That's my ma," he falls on the edge of his bed.

Plopping down next to him I study her characteristics trying to see if their resemblance is noticeable. Although her complexion is lighter, the curves of her nose and face shape allow you to see where some of his traits come from. I can see where his smile originates, but it's the beautiful glowing brown eyes that only a mother could give to her son that convince me this is his mother. How many times do the eyes give it away? "Wow. She was gorgeous."

"Thanks," he attempts to smile. "That picture was taken befo' she died."

Handing the picture off to Billy I question, "When was that?"

"I was eight," I watch him drift into the picture.

❧   ❧   ❧

"Happy Easter," Billy's father places the locket around his mother's neck in front of their bedroom mirror.

"Oh!" she squeals with glee lightly touching it as Billy sneaks into the room on his hands and knees hiding in an inconspicuous corner. "What's this?"

"Just something to show you how much I love you," he pecks a kiss on her cheek.

"Well I love you too," she leans back and does the same. "Why a circle honey? Why not a heart?"

Gently touching her cheek he replies, "Because my love for you is never ending just like that circle. Our picture is on one side and Billy's on the other," his arms drape themselves over her shoulders swaying her gently from one side to the other. Continuing to whisper in her ear he says, "You know being a good farther is the best thing I've ever done in my life. Without the two of you I don't know where I would be."

❧   ❧   ❧

"I wouldn't have a life, my dad told her. To this day I don't understan' how two people could love each other so much," Billy gently places the picture down in his lap.

Politely smiling I feel the need to ask, "What happened next?"

"A few days later they dropped me off at Big Mama's to play wit' DK while they went into town to handle some legal business. I remember how I couldn't wait 'til they got back so I could ask my ma if DK could stay at our brand new house on the good side of town," there's a sudden rise of pride in his voice. I never new he lived on the good side of town. Hell I didn't know there was a good side. "It was aroun' seven forty-five when Big Mama got this call. I remember hearin' a slight scream from in the house makin' all us kids stop our game of ball. We all turned towards the door where she was standin', and it was like time jus' froze ..."

❧   ❧   ❧

With tears in her eyes Big Mama calls Billy to her. "Billy sweetie," she wipes her hands on her apron, "come here."

Her tone was the indicator that something wasn't right. Rushing over to her, his big brown eyes full of hope that her tone was misleading, Billy questions like any good kid would, "What's wrong?"

In one clean swoop she's cradling him in her round, cushy arms. Sitting down on the porch steps together, she doesn't let him go. "You're parents won't be coming to get you."

"Yay!" he squeals. "That jus' means I can stay here longer wit' ya'll. Guys I can play basketball even longer," he calls out to the boys, until Big Mama lays a hand gently on his leg.

"Not like that Billy," her grip gets tighter making him feel like he's being smothered in a pillow. "They were on their way here when a car crashed into them in head on. Then on their way to the hospital ... in the ambulance ..." her voice trails. "They ... they passed away," a tear drops onto her apron as Billy's eyes loose their innocence.

"When you're eight and someone tells you that yo' parents have been taken from you like that; yo' whole life falls apart. The pain eats you alive. There's no one to teach you right from wrong. No one to tell you they love every night befo' you go bed. No one to help you make yo' dreams come true, but worst of all there's no one to be there fo' you. No one to believe in you," his hazel eyes are overwhelmed with tears. I softly run my hand back and fourth over his lower back.

Big Mama mingles with the lawyers in the driveway as Billy and DK sullenly watch from the porch. Gloom was painted on everyone's face that came to the house for the next couple of weeks. It seemed like even the sun was in mourning because it spent that time hiding behind the gray sky.

After the lawyers are in their cars Big Mama scoots her way to them. She swings the locket from her finger handing it off to Billy, "Here. They said she was wearing it when…" her capability to finish the end of that sentence didn't exist. Big Mama simply lifts his chin up, "Keep it safe ok?"

With a nod he lets his fingers tangle the necklace until it sits in the palm of his hand.

"I carried it around everywhere 'til I moved out wit' DK two years ago," his finger tips wipe away the tears. "Now it jus' sits wit' this picture bein' one of the few memories stained in my mind."

My hand slowly drags itself up his tensed back. What do you say to someone after they tell you a story like that? I'm sorry your mom died? Well of course you are. Talk about stating the obvious.

"The lawyers told Big Mama I could have all the furnishing when it came time. There was money saved in the bank for me when I turned 17, which helped rent this and pay for my car. My dad arranged it so I couldn't touch the insurance money 'til this Christmas. It was like he knew exactly what to do if some'n ever happened to 'em. Sometimes I feel like he left me directions on how to financially survive wit' what I was given," his body arrives next to mine.

Somehow I manage to whimper out, "I'm sorry." Eerie silence bounces from wall to wall making me feel more uncomfortable than I already do. "Do you ever wonder what it would be like if they were still around?" Dumb question Kie! Of course he does.

"Yeah. I jus' start wonderin' things like, would I be hustlin' and stealin' my way to try to make ends meat? Ya know I wanted to be a firefighter? Not a weed dealer. God hands you some pretty fucked up entrees, and you're forced to pick yo' main course even if it's some'n you never wanted a day in yo' life," Billy's hand slides itself with mine. "No one gave a damn about me except Big Mama and DK."

As much I want to hate DK for his messed up ways of life, I can't. If he hadn't been there for Billy who knows just how worse off this boy could've been. There's a small chance his life could've prevailed.

"That's the secret to my screwed up life," he sniffles away his last few tears. "The explanation to why I'm a failure."

Taking a playful tone I nudge him in the side, "You're not a complete failure."

Jokingly he nods back, "Thanks."

"No problem," I shrug letting go of his hand.

Billy's hand gently slides across my lower back, "I know you only want the bes' in yo' life."

"'Tis true," I moisten my bottom lip as his hand slides it's way around my tummy and up my arm.

"You wouldn't ever date someone less than what you deserved," it plants itself on the back of my neck. Swallowing hard he shyly asks, "Do you think I um … have a chance?" Billy leans in making it too damn hard to resist him.

Ok a little kiss can't hurt anyone right? Shoot me if I'm wrong, but doesn't he deserve another chance to be someone I could really be into? I whisper back, "Yeah." Leaning in I moisten my lips for preparation to meet his.

Before our anxiety can be resolved with the touch of anxious lips, I hear three loud sharp pops. It sounds like firecrackers are going on right outside of Billy's window. Wait a second. Those are … gunshots. He yanks me onto the ground rolling on top of me. I can't breathe, and that's not just because his heavy ass is trying to protect me. I knew it! I always go against my better judgment. See. This is exactly why you don't get involved with thugs. Wherever they are danger is trailing not far behind them.

My heart continues to play drums on the ground as my brain comes up with the worst-case scenarios for what could be happening to my best friend in the other room. I swear if she gets hurt in the slightest way there will be bloodshed for days when I'm done with these two morons. If anything happened to her I would blame myself for the rest of my unfortunate life. Finally, an eternity later, the shots cease only leaving me with Billy's heavy breathing in my ear.

"DK!" Billy yells in my ear. Nearly dead and now deaf. What a day.

"Yeah?" the idiot calls back.

Billy screams again in my ear, "Mia!" He's really lucky I can't move.

"Yeah," she hollers back relieving that amount of stress off my brain.

Attempting a whisper in my ear he questions, "Kie you alright?"

"I can't breathe."

Quickly, he feels my back in a panic, "What? Were you shot?"

"No. You're crushing my air passage way," I push to say with the breath I can get.

Like a ready pop-tart he jumps, "Oh my bad." He helps me up and checks if there's any damage to the goods he had his hopes set on. "You ok?"

"Am I ok?" I scream at the top of my lungs. "I was just shot at only god knows how many times!" Suddenly my voice reaches another octave as I shove him out of my way, "Take me home now you son of a bitch!"

Billy desperately attempts to save himself as I fling the door open, "Kie ..."

"Now!" I demand marching towards to the living room.

If there was another attempt made I wouldn't have heard it through my angry breathing. Grabbing my shoes I scream, "I can't believe I gave this another chance!"

"Kie ..." he makes another hopeless attempt.

Snapping around I continue screaming, "We were shot at! Do you understand that if I stay here with ya'll this will no longer be a vacation but a hospitalization?"

"OK Dr. Seuss," DK rolls his eyes.

"I think you're over reactin'," Billy sits down on the couch reaching for his own shoes.

"Excuse me?" I storm my way to in front of him.

"I said—

"I heard what you said!"

"Then why'd you act like you didn'," DK mumbles, but quickly shuts his mouth when I shoot him a glare.

Grabbing Billy by his shirt I yank him forward, "Over reacting? You may be accustomed to death knocking at your door, but I'm not. My life gets put on the line because I made the stupid choice of coming here against my better judgment. So you listen to me Mr. I Think I Have the Right to Tell You How to Feel," my grip tightens, "I will react however I see fit. After being shot at I feel scared and very *very* pissed off. My suggestion to you is to take me home before you I introduce you to the Grim Reaper."

Billy, DK, and Mia's jaws are all on the ground.

He stutters through the fear that I instilled to simply say, "Ok."

"Good," I let him go, push him backwards, and begin to walk away.

"Damn," DK mouths at Billy.

"Give me a minute," he says to me like I'm supposed to wait around here another minute for someone else to shoot at me.

My head wheels around, "Sixty seconds."

Getting up to make his way to DK he sighs, "Please jus' take my keys. I'll be right there."

I snatch the keys and walk out the door to go to his car. My glance falls on Mia, which is when I notice her eyes have tears in them. I wrap an arm around her hoping to provide security. It's easy to ease her when she's pissed because her mouth is moving a mile a minute and all you have to do is listen, but when she's scared, she's silent. The sound of her voice is more comforting to my heart than the sound of her tears. Could I really have been any dumber than to come here?

Billy and DK move into the kitchen once we're out on the house.

DK opens the drawer closest to the kitchen table, "Yo take the glock wit' you."

He resists by pushing it away, "Naw."

They struggle back and fourth until DK's eyes force it on him, "Jus' in case."

Looking at the gun Billy slips it into his back pocket. "Who was it?"

"I bet you it was that punk Dunk," he slams the drawer. "I hit his block hard last week after he cleaned us out."

"Yeah well, we can't be dealin' like this. This shit is bad fo' business, and now it's slippin' into my personal life." With a few adjusts his shirt covers the gun. "Besides, I ain't ready to die yet."

DK folds his arms across his chest, "Nigga I know."

After a deep sigh Billy rubs his temple. "A'ight. I'm gonna take these females home. Maybe I can undo what you did," his chuckle lightens the mood.

"Be careful," he calls to Billy who's moving towards the door.

Opening it he yells back, "Don't worry 'bout me. You jus' see where the fuck those bullets went. I don't like my shit damaged."

Billy approaches the car making my teeth cringe. I can't believe I compromised my goodwill for this. I nearly die because everyone wants to push me to be with him. 'He's a good kid.' 'What's the worst that could happen?' I knew I was right for over analyzing my every move regarding this creep.

"I'm sorry," he starts the car. "Bad business."

Before I decide to respond I glance back at Mia who hasn't drawn her tearful eyes away from the window. "Shut up and drive."

Billy backs out of the parking lot. This was the last straw. The only thing that seems to happen around him is long-term psychological damage. Everyone knows the saying, no pain no gain. Well in my case it's no pain, stay sane. No one has ever driven me this crazy without me returning the favor.

I lay my head against the headrest hoping for a moment of peace.

Accelerating he finally speaks, "It's ok Kie. Ya'll are safe now. You're away from all the bad."

"Except you," I murmur.

His eyes shift to me, "Say wha'?"

"You heard me."

"You think I'm bad?" his voice raises. "I'm not. I'm really a good guy."

Two short giggles escape me, "Good guys don't have people shooting at them. You're not a badass because you go through things like this. You have to be the worst influence that's ever walked into my life. I know who good people are, and let me be the first to say you're not one of them. Just do the world a favor, and stay out of my life."

His silence is another point for me. Billy stares straightforward at the road. I hope I've pushed him so far that he gives up on trying to be with me. There is no room for him in my life, and honestly, I don't want a place in his. Game over.

CHAPTER 4

Expensive Propositioning

Naptime is the best time because it comes right after your delicious lunch, which in my case was a sandwich and some nearly stale potato chips. But that's not the point. All that matters now is me sleeping peacefully on the couch while Big Mama pretends to be shocked at very probable outcomes on her soap operas. After an undisturbed forty-five minutes I feel someone disrupt my tranquility by annoyingly shaking me.

"Kie," Mia continues the shaking. Can she not ruin my sleep like she ruins my consciousness?

I shuffle around on the couch groaning out, "What?"

She continues the motion, which makes me wonder does she not know I'm awake even though I'm staring at her in the face. "You have a visitor."

A visitor? What am I in jail? You know on second thought, what was my crime to have to be forced into this hellhole? I didn't murder anyone, I didn't steal anything, and hell I didn't lie to anyone. Besides that I thought there was a rule against cruel and unusual punishment. Correct me if I'm wrong, but spending time with DK is *beyond* cruel, and being pressured to fall for some dickhead who's not worth the time of day is *very* unusual. Why didn't I just get the death penalty? Wouldn't that have been easier? Oh my bad. I came close to that last night.

"Come on Kie," she starts to yank my arm. Can she not control the violence?

I moan sitting up, "All right. All right." Might as well go see who took their dear, sweet time to pay me a little old visit. Well at least I know it's not Billy.

He's got enough sense not to bring himself around me ever again. Maybe it's one of Big Mama's children, who want to tell me how much I've grown since the last time I came here.

Yawning, I stretch slowly, hoping if I take long enough they'll get annoyed and leave. At least that way I can go back to my nap with no more interruptions.

"Rápido," Mia exclaims like speaking in Spanish is really going to make me move any faster.

"Don't get your thong in a twist," I mumble getting up. As I follow her out of the room I pull down my Lakers jersey.

"I heard that," she says matter of fact.

I tighten each of my low pigtails that are sitting on my shoulders, "You were supposed to," and then pull up my sagging jeans.

She rolls her eyes and opens the front door while I glance down at my clothes to make sure I look presentable. Looking back up as I hit the front porch I see Billy leaning against the pillar.

Oh when she said visitor I didn't think she meant another inmate. I thought I told him to stay out of my life forever? Was that not a clear point to never show his face again? Did the yelling, screaming, and aggressive grabbing not push my point over the edge? Is he really that moronic?

Folding my arms I lean against the front door frame, "Now that you've ruined my day yet again, you can go home."

"Nice to see you too Kie," the corners of Billy's mouth turn up.

"I never said it was nice to see you."

"Kie," Mia snaps from beside me.

"I don't think it's nice to see him. In fact it would be nice NOT to see him," I whisper loud enough for him to hear. "Let's get right to the point Billy. What do you want?" My eyes roll back to his, "How do you want to make my life a living hell today?"

Jingling his keys around he answers, "I have a proposition fo' you."

With a baffled expression I raise my eyebrows, "Proposition? What do you think you possibly have to offer to me?"

"A win, win situation," he stands up straight.

"Win? Win?" Be a bit more specific.

"Yeah," Billy nods. "I would like an opportunity to change yo' distorted image of me." Distorted? Someone's been looking at his word a day toilet paper. And what's with him wanting everything? Better yet, why does he always come to me when he wants something like I can grant his three wishes? It doesn't say genie across my head. He wants this, he wants that, and of course I am unimportant in his "me me me" world.

I giggle a little under my breath, "Opportunity?"

"Yeah. It's like this," he leans back against the pillar. "All I want is a chance fo' us to get to know each other one on one. Jus' you and me. Not me you and DK, or me you and Mia."

"I know what one on one means idiot."

Mia pops my thigh, "Kie."

"Tomorrow night from seven 'til whenever it is you have yo' famous dramatic fit where you yell fo' me to take you home. If you still despise me afterwards you won't have to see me ever again." He takes a long deep breath and emphasizes the last word, "Ever."

Does he think he's funny? Dramatic fit … what a jackass statement. There's a catch to this whole thing because if getting rid of him were that easy he'd be long gone by now.

"A date?" I ask unfolding my arms. "I'm sorry. Why would I go on a date with you? You got me shot at."

"I said I was sorry."

"Yeah because that would have revived me from death!"

"You didn't even get hit! It's not like they were shootin' at you."

"Exactly! They were shooting at you! So tell me one more time why I would go on a date where somewhere between dinner and dessert a bullet magically finds it way through my water glass?"

Resisting the urge to say a smart remark back he sighs out, "Because I *know* you have feelings for me."

"Ha—

"Not hateful ones." Billy takes a few steps until he's in my face, "Real ones." Leaning in he whispers, "Last night, when my hand softly traced yo' face," he pauses to lick his lips, "and gently touched the back of yo' neck while you were starin' into my eyes I know you felt some'n. You can't deny it." I had feelings for him. Key word is had. Past tense. The doofus I'm staring at isn't the sweetheart I was talking to last night.

I lean in as well, "Hm. I remember last night when your lips were begging to touch mine …" my tongue grazes my lips as well, "quickly being cocked blocked by a bullet!"

Irritated he snaps, "Can't you jus' let that go?"

"Did I get hit by a bullet? Am I talking to you from beyond the grave?"

With a deep sigh he mumbles, "I'll take that as a no." Raising his voice to my level, he focuses back on his original plan, "So ... what do you say?"

"I say that you need to sell the weed you smoke because obviously it's finally gotten to your brain," I shrug as I slip my hands into my pockets.

Chuckling a little he nods, "I knew you'd say some'n like that."

"If you knew then why are you wasting time?"

Billy crosses his arms, "'cause I thought I'd at least let you come at yo' own free will."

"How do you plan to *force* me to go?" I step forward.

"Oh I know *I* can't force you to go," he stands his ground, "but manipulation goes a long way."

"Come again?"

"Well let's think about it. Big Mama seems to want you go out wit' me, so I bet if I ran it by her she'd more than find a way to make sure you go. She'd probably put you in my car herself," he grins widely. Cocky bastard has a point. "Then again," his stance becomes a lean halfway through the doorway considering the fact I'm in the other half. "Yo' mom seems to be diggin' me. Perhaps I'll mention it in front of her, and she'll convince you to go," Billy ever so bravely leans in. "So Kie. Tell me. Do you wanna go willingly, or do I have to work my magic," his fingertip gently brushes my folded forearm.

"Do not touch me," I growl before I lean in closer. "You think you've won? Fuck me over again, and next time the bullet won't miss. Got that?"

"No worries. I won't hurt you," Billy winks.

My fist tightens, "Well I can't guarantee that on my half. Despite that," I lean back against the doorframe, "I don't have anything to wear." Now I know this excuse won't do anything except buy me time, but hell that's enough for me.

"Oh, I gotcha covered," he jingles around change in his pocket.

"You think chump change is really going to buy me a decent outfit?"

Mia murmurs her first sentence in quite sometime, "You're gonna buy her an outfit?"

"If I recall correctly ..." ugh. I swear if he tries one more time to sound like he actually graduated from high school I might punch him in the face. "Someone's clumsy ass spilt Kool-Aid on what looked like an expensive shirt. I'll jus' buy you a whole new outfit instead. DK and I are already on our way to the mall," he points to DK who's blowing out smoke on the hood of Billy's car, which I was told didn't come out of hiding often. Liar. "You two should jus' tag along."

"No thank you," I smirk; turn around to head in the house, until Mia stops me with a glare. Turning back around I plant my hands on my hips, "I can't be bought." Where does this fool get off trying to buy me like this? Does it say gold digging tramp across my chest?

"I'm not tryin' to buy you," he steps down again. "Besides there's not enough money in the world to do that." I feel like the intention there was supposed to be sweet. "So?"

Glaring, I glance at the open doorway before storming inside, "Let me get my phone."

"All right," he waits for me to go inside before he heads to his car.

Mia follows in behind me. I feel flattered because he's doing everything in his power to make me see something I don't and annoyed that he's trying to blind side me into seeing something that isn't really there. Guess this is God's way of saying 'Kie do what I say before I come down there and make your life something you really don't want it to be.' It could be worse right? I could be going on a date with DK. Note to self: Thank God about that later.

"Billy," DK puts out his cigarette. "What the fuck is wrong wit' you?"

He leans against the trunk of his car, "What?"

"This girl has done nothin' but cut you down, cuss you out, and treat yo' ass like you're a rock in the middle of the road that keeps gettin' in her way. Why are you still after her?" DK hops back on the trunk and pops a tic-tac in his mouth.

Billy just twists his Lakers cap around.

"Let's think 'bout this. They're has to be at least 3,000 fine girls that go out partyin' every weekend between here and Dallas, and I know you could probably bone at least half of 'em," he looks at the side of his face.

"True."

"And the other half is dyin' for you to screw 'em instead. So please explain to me why this trick has yo' ass pussy whipped already," he stares waiting for him to turn his direction.

Continuing to look off in the distance he sighs, "You're righ'. I can have any chicken head I want."

"That had to be the point you were tryin' to prove when you first went after Kie," DK looks off down the road too.

After he rolls his eyes in hesitation, he admits, "It was. But things change."

DK glances back at the side of Billy's head, "You mean to tell me you actually like that runaway mouth?"

"Yup," he nods slowly trying to let it sink into his own mind. "I think I do."

"You think you do? Fo' all this bullshit you betta' be 110% positive."

"Ok then. I do."

"Why!" DK yells making Billy swerve to the side. He then mumbles, "What's wrong witchu?"

"It's like this," Billy turns around to rest his arms on the back of the car.

He faces Billy, "This betta' be good."

"I've had girls wit' all the right features. I'm talkin' soft skin, beautiful brown eyes, lips to die fo', wit' so many curves it's a surprise they didn't walk around wit' 'Caution' written on 'em."

"Damn," he begins to reminisce about the girls he's had that resemble that description.

"And ya know what they had to offer?" Billy slouches down.

DK peers at him with a hopeful gleam, "Off the chain, mind-blowin', out of this world sex?"

He shakes his head, "Nothin' that really means anything."

Confused he ponders, "Since when does sex not mean anything?"

Ignoring him he goes on, "I've had them ghetto girls wit' weave fo' days and an attitude to match."

"Like Chanté."

"Yeah, which by the way I don't appreciate you lettin' her know where I was the otha' day."

"Oops."

"Anyway, what did they have to offer me?"

"Really great sex?" DK hopes he's right again.

"Nothin' that means anything DK," Billy raises his voice. "Try to keep up."

"Well if the damn question wasn't so hard maybe it would be easier to …"

Billy cuts him off and continues with his point, "Hell, I've even had them up class hunnies who swear they're too good fo' a nigga like me."

His eyes shift back at the house as DK grumbles, "Fuckin' Kie."

After taking a moment he glances back at DK to ask, "What did *they* have to offer me?"

"Pretty good sex?"

Rolling his eyes Billy stands straight up, "Not a damn thing that matters. Why do I like Kie? Why?"

"Yes Billy! Please answer the million dollar question that started this useless conversation," DK swings one of his hanging legs.

"'cause she's different," he leans back against the car.

He sarcastically remarks, "Didn't see that answer comin'." Clearing his throat he moves on to a more serious question, "How? Is it 'cause you have to sell yo' soul to Satan to be in her presence?"

Billy slowly turns his head back around with his eyes darted down.

"Damn kid. I'm messin' wit' you. What does she have to offer your annoyin' ass?"

"A chance at a real life," he says as if he's questioning the statement himself.

DK digs for his cell phone in his pocket, "Excuse me? Real life?"

"Life. Ya know, the four letter word that you think is all 'bout money, bitches, blunts, and expensive alcohol you can't pronounce."

Scrolling down through his missed calls list he argues, "Oh you mean she'll turn you into some preppy ass nine to five nigga who works his fingers to the bone to neva' be good enough fo' her unreasonably high standards?"

"Man it ain't even like that," Billy crosses his arms. "I feel like this girl can give me some'n I neva' thought I could have again."

"And you feel that way after three days wit' her?"

"Call me crazy," he looks back down the road, "but yeah."

"You've fuckin' lost it. You have a great life. A roof ova' yo' big ass head, weed, and all the bitches you could dream of. You don't need more than that. What? Yo' ass wants a job? Here's a job, quit bein' a pussy and realize yo' boy's got you," his voice sounds more threatening than compassionate. "There's nothin' that trick can give you that I can't."

Billy kicks a rock his head bowed head and mumbles, "Whatever DK."

DK dials a number. "Can yo' whinny ass hold on while I call Mike?"

"Do what the fuck you want," Billy looks back out at the road again. It's pointless for him to talk to DK about moving onto to better things. Any time Billy's ever brought it up, DK flips it so that Billy feels like he's abandoning his best friend, which is enough guilt to make anyone put their feelings on the backburner. Sometimes people will play their best friend's shadow to prove they'd never abandon them.

I pick up my cell off the bed and glance at Mia who's slipping into her flip-flops basking in her happiness. The one person I depend on other than myself for some aid is the girl who's against me this time. Aren't your best friends supposed to be the one you call in for air support when you get caught in situations like this?

"I sense a bit of antagonism." Antagonism? Has she been going behind my back to read the dictionary? Of course it's not kind to think things like that, but right now I could care less after she left me high and dry to fry in the pan of Billy.

"Oh *NOW* you sense something? Well Ms. Intuition I bet your inferring I'm not real ecstatic with you or my situation right now," I snap slipping my phone in my rear jean pocket before I storm out of the room.

"Kie," Mia calls to me following me down the hall.

"Busy," I yell back. You would think your best friends have your best interest in mind when they make certain choices, but I guess not. Or maybe that's just mine. "Mom," I stroll through the wide-open kitchen noticing the leaning tower of scum dishes. Will someone please point me in the direction of civilization?

"In here," my mom looks up from her hand held card game. "What is it?"

Stopping in front of her I slouch and let my head fall to the side. This is my classic 'I don't want to go' pose, "Do you care if Mia and I go to the mall with Billy?"

"Sure." Her answer makes me growl under my breath. She looks up pressing another button, "You say something honey?"

"No," I shouldn't have to. How do I get the point across once my body language and attitude fail miserably?

Slowly strolling from the hallway next to the kitchen where her bedroom and bathroom reside Big Mama asks, "You're going out with Billy again?"

I cringe a fake smile, "Yes." How do you get people committed anyway? Do they take you if they think you're in your right mind, but the rest of the world swears you're a nutcase or in her case off her rocker?

"Oh good," she squeals moving towards her favorite chair. "Maybe he'll ask you out on a date."

As I prepare myself for a silent exit Mia chimes in, "He already did." I scrunch my eyes shut. You bitch.

"Really?" Big Mama and my mom turn around shocked.

"And you didn't tell me," my mom puts her game down.

I swallow nervously and then put on a grin turning around slowly to Mia. "And thank you for that," I mumble out between my gritted teeth. She's just racking up the brownie points. Any more and she will get a special well-deserved ass whooping.

"How sweet!" Big Mama plops down. "Tomorrow night?"

I nibble on the inside of my bottom lip, "Yes." That is if I don't kill myself between now and then. "Yes it is." You crazy old bat.

"Well then you get yourself something nice at the mall," my mom reaches beside her into her purse to pull out a twenty. What am I supposed to buy with this? A bat to beat him with? Maybe a bullet proof vest will match my jean skirt I brought.

Snatching the bill I manage to say, "Ok." I turn around again to see Mia smiling at me. If one more person smiles at me I might be tempted to smack them. Her fingers wave at me a little while my eyes follow her up and down noticing she changed into a yellow t-shirt with the words 'yeah right' written on the front. I got that as a gift for her fifteenth birthday. Sure hope she doesn't think that wearing that shirt is going to help her migrate to my good side.

Mia drapes an arm around me as we leave, "I love you Kie." She usually attempts to make the situation better with those words.

I hate you, "Whatever."

Love? There's a four letter word no one knows the definition of. If a person goes out, meets someone, starts a mediocre relationship, and has great sex, they think they're in love. Others go out with a guy for a couple of weeks and are somehow madly in love. Then there are those people who claim they are in love like the nerdy girls who long to be popular. It's sad that love is a four letter word that has lost its meaning. People use it as an excuse to be with someone, an excuse not to let go of something, and a justification for sex. I always thought love was a connection made mentally, emotionally, spiritually and least importantly physically. Guess I'll never know.

I walk down the path and go out the gate to see Billy get up from leaning against his car. Let the games begin.

"Thought you took DK's car everywhere," Mia flips her hair out. "Where's it at?"

"The shop," Billy answers glancing at the both of us.

Smile at me. Please smile at me so I can give you what's coming to you. As much as I wish I could use telepathic ways to get what I want, I can't. Slouching over the fact Billy won't smile at me; I turn and look at DK who hangs up the phone and smiles at me. YES! That's all I needed. I take a step closer to him. Smack. Talk about a bitch slap that will go down in history.

He touches his now hand printed cheek and with a raised voice he asks, "What the fuck was that fo'?"

Mia and Billy look more shocked than DK. I hope he's in pain. "I slapped you for being the bases of this date." It's a lie, but they'll buy it.

"That fuckin' hurt," he rubs his cheek.

"Oh suck it up," I roll my eyes as I climb into the seat behind Billy.

"Fuck you," he growls.

"Not for anything in this world," I buckle myself in while Mia is giggling as she does the same.

"Can you two just get along?" Billy sticks the key in the ignition after putting on his Lakers hat.

"Do I get out of this date?" It's worth a try.

"No," he adjusts his rearview mirror to look at me.

"Then shut the hell up and drive." This will be a give and take relationship. You know like it says an eye for an arm.

"What the hell jumped up yo' ass?" DK buckles his seat belt as Billy starts down the road.

Leaning against the door I say, "It's not a five letter word or less, so I don't think you'll know what it is."

"You don't have to be such a bitch all the time," DK leans back in his seat.

Point proven. "Outspoken woman, bitchiness included," I sneer. "If the world wasn't so busy trying to make me date that," I point to Billy. "There would be much less to bitch about."

Switching lanes Billy sighs, "Aw Kie, I love you too."

I flash him the middle finger and smile. No reaction. See sometimes he knows not to speak like a good dog.

DK looks around his seat at Mia who's playing a game on her cell phone, "So while they're out on a date we'll be—"

She wastes no time cutting him off, "Chillin' at Big Mama's."

"Oh so our very own lil' date," he winks at her.

"Look DK. Sure makin' out with me was fun for you, but face it sweetie. You can't handle me."

"Girl *you* can't handle *me*."

"Anyway," she moves on ignoring him, "with that put to the side, I don't date losers. So, you need to let your little boy fantasy go."

"Lil' boy? Who you callin' a little boy you—

Billy chimes in before the fighting gets good, "Leave her alone DK."

"Naw," Mia smacks her lips. "Let him finish, so he can get another taste of what death is like."

The two morons in the front seat have a stare off at the stoplight. Why can't he just let them fight so I have some sort of fun? Must he ruin everything for me? DK turns back around leaving Mia to her cell phone games and me unhappy once again. Damn it. Is there any hope here?

We arrive at the mall about twenty-five minutes later. Of course as soon as we get there the two of them see someone they recognize. This trip would be slightly more enjoyable if every five steps they didn't have to say hello to someone else.

"Ain't that that girl Shauna you know?" Billy points, as I look the opposite direction looking for the most expensive store in the mall. It might teach him I'm too high maintenance.

"Shit. It is," he nods. "Damn. I don't wanna talk to that trick."

"Yo Shauna," Billy yells to the girl walking a few feet in front of us with a little girl and a stroller.

He shoves Billy a little. At least I'm not the only person's life he makes hell. "What the …" DK panics for a place to stash himself.

She turns around quickly and smiles widely at Billy who looks extremely excited. Did he build his life on cloud nine? Seriously. No person should smile as much as he does about everything. It should be some sort of crime against nature to be so damn cheerful.

"Billy?" she turns around. As we approach closer DK tries to disappear between Mia and me. Oh that's smart. You're taller than the both of us, so it's not going to do anything but delay a few seconds for you to see her.

"Hey girl," he leans forward to hug her leaving space between them. She probably wishes he wouldn't have stopped her. I don't blame her.

"Just takin' these bad ass kids of mine out fo' the day," she looks down at her three-year-old daughter who's clinging to her leg. Awe. She's so cute with her high pigtails, denim skirt, and her American flag t-shirt.

"Is that Kaitlyn?" He glances down at her.

"Yup," she flips out her unbeweavable hair with her fake nails. See that's exactly why I don't wear phony things. I couldn't stand looking that fake. Plus the sound of those long ass nails clicking bothers the hell out of me.

"Damn girl," he squats down. "I ain't seen you since you were like one and a half. Look at you now. You've grown into the mos' beautiful lil' girl I've ever seen," he picks her up. "You 'member me?"

"Billy," she says slowly. No surprise there. Do you know how hard it is to forget a smile like that, and how annoying he is?

"Aw you do remember me," he tickles her stomach a little. "You really are one of the prettiest girls I've ever seen. How old are you now?"

"Three."

"Quit playin'," he smiles widely at her. "You ain't three."

"Am too," she giggles. Holding up the number seven on her hands she says, "My birthday was dis many days ago." Well at least she's not one of those cute little girls who've hit her bad stage.

"Fo' real? Well you almos' grown then," he winks at her.

Kaitlyn points to me, "When I'm grown can I be pretty like her."

Now that's just too precious. She thinks I'm pretty. Aw. I smile and then glance at her mama who's giving me a bit of an evil eye like I brainwashed her child into calling me pretty.

"She is pretty isn't she?" Billy turns to smile at me. Gross. "I'm sure you can be that pretty," he taps her cheek. "Jus' make sure you become real smart. That way you can be pretty and smart like Kie." Fuck off. The compliments are not winning me over.

Twirling one of her pigtails she whispers, "Is she yo' girlfriend?"

The poor little girl doesn't know any better because if she did, she'd know that you don't date things like that. They're bad for your health.

"Naw," he licks his lips at me. Looking back at her he whispers, "Workin' on it."

I suggest that the cocky bastard better start looking for a new job. Working on it? Is trying to get me like fixing a car? 'Yeah Jimmy I'm a need a few more parts in order to make sure this baby's motor mouth runs right.' Can he really not make the appropriate word choices?

"Oh," she looks sad. "Can I have you if she don't want you?"

I open my mouth to tell her she can have him now when Mia's elbows in my side shuts my mouth.

Billy smiles at me because he knows what I'm thinking. Maybe he should just pretend he doesn't. At least then he could keep his self-esteem up.

"Yeah, but only if I get a hug," he bargains tilting his head down to touch hers.

Kaitlyn tosses her arms around his neck and hugs tightly, "Deal!"

Ok on a positive note; he does well with the little ones. She seems to like him for some odd reason, but I guess when you're little you don't know any better. Though I think that's a good thing. If the world were to see things through the eyes of a child I doubt that there would be so much animosity. I bet we'd live in an environment where people see the better in a person, forgetting their flaws, trying to give them a chance to show who they really are without being prejudged. Hm … pretty much like I'm doing to Billy. Damn it. I hate kids.

Leaning down he peeks in the stroller, "Who's this lil' fella?"

"Dat's my baby brother," she innocently twirls back and fourth.

"Really?" he leans in towards the baby. "What's his name?"

"De Monte," she answers as Billy picks him up.

"Hi De Monte," he holds him close to him. Bouncing him up and down a little talking in a baby voice he coos, "Hey lil' man what's up?"

Look at him. The way he's holds the baby gently, talking baby talk, and tickling him makes my heart just melt. He's so sweet. Maybe he does have something to offer me. Wait. No. No he doesn't.

As Kaitlyn pulls on her leg Shauna asks, "Where's DK?"

Continuing to play with the baby Billy leans against the railing, "Tryin' to hide behind Mia." Nark.

She smacks her gums as she picks up her daughter, "Nice to see you too DK."

"Yeah," he slowly moves up towards her. "How ya been?"

Licking her lips she pouts them, "Good."

"I see you got anotha' kid," his eyes slide at the one Billy's holding. "Gonna try to pin him one on me too?"

"Fuck you DK," Kaitlyn shuffles her way down. She shouldn't cuss like that in front of her little girl.

"Been there. Did that. Wasn't worth it," he slips his hands in is pocket.

She snatches her baby from Billy as she mumbles, "Bastard."

DK smirks proudly and winks.

Shauna bounces her baby before making the choice to leave DK's pathetic presence, "Well it was nice to see you again Billy. Sorry we couldn't stay and talk longer." Buckling the baby back in the stroller she notices us out of the corner of her eye. "I'm sorry fo' bein' so rude. What were yo' names?"

"Mia," she politely waves.

It's not like I matter to her anyway, but I smile for everyone's sheer amusement. "Kie."

Not even attempting to make eye contact she sighs, "Well nice meetin' you."

"You too," Mia and I say in unison.

Her eyes jump over us straight to her favorite person here, "Billy it's always a pleasure to see you. Hope to again real soon," she tugs the bottom of his plain white t-shirt. Wow if I didn't know any better I would say she's got the warm fuzzies for that freak. God she can have him too.

He twists his cap backwards, "Bye."

"Why you gotta be like that?" DK rolls his eyes. "You know I can't stand that ho."

"Nigga please. If I had to stay away from every girl you ever messed wit' I'd have to move. Besides, she ain't that bad," they begin moving forward in front of us. I wonder if we could escape by slowing down and getting left behind in the crowd.

"Bitch tried to pin that lil' girl on me knowin' damn well I ain't dat baby's daddy," he strolls off walking cockeyed, which actually makes him look shorter and dumber.

"Aight DK," Billy shrugs. I don't think he enjoys the subject. I wonder if it's the same old story I always hear. Guy meets girl, girl is already pregnant, but you can't tell, the two screw, and the next thing you know she's calling him the baby's father. I'm more than likely right. "Where you girls wanna go?"

We stare back at him like he's an idiot because well he is. It's not like we shop here every weekend giving us a chance to develop a mental directory or a chance to establish a favorite store.

Continuing to walk he nods, "Ok … How 'bout I take you two to this store where they sell nothin' but sexy things?"

Ugh. "And what makes you think I would ever wanna dress sexy for you?"

"'cause you always do," he slows his speed, so he's walking next to me.

"Excuse me?"

Smiling he sighs, "It doesn't matter what you wear. You're sexy in everything."

"That line is so overplayed dickwad."

"Kie!" Mia smacks my arm, DK snickers, and Billy lets it roll off of him like every other insult.

"She's crazy," DK mouths to Billy.

I prepare to rip him to shreds, "What was that?" I ask. Why does he have to ruin the moment by opening his mouth?

"You're crazy," he reiterates this time directly to me.

"Because I'm the one running away from child support charges?" my stab is quickly covered by another insult Band-Aid.

He stops abruptly and leans against the railing, "you're even crazier than psycho sally over there fo' going after her."

Butting in before he can defend himself I snap, "Even if he is, at least he's trying harder to get himself the piece of ass he's been after."

"Ya know what? I'm tired of yo' smart mouth and bitchiness," DK attempts to get in up on my face.

"And I'm tired of your lip and dickhead ways," I return the gesture. "All you do is talk trash. Your unintelligent language, your 'I think I'm the shit' attitude, and worst of all your inability to care about anyone other than yourself, all prove you're nothing but a little boy who plays little boy games," I smack my gums in his face. "Why don't you try acting like a grown-up?"

"You trick—

Billy interrupts, "Try this store." Suddenly I'm being gently pulled out of DK's face and being asked, "How much do you need?"

I rip my arm away from him, "I don't know."

"How 'bout a hundred?" he slides the bill from his pocket. "Is that good?"

Quickly I snatch the bill, "I guess we'll see now won't we?"

I start towards the glass doors as Mia growls my name, "Kie."

Whirling around I try to say as polite as possible, "Thanks."

"You're welcome," Billy fights the urge to smile as he leans next to DK. "We'll be in the food court when you're done."

"Whatever," I whisper as I roll my head back to the direction I am going.

DK strolls off down a little further looping around the cross over path to get to the other side, "A hundred dollars on that fuckin' bitch. Man, I swear—"

"Stop."

"But—

"Just stop. Let it be DK. Except the fact this is the girl I'm tryin' to be wit."

"They're definitely takin' playa' yo' card away for this ..."

"I'm a one woman nigga."

"You a pussy whipped nigga; that's what you are," he rubs his nose as they stroll into the open food court.

"I ain't pussy whipped it's jus' ..." Billy drifts off.

DK points off to a group of guys standing around a booth, "Look there they are."

Billy rubs his hands together and gets a gleam in his eyes, "Time to make that money."

"Kie," Mia says to me as I make my way around racks of clothes.

Skimming through the racks I hum, "Hm?"

She leans against the rack directly in front of me, "I'm sorry." Oh, an hour or so later she decides now is a good time for an apology. Beautiful. "I guess I just sided with what Billy told me."

Nonchalantly I look up, "Which was?" Mia's supposed to be the cold hearted one, and I'm supposed to be warm. When did it say we were supposed to switch places?

"He told me not to tell you."

I roll my eyes and walk away to a pants rack, "Of course he did."

Following me she attempts to revive the situation again, "Billy said he didn't want me to tell you because …"

"Because what?"

"Because …"

"Mia."

She sighs, "He feels he would be trying to charm you into liking him." Wow. He's playing her like a good poker bluff.

My expression reveals just how unimpressed I am. Two can play this game and the saddest thing is that I play it much better. "It's not charming me if he really means what he says."

Mia debates for second that my point, while it's a load of bologna however is a good one, and decides to spill, "Well I guess it's ok tell you then, but first we need to be looking at skirts and dresses."

After stopping in front of a rack I let her drag me to I instruct, "Go on."

"When you started napping I went back towards the room to get a piece of gum from my bag when I saw Billy coming in. He knew better than to try to even talk to you, so he asked could we talk for a second. Our conversation starts out as an argument, but before I know it he asks if he would be crazy to say he could see himself falling in love with you," I glance over at her with raised eyebrows. "Yes the L word girl. Now you know these clowns no nothing about that emotion, so he had my attention. I asked him what he was smoking to think he had a chance for that heart of yours, and well he just said he owed it to himself to at least try. Now I know you think it's nothin' except game he's runnin', but he looked me in my eyes Kie and pleaded with everything he had for me to help him." Grabbing a little black dress she sighs, "I couldn't resist. Before I realized it I was helping him plan his attack."

Silently I start towards the dressing room with the dress in hand. Again with that word love. It seems more like a curse than a blessing. I know all the evil that lies behind it. All the pain, hysteria, and anxiety it causes. Personally pain to me is not pleasure. If pain must be inflicted on me I would prefer it self inflicted because to me that would easier to deal with.

Love also comes with responsibility, which would be a word he can't define. It takes a lot to make love, and I don't mean the psychical act. Making love, let me rephrase that, a loving relationship takes feelings I don't think he's capable of; on top things I don't think he can handle. How can he say he thinks he can see himself falling in love when he has no idea what it is? Besides I'm no one's love tutor.

"It wasn't like I wanted to make you mad. What can I say? He just kind of got to me," Leaning against the wall outside my dressing room door, she lets out a deep sigh. "I'm sorry."

I mutter as I strip out of my clothes, "It's ok." I hate giving into her, "I understand you were just trying to do something for me. Usually it's me getting you into dates." After I give a slight chuckle, I open the door with the dress on. "Guess you just think it's my turn to get into one."

"Yup. And in that dress you will get a lot more than that," she gives me a hard look over. "Damn."

Allowing a giggle to escape I look at myself in the mirror. "I guess ..."

"There's a matching earring and necklace set out there," she smiles as I turn around again letting her check it a final time. "Oh and a toe ring," she points to my feet. "I think we'll do those ourselves tomorrow. Oh my gosh we can finally have our own get ready date night for you!" It's not like I never go on dates. I'm just a little bit choosey.

A disgusted look paints itself on my face. As nice as it is to be pampered for once, that doesn't erase the fact of who's taking me out. Nothing in this world could make me forget the demon that is going to risk my life again.

When we leave the store Mia is carrying the bag of accessories, and I'm carrying my dress. We discuss the last battle on our hand, which would be the task to find shoes.

Somehow shoe talk morphs into a debate on the idea of me warming back up to Billy, "Speaking of Billy, I wonder where those boys are at."

Mia aimlessly looks around as I point straight ahead. They're leaning against a booth like they have nothing better to do, "In the food court where they said they would be."

We start towards them when I see exchanging of money for something. What is that? Is that a bag? A Ziploc bag? Leaning forward I squint like I'm trying to read the fine print in a document. That couldn't be ... that wouldn't be ... my god it is. Weed. They're selling weed in the mall. Ever so slowly we look at each other. On her face is a look of ultimate shock, and on mine the obvious annoyed anger glare, which we all have come to know as my signature expression. See. That's the kind of dumb shit I'm talking about. I don't need to get involved with people who smoke weed let alone sell it.

Mia watches any sympathetic feelings I had towards him go bye bye. She makes a small gesture towards me as if trying to make a plea for her client. Ignoring it, I storm full speed ahead like a locomotive train. It's like that boy put bullshit in a shot glass and downed it until he became dunk. No way is that trained monkey capable of doing anything that brainless fool next to him hasn't instructed him to do.

"Yeah," DK laughs slipping half the money in his pocket, and the other to Billy who's now sitting at the booth.

"Thanks," the guy strolls away from them as we arrive.

"Yeah," he looks back at Billy who's twiddling his thumbs.

With a perky attitude I question, "Selling weed are we?"

"Bein' nosey are we?" DK snaps.

"Doing it in public makes it an open forum. And in case that word is too large for you to define, it means discussion."

DK grunts, "Fo' the love of god, what are you whinin' 'bout? It jus' bought yo' ass an outfit, and who knows what else. Be thankful."

"Wait a minute. You bought me an outfit with drug money?" I toss my bag on the table so hard it slides and hits Billy.

He begins to stumble over his words, "I … uh …"

"So what if he did. It was good enough to pay fo' yo' tramp outfit wasn't it?" DK jumps to his defense.

"It wouldn't have been if I knew where it came from," I place my hand on my hip.

DK shakes his head, "Oh come on. Don't try to play dumb. You know damn well we ain't the nine to five types."

My eyes slide over to Billy on that note and I let my eyebrows rise, "Pardon me, how could I have forgotten? Why on earth would I ever think you would do something the right way?"

Billy slightly hangs his head as he slouches down.

DK slides himself in the booth to mumble, "I don't know."

I open my mouth to hit the ping pong ball of insults, but I get stopped by Mia who turns me towards her, "I'm thirsty. Will you get me a lemonade?"

"God gave you legs for a reason," I snap. Her eyelids shift downward forcing me to submit. "Fine." Within seconds I'm disappearing from everyone's sight.

"What's wrong wit' yo' home girl?" DK asks tilting his head towards her.

Bluntly, she states the obvious, "She hates you. You're the epitome of everything she believes is wrong with the opposite sex." Immediately she diverts her attention and points at Billy, "And then there's you."

"What I do?" his voice rises as does the innocent expression.

Mia plops down next to DK. "What did you do? What did you do? She's trying to see whatever good is left in you, and you sell this shit where she can see? Does the word discrete mean anything to you?"

"I—

"You know you could have waited until you took us home to do this shit. Use your better judgment for Christ sake. Billy I can only help your ass out so much. This is give and take. You have to meet me half way," she relaxes.

"He don't need help—

Mia turns toward him, "Was I talking to you?"

"Naw, but—

"What part of this conversation was an invitation for you to join?"

"But I—

She puts her hand in his face, "But nothing. Shut up when no ones talking to you." Facing Billy she continues, "Now sure Kie's a bit difficult—

"Difficult? No. School was difficult. Gettin' a job is difficult. Hell, livin' wit' DK is difficult. Tryin' to hook up wit' Kie is like—

"I don't care. I don't wanna hear it. You don't wanna do the work and effort it takes to be with a great girl like her then don't sit here and waste my time. It's just that plain and simple," her voice comes to a halt as I slam her lemonade down in front of her.

I sip my own lemonade, "What are you guys talking about?"

"Shoes. I was telling Billy you two are going to go get shoes while DK and I get some'n to eat. Girl you know I'm starving," she begins to gulp down her lemonade.

A sarcastic look comes across my face. I cock my hip to the side, "What?"

"It's ok," Mia tugs on the bottom of my jeans. Did she already forget what just happened? What does he do to make girls putty like that? I look down at her puppy dog eyes, "Trust me Kie."

I snatch the Lakers hat off of Billy's head and put it backwards on mine, "Fine. Let's go then."

"All right," he slides himself out clutching my bag.

"Pussy whipped," DK mutters under his breath making Mia kick him under the table as we walk off. The last thing I hear him grumble is, "Ouch."

Rubbing his head he asks, "Can I have my hat back?"

"No," I step onto the escalator with the assumption we're going down.

"But—

"It doesn't match your ensemble," I sip my lemonade.

He smirks to himself like I can't see.

"Will you wipe that god awful thing off your face?"

"What thing?"

"That thing …" I glare. "The corners of your mouth keep going up, and it's becoming really annoying."

"I'm sorry. Not everyone has the capability to scorn for a livin'," his tongue grazes his lips.

With a deep sigh I shove the straw back in my mouth to sip more lemonade.

Attempting to change the subject and lead the conversation up pleasant mountain he asks, "So you didn't see any shoes in there that matched?"

"I just didn't see any that I liked." That's when it hits me that he's still holding my bags. He's got gentlemen skills after all. I cover my smile by pressing my lips together.

"Oh," he steps off the escalator behind me. "Can I see the outfit you bought?"

"No," I exclaim quickly looking back at him. Lighter hearted I say, "It's a surprise, so don't even try to peek."

"I swear I won't look in the bags," he puts up his hands in an innocent manner.

"Better not."

After a few moments he grins, "So you got me a surprise?"

"Don't flatter yourself," I tuck my lemonade free hand in my back pocket.

Billy laughs a little and nods.

"Where is this shoe place anyway?"

"There," he points to a store where I see lots of shoes in the display. I love shoes in different colors, different names, different styles, and different prices. I love them all.

In awe I say, "The Shoe Palace."

"Yeah I got a friend that works in here. We can get a discount," he says following behind me. Quickly he corrects himself, "Not that we have to." Damn right I'm not cheap.

I continue drinking as we walk through the sports shoe section and into the dress area. Coming to a stop, I sit on the bench to look at all the shoes that have this wonderful golden glow around them. My inner shoe shopper is clawing its way out.

"Are you ok?" Billy interrupts my blissfulness.

Reaching for the shoe in front of me I mumble, "I'm fine." For a moment I drool over these red two inch high heels I know I don't need. As I slowly put the shoe back battling the impulse buyer that shares a brain with the shoe shopper, I say to him, "I need a pair of black heels."

Politely he asks, "Would you like me to go find you a pair?"

Giving him my famous sarcastic look I shake my head. He can barely tie his own shoelaces, so why on earth would I give him a task as precious as picking out *my* evening pumps?

"Wha'? You don't think I can do it? You think I'm incapable of findin' a pair of black heels?"

Placing the straw to my lips I nod, "That's right."

"Come on. Give me a chance Kie."

I guess I'll let him amuse me for a few minutes, "Fine. I need a shoe particularly with straps in a size nine. Is that too difficult to remember? Do I need to write it down?"

"I got it," he sneers. "I'll be right back." I watch Billy disappear around the corner.

Hm. I wonder what kinds of crap he will bring to me. Probably just the normal ugly shoes any guy would pick out. If his taste is a reflection of how he dresses I might not have too much to worry about, but then again let's not place that much faith in him.

After finishing my lemonade and aimlessly twirling my hair, I look back up to see Billy stumbling around the corner tripping over a shoe that's lying around. I try not to laugh as Billy sits next to me with seven shoeboxes.

He desperately attempts to catch his breath, "Here you go."

"Why are you all worn out?"

"I had to fight fo' some of these," he puts the boxes on the floor. "They weren't all that easy to get."

Laughing at him I put my cup on the floor before I solute him, "Good battle solider."

Playfully he smiles back grabbing a shoe box, "Now 'member I made due wit' all I had to work wit'. Black and straps."

Billy pulls out something that looks like a deformed flip-flop causing me to snap, "What the hell are these?"

"Shoes! You told me shoes wit' straps."

Rubbing my head in frustration I wait to see the rest. The selection is so pathetic I don't know why I thought he would pick something decent in the first place. "Would you like to attempt to redeem yourself, or should I just go and find my own shoes now?"

"No!" he exclaims. "I can do it! Trust me I can!"

With a sigh I shake my head, "Ok. Just remember. Dressy but causal shoes."

Maybe if I give him the benefit of the doubt I'll be more amused when he returns with more hideous crap.

Between the time he left and the time he gets back I could rip out every single strand of hair from my head. Did he get lost? Who gets lost in a shoe store? Especially when the girl you're getting the shoes for didn't move? Well he is stupidity at its finest.

Billy pops up behind me, "Hey."

"Took you long enough. Where'd you go? France? Designer make them by hand himself?"

Offended he sits down, "Why yes he did Cinderella. I wanted to get the perfec' shoes."

"How do you know their perfect?"

"'cause I do."

"I highly doubt that, but let's see." I reach for the box.

"No," he moves the shoes away from my reach. "In fact I don't think you deserve 'em wit' that attitude."

"Whatever. Let me see," I grab for them again.

"No," he playfully grins.

Trying to snatch for it continuously I fight, "Yes."

"No," and he's laughing now.

With a deep sigh I feel an overwhelming anger slump over me. It's like he loves to piss me off.

"Now apologize," Billy demands.

"Excuse me?"

"You've been nothin' but rude 'bout everything, particularly 'bout these shoes. Now apologize," Billy crosses his arms.

There's a first. He finally wants to stand his ground. His eyes narrow down and force me to back up some.

Intrigued I answer, "I'm sorry. Can I have them now?"

"You realize that has to be the nicest thing you've said to me all day," he lets them go.

"Well don't get use to it. Especially if the shoes aren't …" I say lifting the lid to reveal wads of paper and a weight. I look up and put the box down. Slowly I start, "Billy …"

"What?" the innocent tone in his voice annoys me.

"Where are the shoes I apologized for?" I toss the box on the ground.

He tries to contain his laughter, "Those are them."

"Dumbass that's a wad of paper and paper weight. So you just lied to me?" I get ready to make my dramatic exit when a sales lady taps my shoulder.

"Excuse me," she politely gets my attention. "Are you Kie?"

Puzzled I nod, "Yes."

"The other sales girl told me to give these to you. She had to take an emergency phone call, but she said she hopes you like them. Call me if you need anything," the sales lady strolls off.

In one swift motion I look at Billy, who by the way is smirking now, hit him in the head with the lid to the box, and give my foot a stomp.

"Do you really think I'm that stupid?"

Of course I do, but I chose not to answer out loud.

"You do; don't you," he scoots closer to me. "Sometimes I wonder why I even ask."

"So do I …" I stare at the shoes that have just enough heel to give me a lady-like lift. They buckle around my ankle with a fake diamond jewel that hangs down. There's one strap, which has jewels on it, that goes right across my toes.

Impressed I quickly questioned, "*You* picked these out?"

"Not at first. See, I picked up all these shoes and kept askin' my friend Trina fo' her opinion. After hearin' no so many times givin' up seemed to be my only option, I found those, but not in yo' size. She went in the back, and I decided to divert yo' attention durin' the wait," he shrugs. "I was jus' tryin' to have a little fun."

"Real cute," I smile and take my foot out my shoes.

"You're not mad? 'Cause I don't need to do anything else to get on yo' bad side."

Well at least he cares enough to try to make the situation better. God. He tries so hard and never gets enough credit, "No." In a nicer tone I say, "Help me try on these shoes please." I inch my foot closer to his crotch.

He looks down at my foot that's now sitting in front of his pants causing him to get an even wider grin. "Watch out girl. Don't kick nothin'."

As he takes it from me I giggle, "Better continue to be nice to me then."

I allow him to roll up my pant leg before I slide my foot in the shoe, "Of course. No one likes the dog house."

"Mm," I continue to watch him gently adjust my pant leg. Every time he touches me he's so careful. I wonder how a guy who is classified as rough can handle me like I'm a dying flower he's not quite ready to get rid of.

Billy buckles the shoe around my ankle and looks back up at me. "What do you think?"

"I like them," I glance down and let a smile slip on my face. Looking back up I say, "I like them a lot."

"Me too," his eyes fall into mine.

With a deep sigh I bite my bottom lip, "I think it may be a perfect match." And I don't just mean the shoes.

CHAPTER 5

And Then There Was Billy

Why is it girls take such pleasure in getting all dressed up? Better yet why does it take so long? Let's do the math shall we? It can take up to five hours to get ready for a two hour date, and it can take all day literary from the time a girl wakes up until a few minutes past when their date arrives to get ready for a possible four hour date. The proportions make no sense, the math makes no sense, and now that I think about it, it's ok because females don't make that much sense either.

As I scrub my arms I giggle at the simple fact I started at four, and it's now rounding seven thirty. He pushed it back from the original time due to business reasons, which I hope is his real job and not his child's play. Either way I'm not complaining that I have more time to prepare for the date that I'm slowly but surely coming around to.

There's a knock at the door. "I'm in here!" I hate taking a shower in this place. Guys constantly knock like they don't know I'm showering. Then they act like there's only one bathroom, but I know it's just part of their plan to give me a complex before I go on my date with one of their kind. They better be careful because I'm just as tense as I was before they began to annoy me with their continuous knocking.

At least I know he's not freaking out right now. After all, the most he has to worry about is remembering to bring money, and where we're going. How hard is that?

"Where the fuck is the money DK?" Billy yells pulling down the sleeves on his black Tommy shirt.

"What the fuck is yo' problem?" DK strolls out the kitchen with an envelope.

"Nothin'." Snatching it he snaps, "I don't have time to play today."

"Nobody's tryin' to play wit' yo' dumbass," he walks around. "You need to loose that funky ass attitude of yours." As he plops down on the couch he pauses to laugh at his own sarcasm, "It ain't like you're 'bout to go out wit' Janet Jackson or something."

In one swift motion Billy rips the envelope open and quickly transfers the wad cash into his wallet, "I don't need you tell me I have a funky ass attitude. I jus' need yo' ass to get up off that got damn couch, get the merchandise, grab the movies, and my keys while makin' sure that you don't fuck up this business deal like you did the last one."

Slowing getting up he mumbles, "Damn foo'. A'ight."

I bet Billy and DK are getting off to soft-core porn or something. All I know is I'm going to look stunning, and he better be just as decently dressed, though to be fair this hasn't previously been a problem.

Now this is his last chance to measure up to what I'm looking for in a person. Notice I didn't say boyfriend, someone to date, or even friend. I specifically said person. As in person I can associate myself with respectfully.

Turning off the shower I grab my towel off the rack to wrap around me. Wow. With all this fog in here I can't see what time it is. Oh well. My motto has always been if I'm that important then I'm worth any wait. Besides I don't think the time is very important. Heaven knows it's not like I'm jumping up and down for joy to go on this awful thing. It's not going to be that bad right? Hey, maybe this date will be the best thing to happen to me. Maybe I'll get lucky, and everything will be just fine. I spitefully laugh. Yeah, I didn't believe that load of crap either.

Thirty minutes later Billy walks through the front door of Big Mama's with DK at his side. He glances down the hall our direction before making his way to the living room where my family and Big Mama's are bonding over a game of spades.

Slipping his hand into his ironed khakis he strolls his way into the room, "Hey Big Mama."

"Hey baby," she says in her little old lady tone while dealing out the cards.

"How are you?" He leans down so she can hug him and kiss him on the cheek before starting the game.

As she picks up her cards she sighs, "I'm tired darlin'. How are you?"

"Pretty good. I'm nervous though," he jiggles his keys around in his pocket.

"Why's that?" she sweetly asks. Making eye contact with her partner across the table she says, "I got four."

"Jus' want her to like me that's all," he glances at my mom who's sitting on the opposite team of Big Mama's. Anxiously he shrugs, "I really want this date to go well."

"Don't worry. I'm sure it will," she reaches up to pats his cheek.

"Hope you're right Big Mama," Billy sighs and turns to my mom. Politely he asks, "And how are you this evening?"

"I'm fine," my mom smiles at him before jotting down both of the team's bids. "So you're nervous about taking Kie out?"

"Yeah," he begins to wonder where DK disappeared to.

"Well don't. She doesn't bite," my mom tosses in the first card before mumbling, "hard."

Smirking at the joke he nods and prepares himself to exit when my father's voice haults him like a game of freeze tag.

"Who's taking my daughter out?" my dad leans around the corner of the couch.

Adjusting the collar on his long black dress shirt he changed into, Billy bravely faces him, "I am sir."

My father slowly rises as if trying to be intimidating. He approaches him like he's attempting to be the silent yet deadly type. When Billy was a child my father had quite an idea of what he was like, but since then he hasn't gotten the chance reacquaint himself. What makes matters even more frustrating for my father is, he tried a few times prior to this date to rekindle his knowledge, but I managed to ruin every chance forcing him to have this uncomfortable interview process. "Name?"

Extending his hand cautiously he introduces himself, "Billy."

Quickly he shakes and folds his arms, "And who are you exactly?"

"The guy who would like to take your lovely daughter out."

"What do you do Billy?"

"I uh …"

"Do you go to school young man?"

"Not at the moment sir."

"And why not?"

"Well I—

"Do you have a job?" my father clears his throat.

"Actually I start tomorrow. Really I jus—

"Do you live by yourself?"

"No. I live wit' my friend, DK. We've been friends since—

My father's eyebrows raise, "Hm. If you don't have a job, how do you pay for rent?"

"Well I—

"Where do you get money to pay for bills? And money to take young girls, like my daughter, out?"

Nervously he fumbles as his jaw bobs for the right words.

"So you don't go to school, and you just got a job, yet somehow you've managed to pay rent, bills, and have extra money to take my daughter out?" My father's eyes lower, "I don't like the way this looks. Tell me why I should let a nigga who didn't even have the curiosity to introduce himself when he first began hanging out with my daughter, now take her out."

"Darryl," my mother scolds, her beer hitting the table.

Billy takes a deep long breath to gain his composure. After scanning his thoughts he presents the best answer he can, "I apologize for not bein' a man and steppin' up to you when the idea first came to me. With all due respect sir, I like your daughter a lot and would jus' like the chance to get to know her better. I'm sure I don't look like a grade A date at the moment, but I'm different from the others because I'm tryin' to better myself. There's not much more I can do than try sir."

"Well," my father hums. "That answer will have to do for right now I suppose. Be careful with her." He strolls away back towards the couch finally giving Billy the chance to breathe as he leaves the living room area.

He migrates to the hang out space behind the TV, which has a dinning room table, a stereo system, a computer, and right now a crowd of guys around the same age as Billy and DK, who has already joined the pack.

"Craziness runs in the family," DK jokes. Of course he overheard the interrogation process.

Billy tosses him the middle finger.

"So you the dumb nigga takin' Kie out," Marq' stands up greeting him with the male handshake embrace.

Chuckling he says proudly, "Yeah."

Rick who happens to be sitting next to the stereo turns it down and asks, "What kinda weed you been smokin' 'cause that's definitely gotta be some good shit."

"Fo' real though. It's gotta be off the hook fo' you to take that girl out," Marq' jumps back in the bashing while scratching his light black skin.

"Stop trippin'. She ain't that bad," he argues leaning against the computer desk beside DK.

Leaning forward in the computer chair Mario tosses his two cents in, "The girl is a straight up bitch."

"Jus' leave her alone a'ight?" Billy's pathetic attempt to defend me only eggs them on.

Mario tries to justify his words, "A nigga is jus' tryin' to help *you* out."

"Look, I know what I'm doin'. So just mind yo' biz," he slides his hands back into his pockets.

DK shakes his head and sighs, "The nigga don't listen to nobody."

"I don't blame him fo' not listenin' to yo' ass. Everyone knows you don't know shit 'bout women," Marq' chuckles.

"Yeah the mos' you know is how many beers 'til they're legally too drunk to consent to sex," Mario joins Marq' and Billy who are laughing.

"Oh like you two got game? Where yo' chicks at?" DK defends himself.

Marq' responds for the both of them, "Where's yo's?"

Obtaining a cocky grin he looks at them, and licks his lips like a champion, "Her hot little friend ..."

"You won't be touching," Mia folds her arms approaching them.

The guys snicker under their breath and Mario whispers, "Didn't think so."

DK scratches the back of his neck and mumbles in a low-key tone, "Sup Mia."

"Uh-huh, hi DK," she sneers leaning against the kitchen counter. Quickly she turns her interest to Billy, "I came to see if you were here and ready for your breathtaking date." Mia deviously folds her hands behind her back.

"More like bitchy date," Marq' clowns until he gets a swift kick in the ankle from Billy.

Standing straight up he replies, "Yeah I'm ready. Is she?"

"Yeah. Let me go get her," Mia turns around flipping her hair out.

DK flashes her the finger.

"In your dreams moron," she calls back rounding the corner out of the kitchen.

Frustrated DK grumbles out, "Damn that bitch is fine."

"Yeah, and you won't be tappin' it," Mario begins to lightly laugh.

"She wouldn't fuck you either. Hell let's look at yo' pussy tally," DK pretends to look at list, "None. A virgin. Jus' like Kie."

Billy get's ready to say something when Marq' chuckles, "I would definitely pop that cherry if I hadn't heard her talk."

Not being able to control himself Billy snaps. "Fuck. Would it kill you to show the girl a little respect?"

"Probably," DK mumbles under his breath.

Rolling his eyes, Rick decides he'll sway the conversation in a politer manner, "Where you goin' anyway?"

As he fiddles with his cuffs he answers, "To eat, and then I got a lil' some'n special planned fo' her."

Mario twists around in the chair, "You got enough dough?"

"Of course he does," DK assures everyone. "We took care of business."

"Which I would appreciate it if you didn't mention it 'round Kie," Billy turns to look at DK.

"Yeah, yeah."

"Not a word."

"Got it," DK snaps in his face.

I clear my throat demanding acknowledgement.

After taking a moment to break eye contact with DK his head shifts towards me. With an instant his jaw drops, his breath abandons him, and his eyes leech themselves on me.

Starting at the top of me he lets his gaze travel from my hair that's got tight curls on the end that bounce, to my halter-top dress that only hugs me in the right places. Of course the right places being my more than decent busty chest where the dress slightly dips, my hold me all night wide hips where it clings for dear life, and squeeze me during the right kiss thighs, which is approximately two inches from where my outfit stops. I know it's almost unheard of for a girl to wear a date dress that stops so close to her knees, but I'm a firm believer in leaving something to the mystery.

I flip my hair back behind me letting it cover the string that ties at the top. It matches the one that ties in the middle, which is the only coverage on my back until my dress comes back together a few centimeters right before my butt.

"Well I'll be damned," Rick mumbles out.

"I never knew evil looked so good," Marq' grunts out.

Mario lets out a deep groan, "Definitely wish she were a mute."

Popping my leg out innocently I sigh, "I'm ready."

Billy's jaw hasn't moved, so I assume his mind is still trying to comprehend just exactly how stunning I look. While I watch his mouth struggle to make words, I tap my heel.

He swallows deeply as his eyes journey a final time, "You ..." I wait for another word to be said, but am firmly disappointed when all I hear is, "You ... you ... you ..."

"I'm ready to go?" I try to help him out of the word slump he's managed to get himself into.

Continuing with his battle to regain consciousness he attempts to move on, "Well then um ..."

"We should go ..." I dangle my dainty black purse in my right hand.

"Yeah," he clears his throat. Turning to face the guys he mouths, "Damn!"

"Mom I'm not taking my phone, but Billy has his if you need us. You can get the number from DK," I say while Billy struggles to stop his fantasizing.

Acknowledging me with a flick of her wrist I look over Billy a lot slyer than he did me. He looks mighty fine himself. In those hug hip khakis, tucked in black dress shirt with a white wife beater underneath, and pair of black Dockers, he looks like a dream come true. You know I think if I could have imagined a dream date on looks alone, Billy would definitely win.

"Shall we," he captures my hand to intertwine our fingers.

"Mm," I smile. My hand that's holding my purse waves, "Bye Mia."

"Have fun," she mutters waving back as DK makes his way to her side.

"Don't do anything I wouldn't do it," DK smirks trying to wrap an arm around Mia who quickly throws it off of her.

Billy smiles and opens the front door letting me go out first. Good thing I know his gentleman act is just to let him take a good look at my backend. Smiling widely as he opens the car door for me I notice his car has been washed as well as vacuumed.

So he looks clean, smells good, and even went so far as to clean his car. Nice way to start out at an A plus for the evening.

Starting the ignition Billy looks into my eyes, "You look beautiful."

"Thank you," I smile. "You look good too."

"Well ... ya know," he buckles his seatbelt. "I try."

We take off down the road in an awkward silence. The best way to start a date is in a very uncomfortable silence where no chemistry, not to say I want any, could ever develop. Looking down at my dress I notice I've got lint on and around my boobs. Great. At least now I have something to occupy my time.

"How was yo," Billy looks over to see me picking lint off my dress in my chest area. "Wh-What are you doin'?"

Not looking up I sigh, "I've got lint." Hoping I've gotten it all off, I stick my chest out towards him and ask, "Do I have any more?" Really I'm not trying to seduce him. I just need to know if most of it is gone, so I don't look like a lint factory in public.

"I-uh ... well ... I ... um ...-I," he stutters doing his best not to stare at my chest.

"What's the matter with you? All I asked you to do is what normal guys do and that's look at my chest. How hard is that?" I roll my eyes and pull down the mirror. God he can't do anything right.

Switching lanes he defends himself, "You're righ' that's what normal guys do, but I'm tryin' my bes' to show you that despite what you think, I really like you. So forgive me if I'm extremely nervous especially when you stick yo' chest out at me."

"You really like me?" I lean against the door to look at him. "It's not just about trying get me into bed?" Let's see how deep a web of lies he will weave to try to hit it and quit.

His head turns to face me and he bluntly says, "No."

"I'm sure." What kind of a fool does he take me for?

"I admit at first it was," he shrugs. "No bullshit. But things change."

Sarcastically I sigh, "Uh-huh."

"You don't have to believe me since you're convinced I'm the world's worst guy ever born, but it's the truth. I'm bein' real as you get babygurl." Line after line after line. It's like he's reading exactly what he highlighted to pass his first test, the big date.

"Yeah we'll see," is the last sentence I say until we reach the restaurant. Why is it I can hear Mia's voice in my ear snapping, 'if you don't be nice to this boy I will make you wish you had.' I roll my eyes. Come on Kie. You can do it. Just give him another chance.

The restaurant is a pleasant surprise. I'm expecting somewhere mildly decent and end up at a four star bistro. It's one of those places you know you can't get in without reservations, which makes me wonder just how long he's been planning to ask me out.

After the valet takes his car, Billy holds the door open allowing me to approach the host.

The host adjusts his red tuxedo jacket, "Name?"

"Billy," he places a hand on my lower bare back.

I watch as he thumbs through a special yellow list, "In the Elstay room?"

"Yes," Billy replies back.

"Follow me," the host hops and quickly escorts us around tables draped with white tablecloths and wine glasses. Violins are playing, and I quickly catch on that I will be having Italian food tonight.

"What's the Elstay room?" I whisper out afraid to interrupt the atmosphere.

"Our V.I.P. section if you will," the host answers placing us in a section blocked off by gorgeous glass windows, so you are secluded, but can still be seen by every one. Talk about feeling high class.

Our gorgeous wooden table has a red tablecloth and red cushions on the seat of the wooden chairs as if to try and appeal to the guests comfort. In awe I admire the champagne glasses, candle sticks, and silverware already laid out for us.

Billy politely pulls the chair out for me to sit in as the host lights the candles.

"Enjoy your evening," he nods and heads out of the room hitting the lights leaving only dimmers and the candlelight making it a very romantic mood.

"Wow," I do not believe he went though all this, paid for all this, and strangest of all thought of all this.

Taking a seat himself he asks, "Ya like?"

As I look around at the paintings I nod slowly, "Yeah. It's gorgeous."

The waiter arrives, politely greets us, makes small talk, and introduces the specials once the menus are secured in our hands.

Slyly I skim over the prices on the menu to get a general idea that no meal is less than fifty dollars. Well at least his drug money is being put to a better use than tossing it into the pockets of gold digging whores.

After a good ten minutes more of painful silence the waiter comes back to take our orders assuming we know we want. Good thing he lucks out.

Billy hands the waiter the menu after I do, "Let's talk Kie. Nicely."

"Just don't give me a reason to be mean, and I will," I sip from my water glass.

"I'll try," he smirks.

Tapping the side of my glass I sigh, "What do you want to talk about?"

"There's some'n I'm curious 'bout," he starts leaning back in his chair.

"What's that?" I run my finger around the rim of my water glass.

"What happened to yo' las' boyfriend?"

Uncomfortable, I uncross and recross my bare legs. They call them exes for a reason. Ex as in the past, ex as in mistake, and ex as in never to be discussed again. "What do you mean what happened to him? I didn't kill him or anything." I fold my hands, "Though I should have for the BS he put me through."

"What happened?"

I wish we would have waited to have this talk until the food got here, "He cheated on me."

"Oh," he looks surprised. "Why?"

I swallow quickly and give him the strangest look. "What do you mean why? Do I look like I know why guys cheat? Isn't that like one of the world's biggest unsolved mysteries?"

Billy laughs a little under his breath, "I meant, what reason did he give you?"

Suddenly I feel an unfortunate twist in my stomach. The reason just adds to the self-pity I find myself stuck in every sleepless blue moon, "Well you know the old saying, if you don't take care of business at home someone else will."

His jaw slips open like he's actually surprised, "You weren't givin' it up, so he went to a girl that would?"

"Surprised?" I quickly pick up my water glass and begin to drink hoping he'll change subjects.

"No. I mean … that's jus' messed up," he picks up his glass as well.

"Tell me about it," I mumble.

"So you've never …" Billy's sad hand gestures make the indication of asking me the rest of the question. I shake my head quickly, and he tries again, "Ever close?"

"Not that it's any of your business, but no," I answer in a firm tone.

Glancing around for the waiter to see what's taking so long he asks, "Why not?"

Almost fully annoyed I snap, "This really isn't a conversation I would like to be having with you of all people, but the answer you're looking for is … I don't want to. It's different for everyone. In my opinion, sex is something you do when you're ready, have taken all the right precautions, and most of all you're in love. And as of right now I'm none of the above. Not even close."

Billy nods real slowly before fiddling around with his fork, "So you don't have a boyfriend 'cause no guys willin' to wait around fo' you to never be ready?"

Oh that was a nice way of putting it. I won't give it up, so I'll never have a man very long, if at all for that matter. Way to boost my self-esteem, "Well let me ask you. I don't want to have sex with you. Not now and as far as I know, not ever. Do you still want to date me?" Say no so we can be done, and this date can be officially over.

Dropping his fork, bored with it I assume, he answers, "Yeah."

Typical guy answer. Of course they're going to lie and say yes, so I can be the ultimate conquest. Rolling my eyes at the pathetic attempt I sigh, "Of course you do. You'll stick around for a couple of weeks, months if I'm even less fortunate begging for us to do it. And when you get tired of hearing no, you'll leave just like the rest."

"That's not true."

"Oh cut the bullshit Billy. We both know—

"Know that you jus' want guys to say that so you neva' have to put yourself out there. " Chuckling Billy shakes his head, "You really don't get it do you? I like you. I like you 'cause you're this incredible person I want in my life, not 'cause I wanna hit that ass 'til you call me big papa." Graphic content unnecessary. "There's more to life and relationships than sex."

Our waiter enters his way to us right as I ask, "Are you gay?"

The waiter makes eyes at him. I guess our waiter is. Continuing to glance at Billy while refilling our glasses he lets our conversation go on.

Billy makes a point to say in a loud, clear and deep manly voice, "No." I giggle at how uncomfortable I made him. "My number one concern isn't sex, so that makes me gay?"

"Well … science says," I sigh and take a sip from my glass.

He smirks, "Come on Kie. Yo' sassy ways, yo' smart mouth, yo' understandin' and compassion for others—

"Listing my credentials on your fingertips won't get you much more than a phony smile," I insert my two bits.

"Will you jus' let me finish? All that stuff along wit' so much more out weighs any sexual thing you can do. I mean any twist, turn, pop, suc—He looks up to only realize his gruesome rambling on was about to get him a fist in the face. Billy clears his throat to continue, "I mean sex has it perks, but so does all the other stuff and push come to shove; I'm not a complete idiot. I know which one to pick. What do you think they invented porn fo'?"

His attempt to do the three things that woo girls over only slightly annoys me. The text book says: always be sure to compliment, make it known you're open to compromise, and don't forget to end the conversation on a comedic antidote.

A silence fills the table, which is when I assume he's waiting for me to bridge the gap, "So was your ex girlfriend the one you cheated on?"

"No," he sighs like he's the uneasy one. Touchy subject? "Chante was."

"Was your ex girlfriend, or the girl you cheated on?"

"Cheated on. At the time we weren't exactly in a relationship. One night some girl was throwin' herself at me, and I didn't wanna say no. Short version, I slept wit' her, and Chante wasn't too happy 'bout it."

"I could tell," I smirk. "You didn't wanna say no? Honestly that's not something that sounds appealing to me. A guy who can't say no isn't the type that I'm bending over backwards to be with."

"Well what did you want me to do? Lie? Everyone makes mistakes Kie. I'm human. It's jus' a matter of learnin' from them," he folds his hands in his lap.

"And did you?"

"To say the very least," he sighs. "Ya know chicken heads are pretty crazy, jus' imagine how crazy one gets after you cheat on her."

Giggly I move on, "So what happened to your last girlfriend?"

After taking another long sip of his water he answers, "I broke up wit' her 'cause she was the one sleepin' wit' someone else."

"She cheated on you? There's a shocker." We all know girls cheat. It's just we're hardly caught.

"Yeah. Girls cheat too."

"I know," I snap back. "Sorry she cheated on you. I think if someone cheats they never really loved that person to begin with."

"I agree ..." his voice trails off as we start to stare into each others eyes for a brief moment.

The waiter finally arrives with our chicken fettuccini. Damn, what did they have to do? Catch the chicken, kill it, pluck the feathers, and cook it? The taste better compensate for the wait.

While the rest of dinner is filled with obvious small talk such as other exes, music we're interested in, and so on, it's after dinner, on our way to dessert, where I'm expecting another conversation to take off.

Trying to keep me interested in him and not the cars we're passing, Billy turns the radio down, "Ya know you can ask me anything righ'?" he smiles. "I swear I'll answer."

That's a very dumb, dangerous thing to do. He just placed way too much power in my hands. It's like giving a shopaholic teenager a credit card with no limit and allowing her buy whatever she wants on it. Well if he's dumb enough to give me the power then I'm damn sure going to use it.

I twirl a curl around my finger. To use my power for good or evil? "What's one of your biggest fears?"

"A fear?" he questions. Did I stutter? Billy repeats himself to buy more time, "A fear ..."

Maybe he'll have to think so long I can enjoy some peace and quiet. Forgive me for wanting some time to contemplate over my feelings for him in silence, but a girl needs her time. This guy takes every angle and every opening he can to try to keep me interested, which is frustrating in the same since it's sweet.

"Public humiliation," he lets it slowly slip off his tongue as if still deep in thought.

"Like your pants falling down in public while everyone points and laughs?" I lean against the door trying not to snicker.

"No," Billy snaps like he doesn't appreciate me mocking him. "Ya see when I get up in front of a crowd, the fear that they're not gonna like how I sound isn't there at first, but then deep in the back of my mind I know there's a big possibility someone, somewhere is laughin' at me. And that leads to the fear the laughter from that one person will spread like cancer and everyone will be laughin' at me at the same time. Then they'll be yellin' I suck, and it's all downhill from there ..." his voice saddens.

Confused I tilt my head to the side, "But you're DK's R&B side kick. How can you be afraid of being able to sing in public? I mean that makes next to no sense."

"All I do is sing in a booth, lay the tracks down, and I'm done. I've always figured I'll never really have to be live wit' DK anywhere. I'll jus' be the background vocalist. It happens all the time."

Sighing I look out the window for a moment. Wow he's an idiot. Singers aren't supposed to fear humiliation. I should know. I am one. "Billy you're going to have to get over this fear. It's very irrational, especially being a singer. No matter what you do you can't worry so much about what people think. You just have to do your own thing. When you let go and realize you like what you're providing, people will too. It's a very simple science."

Biting his bottom lip, like I tend to do, he changes lanes. I get the feeling he doesn't like being analyzed or offered help. "I guess on another level I jus' feel like I'm bein' judged by some'n that's superficial, and that's not how I wanna be judged. If you're gonna judge me, judge on some'n deeper 'bout me than jus' how stupid I may look in front of you."

"Confidence," I quickly snap at him. "The key is confidence."

Attempting to smile he nods, "I'll keep that in mind. How 'bout yo'self? What are you afraid of?"

Bluntly I say, "Trusting people." Unlike him I don't have to think it, and I'm not ashamed to admit it. "I live in this very comfortable, well organized, and controlled world that I'm the boss of. When people come into my life I think everyone has the intent to mess it up, yet I'm not closed off from people. Actually, I'm really friendly, but just at an arms length," I pull my hair to the side.

"You can't keep everyone at an arms length Kie," he takes an exit. "As much as you love that world you've created fo' yo'self you'll never make it through life that way. The changes are goin' to be scary when they happen," he grins, "but they're long over due. Believe me babygurl. It's better to open yo' world than have someone bus' the door down."

And thank you, Dr. Obvious. I hope he doesn't think he's enlightening me. Rolling my eyes I notice we're pulling up to a cozy little restaurant that looks packed. Well at least I know he's living this date up, since it's the only one he gets.

I reapply my lip gloss as Billy walks around to kindly open my door for me. At least his gentleman ways haven't disappeared. We stroll in together this time with a friendly gap between us. How should I celebrate the end of our relationship or lack there of? I'm thinking a big ice cream sundae.

Following behind Billy we approach the bar where his friend works. Who does he think he is? A celebrity? This isn't Hollywood. It's Fort Worth, Texas for heavens sake.

"How's it goin' Dave?" Billy leans on the bar.

"Kinda busy. It's karaoke night. Ya know how people love to come and laugh at the talent."

My eyes light up as I smirk deviously. Now this shall be a treat to me. The perfect goodbye if you will. Something to teach him I'm not a force to be reckoned with.

"Well we're gonna take a seat up front. Jus' send someone to us when you get the chance," he sighs and walks towards a front table with me behind him. Billy smiles as he pulls the seat out for me.

"Thank you," I say trying to hide my idea that's boiling underneath my skin dying to get out.

"You're welcome ..." he says almost suspicious of how chipper I said thanked him.

"Good seats for the show," I point to the vacant stage.

"Glad you like 'em," he sighs sitting down in the wooden chair beside me.

Well I do love the cozy little wooden table that has crumbles lounging on it, and the advertising for a giant sundae which I guess is their attraction dessert, but what I really love is the ring left on the table from a cup that couldn't have been there any longer than five minutes ago. Don't worry though. All the disgustingness will pay off in just a few moments.

"What are you in the mood fo'?" he asks looking at the advertisement while I look at the stage basking in my wonderful idea.

Smirking I say, "Entertainment."

Billy stops touching the menu and looks up, "Huh?"

"I want you to go sign up for karaoke," I point to the sign up sheet noticing there are still a few empty spots.

"What?" he clears his throat after it squeaked.

I try to maintain a straight face, "I think it would be good for you. It'll help that fear of yours."

"Are you crazy?"

"I'm pretty sure we established that already," I bite my bottom lip. Giving me a chuckling nod he lets me continue, "Come on Billy. You wanna impress me? You wanna show me that being with me actually means something to you? Go up there, and sign up for the karaoke contest."

Nervous at the very thought his eyebrows dart down, "You're serious?"

"As a heart attack," I whisper as I dangle my index finger innocently next to mouth.

Billy stares at me intensely like I'm going to back down. Oh yeah since when have I ever backed down to him. You know he's the one who wants my heart. The sooner he realizes it's a loosing battle; the sooner we can all go home and rest peacefully in our beds.

A few seconds later, after his contemplation is ceased, he simply responds, "All right. I'll do it."

With an intrigued expression I smirk, "Really? What about the bright lights beating down on you, while that one person in back rubs his hands together preparing to laugh you off the stage?" I watch him shift in his seat, "Or the one girl who leans over to whisper to her friend about how pathetic she thinks you are? Maybe the entire crowd congregates and decides to get you off in one long, loud boo? Can you really handle that?" I watch as Billy pulls the collar of his dress shirt nervously. "You ok?"

He gaps for air for a sec, "Yeah. I'm jus' a little hot."

"So," I press my lips together. "Are you sure you wanna do it?"

Being as brave as he can, he nods, "Yeah, but only for you." He quickly gets up and heads towards the sheet of paper where he will be signing the end of our date.

While I watch him struggle to write his own name, probably the first time since he learned to write, I twiddle my thumbs. Oh big deal. He signed up, but that doesn't mean he won't back out when the time comes for him to go through with it.

I smile as his friend casually drops off a couple of menus about the time Billy makes his way back to the table. He sits down giving the impression he's calm until he attempts to hold his menu that ends up shaking like an earthquake.

"If it terrifies you that much you can take your name off the list," I open my menu nonchalantly.

Trying to convince himself as well as me he sighs, "If makin' a jackass of myself helps you see jus' what I'm willin' to go through jus' fo' a chance wit' you, then I'm gonna do it."

Since the fear I tried instilling before didn't work, let's try another round, "I'm glad you're ok with music blaring that you probably don't know the words to, and people routing for you to fail so that they can laugh at your expense." Pulling all my hair to one side I sweetly sigh, "Ya know the hot fudge sundae looks pretty good."

Gasping for air again he agrees, "It uh … yeah."

"So you know that if you win this contest then our dessert is free?" I recall the sign by the karaoke list. "No pressure or anything though."

Billy unable to really form any more words just nods. Now why didn't I think of this earlier? All the good opportunities to shut him up come long after they're really needed. Talk about great luck.

After deciding to hold off on ordering until after Billy goes, I make continuous small conversation to try to restore some of his speaking abilities. I don't want him to go up there and make a *complete* ass of himself. I at least want him to be able to sing, not just stutter. Will I be able to forgive myself if they laugh and boo him off stage? Of course, probably not right away though. Knowing me I'll have to give myself a good five minutes to feel forgiven.

While watching the few people in front of him, I play with the napkin holder, condiments, and anything else on the table I can find to keep me company while he makes a useless effort to gain his composure.

Having to resort to fooling around with my hair again, I point towards the stage, "You're up next." He acknowledges the statement with a nod. "Make sure you shake some'n too," I begin to ruffle his feathers again. Glancing at his butt for effect I pout my lips, "Girls like a nice piece of meat to drool over."

"Oh you think you're funny?" his voice cracks. "You know wha'? I'll get you."

"Let me guess … and my little dog too?" I giggle as he rises up.

Resting back in my very hard chair I look at the rest of the front row audience. It's full of females giggling with their best girlfriends. My eyes roll back towards the dusty stage steps and up to the single microphone where Billy is trembling. While looking around for the teleprompter I end up noticing the bartender smiling widely and giving Billy his full attention. Would it kill him to take that yellow smile down a few notches from creepy to normal? My eyes wander back to Billy, who better give me a good show, or this night will haunt his dreams for the rest of miserable existence.

Tapping the microphone with his quivering hand he croaks out, "Mic check."

I cover my mouth as I giggle to myself. Just how forgiving is god? Because I know this will definitely go on in the big book of reasons *not* to let me in. Come on this is borderline inhumane.

Uncrossing my legs, I cross them again the opposite way. My elbow rests on the non-sticky part of the table as I watch Billy barely open his mouth to let the words come out.

Now really, how much easier could he have gotten it? It's R&B night, and that's the sort of singer he is. Beginning to loosen up a tad in the middle of the first verse, he let's his death grip on the microphone go. Good start kid. As the words continue to follow beautifully out of his mouth his eye contact gets directed at me. I mouth loosen up trying to soften my offense.

Smiling at me he does as instructed and starts to move his hips a little. Now that's better. The chorus starts and out of nowhere Billy gets guts as well the microphone. Confused at the miracle, I look around for the shelf he snatched his courage off of.

He sings along in the right key and moves towards the crowd of girls who are gawking over him. Billy reaches out towards one of them making her squeal. I shift my weight. Wait. Shouldn't he be singing to me? Which one is his date? Whose fault is it he's even up there?

Continuing through the second verse he croons another girl at the parallel table. What do I have to do to get some attention? I spend all night with him, listening to him whine, listening to his problems, and even pretending I would give him a shot at a relationship, and this is the thanks I get? Ignored, when I actually want the attention that's being handed out like candy to the other girls in the audience?

Not hiding my pout very well, Billy eyes me, leaving them behind. Yeah. Now he wants to notice me. Working on his fear sure is bringing him lots of luck with the other females. Ironic. At least I know not getting into my pants won't put a crimp in his game. He reaches our table to see me upset, which only fuels the fire for the plan I assume he had already devised.

With a stretch of his hand Billy slides his way back into the chorus again expecting me to put my palm in his. Reluctantly, I join him on the stage, and suddenly become the center of his attention. Every word he's singing I feel like it is what he wishes he could say to me.

I smile when his hips start to move with mine as his free hand moves itself around my body. Must admit, the boy is a natural born performer. Wrapping his free arm around me, he continues to sing. Billy takes feeds off the crowd who is clapping along with him.

Sliding his finger up he let's them know he wants to have a moment just between us. The slow middle verse is the most intimate part, which is why when he glides his hand across my face, licks his lips, and seduces me with his beautiful hazel eyes, I find myself incapable of holding my smile back.

As the music fades he lightly presses his forehead against mine. The crowd starts whistling, clapping, cheering, and there are even a few standing ovations. He chuckles slightly embarrassed and bows. Moving aside I join in the clapping. I must admit he deserves every ounce of love being showed up here at him. Nice of him to finally take off the mask he's so nicely glued on his face to try to impress me. Can you keep a secret? I wouldn't mind dating him so much after all. Actually I've never wanted to date a guy nearly as much as I want to date him right now, but that could just be a rush from all the excitement.

"Yeah!" the bartender jumps out from behind the bar and rushes the stage as I shuffle my way off the stage before anyone notices that I'm still loitering "That's my boy!" Taking the microphone from Billy's hand he says loudly into it, "That's what I'm talkin' 'bout! It's anonymous. The crowd has spoken and crowned you as tonight's karaoke winner!"

"Thanks," Billy takes the frame with a proud smile.

"Your dessert is on the house," he laughs and pats him on the back. "Ya'll give it up one more time for my homeboy Billy."

I smile and look over at the floozies who were fawning all over him. They're still drooling and giggling like one of them will actually take him home, but I've got news for them. He's coming home with me. I dare one of them to try to stop him.

Billy strolls down the stage and sits confidently in his chair, "That was fun …"

My elbow rests itself on the table, "I'll say."

As the bartender comes to us, we over him bragging on his cell phone, "Yeah I thought he had too and then there was Billy. He blew 'em all out of the water." Putting his friend on hold he asks us, "What can I get for you two?"

With a gleam in his eye Billy winks at me, "How 'bout that sundae?"

Twenty minutes later we're back in the car with tummies full of hot fudge, ice cream, nuts, whip cream, and of course my tummy got the cherry. We're quietly enjoying each others company and holding hands when his cell phone goes off. That better not be one of his boys calling. I bet it's another girl.

"Yeah," he answers the phone letting my hand go. "Why are you callin'?"

Ain't this a bitch? I knew he'd screw up the evening just like he does every other perfect moment. Couldn't he have put his evening sex toys away for the night or at least until we were done on our date? Is that really too much to ask?

He holds it out in front of me, "Phone."

"I'm sorry. What?" How is his phone for me?

Dangling it he sighs, "Phone call."

"Hello …" I answer it slowly looking out the window.

"Hey girl," Mia says cheerfully into the phone.

I shake my head and roll my eyes while Billy laughs. What the hell is she calling for? Doesn't she recall she helped me get ready for this date? It's a date meaning you don't call unless it dyer important, and I'm more than sure nothing she was to say is dyer important right now. "What is it?"

"Just called to see if he was still alive and breathing, or if you needed help stashing the body," she laughs at her joke.

Mia looks at DK whose lips are sailing towards her like Columbus thought he was to Asia, "Everything is fine in fact," she shoves him hard away from her accidentally making him fall of the bed causing a big thump, which cuts off my comment, "—What the hell was that?"

"Nothing. When will you guys be back?"

"Not sure, but I'm going now. See you later," I quickly hang up the phone. Sheepishly I apologize, "Sorry."

Slipping the phone out of my hands and tossing it in the back he questions, "Felt that need to check up on you?"

"Unfortunately," I sigh crossing my ankles.

"You trust her huh?"

"Of course."

"Wit' yo' life?" he exits off the main road.

"Most def," I nod. If you can't trust your best friend you've grown up around, whom do you trust? The stranger who walks into your life looking for something to steal or screw up?

He enters his way onto a dark road that looks like no one has drove on in awhile. There aren't many streetlights, and the road is somewhat narrow surrounded by tons of forest. I hate roads like this. I always feel like a killer is just waiting to jump out in front of your car and snatch you to take back to his secret hideaway. What a romantic place to drive, "So are you willin' to open that trust to me?"

Did that bush just move? "What?"

"Do you trust me?" he glances at me.

I sarcastically look at him. That's a stupid question. Wow now I see I give him too much credit for how intelligent he is.

"I asked you a question," he gives the road a quick look then his eyes are right back at me. "Do you trust me?"

I wish he would watch the road. What if another car starts to come towards us while he's staring at me? The next thing you know BOOM we're all dead, and I'm coming back as ghost to haunt Mia. Pointing forward I sigh, "Billy watch the road."

"I told you Kie. There are people who are gonna knock and those who are gonna bus' through. I'm knockin'," his eyes don't meet the road again.

Now is not the time for his feeble metaphors. "I'm not answering," I play back.

"Which would you prefer me to be?"

"Neither," I sneer. Way to begin to ruin this evening.

"Knock. Knock." I give him another sarcastic look. "No answer?" He takes one hand off the wheel. "I need you to trust me."

"I barely know you. You're driving dangerously, something I loathe, yet somehow you still expect me to trust you?" I look ahead to make sure no one's coming towards us on the opposite side of the small curvy road. "I think that ice cream went straight to your head."

He answers showing no sign of resistance, "I wanna hear you say you trust me."

"And I want a golden pony. Hate to break it to you, but you'll probably die before you hear it," I utter watching the road.

"Knock Knock Kie."

"Go away …"

"Knock. Knock."

"No thank you. I don't want to buy anything today."

"Knock. Knock."

"You should really tell the next part of that joke."

"Knock—

"Billy," I cut him off. Talk about being stubborn.

"I'm not gonna look back at the road 'til you do," he lightly presses down on the gas pedal increasing the speed to fifty miles per hour.

Trying to maintain a calm attitude I ask, "Excuse me?"

"You won't answer my knockin', so I'm gonna bus' my way in," he switches hands.

Has he lost his damn mind? How smart is it to put someone's life at risk and say 'oh yeah trust me'. I point feeling us go over a few bumps, "The road." Nervously I shake my knee up and down. This crazy ass muthafucker has me out here in the middle of the woods, speeding like a maniac while he doesn't watch the road screaming trust me. I swear if this ride doesn't kill him I will.

"I need you to trust me," he leans in. "Trust me. Say you trust me."

"I did trust you to get me home safe, but now I'm not so sure," I shake my head watching the road.

"I need—

"You always need something."

Clearing his throat as he stands his ground he makes this situation even worse, "The longer it takes you to say it; the longer I'm going to stare at you like this."

"No thank you."

"It's not an offer Kie."

I nervously swallow and shake my head. "Well I can't do it Billy, so just look forward again."

"I can't isn't what I need to hear," he tilts his head to side.

"I don't care what you need …"

"You're 'bout to."

"Stop joking around, will ya?"

"No one's jokin' Kie."

A lump grows in my throat, "So you're so serious?"

"As a heart attack," the spite in his voice makes it click this is a lesson he's going to teach me.

"I get it. You're trying to make me feel bad for what I did to you, so here it goes. I'm sorry Billy."

"No it's bigger than you tryin' humiliate me and pass it off for therapy. This is about you needin' to find it in you to trust people. Startin' wit' me."

"Will you let this go already? It's really not something you can fix in the blink of an eye."

I assume he brushes off what I said when he remarks, "I know you're nervous."

"And I know you're fucking crazy," I grip the door handle slyly.

Beginning to sound like a broken record he says, "Let me hear you say it."

"No you psychopath," I argue back glaring at him.

"Callin' me names isn't makin' my foot get any lighter on the gas pedal now is it?" I lean over noticing we're doing seventy. "Are you scared Kie? Are yo' palms sweatin'? Yo' adrenaline rushin'? Heart poundin' so loud you think it can be heard in another country?"

I cover my mouth whining, "Billy."

"My foot is like lead on the pedal wit' every breath you take, the engine is burnin' up as yo' fear increases, and the rubber on the tires is blazin' from how fast they're spinnin', and all you have to do make it stop is let me help you."

"But—

"I told you that it was gonna be scary, and that it was long overdue. I'm waitin'."

Breathing out deeply I try to devise a plan. Why don't I know how to handle this situation? School is now officially useless. They don't show you how to deal with situations like this or people who are borderline mentally insane. I know. I know. I could sit here and lie, but I can't do that. A person's word is the only concrete thing they have, so if I lie and don't mean what I say then I'm no better than DK or any other person who I consider lousy. "I-I-I," I stutter out loud. Believing I see a car head I yelp out, "There's a car."

"Then you better hurry and say it," he presses down harder.

"Billy," I scream at him putting my hand on my forehead.

"Yes …" and now he's doing eighty down the dark road.

I bounce up and down feeling the knot in my stomach a person get's right before they're going to cry. He wants to see my cry. That's all he wants. I squeeze my eyes and pray the tears don't fall.

"Ya know what will make me look forward—

"And I can't give it to you—

"Won't. The word is won't. Come on. Overcome yo' fear that I'm gonna destroy yo' life. Kie I need you to trust me if we're gonna pursue anything," he says to me as I feel a tear fall. "I need you to trust me wit' yo' life. Knock. Knock."

Shaking my head I belt out, "I—

"Give me that chance to show you I won't hurt you," his free right hand drifts its way towards mine.

I look up with watery eyes. Here I am scared for my life, and all this fool wants is for me to say is I trust him. I can't do that. I mean won't do that. Oh god whatever. It's not going to happen.

"Three words Kie. I know you'll mean 'em when you say 'em," he lifts my chin up. "Please."

You know I didn't endanger his life to help him conquer his superficial fear. At least mines profound. "I … I …" am going to pass out from the lack of air getting to my lungs and my brain.

"You can do it Kie. I believe in you." I'm glad one of us does.

At ninety five miles an hour I shut my eyes and cry out with everything in me, "I trust you Billy."

Smiling Billy presses down slowly on the break gliding us right up to a stoplight. He turns forward and looks at the gas station on the corner, and the empty four way stop.

Slowly reducing my hyperventilation I look up to see the city I've come to accustom to hating. I see a parked cop car, other parked cars, and many street signs. I've never been so thankful to see traffic signals. My make up is all over my face, air is struggling to burry itself back in my lungs, and my life that just flashed before my eyes is doing what it can to erase that from my memory.

Billy makes sure he's staring straight ahead as he makes the effort to lighten the misery he created, "I only needed to hear three, geez."

Glaring through my splotched eyes I feel hate bloom like roses beautifully back out of my heart.

"Don't be mad at me Kie," he shakes head switching lanes to turn into a neighborhood. "Do not go back to bein' hostile.

"You scare the living shit out of me for your own sick pleasure and expect me not be irate?" I growl very low.

He smirks as he turns down a street with nice cookie cutter houses, "Ya know, fo' a girl who's very bright you sure don't act like it."

I prepare my hand to smack him, "Excuse me? You scare me and now you insult me?"

Placing a tissue in my hand before I can use it for an attack, he turns down another neighborhood road continuing to try to make up for his behavior, "I didn't mean to insult you or make you cry. I jus' needed you to trust me."

He turns down his final road as I ask, "So putting my life in jeopardy is how you go about it?"

"To be completely honest Kie, no one ever goes down that road ..." he trails off pulling into a parking lot of a park. "It's a back road people stop usin' once they built the short cut. In fact mos' people have either forgotten it existed or jus' don't know. So technically I wasn't really puttin' yo' life at risk." Son of a bitch! "You know everything you felt jus' then you made me feel back in fron' of those people. I've jus' got a braver solider face than you."

Wiping my run away make up I avoid eye contact letting the last few minutes process. So I had to face my fear as I made him do meaning this must be one of those an eye for an eye situation. Ya know I should strangle him for what he did to me. He's put me through a lot of hell and for what reason? I take a second to recall for a second that I've treated him pretty shitty and done some pretty horrible things myself, which almost rectifies his behavior. Damn it. Fucking karma.

"So what, we're even now?" I ball up the tissue. I should throw it at him.

He slides the keys out of the ignition, "Yeah. We can't start a relationship wit'out trust. It doesn't work that way."

Ignoring his talk show host advice, I look straight ahead at a playground in the middle of a very nice park. Why am I looking at a park? Better yet why is this park nicer than the one back home? Where the hell am I? "What are we doing here?"

There's a swirling slide painted yellow, a giant swing set, a balance beam, and a seesaw, all spread out over baby rocks. It looks like something you see out of those badly done sitcoms.

Billy innocently shrugs, "We're here to walk around and stuff."

"I'm sorry you might wanna get that off yo' face," I glance at him.

In a rush he pulls his mirror down, "What? Food?"

"No. The word crazy that's stamped on your forehead."

Annoyed he asks, "Why am I crazy now?"

"It's after ten, and you want to take a leisurely stroll around a park ..." I say real slowly. "Do the words mug, rob, beat down, or rape register?"

Laughing he rolls his eyes, "You watch too many cop shows. Don't worry. We're in a good neighborhood." I do not. He's just naïve.

"What's good? Better than one you live in because if that's the case then there are dark alleys that are better than that," I slightly tilt my head to the side.

"Such a smart ass," he mumbles to himself. Uh … I can hear him. "I use to live here befo' my parents died. We're in the 'burbs now. You should know 'em real well." Was that a stuck up comment? Who verbally abuses me twice in the same sentence? "Besides you do trust me don't you?"

I wrinkle my nose and open the door, "For now … But if something and I do mean the slightest thing puts me in any kind of danger while we're out here, not only will I kill you, I will serve you to DK as breakfast the next morning."

"Gross enough," he shrugs meeting me in the front of his car.

We head the direction of the playground running into a ledge that I won't enjoy making in heels.

"Let me help you up," he steps up and holds his hand out. How is it he maintains his gentleman qualities through all my bitching?

"Why here?" I ask feeling a few rocks slip into my shoes as we make our way to the swing set.

Billy pauses feet in front of it being swept into a memory.

❧   ❧   ❧

"Billy, tell dad what you want to be when you grow up?" his farther says pushing him on the swings.

"I don't know," he says kicking his feet.

"You can do anything you want to do," his mom encourages him from behind the camera. "Don't ever forget that."

"Ok," he says like any other seven year old would. "Anything?"

"Anything," she struggles to focus the camera.

Chuckling he starts kicking more rocks as his father slows down, "I want to grow up and be happy."

His father speaks up letting go of the swing chains, "Just happy? Not a fire-fighter or a police officer like daddy?"

"Just happy," he shrugs scratching his slightly curly head.

❧   ❧   ❧

"Billy," I say hoping I didn't ruin his special flashback I assume he was having. I sit down on the swing he was staring at, "Are you ok?"

Holding back tears he clears his throat, "I'm fine."

"Why'd you bring me here?" I ask again gripping the chains.

"To talk," he states the obvious.

"Ok. About?"

After he starts to push me on the swing he hesitates to say, "I don't know what I wanna do any more." Waiting for him to continue I lift up my feet. "What we do jus' isn't what I want. Ya know hustlin' is the kinda game you gotta have heart to survive in. I'm afraid if I don't get out now it'll kill me."

"So get out," I quickly say. "You shouldn't be in anything that dangerous anyway."

"It's not like I haven't tried, but there's not much else I'm good at."

He gives me a soft push, "You can sing. Hands down."

"I know, but I'm not DK. I don't wanna work my ass off to try to make a baby footprint in a game that's over done and not real welcomin' to new comers. That's his thing. I mean I wouldn't mind doin' it along with some'n I'm passionate 'bout."

"Well what's that? What are you passionate about?" I wiggle the rocks out of my shoes. "Do you wanna be a doctor? A lawyer? A circus freak?"

Letting out a slight laugh he continues pushing me, "I don't know." Well idiot that doesn't exactly help now does it. "Maybe a chef," it accidentally slips out.

Restraining my laughter I mumble out, "A chef?"

"Maybe. Own a restaurant or some'n," he pauses in between his career fantasies, "Or own a nightclub. That would be pretty tigh' too."

"A nightclub?"

"Yeah. You know, have it blow up wit' celebrities rollin' through and chillin' wit' me in the V.I.P. section," the grin on his face grows.

As easy as it is right now to throw his out there dreams away I won't. If I were to do an evil thing like throw away the small amount of hope left in him, it would probably push him further into the game, which is exactly what I want him out of.

"So why don't you do it?" I return to dangling my feet.

"I can't," he mumbles not pushing nearly as much as before. "I can't afford to go to college to get a degree in business or some'n. Besides I wouldn't even have enough money to open a place."

"Sure you would," I glance back at him. He begins pushing me at a faster speed, "That money your dad left you. Save it, and add to it, so you can open up your own place. I mean I'm sure you've got connections with people who know what their doing in the business ..."

"I don't know if I can do that Kie," he slows down again. Damn it boy; push me at one steady speed not four annoyingly different ones.

Running my fingers along the chain I sigh, "You can do anything you want." How is it he only exudes confidence every other twenty minutes?

Billy's hands disappear off my back as his body takes on the shocked form, "Wh-what did you jus' say?"

I repeat myself and watch his emotions circle around inside him. Sometimes I wish he would tell me what's going on in that normally out of work mind of his.

"Maybe when I was younger, but not now," he toughs himself back up. Billy slides himself into the swing beside me, "I use to buy into that crap, but now I know better. You can't do anything you want. People look down on you, discourage you, hurt you, and hold you back. No matter how much you want some things you can never have 'em."

Boys got a point, but I don't think he's completely right. "You're right. There will be people who do those things, but you can't let them stop you. You have to do what *you* want, be who *you* are, and live *your* life. Like I told you, you have to do your own thing and when you love what you're doing and giving others will too. If anything remember this," I turn to face him. "You have to learn when it's time to put *you* first."

"Wise woman," Billy looks down as he kicks a rock.

"I like to think so," I gloat proudly. "You learn a few things after awhile."

"Mm," he hums out. "Where'd you learn so much from?"

I know it's an attempt to part his way into the world of me he doesn't know. "I've learned by example. Being raised by a strong mother and a strong older sister will do that to you. The way I lead life, the way I was taught, there's no time for doubts and fears like yours. I have no time to be weak and inferior to the rest of the world," I look out to the road ahead.

"But you can't play superwoman twenty four seven," my eyes find there way to his. "It's ok to be strong and independent as long as you learn that sometimes you need to let someone else take care of you ..." his hand slips into mine that's dangling between us.

Intertwining his fingers with mine I buzz, "Hm. Like you?"

"I don't know. Bein' Superman is a very hard job especially wit' you as superwoman. That's a lot of crime to clean up. I mean I don't know if I can handle it," he playfully smiles at me.

"Well I guess if you're not man enough ..." I shrug innocently.

"Oh I'm man enough," he leans in my face. "Believe me."

"Prove it," I lean as well.

Billy places his hand slightly under my chin and presses his pre-moistened lips against mine. My eyelids fall immediately as it sends a shiver down my spine. He gently moves his lips with mine sucking my bottom lip into his mouth making my knees weaken. I feel like I'm about to fall off the swing. Billy casually parts my lips letting his tongue slowly enter my mouth barely touching afraid it's not what I want. I wouldn't have parted my lips if that's not what I wanted. Pushing my tongue towards his they take their well overdue meeting. He slowly massages his tongue with mine giving me those things people call butterflies. So that's what those feel like? Wow. His tongue is like sweet candy that I just can't get enough of. Continuing to let his tongue linger with mine I feel my entire body fall into a warm comforting feeling I don't remember ever having. Well if kissing were an Olympic sport we all know who would be taking home the gold tonight. Billy slowly slides his tongue out of mouth, capturing my bottom lip once more before pressing his lips against mine as softly as he started. Four stars and two thumbs way WAY up.

Billy smiles at me as he removes his hand. Still staring into my eyes he shakes his head, "I'll never understand how lucky I am to have you here wit' me."

As I slither my way back into reality I jump on the first chance he gives me for a flirty joke, "Neither will I."

Preparing his lips for what I hope will be round two he leans over and says in a low voice, "One things for sure."

"Uh-huh what's that?" my voice is anxious to have the conversation with our voices end, and the one with our tongues begin.

"It took me this long to finally catch you, and I'm not letting you go," he whispers and gently moves his hand edge of my face as we embrace our lips once again.

I may be hard to catch, but if you continue kissing me like this I won't be hard to keep. Laughing inside I find myself happy and scared; two things I didn't think I could be at the same time. I guess you could say that my fairy tale came true, minus the whole big dress and glass slipper thing.

CHAPTER 6

The End is the Beginning

Why is it when your night wonderfully ends sleeping is the hardest thing? I tossed and turned for hours once Mia and I swapped date stories. After hearing 'I told you so' numerous times, we eventually passed out or at least she did.

For some reason I just couldn't help but wonder what was going to happen to Billy and I. Are we going to date long distance because that almost never works. Then again there's still that slight chance that something could progress. I mean there's something different about us. We aren't exactly 'normal'. Nothing we have done has really been 'normal', so who knows what could happen.

Eventually I got to the good point, you know where your entire body is so dead that it doesn't matter how fast your minds racing it stops allowing you to be at rest, when someone starts to gently shake me. Let me get this straight; it's not bad enough we have to wake up at seven to beat the 'morning traffic', but now someone wants to snatch up the few hours I get to sleep in a bed. Perfect. Perfect night about to be a very perfectly grouchy morning especially for whoever just decided it would be a good idea to wake me up.

Rubbing the sleep out of my eyes I barely see a blurry figure in front of me. I hate wearing my contacts to sleep, which means I have to wear my glasses in the morning when people wake me up like this. Personally I think my glasses make me look more intelligent, but not necessarily more attractive. After I grab them off the nightstand, I quickly put them on to see Billy hovering over me. What the hell is he doing here?

I roll onto my back and readjust my pillow only to hear him whisper, "Good mornin' beautiful." Billy plants a kiss on my forehead.

"What are you doing here? What time is it?" I yawn and pull the covers over my bare shoulders.

"Is there a time of day when you don't ask a lot of questions?" he continues to whisper. Smartass. I didn't ask for him to wake me up let alone give me hell this early. I merely smile and roll my eyes at him. His mint breath rolls out the words, "It's 6:30, and I brought you breakfast." Well it looks like someone brushed their teeth, which sucks because I probably have morning breath that could bring down a giant.

Yawning again I spray my nasty morning breath all over him, "Breakfast?"

Dangling the brown paper sack in front of me he nods, "Yeah."

Awaking from the few moments of sleep I've actually gotten, I notice he's now in navy jersey shorts, a wife beater, and a plain white baseball cap. Well at least he changed. "You bought me breakfast?" Was that high-priced meal last night not enough?

"No. I made it …" he proudly grins.

I stare at him blankly. Who wastes perfectly great hours made for sleeping to slave over a hot stove to make me of all people, a non-morning person, breakfast. "What? When did you get up?"

"Get up? Girl I ain't been to bed," he winks at me. What moron doesn't get some rest after an exhausting evening like the one we had? All the yanking, tucking, primping, flirting, testing, yelling, arguing, laughing, smiling, and kissing makes me tired just thinking about it. I couldn't imagine not getting any sleep after it. Although I'm not too proud of the three hours I've barely been able to capture.

Making the gesture for him to explain he just smiles again.

"After I brought you home, DK and I hit this party at our boys' crib. By the time we lef' there it was nearly five, and on the way home I decided why not make you breakfast as a goodbye gift." Quickly he adds, "Ya know wit' our whole talk las' night I figured why not try my hand at it?"

"Well isn't that sweet …" I sigh.

"Only if there's some for me," Mia rolls over to face us. I smile at him as she reaches out for the bag.

"Of course," he takes out a clear container. "This one's fo' you."

Suspicious she sneers, "Why you say it like mines got poison or something?" I laugh under my breath. Spending too much time around DK has got her more paranoid than normal.

"You're not a mornin' person are you?" Billy slides a similar container next to my thigh.

"I'm just a careful one," she shrugs removing the lid to inhale the smell of eggs, bacon, toast, and hash browns. Mia looks down and licks her lips catching the drool that almost fell off. "You brought us food, but no utensils? No syrup? No napkin?" Would it have killed her to compliment the food first?

Billy hands her the brown paper bag I swore was empty. Mia peers over the top and removes everything she asked for along with a ketchup bottle.

"Mm," she licks her lips again eyeing the toast like a wolf that hasn't eaten in two days. I have a feeling that toast has no chance of survival. "Thank you Billy ..."

"No problem," he grins as I cover my mouth to yawn once more.

I'll see if Mia likes it. Sometime ago when our friendship first began I learned that Mia has excellent taste in food. Since her step-dad is a chef it makes her taste buds critique everything that touches her tongue and anxious to try new things, which I find useful since I'm naturally very picky about my food. At least if his cooking isn't all he hopes it to be, I'll find out before I try it. That way I can prepare myself to use some of my acting skills.

She chews partly with her mouth open, her shoulders continue to slump, and her eyes keep rolling themselves back into her head. All clear signs it's too die for, but not in a literal sense.

"This is so good," she points to the egg crumbs that managed to escape her cave of doom. "Oh my gosh Kie," she swallows a bite of the bacon and looks in the bag pulling out a bottle of orange juice. What the hell is that? A magic bag? "You have to try it. Billy I don't know what you did, but food should never be this good. Hell if DK could cook like this I would date him."

"Yeah, too bad he can't," Billy shoots me a wink.

"Thank god," I mumble.

After a moment more of watching Mia suffocate her breakfast in silence, Billy leans over to whisper in awe, "She's like a garbage disposal."

"We shouldn't stare. It seems to only make her suck down more," I try to draw my attention away. She's got jelly outlined around her mouth along with crumbs on her shirt trying to escape. "It's like those animals in the zoo. They say you shouldn't watch them, but you do it anyway because not to stare would be a crime in itself."

Billy slightly lets out a chuckle as we watch until every last crumb along as well as every last drop of juice is gone. Damn.

"So good," she licks her fingers and puts the lid back on the container. Slobbering on the other set she says, "Thanks Billy. That was a good wake up. I think I'm going to take a shower, and let you two be alone for a little while."

We glance at each other and then back at her watching as she snatches her bag off the floor. Why do I feel like she's in fast forward, but we're stuck in pause?

She prepares to exit the room but announces herself leaving a final time before closing the door shut.

"That was ..." I continue to stare in the direction of the closed door. "Graphic."

"To say the least," he nods pulling his face back towards me. "But that's yo' friend."

"Do we need to talk about yours?" I start to laugh as I feel Billy roll his fingertips around the leftover curls from yesterday. Oh my gosh. I was so worried about my morning breath I forgot about bed head. I quickly try to pat my hair over to keep from my infamous Alfalfa look.

Clearly aware of what I'm trying to accomplish Billy's fingers slip into mine, "You look beautiful jus' the way you are." His lips lightly press against mine making those damn butterflies go wild. He captures my bottom lip and then switches to my top as we lean back onto my pillow. I glide my arms around his neck as our tongues softly roll around each other's. Around the time I get deep into it, he slowly draws his lips away from mine. Tease.

Surprised himself that he had the strength to pull away he whispers, "I've been waitin' to do that since the moment you lef' my sight."

Feeling my cheeks warm up I sigh. "I know how you feel."

"I made you breakfast," he puts the container in front of me. "The reviews are raving though all I did is jus' whip up a little some'n some'n."

"Well," I reach for it as he puts the silverware, ketchup, and syrup in front of me. "Let's see what this critic thinks." Peering down at my organized meal I notice it's the same as Mia's minus the toast. I point to the pancakes that have the whip cream hearts drawn on them, "Aw. You drew on my food."

"Yeah. I'm an artist," he looks a bit embarrassed. What a softy. It's funny how a guy who spends most of his time trying to be a hard ass can become softer than mash potatoes when no one's watching.

"Aren't you special," I reach for the fork, but Billy grabs it first.

"Let me feed you the first bite," he looks hopeful. I drizzle syrup over it and figure I might as well give into his one request. It's the least I can do since he did make me breakfast. Billy cuts a piece of a pancake with the fork, moves it towards my mouth, and I close my eyes. When the light, fluffy pancake touches my tongue I nearly faint. I don't know how anyone could make a simple pancake taste so damn delicious, but I know he could make a hell of a lot of money if he were to become a chef.

"Oh my gosh," crumbs fall from my mouth. "I would hurt someone over these," I point to the plate in his hand. Casually sliding the plate out of his hands into mine, I gracefully take the fork to dig in.

"Good to know," he smirks widely and starts telling me about the party.

The explanation starts what he did, who he talked to, something about some girl who was drunk, and before I know it he's telling me about DK being all over a different girl to regain the dignity he lost with Mia.

Fifteen minutes later, about the time I'm done sucking down my breakfast, he finally finishes his story about his night out after me.

I wipe my mouth as I move the container to the side of me, "Sounds like someone had fun last night at the party."

Leaning in towards me he whispers, "Not nearly as much fun as I did wit' you."

"I sure hope not," I giggle and lean back towards him. Gotta love the obvious kiss set-ups.

"Ya know the bes' part of the evenin' though," he strokes my cheek, "was when you said you trust me."

"THAT was the best part?" I question with a confused look. "Am I just that bad of a kisser?"

Shaking his head he prepares to put his anxious lips on mine when Mia walks in to interrupt.

"Geez get a room," she tosses her towel in a laundry basket near the door.

I cover up the fact she ruined a craving I probably won't be able to fulfill for a while with a laugh and a bit of sarcasm. "You asked for this, so don't complain."

Rolling her eyes she ruffles her hair, "I guess I should be careful what I wish for."

Billy slides his fingertips into mine and prepares to go back into the moment.

"Kie," my mom calls opening the door with her cup of coffee clutched in her other hand. "Oh you're up," she smirks at me. "What are you doing here Billy?"

Please answer wisely. If he says something that perks my moms thought of me dating him for longer than a week, she'll freak out. You have to learn to read in between my mom's lines. 'I don't mind you dating him Kie' really means 'I know you wouldn't ever fall for that no good thug charm he tries to shower on you'. Horrible huh?

"I came to say bye to girls. I brought 'em breakfast," he shows her the empty container. Ok why did she need to see the container? Would it be that hard for her to believe he brought me food? Yeah. It would be.

"That was thoughtful," she leans against the doorframe and clinks her nails on her coffee cup. "Kie, go get dressed. We're going to leave in a few."

"All right," I smile watching her walk off down the hall. Tugging at the bottom of his shirt in a flirtatious manner I sigh, "I guess I have to get dressed."

Not going anywhere he says, "Yeah. I guess I have to move."

"I guess you do," I don't move either.

"Oh my god would you just kiss already?" Mia snaps shoving her make-up into her bag.

Billy kisses me on the lips softly and quickly. I reluctantly move after he does. As he watches me grab my stuff I snicker at the fact I know he's staring at my butt in my pajama shorts. I bend over and pop a bit to grab my clothes. Well I have to give him something for that delicious meal. I hear Mia giggle as she brushes her hair. She knows I'm killing the poor boy.

"I'll be back," I stand back up. "Mia don't try to kill him like you did DK last night."

She defends herself, "Since when is trying to smother him with a pillow considered attempted murder?"

"Since all fifty states decided too many husband's deaths were going unaccounted for ..." I stroll out of the room.

Once I'm clearly out of ear shot, Billy says what's been on his mind to Mia. "Ya know you've got DK trippin' bad?"

"Like off a cliff?" Mia proudly smirks as she continues to brush her hair.

"No like over himself."

"You don't say ..."

"Las' night you were all he could complain 'bout 'til he got a few drinks in him, which is when he started obsessin' over how hot he thinks you are in yo' pink thong. Some'n I didn't ever wanna know," Billy hakes his head. "DK's not the type to dwell on anything fo' longer than he has to."

"Well that shouldn't have been more than a minute now should it?" She flips her hair over and begins to brush it again.

Refusing to call his boy out like that he bluntly says, "Look I'm jus' sayin'—"

"Uh-huh. What about you?" Mia stops to run her fingers through it for a sec. "What's Kie doin' to you?"

He rubs the back of his neck unable to keep a gin off his face. His eyes divert to the ground, "She uh … she's got a nigga fienin'." When he finally looks back up at her his smile is even wider than before.

Smirking cockily to herself she nods proudly like she had something to do with it. "Well be careful. It took a lot of balls to make Kie cry, and if you know what's good for you then you won't make that mistake twice."

"And what are you two talkin' about?" I stroll into the room dressed in jean shorts, a wife beater, tennis shoes and a UT baseball cap.

"I was just tryin' to scare him away," Mia tosses the brush into her purse.

"Thanks," I sarcastically laugh finding myself leaning against Billy's hips.

"Don't worry. She can't scare me away from you," he winks wrapping an arm around me. "I've handled a lot more things scarier than you."

Throwing her bag on the bed next to mine she mumbles, "Gunshots are the only thing scarier than making Kie cry."

Giggling I plant a kiss on his cheek. I slip away as he says, "I guess I might jus' have a scary girlfriend."

Mia and I both give him a stern look before I shake my head, "Shh with the G word. One date and a few kisses don't make me that."

"Told you," Mia mouths at him as she zips her bag shut.

"Sounds like someone has commitment issues," he watches me finish packing my bag on the bed.

"No issues. We're just not that far yet." I hate repacking. It's so much harder, and it feels like I have more stuff when I leave then when I came. "Don't get cocky."

"I'm not tryin' to be cocky," he argues while watching me struggle to pick up my bags. "I'm jus' tryin' to be confident."

"Same, same," I roll my eyes. Staring angrily at my heavy bags I debate how long it'll take him to offer to carry them for me.

Receiving my telepathic messages he picks them up, "Let me get those."

"Who knew you'd start this vacation carrying my bags out of hope to be with me," I slip my purse on my shoulder.

"And end it out of hope to stay wit' you," he starts out of the room ahead of us.

"He's charming Kie," Mia whispers beside me lugging her own bags. "Don't set him up to fail."

"I would never—

"You've already tried."

Sighing I let her pass me by. Come on. Who sabotages their own relationships? Tell me who constantly puts down a guy hoping he'll stay down for the count? And who has a strong inability to share her feelings with others? Oh.

"Mom, keys," I ask going into the kitchen while Billy heads towards the front door.

"Here," she tosses them to me. "Where's your stuff?"

"Billy's got it." She gives me a confused look. "He's just being polite."

With a shake of her head she dismisses any other explanations she was considering.

I go out the open screen door witnessing Billy and Mia laugh as they go to the car. At least I don't have to make the two of them like each other due to the pre-orchestrated alliance they formed.

Hitting the unlock button I give them the chance to load the bags into the back. Mia tosses her bag in the very back seat while Billy squishes my bags carelessly. The nigga better not break anything. That's all I'm gonna say.

"Mia," I meet Billy at the back. "Be a good friend, and play look out."

She rolls her eyes as she climbs into the very back seat of the suburban.

Billy closes the door and leans against it. Sliding his fingers into mine I watch a frown appear on his face, "I didn't think I'd have to say goodbye so soon."

"Up until last night I couldn't wait for this day," I laugh a little moving my body into his.

Nodding he chuckles, "Well I'm glad that you changed your mind ..." Billy falls for my tactic. Damn I'm good. "This isn't goodbye though."

"I know we're gonna talk on the phone," I smile unfolding our hands to run my finger down his chest.

"Yeah, and I'm gonna drive up there on the weekends to come see you," he moves them together again. "Give me a chance to see yo' world."

"It'll be just as traumatizing," I toss my head back in a flirtatious giggle. It might be a good idea to stop before I go overboard.

"I wouldn't have it any other way."

"Don't be messing around on me with any chicken heads," I scold him a final time.

"No worries." Pulling me into an embrace he whispers in my ear, "I'm gonna miss you."

"I know," I smirk wrapping my arms around his neck.

"Do you know how much?" he asks resting his forehead against mine. Ok not to be like a total drag or anything, but all this miss you talk isn't what I wanted. I mean sure I like to hear I'm gonna be missed and what not, but what I really want is for him to just kiss me already.

"Can you show me?" Maybe this will speed up the process of that kiss before my mom or dad comes.

"That I can do," he pulls me into as he leans back against the car.

Finally he plants his lips right where they belong. He teasingly slips his tongue towards mine causing my knees weaken beneath me. I'm melting so bad Billy glides his arm around me to keep me propped up. His tongue circles around mine a bit slowly before pushing against it softly. I wonder how long this honeymoon state will last.

"We love you too Big Mama," I hear my mom call to her on the way out.

I better pull away before she catches her daughter playing tonsil hockey. Slowly I draw my tongue away from his, but feel him anxiously recapture it making my knees shake again. Talk about making this hard on a girl. Somehow I find the strength to pull away before it's too late.

"Kie," I hear her call to me right as I open the car door while Billy wipes away the lip-gloss flavor with his tongue.

"Yeah," I answer innocently.

She instructs as she hops in the driver seat, "Go hug Big Mama goodbye."

"All right," I slide around Billy watching him resist with every bone in his body to touch me the way he wants.

Hugging her I inhale the sweet sent of roses and cough drops, "Love you Big Mama."

"Love you too baby," I giggle as she kisses me on the cheek. Knowing what my parents don't she whispers, "Go hug Billy bye."

With a gleam in my eye I wonder how is it she knows. It's amazing how she knows everything that goes on underneath her roof. "Ok."

Billy's strolling back towards the house when I meet up with him. Tossing my arms around his neck he says softly, "I'll call you tonight."

"Get your ass some sleep first," I wink as I pull away to his smiling face. Sneaking around is kind of exciting. It's something I never thought I'd have to do, and now that I'm doing it, it feels good.

Letting go he slips his hands into his pocket, "Anything else?"

"Be good," I stroll away towards my side of the car.

"I'll try," he nods before watching me get in.

I look at Mia who's made herself so comfortable in the very back seat. She smiles at me as I climb over the seat. We all know why she's smirking like that. It's more than obvious after you see us hug.

As I wave, Billy waves back still standing next to Big Mama. Who really likes to say goodbye, or see you later to someone they really like? Seeing him fade behind the trees, I slouch down.

I glance at Mia who's basking in her glory. I don't feel like listening to her gloat about how she was right from the beginning and blah blah blah. All I want to do is rest against this window and go back to sleep. How hard is it going to be to not miss the fighting or the waiting for him to pop up to secretly make my day?

Looking back one last time knowing he won't be around on a daily basis any more, I realize it's a lot harder than I'm letting on.

About three hours later I awake to find everyone, but my mother of course, sleeping. The radio is on low, and my moms tryin' to rap along on the cool. People do the best things when they think no one's looking.

I look over to see Mia drooling on my damn pillow. Again with the drool! Next time we go somewhere she's bringing her own pillow or sleeping on her damn hands. I groan at thought of having to sleep on that ever again.

Glancing down at my cell phone I notice that I have a new message. God I love this thing. It was the best sixteenth birthday present ever. At first it was only so they could reach me at rehearsals, but somewhere between Mia constantly calling and me being a non-stop text machine, they gave up on that idea.

I dial my number and press the button to listen in. Voicemails are exciting because I rarely get them. That's just what happens when you actually answer your phone when people call.

"One new message," my machine says like it's being diced like a cucumber. Why does it have to be so monotone? Can't it sound excited I have a new message or something? Stupid machines. "Today, at 9:15."

"Yo, it's Billy. I was jus' droppin' a line. I'm on way to the hotel. Don't worry I'll get some sleep later," he says like he can see the look I'm giving him. "Call me when you get this, or it's convenient or some'n. Peace."

Doesn't he get more sophisticated every day? Talk about a rambler. I erase the message and go straight to text messaging. What? I can't call him. I mean come on. Look at where I am. I'm in the backseat, next to my sleeping best friend, behind my sleeping father, and my crazy mother who looks so into her 'groove' she'd throw me out of the car if wrecked it. It would not be in my best interest to wake anyone up. I turn my CD player on and slip into my headphones.

"Nice message kid. I can't call u because I'm in the car and everyone is sleep. Text me back if u can. Muah." Happily I send the message and lay my phone back in my lap.

Moments later I feel my phone start to vibrate. I quickly open it to read the text, "Sup baby? I'm jus' hangin' out wit' DK and then I'm off to bed until work. I swear. Miss you."

Smirking I type back, "Good. I'm going to hang out with Mia this afternoon. Call me after 7 or when you get off. Miss you too."

"Call you then BG. Muah right back at ya."

I smile a final time as I put my phone back in my lap. Muah. Aw isn't that cute? He gave me a phone kiss. Wait. Remind me again why I'm being all googoo over him? He's not even my boyfriend yet. We're not even an official couple. I'm getting ahead of myself. What if it doesn't work out? I mean what if this was just a once in a lifetime sort of thing? I just wish I could get a sign from above. Something saying, 'Hey you! Yeah you down there! That guy who's getting on your nerves because he won't give up … yeah he's the one for you.' Good thing life works that way.

Closing my eyes I start to wonder why I don't just let good things happen to me. I guess that's what happens when they don't happen very often. You become trained to respond to it like it's a bad thing. Good thing this is far from goodbye. Don't think so? Haven't you heard the end is just the beginning?

PART II

DATING

CHAPTER 7

Fireworks

As nauseating as watching my classmates hang around like monkeys, guzzle down alcohol like drunks, and grope on each other like porn stars is, I have to admit that I have nothing better to do on the Fourth of July. Pathetic isn't it? Normally Mia and I would be hanging out with her family watching the fireworks go off in the park, but because they went out of town she felt it was her adolescent duty to throw a party with me of course being her right hand in helping, planning, decorating, and liquor collecting. I guess that's what best friends are for.

Now one concept Mia missed in the eventful guest gathering is whether or not we invite 'the cool crowd' or how I prefer to refer to them 'the future alcoholics and drug addicts of America'. They will be here to critique and drink, which will bring either Mia's credit up or down.

Regardless of their grading system I know where I stand on their social pyramid. I'm known as the threat. I'm popular without having to convert my wardrobe or open my legs wide. My peers ironically enough flock to me because I'm fun to hang around, easy to talk to, and very kind. Sure none of that's apparent in the way I treated Billy and DK, but they weren't on my good side. Their difference is literally a heaven and hell sort of situation.

Speaking of Billy, he's coming tonight to hang out with us. Lame I know, but he insisted on joining his 'girlfriend'. While I'm dodging that name like bullets in the Matrix, he manages to throw it out there every chance he gets, and it's really starting to feel like a bolder in my shoe.

I'm sitting on Mia's countertop in the kitchen near the keg when she hits my swinging leg, "Answer your phone."

"Oh," I pull it out from my pocket. Guess I didn't realize that it was ringing over the loud alternative music that needs to be changed immediately. "Hello."

Billy sounds like he's whispering my name, "Kie."

"Yeah," I scream into the phone.

"I'm jus' now hittin' Austin, so give me an hour and a half," he yells back hearing the music. "I gotta stop by A.J.'s befo' I come."

"Ok," I yell back plugging up my left ear. "You got directions right?"

"Yeah," he yells again turning down the radio. "I'll see you 'round 10:30."

"All right," I prepare to hang up, "Bye." That means there's the perfect amount of time to sit here and swing my legs to this shitty music that I'm just too lazy to change it.

"Hello ladies," Andrea, a fellow group member strolls up beside us.

She runs her fingers through her dirty blonde hair before slipping them into her jean skirt pocket. Now why can't I pull off an outfit like that? Her jean skirt is being accompanied by a designer off the shoulder red shirt that compliments not only her average sized chest, but her little to non-existent stomach. The overly priced heels on her feet quickly remind me of exactly why I don't and can't dress like her. My mommy and daddy can't afford it. Sorry if that sounds a little resentful, especially since she's one of my best friends.

With a pleasant smile she asks me, "What are you doing in here?"

She moved here from L.A. freshman year. While her parents are loaded meaning she'll never have to work a day in her life, she chooses to go after the Californian dream of being a singer. Too bad her parents aren't really into funding it because otherwise we'd have it made.

"Nothing."

"Well don't you think you should do something," Natalie appears almost out of nowhere. Aw. It's our cute little country girl sporting her tan cowboy hat, yellow halter top, low rise jeans, and sandals. As innocent as she looks, it's a shame it's all an act.

Jerking my attention her way I quickly snap, "Like?"

Stuttering she shrugs and slips her hands in her back pockets like she so often does when she's embarrassed or at a lost for words. It's so sad she's trained herself to act like that. Usually this is when her parents, who are also pretty loaded, would apologize for the attitude and give her whatever it is she desires except the money she needs to start her singing career with us of course. Gotta love how their parents don't believe in them the way Mia and mine do. I guess that just proves money isn't everything.

Somewhere between the appearance of the two of them, Mia has disappeared. Great. Her party that I help plan and she ditches me. I appreciate that.

"Thirsty?" Mia pops up holding out shot glasses of green Jell-O on a tray.

"A little," I wiggle one around. "Is there alcohol in that?"

"Do you not know me, but at all?" she rolls her eyes. "What sort of friend do you think I am?"

"Crazy," I mutter.

"A damn good one," Natalie snatches one of the glasses.

Andrea raises one of the shot glasses up, "I'll drink to that."

Sounding like a downer I say, "I don't know if I should be drinking this." I swish it around letting it hit the sides of the glass.

Mia grabs the last one on the tray, "And why not?"

"I don't want to be drunk when Billy gets here," I sigh. Honestly, I would rather not drink until he gets here, but life doesn't seem to give me that luxury.

They all roll their eyes, and Mia tries to be the one to persuade me, "One shot won't kill you."

"I know," I look back down at it and mumble, "It's the other five I'm afraid of."

"To the Fourth of July," Mia proposes a toast, and we clink.

We take the shots in a quick manner and giggle. We've all got a bit of green on our lips.

"How about another?" Natalie suggests noticing there are more within our perimeter. That girl has an alcohol detector that's unbeatable. If what she wants is within a seven feet range she knows about it.

"Sure," I sigh. And so it begins.

Shots later I'm lounging against a wall bouncing my head along to a hip-hop song. I don't feel like I know the words well enough to sing along, so a simple bob will have to do. Even though I feel a bit more relaxed and a lot freer than I normally do something tells me I'm going to regret drinking. If I know anything about when I've had too much to drink, it's that I become a bit of a giggle box and a little too friendly.

"You wanna dance?" Some beach blond surfer boy look-a-like touches my hand. No way can he surf. The only ocean this fake tan boy has seen is the shots in Hollywood blockbuster films.

"Sure!" I squeal and quickly get up off the wall. Wow. I've never been that enthusiastic before. Maybe I should drink a little more often. I try to stop giggling since he hasn't said anything worth laughing over.

I start to move a little to the music and notice the people dancing. It's like watching porn for the inexperienced. Hands are under shirts and skirts, while tongues are in places I would rather not mention. There is no dancing actually occurring, and it's so graphic you need a condom to just walk through them. It's probably because they're all liquored up. I start to giggle again. Liquor. Lick her. Get it? Lick her? How ironic.

He moves his body closer to mine and says in my ear, "I'm Calvin." Like the cartoon character? Weird. I'm dancing with a cartoon character. I gently brush up against him to make sure he doesn't feel like paper.

Slurring my words I manage to say, "I'm Kie." The giggles continue.

I think he attempts to compliment me, but it's hard to hear between chuckles. Why can't I stop laughing? I feel like I was injected with the giggles, and I need to find the antidote.

Now there's nothing wrong with dancing when it's harmless. Harmless however is not a hand creeping up my thigh towards my butt. I casually move away to only find him prowl after me. My hips attempt to inch away but find themselves stranded next to his hard on that feels like a fallen tower rebuilding itself. His hands are moving up my bare back towards the knot in the middle where my shirt ties. I always triple knot it, but in this case I don't think that'll slow him down much. Attempting to shove him away he catches my wrist and pushes me backwards against the wall.

"Relax," he whispers in a very movie mystery killer sort of way. "You know you like it."

"No," I attempt to push back with my wrist. God I wish my coordination wasn't off. Something tells me I would have a lot more power and skill to get out of this situation if I hadn't been drinking. Then again I also probably wouldn't be in this situation.

"Yes you do," his giant pink fungus lips attempt to cover my face.

"No I don't!" I shove at his chest. Stomping on his foot I scream, "Let go!" I'm attempting to make myself heard although I don't think they'll stop from shooting their porn video to help me.

Ripping one of my knots undone, he shoves me and fusses, "Stop being pissy."

I wiggle out of his grip and smack him across the face hoping that leaves a window of enough time for me to at least start in the direction of help. Unfortunately for me it seems to just get me in more trouble. He twists my wrists together in one hand and pins them above my head against the wall.

"You'll pay for that," he whispers nuzzling his face against mine. The second I reach my leg to knee him in the balls, his free hand stops it before slipping it between my thighs on the outside of my khaki capris.

Still struggling he continues to mutter, "If you don't fight you won't get hurt."

With my eyes shut as tight as they get, I feel water fill my eyelids. Don't cry Kie. Gritting my teeth I try not to let a tear fall. If he sees me cry he finds me vulnerable. And if I am found vulnerable there is no way of escape. Do not cry Kie.

I start panting deeply as the touching becomes more and more uncomfortable, "Please. Just let me go."

I feel my body start to tremble at the feeling of him struggling to undo my belt, "When we're done."

This is exactly why I don't come to parties. I know there is always at least one sleazy guy looking for a half drunken girl to try and score on. Not to sound cocky or anything, but I never thought I'd be that girl. Then again, who ever thinks they will be?

"What's up Billy?" Mia giggles handing her empty glass to someone behind her.

"Nothin'," he shakes his head a little at Mia's drunken behavior. "Where's my baby Kie?"

"She's um …" Mia twists her hand around and looks behind her. Quickly she shrugs, "I don't know. She went to dance with some dude."

Uncomfortable at her answer he nods slowly, "Ok … I guess I'll jus' look around fo' her."

"You do that," she snatches a cup from another guy and walks off towards another crowd of people.

The cartoon character is now trying to keep me from screaming by forcing his mouth on mine. For some strange reason it doesn't matter if I bite, spit, or scream while his tongue attacks mine. It just excites him.

I feel his hand struggle with the button and zipper on my pants. Must be his first time trying to rape a girl because a professional wouldn't have nearly as much trouble … if that lightens the mood any.

"Kie," Billy calls towards me moving though the crowd. Tossing girls hands off of him to continue his search I hear him call again, "Kie."

Thankful that he's become so frustrated and too distracted with my 'complicated button' to hear someone's looking for me, I take this time to try to yell back.

"Help," I yelp out of breath from the fighting. I don't see him. With every ounce of hope in me I attempt again, "Billy."

While fighting with me once more I see him round the corner. Somehow his eyes find me like Waldo on an easy page. Billy darts towards me pushing people out of his way saying excuse him of course.

What he does next happens so fast that it takes a moment for it to process. He yanks Calvin off of me, right hooks him sending him backwards, swoops me into his arms, and rushes me up the stairs like a true damsel in distress.

Mia's parents' room, which happened to be the nearest unoccupied room, is where Billy gently puts me down. He shuts and locks the door while I button myself back up.

"Kie," I hear him pant out like he's panicking worse than I am. Billy kneels down in front of me, "Are you ok?"

I rub my bare arm and look around. How do I get myself in these positions? Do I just look like the perfect target or something? Do I send out molest me vibes? You know people don't understand that no matter what you say you would do in the situation, that it's not always possible. I guess I'm thankful Billy's always there to play Superman. Although, I'm terrified to know what would happen if he wasn't?

Putting his hand on top of mine he says to me again, "Kie ..."

I do my best to put those thoughts in the back of my mind. In a slur, forgetting I've had too much to drink, I answer, "Yeah."

"You ok?" he questions me like an innocent child who's fallen off their bike for the first time.

"Yeah I'm fine," my words slur more, creating a giggle in me. Good job Kie. Make sure he knows you're drunk.

Keeping eye contact with me he asks once more, "You sure?"

"Yeah," I say getting an attitude. "What's with all the fourth degree?"

"Don't you mean third degree?" he questions me again. What's with him and all the questions? I didn't sign on to play twenty questions. "Kie are you drunk?"

"Psh," I make one long sound and start sniggering a lot. That has to be one of the funniest sounds. You have to try it out loud. It's so much fun.

With a smile he instructs, "Stick out yo' tongue."

"Stick out YOUR tongue," I poke him on his chest.

"Kie," he says in a firm tone.

"Bilwee," I laugh until I snort as I attempt to retie my halter top at the top where he managed to get one knot underdone as well.

Trying his best not to laugh he says, "You're drunk."

"Nopperz," I shake my head, "but will you tie my shirt in the correct number of knots pwease?"

"Only if you stick out yo' tongue fo' me," he attempts to bargain with a drunken girl. That's real smart. Where did he learn that? Bartending School?

"Deal," I smile and stick out my tongue as far as I can revealing it's bright green.

"Yo' tongue is green."

"And your tongue is pink," I hiccup.

Billy shakes his head as he stands to tie my shirt. "How many Jell-O shots did you have?"

"Mmm," I sound off putting my hand on my stomach. My tummy is starting to boil just like lava. Shrugging I squint like I'm thinking hard, "Lost track after seven, but I don't sink it was many more after dat …"

After making sure they're tight he backs away to look at me, "Seven? I thought you didn't like to drink that much?"

"I don't, but it was just Jell-O," I smirk clinching my belly with closed eyes. Oh god please not this. I hate to throw up. I really *really* hate to throw up.

"Kie …" he backs up.

"I think I'm gonna throw up," I cover my mouth. If I throw up on her parent's sheets they'll know we were drinking like crazy. I dash towards the open bathroom that's connected to their room.

Billy watches me plop down in front of the toilet and begin heaving my brains out. Every breath only creates more of the urge to throw up. He holds my hair back as my head drops further into the toilet bowl. I knew I shouldn't have had that first shot let alone the second.

A mouth of puke comes out of me again while Billy rubs my back trying to comfort me in the situation. Why is he still in here? Shouldn't the stench and the sound make him run like most guys?

Like an idiot I take a whiff of the smell and continue to spew out everything I've eaten in my entire life.

Could this day be any worse? I'm throwing up, I was sexually harassed, and the guy I'm dating has to witness me in the worst state ever. Those thoughts make my stomach more uneasy, and I continue to throw up. I'm gonna kill Mia for this. It's her fault I had to come to this party, it's her fault I had the drinks, there for it's her fault I'm throwing up things I can't identify. Isn't it funny how teenagers love blaming everyone else rather than themselves? In some cases I guess it makes sense to blame others, but sometimes we just gotta take responsibility. I feel my stomach rumble again. This time I choose to blame Mia.

Coughing the last bit of puke in the toilet I keep my eyes shut. I know if I open them I will be throwing up for hours, so I just ease backwards.

Billy helps lean me against their Jacuzzi bathtub. I'm not sure which is worse, the way I look, sweaty, messed up hair, with puke drizzled around the edge of my mouth, or the way I feel, exhausted with puke still deciding whether it's done coming up or not.

Casually flushing the toilet he reaches for a towel off the rack. I try to smile while watching him come at me again. He shakes his head as he straddles himself in front of me, one leg on each side of me. That boy better hope I don't have to throw up again.

My eyes fall down to the carpet and attempt to close themselves. I feel a bit ditzy and lightheaded. This is not a good feeling. "No Kie. Look at me," he raises my head up.

I shake my head and keep looking down as he gets up scrambling around for something. What's with him? Can't I suffer alone? Not fighting to keep my eyes open or my head up, he raises my chin again, "Look at me."

"Look at yourself," I grumble out as I remove his hand.

He smirks as he begins to wipe the puke off my face. "The smell will make you wanna puke more." Oh so he's not as conceited as I thought, surprise surprise. Suddenly he holds out a paper cup in front of me full of water, "Drink this."

Shaking my head I push the cup back towards him. He slides it back into my hands as I whimper, "I can't drink anything."

"Trust me," he continues holding it. "Drink some."

"You drink it."

"Kiara you—

I snatch the cup and close my eyes once more. Why is it he thinks he's right about everything? I hope I do throw up again, so I can throw up on him. The cold water soothes my throat and my temperature for the moment.

Putting the cup down as Billy wipes my sweat off my forehead I sigh, "Thanks."

"You're welcome," he lets the towel fall into his lap. "Now tell me again how many Jell-O shots you had?"

"Nine I think," I mumble wrapping my arms around my over worked stomach.

His jaw hits the towel, "Nine? I didn't think you could handle nine."

I glance at the toilet then back at him with a sarcastic look.

"You shouldn't ever drink that much especially not at sixteen," he begins to gently rub my legs.

"And who are you now? Dr. Phil?" I sardonically say as I feel a headache hit me like a freight train.

"Look," he points a finger at me. "Don't come at me like that. I'm jus' lettin' you know it's not healthy. Not only does drinkin' like that screw up yo' stomach but yo' ability to fight back. If I hadn't come in when I did—

"Can we skip the lecture on youth mistakes and the possibilities of what could go wrong?" I interrupt him. My head just can't handle him trying to overheat it with his juvenile talk.

"Pardon me fo' givin' a damn," he snaps back at me. "I just—

"You just were jumping down my throat. Give me a break, damn," I let my eye lids fall.

"Kie, do you remember what he was tryin' to do to you?" He forces eye contact on me. "He could have raped you wit' a possibility of it bein' passed off as consensual sex because you were under the influence of alcohol." And when did he get all Court TV on me? His hand moves on top of mine, "Do you know what I would have done if that would of happened?"

With a deep exhale I look into his eyes. I take a deep look to see that he's not trying to be the over protective boyfriend, but the caring, loving, very concerned, gentleman who makes the perfect boyfriend. Geez I'm such a bitch. Here I am chewing him out as he tries to express he cares. "No. What?"

"Killed him," he answers bluntly. I have a feeling that wasn't one of those say it and not really do it. "I swore I'd never let anyone hurt you, and the fact I'm sittin' here calmly is a surprise. I'd love to jus' pop my trunk and—

"I get it," I touch his hand, which seems to calm him down a bit. Curiously my mind wonders, "You pack in your trunk?"

"Business purposes," he avoids eye contact for guilty conscious reasons. "That's not the point. The point is I would not have hesitated to pop him."

That's sweet in a weird, scary sort of way. "I'm ok. A bit violated, but I'm ok," I rub the back of his hand. "A bit nausea still ..."

"Feels like someone is tryin' to squeeze yo' guts out like toothpaste from the bottom of the tube huh?" The graphic image he paints hits a weak spot in my belly causing it to turn. Thanks kid.

"Pretty much," I run my fingers through my hair.

"Glad you're ok. I meant what I was sayin'. Don't drink so much. Yo' hangover right now is pretty bad. Give it a few, and the pain will ease up. Ya know that's how mos' girls get scored on? When they're drunk at parties and clubs …" his voice trails off once more.

Snatching him out of his thoughts I try to slightly sway the convo in my direction, "DK get laid often that way?"

Noticing my desperate attempt at humor he shrugs, "Use too. He's knows better now."

"Now?" I question picking up the cup again taking another drink.

As he removes his hand from mine he declares, "Court will do that to you, but let's just end the subject of DK at that."

I nod and look down into the cup. As it swishes around a little in a circle I notice its striking resemblance to toilet water. Inhaling a deep breath of the water I feel my stomach rumble again. See. I knew there was no way I was done throwing up. You would think by now I wouldn't have anything left to toss up, but how wrong you can be.

Cupping my mouth again I try to shoe Billy out of the way, but I don't make it in time. I throw up on his navy blue collared shirt. Slowly he looks down at the puke on his shirt and scrunches his nose with closed eyes.

I mumble out, "Oops."

Billy tugs off his shirt and sighs, "Yeah."

"I didn't mean too," I lean back again against the tub, grab the towel from his lap, and quickly wipe my mouth off.

"It's ok," he gently tosses it in the bathtub behind me. Taking the towel from my possession he tries to laugh it off as he wipes off the wet excess on his chest, "Rather my shirt than my jeans."

My head is throbbing like it's my heart and been overworked. "I'm sorry."

"Don't worry 'bout it baby. It's jus' a shirt," he smiles at me again. Did he just call me baby? I believe that's the first time he said that. At least it wasn't like a cheesy or sexual baby, which in either case I more than likely would have smacked him.

Wishing I could see clearly to be able to gawk at him shirtless I ask again, "You sure?"

Billy touches my cheek softly, "The only thing I'm worried 'bout is you. Now do you think you can get up, or are you still too nauseated?"

I pause for a moment and rub my eyes. Should I get up? Other than Billy, who cares if I do? My best friends have some how let it escape their mind that

I'm here. I repeat that alcohol is not a good thing most of the time. "Yeah I think I can."

I put my hand into his and let him help me up. "Good," he says looking at me standing. "I've got you up. Do you think you can walk?"

"Yeah," I start to wobble towards the sink. Billy quickly catches me the second I start to sway too far to one side. Coming to the conclusion my breath smells like Jell-O, leftovers, and vomit I decide I have to brush my teeth. It's more vital than walking down stairs. I prop myself up against the sink, "Do me a favor and look under the cabinet for a toothbrush." Something tells me if do too much up and down activity I will be right back where I started.

"No problem," he bends down to look through the cabinet. 'Well hello Mr. Ass. Billy sure has been treating you nicely if I do say so myself.' I nibble my bottom lip while attempting to keep the drool in my mouth. He rises with the toothbrush as I pretend like I was rubbing my eye, "Here."

Chuckling he asks, "Enjoy the view?"

I roll my eyes innocently and snatch it. Gently I mutter, "I was."

"What did you say?" the corners of his mouth start to turn up.

"Thanks," I point the toothbrush, now out of its package, towards him. Wrapping my arm around my aching side I attempt to reach for the toothpaste with my other hand.

"Let me get that," he quickly picks up the tube, spreads a fine thin line on the brush, and hands it back to me. Billy places his hands on waist to help me keep steady or at least I assume. Ever so often he gently rubs my lower back.

I begin brushing my teeth carefully and slowly. Too much quick movement will send me into automatic vomit shock. Moving it around to get every knick and cranny, I spit it out and make the gesture to put more on my toothbrush. I love how Billy gets what I mean without me even having to say it.

After placing another strip on it, he goes back to soothingly rubbing my back. Talk about a horrible after taste. I think I would rather eat broccoli with bugs melted on it than ever have to taste this again.

While I continue brushing, my phone begins to vibrate and sing loudly in my pocket. Casually Billy reaches his hand into my pocket to answer it. Excuse him. This isn't his phone, and I damn sure don't have a secretary.

"Speak," he holds the phone between his ear and shoulder.

Now is that anyway to answer a phone? Let alone a phone that's not yours? Better yet, my phone? I don't think so. He better hope it's not my mother otherwise that's double the obvious trouble.

Pouring mouthwash into my mouth I begin to shake it around when Billy says, "Naw girl she righ' here. Her mouth's a bit busy though."

He snickers as I spit out and quickly wipe my mouth. I run my tongue across my teeth before mouthing, "Who is it?"

"Mia," he covers the receiver.

"Give me the phone," I try to pull it from him.

He holds up one finger telling me to hold on. Excuse him. "Suddenly her mouth jus' freed up. I guess now that she swallowed; she can talk. Hold on."

I drop my jaw and smack him in the stomach. That dirty, filthy, ew. How could he say that? Hitting him again in those rock solid abs that don't seem to move I answer, "Hello."

Laughing at his own sick perverted humor he slides away to rinse out his shirt in the tub.

"Please tell me he was joking," Mia pleads throwing cups into the trash bags while people keep dancing around her.

"Of course that nigga is just kidding," I shake my head at him while he continues to chuckle under his breath. "You know better."

"Where are you? I heard someone got decked, and the next thing I know you're gone, Billy's gone, and there's a guy just now waking up from being unconscious. I need some fucking explanations here," she tries to say calmly while putting the lid on some of the alcohol bottles. "So I ask again. Where are you?"

Billy finishes and leads me out of the bathroom back to Mia's parent's bed. He asks me for a shirt. I tell him to hold on the same way he did me. "Upstairs in your parent's bedroom."

Pausing she nearly spills the trash. "You better have a damn good reason why. And to create sparks in the bedroom for the first time in your life is not a good reason."

"I'll let that one go. It's a long story that I'll explain later," I say watching him walk around the room as if looking for the closet door that's right next to bathroom.

She continues cleaning, "When's later?"

"After we make rabbit love on your mom's bed."

"What?!"

"Just kidding. In a few. I will tell you in once we get downstairs ..." I say and point to the closet making Billy smirk for feeling stupid about not knowing where it was to begin with.

"OK," she says calming down. "Call me when you get down here."

"Sure thing," I hang up and toss the phone next to me.

"Kie I don't think any of these will fit," he scavenges through the shirts. "Is her step-dad a really lil' guy?"

I think about Mia's step-dad as a bite-size candy while Billy is a big chocolate bar. Now where did I get the idea that he could squeeze his broad shoulder, overloaded guns, and swole chest into something that would fit a ten year old boy?

"Excuse me," Billy waves his arms in front of me. After he shuts the door he strolls towards me, "I need some'n to wear."

Touching his abs I feel my knees weaken. Good thing I'm already sitting down. With a giggle I smirk, "You could go down there shirtless. I know I wouldn't mind."

He leans over me, lips dangling dangerously close to mine, "'til others girls start to flock to me."

"Well then they can have you," I whisper back to him straight in his face. Wish he'd kiss me already. My breath damn sure is ready for it.

"All right," he removes himself from lip-lock distance.

I play off my disappointment with a smile. Where does he think he's going? I was just kidding. After everything he's put me through I have first dibs on him, and I haven't given up my rights yet. "Where are you going?"

Playfully he answers, "To get a shirt."

Billy slides open the dresser drawer. I fold my arms, "Thought you couldn't fit into his shirt."

"Can't," he shrugs. "But if he has a wife beater then we're back in business."

"Oh well then," I lean backwards to be lying on their bed. "You're looking in the wrong spot." He quickly shuts the drawer. The only thing he'll find in there is underwear, bra's and condoms. I point to two drawers below it, "They'd be in there."

"How did you know they'd be in here?" he questions digging for the largest one he can find.

"Mia and I put up clothes all the time. You get a hang of where things go," I close my eyes wondering where the aspirin is. "Look in the second drawer on the left for the bottle of aspirin please."

He digs around tank tops to find a half empty bottle. Like a good boy he brings me two along with a cup of fresh water from the bathroom. Helping me sit up he drops them into my hand and waits to hand me the cup. Once they're down I smile to thank him.

Billy slips the shirt over his bare upper half and remarks, "Guess it's time to feed me to the piranha whores at the party." I snatch him by the bottom of his shirt when he pretends to walk off.

"I don't think so."

"But you said they could have me," he tries to argue falling next to me.

"I changed my mind," I draw him closer to me. "Superwoman can do that."

Nodding, he cheerfully smirks. Do I really have to do everything myself? I gave him two set-ups to kiss me and still he hasn't gone in for the kill. Should have known better. I lean over and place my lips softly on his. Wasting no time to react, his arms cradle me close to him, holding me securely and reassuringly that not every guy is going to try to do what that creep did. He holds me gently as his tongue greets mine. My stomach turns a little unsure about rushing into kissing. Reluctantly I pull away and shake my head.

"Too soon?" I nod my head as he rubs my back a little. "I understand." Hopeful eyed he leans his forehead against mine, "I'm sorry."

"It's not your fault," Trying to shake it off I let out a deep sigh. Get a grip Kie. I got away before anything could happen. Remember you're in the arms of someone who cares about you and would never do that to you.

He proposes, "How 'bout we go downstairs? You can introduce me to yo' friends."

"All right," I stand up with him folding our hands together. Rubbing the back of my hand, he waits for me to open the door and then follows me out.

We stroll down the stairs smiling and giggling about his trip here. I don't really capture it all between the blaring music and constant fear of running into that cartoon freak, but I get the just.

The two of us slide into the kitchen where my girls are gathered in the same spot they were a couple of hours ago, this time without the Jell-o.

"There you are!" Natalie exclaims more sober than I would have guessed. "And who is he?"

"Billy I would like you to meet Natalie and Andrea," I introduce him.

He kindly says hello shaking each of their hands.

"You didn't do him justice," Natalie licks her lips.

"Damn sure didn't," Andrea reemphasizes.

I scoot closer into Billy's arm when Mia puts her arms around each of their shoulders, "Down girls."

Giggling it off I make sure that Billy's marked as mine. Now I know I'm having issues with being the giant g word, but that doesn't mean I don't feel the need to make sure the world knows he's off the market. We all know the girls were just kidding, but as for the triflin', no good sluts here, that's another story.

Natalie shakes her head, "We're kidding."

"About wanting you," Andrea corrects her. "Not about you being hot."

Billy smiles cutely and begins making small talk while my head starts wondering else where. I'm scanning the nowhere near empty house to only find the same drunken horny teenagers as before.

"We should get going," Andrea pulls out her keys from her pocket. "I have to find Anthony to drive us home."

"Designated driver?" I ask making sure they don't endanger their careers, but more importantly their lives.

"Yeah. He was Natalie's date," Andrea gives her a special look.

"Was?" Billy quickly questions. "Don't you mean is?"

"All the same with Nat," Mia jokes letting them go.

"She's been dodging him after he began to get a bit too clingy," I whisper in his ear.

"Yes, yes. We all know how my love life works. Now if you'll excuse us," she grabs Andrea's arm. "Nice to meet you Billy."

"You too," he waves as they disappear. "Nice girls."

Mia and I give a long stare. Poor boy has no idea what they're really about, yet I'm not sure if that's necessarily a bad thing.

I quickly try to get a change of conversation with a suggestion, "How about we dance a little?"

"Sounds good," he takes the initiative to lead me into the living room while Mia returns to her active cleaning.

The second we reach it I see Calvin in desperate search of the guy who knocked him out. When Billy and him make eye contact I know any chance of a calm night is ruined.

Calvin shoves Billy, which also shoves me a little. Has he not already done enough damage to me? "Why the fuck you hit me?"

That wasn't the smartest thing to do to a guy who just knocked you out for nearly half an hour. Billy snatches his hand away from me and his eyes dart down to a glare. Warning shots.

"'Cause yo' punk ass was tryin' to rape my girl!" he yells shoving him back.

Did he have to blurt that out like that? Now this will never die down. It'll be the talk for weeks, and I'll either end up looking like the crybaby drunken slut or miss too good for sex while intoxicated. Whether or not that's the truth it doesn't matter. Our school is just like a tabloid. The story that sells is the one that's told and nine times out of ten it's not the truth.

"I wasn't trying to rape her. She was begging me to taste her," he winks at me pissing Billy off more.

"You son of a bitch," I scream. Attempting to take matters into my own hands by rushing towards him to give him a taste of what Billy did, I'm stopped by his strong arm right in my stomach. He's holding me back? Why is he holding me back?!

"That's bullshit, and you know it. She told you to stop, but you forced yo'self on her 'cause that's what kind of pathetic maggot you are," Billy steps in his face.

"What can I say?" he shrugs smirking to the crowd. "I know she liked it."

Billy snatches him up by the collar of his shirt and growls, "I'll show you what she likes."

Catching wind to the all the excitement Mia quickly interrupts them. She throws down the trash bag in her hands and screams, "Hey!" Everyone's attention diverts to her. "Take it outside!"

"Gladly," Billy drops him like a cigarette bud. "Come on chicken shit."

The cartoon character rubs his neck and heads for the door. I reach out and grab Billy by the arm.

"Billy don't," I plead.

"Kie stay out of this," he snatches his arm away from me.

"Out of this? This is all about me moron! And as the cause of it all I'm telling you not to do this," I fold my arms stubbornly. Let's see if he listens to the girl who's supposed to trust him.

"I have too," he shrugs turning to look at me.

"Spare me the male macho bullshit." This is just way too much male testosterone for me. I thought maybe he was a bit different, a bit more self controlled. Why did I waste time trying to fool myself?

"Maybe if you considered yo'self my girlfriend then I'd take the time to listen. How's that fo' male macho bullshit?"

My jaw drops at his pathetic attempt to throw that in my face. He has a lot of nerve. As my heart sinks and freezes over once again I bite back, "Fine! Kick some ass, restore my good name, and come out the hero." Shrugging I watch him walk away, "But see if you get that chance to call me yours when you're done."

With a hard cold look he takes a deep breath and swallows. Billy turns his back to me and walks out to take his place in the street. Thug changing my ass.

He's still the inconsiderate, pig-headed, jackass he claimed he wasn't. The nigga is just like those ghetto cars you see where he came from. Just because you slap a new coat of paint and pair of dubs on the car it doesn't change what's under the hood.

I turn and look at Mia who looks disappointed. It's not my fault he's being this way, and it damn sure ain't my fault that this is probably as far as our relationships goes. Ya know I'm better than someone who's just going to throw shit at me like that. She curiously glances at the window. I know she wants to watch the fight just as bad as I do, even though I don't want it to happen.

We stumble our way over to the big living room window to watch. I may not encourage it, I may not support it, but I damn sure want to watch it. Call it human nature. I sure hope Billy whoops his ass for putting his hands on like that.

The cartoon takes the first swing. It's bad too. It's like he's watched one too many choreographed fights. Billy on the other hand has no problem whatsoever nailing him in the stomach. I guess all those days at the gym are going to pay off. You would think a blow like that would make the guy to fall to the ground and play dead, but it does just the opposite.

After the clenching and a few groans he takes another swing at Billy popping him right in his jaw. DAMN!!! Now that look like it hurt. Too bad that little smack to the jaw didn't seem to do anything except irritate him.

"It's like watching a video game," Mia mumbles in my ear.

Smiling, I focus back onto the fight afraid to miss something. Billy throws the guy a right punch and next thing I know I see a right uppercut from Calvin. I can sense the outcome of this fight will not be pretty.

Billy pounds the guy in the chest once more with his fist before using his knee. I've seen that move in the video game for sure. The cartoon character is clutching his stomach while Billy wipes away the small line of blood off his lip. Nope. Definitely won't be kissing those bloody lips.

The cartoon character tries to take another punch at Billy, but he grabs his fist, twists it, punching him one last time with his left. Calvin falls onto the street in pain with blood across his face when we hear the sirens. Someone called the cops. Why is it she has those paranoid neighbors you only see in the movies?

Mia sighs, "Cops ..." Kicking the garbage bag in frustration she yells, "Fuck!"

Cops coming to bust in here would lead to double homicide with our parents as the killers. I watch Mia do what she does better. Intimidate.

"Get the hell up out of here," she yells to everyone yanking some people off the couch. "If the cops catch you I'm labeling you all trespassers, so get the hell up out of here." Her yelling is now being directed towards the stairs. I just watch laughing under my breath as they run like jailbreak.

"Now! Hey you," she says to a thin blond girl sucking down chips at the table. "Get you're Barbie doll skinny ass out my house!" The girl throws down the chip and storms out behind a few other people.

I look back out the window to see everyone scrambling to their cars, hopping in, and driving off. Where on earth is Billy? Better yet what time is it?

"Heifer," she points to a lingering girl by the stairs. "You better get your ass out of my house before we have a throw down of our very own."

"But I need to pee," our head cheerleader whines innocently.

"No. You need to get your ass out of here before you end up in one of these trash bags," she glares. "Ya dig?"

The girl quickly scatters out of the house leaving just the two of us. Laughing I shake my head gathering more paper cups off the floor. Why she can't keep a boyfriend is a mystery to me.

Billy stumbles in with a bit of blood on the side of his mouth where he's cut. I can see his jaw a bit bruised which makes me only image what it looks like under his shirt. I don't want to rush over to him like I'm some bimbo, but I don't want to just ignore him like I don't give a damn. What to do; what to do? He shuts the door behind him as the cops run the siren down the street passing her house.

"Thank god," she sighs relieved. Quickly Mia takes a survey on Billy's face to decide what he needs. "Ice?"

"Please," he gently touches his jaw making a groan of pain.

Tying the trash bag Mia filled earlier into a knot I say, "I told you not to fight. See what—

"Can you jus' turn off the bitchin' long enough for the throbbin' in my head to stop?"

Offended I say, "Well maybe if you would have taken the time to assess the situation then—

"You know what?" he plops down on the couch next to a pile of cups. "One of the perks 'bout *not* havin' a girlfriend is *not* givin' a damn when she says shit like that to you."

"You're such an asshole," I throw down the bag I had begun to tie and walk out the front door. I was just trying to help, not rub it in his face. Finding an empty dry spot on the driveway, I sit down and lean back on my palms to look up at the stars.

Mia throws the Ziploc bag of ice at his bruised abs, "Ouch."

"Why do you insist on being a dick?"

"What?" he moves the ice up to his bruised jaw.

"Are you just that stupid? Why'd you yell at her? Now I understand you might be a bit hostile after that fight in the street, but that's no reason to take it out on the girl who's just trying to look out for you," she sneers at the yards of cups she still has to pick up. "And there is no reason to ever throw the girl-friend issue in the mix."

Ignoring the last part of her comment he snaps, "Look out fo' me? Wouldn't lookin' out for me be cheerin' me on out there? Supportin' me?"

"Now you listen to me, that girl is a very supportive person. I can't tell you how supportive she is when she knows something is justified. Fighting for her honor wasn't the right way to handle the situation. She wasn't trying to be self-ish. She just wanted you to be spared pain," Mia snatches a cup on the coffee table next to him. "How inconsiderate."

Billy moves the ice around and sinks into the couch. He hates to be wrong about as much as I do. "I jus' had to do it ok? He made my girl hurt; I made his ass bleed, lucky fo' him I didn't bus' a cap in his ass," he mumbles the last part.

"Oh spare *me* the boyfriend revenge bullshit Billy. You just wanted to fight to help boost your ego and make sure that she knows what kind of man she has. Well some man you are. Your girlfriend, or was going to be, is outside because her 100% man pissed her off. Hm, could you be any more of a great guy than you're being right now ..." she pauses tossing a cup in her bag. "I don't think so."

My headache is finally starting to fade when a cop car rolls up to Mia's house. Under normal circumstances I would be flipping out, but as of right now, I don't have the strength or patience.

"Excuse me young lady," the cop in the passenger seat stops me.

"Yes officer?"

Suspicious of me he asks, "There was a disturbance in this neighborhood. Did you happen to see anything or anyone?"

"Actually I saw a bunch of kids take off that way," I point the opposite direc-tion I know they went. "They were laughing pretty hard and looked kind of drunk. It made me very nervous."

"Thank you. Don't worry miss. It'll be fine," the two of them pull off. Don't worry miss? Ugh idiots. Do I look like a nark to them?

My attention quickly diverts to the front door I hear opening. Turning around out of sheer hope Billy has some goodness in his heart to come after me, I'm sadly disappointed when I see Mia carrying two large trash bags.

"How ya holdin' hope kid?" She stops on her way to the trashcans.

Miserably I sigh, "I've been better."

"I'm sorry your night sucked," Mia tosses them in. "Hope it looks up."

"Doubtful."

"Well you never know," she wipes her hands on her holiday bought dress. It's a blue jean tube top that I wouldn't mind borrowing to wear on a later date. "Someone might just lift your spirits up …" Mia eyes Billy on her way back to the door.

"Too bad Santa doesn't grant early requests," I grumble staring off back into the road.

"I may not be a jolly fat old white guy, but I can still at least try righ'?" Billy eases his way through the door way, hand cupped on his sore abs.

Mia smirks as she prepares to pass him through the doorway but whispers, "Now that's a man," in his ear first.

Ignoring his last statement I look at the sky where the late night shooters have began letting off fireworks. Billy sits down next to me staring up at them. He stretches out his legs and moves the ice around in the plastic Ziploc bag around on his face. "Did they jus' start?"

"Yeah," I don't remove my eyes from the sky.

Dropping his head he looks at me, "So exactly how mad are you?"

I shrug and don't really give him an answer. How do I determine a degree of anger? I mean it's not like I have an inner anger thermometer that tells me how hot I am about a subject, which if I did it would probably be bursting.

"I really fucked up," he readjusts the ice on his face. "I didn't mean to lash out at you. I shouldn't have said those things like that. Talk 'bout bein' an assh-ole."

"Your lame attempt to lighten the situation is not being well received," I neglect eye contact.

"Kie," Billy brings my face down to his. "I am sorry fo' what I said. I didn't handle the situation right, and I was bein' a jackass. Some'n jus' came over me and …"

"And you took it out on me. Poor defenseless me," my eyes are glazed over in a hurtful color he's not use to seeing.

Letting the ice pack drop into his lap he rubs his thumbs on my cheeks. "Yeah. You didn't deserve what I said. Forgive me?"

His touch sends those butterflies on an uproar in my stomach. He didn't mean it. People say things out of anger all the time. I would be crazy to pass him up. Nodding I prepare to look back up at the sky when he stops me.

"You're not off the hook though," his hands slide of my cheeks.

"Wait. What did I do?"

"We didn't see eye to eye on this situation jus' like we don't on another," my eyebrows rise from curiosity. "I defend you, I protect you, I care about you, and I want to be in serious relationship wit' you, but you won't even let me call you my girlfriend. Now I don't want another fight like the one we jus' had, so jus' be real wit' me Kie. Tell me why we can't be a couple."

Uncomfortable about the situation I leave my mouth shut. Never ever speak about something this vital until you have every single word perfectly looked over and correctly fine tuned.

"Being committed to each other isn't like claiming dibs on the last slice off pizza. I mean once I get known as your girlfriend there goes the labeling and freedoms of being Kie. Instead of meet Kie, it's meet my *girlfriend* Kie. Then it's not what do I think; it's what *we* think. Being in a relationship takes over your entire identity, and if you know anything about me, you know I love mine."

Gently touching my cheek again he sighs, "I get it. Now you get me. I don't mind bein' labeled yo' boyfriend. I take pride in it. To me, it's like one of the greatest things to be called a boyfriend particularly yo' boyfriend. I guess the label doesn't matter as long I know you are there fo' me," he gently touches my cheek. "I want us to be on that path though. And if you're not ready fo' that label then that's fine, but I'm lettin' you know … as long we can get there, as long as we're goin' somewhere wit' this, then I'm cool wit' it. I'm coo' wit' bein' known as Billy or that guy Kie's kinda seein'."

Smirking at his understanding and second lame attempt to help the situation, I lean him backwards. Casually I take out a piece of ice from the bag, lift up his shirt, and gently rub it over his bruised abs.

He winces at the pain, "Easy girl."

The ice cube begins melting over his abs, and he lies down with his hands behind his head. "I want those things too …"

Watching me trace the outline of his abs he chimes, "We don't have to rush anything. You want to hold off on the namin' of each other then that's fine."

"No Billy," I rub my wet hand across his lower stomach. "I want to call you my boyfriend, and it's ok for you to refer to me as your girlfriend."

"My woman …" he cocks a smirk.

"No," I hold up a finger. "Girlfriend. Respectable young lady I'm seeing. But no woman, future baby mama, or hot little hunnie I'm tryin' to hit."

Laughing and flinching at the same time he agrees with a nod.

"Now just relax," I take out another piece of ice and return to rubbing.

"One thing first," he sighs. "Do you mind comin' down here for a sec and checkin' my cut."

I lean down to look at the cut near the corner of his mouth. Before I realize what his game plan is, his lips are mounted on mine. Sneaky. How did I not see that coming? Everyone else would have. Guess that alcohol is still having an effect on my judgment.

The slow movement of his tongue is hypnotizing. I find myself lost in the kiss forgetting how long it's been going on when Billy leisurely draws his tongue away from mine. Ending with a subtle kiss he leans his forehead against mine like he did earlier.

"I like you," he whispers smiling almost childishly.

I whisper back in the same voice. "I like you too."

Billy lays back down as I go back to massaging. "This is by far the bes' Fourth of July."

"I think I agree, minus the whole almost raped thing. What do you usually do?"

"Get drunk and then laid."

"Romantic." I hope he was kidding, and if he wasn't kidding I hope he knows this will not be like the others. His ass may get drunk, but he is certainly not getting laid. I turn my head around and give him a sarcastic look. "How is this better?"

Billy shrugs and rubs my side with the tips of his fingers, "I won't wake up wit' a naked a girl and a hang over in the mornin'."

His repetitive humor is going to eventually annoy me. "Don't you mean only half of it's better ..."

"As good as a hangover feels—

"No. The other half ..."

"Oh. Well as much fun as waking up to a random naked hunnie would be, there's jus' some'n better 'bout sittin' next to the mos' beautiful girl you've ever seen while watchin' total strangers light shit on fire," he sighs like he's trying to be romantic.

His cute attempt to mimic my humor won't go unnoticed. When I open my mouth to joke back Mia's loud and very worn out voice interrupts.

"Not to be a drag or ruin what I hope is making up, but can ya'll help me?"

"Of course," he calls back to her still not lifting his head. "Jus' give us a minute."

She puts a hand on her hip, "I kind of need ya'll like now."

"Do you really want our help?" I yell back, my hands still moving on his abs.

"All right. I'll give you one minute exactly," she glares at me and closes the door behind her.

Billy lifts himself up still groaning in pain. He licks his lips and plants a small kiss on my lips before smiling.

"What was that for?" I grin back.

"Jus' 'cause I can," he shrugs. Leaning in he whispers, "Boyfriend's right."

Someone's enjoying the hell out of being known as that. I shake my head and grab the melted bag of ice as well as the towel it was wrapped in. "Come on before Mia has another hissy fit."

Slowly, he rises up mumbling, "Wouldn't want that."

After three and a half hours of cleaning the house is, it's restored to its original form. In fact, it looks better than the way it was found. Every room was vacuumed twice, along with the couches, and stairs. Dishes were washed and put up away while the fifteen trash bags were magically carried out by my boyfriend. As for Billy's shirt and any other mess made in her parent's bathroom, she cleaned it personally. His shirt is in the dryer and he's lying on the couch with me in his arms with one eye open. I hope this is the last party she ever throws.

Mia flops down on a middle stair and sighs, "Good thing today's trash day. If it wasn't, today would be my death date."

Smiling, I feel Billy start to curl the end of my hair around his finger. I ask in a yawn, "What time is it?"

"Almost six," she rubs the sleep from her eyes. "And my bed time. Goodnight."

"Goodnight," we shoe her away.

"So um," I snuggle into his arms. "What time are DK and your friend expecting you?"

"I have a key. I was told to let myself in whenever I was ready," he starts to raise himself up making me pout. "Guess I should get going."

He stands up, and the next thing I know I don't want him to leave. "Do you have to?"

"What do you mean?"

"I mean … can't you stay the night here? With me?" my voice is hopeful.

"Are you askin' me to spend the night?" he flops down next to me.

"Kind of ..."

"One second you don't wanna call me yo' boyfriend, and the next you want us to sleep together?"

"Slow down buddy," I hold up my hand. "I was just suggesting we fall into slumber in each other's arms. No ... sex ..."

"I know," he starts to chuckle, "jus' didn't think you'd be ready to take that step. It is a step ya know?"

Nodding, I place a hand on his thigh, "I think we'll be all right."

Mia suddenly appears on the stairs in her pajamas. "Are you ..." she slowly points at me, "sleeping in my room?"

"Actually we're going to crash in the guest room," I point to the room just right ahead of me.

"We?"

"Yeah," I give her that 'don't even imagine we'd do anything dirty' look. I wave to her, "Enjoy your bed."

"Ok. Enjoy your boyfriend," Mia disappears once more for the final time.

"Come on," I get up and pull him into the guest bedroom.

"You sure?"

"Positive," I stroll in with his hand in mine. We crawl into bed, under the sheets and snuggle up.

Billy mumbles in my ear, "I could get used to this."

"Well don't. It's a once in a life time sort of thing."

"Figured. Goodnight babygurl," a soft kiss lands on my cheek.

"Goodnight," I say back and let my eyelids fall. Silence falls and before I realize it I can't sleep without knowing a few things. "You don't have any weird sleeping habits do you?"

"Um ... no," his eyes flitter open.

"Snoring? Sleep talking? Sleep walking? Random screams?" You would be surprised who has what sleeping habits. Some are scarier than you think.

"Not that I know of," he says in a confused tone. "Do you?"

"Nope," I close my eyes again. "Do you mind singing me to sleep? It might help me get there sooner."

"Any requests?"

"That song you sang for me at the karaoke place," I yawn. "Make it a little slower."

Billy smiles and starts singing the song he sang to me the night of our first date. What he doesn't know is that after the chorus I'm drifting away. I hope he didn't expect me to stay awake throughout the whole thing. I mean I am sleepy.

The minute he realizes I'm no longer really listening to his voice I want him to stop, so that he doesn't wake me up.

"Kie," he whispers to me after singing the chorus twice.

I don't answer I just deeply breathe out like people do when they're deep asleep. What can I say? I easily drift off to sleep to his beautiful voice. Wow. If I ever have his voice on a CD and needed to put myself to sleep, that would do it.

"Goodnight," he kisses my forehead and rests his head back on the pillow.

Don't you ever wonder what guys dream about? Other than sex, sports, and music what do they dream about? Is there anything left for them to dream about? Girls dream about fashion, shopping, goals they hope to accomplish, guys they'll meet, and tons of other things, but not too often about sex unless of course they just had it and are dwelling on how incredible it was or how much it sucked.

Speaking of sex I know this is a strange thing to wonder, but since I am in this position and going to sleep anyway ... that whole guys waking up with a hard on thing isn't true right? I know guys can't help it, but that's not how I want to wake up. I don't want to wake up to feel something stabbing me in the leg. How come you can never wake up like they do in the movies? You know, warm sunshine touching your face with the smell of fresh cooked breakfast waiting on the table. Oh that's right. I'm not being raised in the fifty's. That explains why I will wake up with the scolding afternoon sun, smell of Mia burning lunch, and a hard on next to my leg.

CHAPTER 8

Carnival

Today of all days just isn't the day I want to play the 'I have nothing to wear' game. I have to be ready to go the carnival in less than an hour, and I'm still not dressed. You know I could own the whole damn mall and still say I have nothing to wear? What I wear is as vital as the expression on my face.

"Remind me again jus' why we're drivin' three and half hours across the state of Texas to take this girl to the damn carnival," DK unbuttons his black shirt.

"'cause she's my girl, and I can do shit like this fo' her," Billy glances at DK who continues undressing himself.

"That's bullshit," he tosses off his wife beater undershirt next. "Give me a legit reason why you're doin' this."

"Didn' I jus' tell you 'cause I can," he moves his hands down to the bottom of the steering wheel.

DK points a stern finger at him, "Nigga you better give me a good reason, or I'm a jack this car and turn it back around to drive our asses' home."

"What do you want me to say?" he glances at him as he starts to wiggle into a baggy red one.

"I don't know damn it. Give me some'n other than that 'she's sweet, she'll change my life, or I jus' enjoy her company ...' blah blah blah," he says in a high-pitched girly voice. "I know she ain't gonna give you any now or ever, so you can't say these weekend visits are fo' sex. Now break it down to a brotha," he slips it over his head. "Try to make me understand."

Billy rolls his eyes and laughs a little. "Why you gotta understand everything I do? All yo' shit ain't got motives; why mine gotta?"

"'Cause my shit don't require us to travel three and half hours to pick up some jail bait hunnie and her friend," DK pulls down the mirror to check himself out.

"No. Yo' shit jus' nearly gets us killed every otha' week."

DK hesitantly nods, "True, but at least it's in our town. Tell me some'n 'bout this chick that might make me understand why yo' ass is already whipped."

"Can't," he bluntly remarks. "Nothin' I say will make you understand why I'm willin' to travel miles to see her."

As he unties his nice shoes and rips off his socks he grumbles, "No shit. Hell you couldn't make me understand if I had been high fo' three days and convinced the world was 'bout to be overthrown by monkeys. Jus' give me some shallow reason to make me feel better."

Billy says in a hopeful tone, "Uh … She's a good kisser?"

"A good kisser? Nigga fo' three and a half hours her ass better be an Olympic gold medal holder, MTV movie award winnin', Oscar nominated kisser," he slips on his crisp white socks.

Laughing he nods, "She is."

DK nods to himself while slipping into his shoes, "I don't believe you. Let me test her out myself."

Billy shoots him an evil glance, "Nigga there ain't no way in hell I'd ever let yo' playa bouncin' lips touch her." Uncomfortable he readjusts himself in his seat, "Besides she wouldn't ever let you get close enough to try."

"I was jus' fuckin' wit' you." Tying his left shoe on the seat he continues, "Don't get all up tight. Damn. I didn't know you could care 'bout anyone like this."

"Yeah well I do," a deep sigh escapes him. "And get yo' shoes off my seat."

"Touchy, touchy," DK mumbles putting his tied shoe back on the ground. "Someone needs to get him some …"

Rolling his eyes he hits his head on his seat rest giving the clock a glance. Great. Forty-five more minutes of having to listen to DK's nonsense. Annoyed, he grips the steering wheel tighter.

"You haven't picked out a shirt yet?" Mia questions as she falls backwards onto my sleigh bed. "What about shorts? Have you picked them out yet?"

"Can you give me a second?" I push through a few pairs of jeans in my closet. "I mean this is an important decision."

Rolling over on her favorite pillow she sighs, "It's not like buying a car."

"No," I pull out my baggy blue jeans I wore when I was up in Fort Worth. "It sure isn't."

"At least when you buy a car there's perks. But I know this is important to you because Billy's traveling a few hours to come see you, and you want him to be impressed," she closes eyes. "Not that it really matters or anything. You could wear a freakin' loin cloth or a coconut bra, and he'd be just as glad to see you."

"Yes. Yes. He Tarzan, me Jane," I grunt and pull out a pair of tight jeans and a green camouflage baby t-shirt with the word 'brat' written in black on it. As I begin to get dressed I make a slight attempt to change the subject, "Aren't you going to be excited to see DK?"

Mia opens one eye and mumbles, "Yeah, like I am about my period every month." She quickly closes it back while I continue to change.

That's Mia for you. For a girl who hates DK while we were in Ft. Worth she sure tried to impress him quite a lot. Then again the obvious explanation comes to mind. She's the kind of girl who's intrigued by a challenge, but once the challenge is gone so is any interest in the guy. Must be a power trip issue.

"Are you almost done?"

"I am done," I strike a pose with my hands in the air.

Picking herself up, she sarcastically remarks, "Classic."

"If only …" I slip cash off my dresser into my back pocket.

"Look Kie, I know you're really worried about what he's going to think about you," she pushes her hair behind her ears, "but you need to realize that he thinks you're adorable no matter what you wear. Boy hasn't given a damn this far; why would he start now?"

As we stroll out of my room I mutter, "That's true."

"Aren't you glad your mom went to see your grandfather, and your dad his mom?" She smiles at the fact we've had an empty house all to ourselves for nearly the whole day.

"Very," I walk through the den to get to the kitchen. Within an instant I'm opening the fridge to grab a soda, "I couldn't imagine if she was home. There'd be no way she'd let us leave with them."

Hopping onto our wooden counter a few feet from the fridge Mia jokes, "Hell she wouldn't even let them into the driveway."

Too bad as far as mommy and daddy know I've returned to dating mysteries of this city, and he's returned to his chicken heads. "Fo' real though," I pop the can and prepare to take a drink from it when Mia snatches it from my grip. Good thing I wasn't going to drink that.

After sipping from it she questions, "Speaking of our ride, where is your superhero and his lame sidekick?"

"Good question," I remove my phone from my back pocket. You know, it might be good idea to invest in a purse. Although, I feel like if I get a purse I'm more than likely going to get it stolen or accidentally leave it somewhere like a goofball. So scratch that. I hit three on my speed dial.

"Yeah," DK answers as Billy looks for my street.

"Where's Billy?"

DK laughs into the phone while Billy rolls his eyes, "Makin' out."

"Still getting more action than you, jealous huh?"

"I'm sorry. I didn't realize 1-800-BITCH called otherwise I would've connected you straight to voicemail." DK changes to an answering machine voice, "Fuck off you—

Billy pulls up to a stop sign, snatches the phone from him, and nails him in the shoulder right as I yell into the phone, "You stupid son of a bitch!"

"Hey to you too," my boyfriend laughs and rounds the corner straight down my street.

"Oh. Sorry. I thought I was still talking to the asshole," I shake my head when Mia finally offers me the last of the soda that was intended for me. "I can't believe he said that."

"Don't worry. He'll pay fo' that. I'm sure," Billy mumbles parking in my driveway.

Leaning against the counter I watch Mia as she watches me, "Good. Anyway, where are you?"

"Hm," he hums and strolls up to my front door, "closer than you think."

"How close?" I question as Mia looks towards the door like she heard something.

"Real close," he smiles looking at my front screen door where he can see his reflection. Desperately attempting not to laugh at his own playfulness he sighs, "Go outside and wait fo' me to make sure I've got the right house."

"All right," I stroll to the laundry room. Once you pass through it you've reached the garage, which is where we come in and out of the house. "Bye." Mia rushes to follow behind me right as I hit the garage door button waiting for it to slowly open.

When Billy realizes I'm not coming through the front door, he darts under the still opening garage door. Swiftly he picks me up and spins me around making me realize just how glad I am that I didn't drink that soda. It would totally be bubbling right about now. I wrap my arms around his neck and shake my head while Mia leans against the door watching us. I bet she's thinking spiteful yet happy thoughts.

Am I supposed to wait any longer before I kiss him? It's been a little over a month since the last time we've seen each other, so I've definitely been missing his sweet candy lips on mine. I slip my tongue into his mouth within seconds I'm fondling mine with his. What makes people wanna watch other people make out? Or a better question is, why stick around while people make out even though we're not quite there yet? It could be a matter of minutes before we are if we don't stop at it now. I tilt my head to the side a little and gently roll my tongue around his a little feeling him grip tighter around my waist. Slowly pulling away from his lips I leave his tongue craving for more.

"Damn," he mutters a bit out of breath. "Hello to you too."

Winking I smirk, "Hey."

Staring at him almost in awe I soak him in. Billy has on a pair of hip-hugging light faded jeans, a sleeveless green Nike t-shirt, and a pair of green and white Addias. Luckily for me during that kissing session I inhaled the sweet smell of his cologne. He looks and smells better than I remember.

"I missed you," he smirks running his tongue across his lips.

Before I can answer Mia snaps, "Yeah. Not to be like rude, but can we go now?"

"Sure," Billy slides my hand into his.

Leading me out of the garage, I slyly instruct, "Mia do me a favor, and close the garage."

"Wouldn't kill you to be a little less lazy," she mumbles as she types in the code.

"You're a brat huh?" he glances at the title on my shirt, "'bout what?"

Nudging him a little in the side I flirt, "You."

He smiles as Mia let's herself into the backseat grumbling, "Kill me now."

When I notice that DK is still in the passenger seat, I rudely say, "Move."

He looks me up and down to bluntly remark, "No."

A glare paints itself on my face, "Move."

"No. His nigga rides shotgun."

"His girl rides shotgun."

"True," Mia chimes in as she fastens her seatbelt.

"Not in this car," DK tries to put his foot down. "I do."

I shoot my boyfriend a sweet, innocent, 'give into me look' and whimper, "Billy ..."

He looks like I've broken his heart and quickly does as any good boyfriend should do. Billy puts him in his place, "Move DK."

"What?!" He snaps watching Billy slide himself into the driver's seat. "How you gon' do that to me? NOB."

"Shut up, and get yo' ass in the backseat," he points next to Mia's who's snickering.

Climbing into the backseat he mumbles at me, "Bitch."

Proudly taking his seat after dusting it off to rub it in, I bite back, "Pinhead."

Billy starts the car and slowly backs out of my driveway. As he fastens his seatbelt DK mumbles to himself angrier than before, "I can't believe you picked a trick over me."

Coming to a jerking halt, he bangs the steering wheel, and puts it in park. With a deep breath he slowly turns around, "Look. It's one thing to call my girlfriend a bitch in the obvious jokin' way, but if you ever call her a trick again ... we bust. Period."

DK opens his mouth to retaliate when he notices a look in Billy's eyes he's never seen before. Out of all the girls that had been with Billy for a decent amount of time this was the only one he had ever stood by, up for, and protected like she was worth more than sex to him. For the first time since our relationship began it's finally starting to sink into DK's head that maybe this is more serious than he thought.

I bite down on my bottom lip as I raise my eyebrows. Yeah ... I don't like coming between friends especially guys who have been down for each other for life. I've never wanted to be that girl. In fact my entire life has been set on not breaking the boundaries and foundations of my friendships, not letting anything come between us, yet here I am being the same variable I set my life to fight against.

Intimidated he slouches down, "Ok."

Billy turns around and clears his throat before putting the car in the proper gear. The awkward silence that fills the car is so uncomfortable I would rather sing a rap song at a Garth Brooks concert. When should I say something, or should I wait for someone else to? See even teenagers get into really unsettling situations. He hasn't even given me a second glance since his minor dispute with DK, so now I'm even more uncomfortable. Somehow he senses my anxiety and slips his hand into mine that is resting on the console.

Relaxing into the seat I look over and force a smile on my face, "How's work?"

"Great," he answers too quickly. With a small laugh he realizes he's being just as uneasy as me. Billy takes a moment to calm down, "I like my jobs, but I don't like the fact I can't come see you every weekend."

"Yeah, well, don't you worry about that. As long as I get to see you at least once a month I'm ok," I push a few floating strands out of my face. Joking I dramatically sigh, "I've learned to cope."

Amused he smiles back, "I haven't. Once a month jus' isn't enough," Billy tightens his grip. "I never knew how much I'd miss you."

"Me either," I look at my reflection in the side mirror. "But long distance relationships are hard."

"Tell me 'bout it. This is my first one, and it's drivin' me nuts."

Softly I smile, "Me too."

"Speakin' of our relationship, today's our two-month anniversary."

Wow. Someone passed math with flying colors. I try not to laugh out loud at my sarcastic comment. It is our two-month anniversary. Our last one I managed to almost ruin by puking my brains out. Good thing I miraculously made up for it by suggesting we fall asleep in each other's arms. "Very good."

"So anything you want tonight you can have," Billy rubs the back of my hand with his thumb.

"As sweet as that is, what am I suppose to get you if the whole evenings on you?"

"You can buy our tickets," he nods. "Fair?"

"That's not fair," I shake my head. "Tickets are like seven bucks a piece to get in to ride every ride. That's only a total of fourteen dollars."

"Right. Meanin' only food is left to pay fo', and I'm sure you and Mia will end up splittin' at least fourteen dollars worth of food," he glances at her in his review mirror.

Nastily she smirks, "I eat more than that alone."

Holding in my laugh I speak up, "Besides food prices are ridiculously high there."

"Well that's the deal. Yo' gift to me is our tickets or nothin' at all."

"Tickets it is," I cross my legs.

"Hey," DK leans in the space between the two front seats. "Not to throw off the anniversary talk, but can a nigga listen to the radio."

"Yeah," Mia leans in the space next to him.

Billy hits the radio on and turns it up making the backseat riders happy. Ya know for a girl who wanted me to be with him so bad; she sure doesn't seem to appreciate how sweet I am being. Now I understand that having to listen to people be lovey dovey is nauseating, but when you're that person being lovey dovey, it's another story. Having a boyfriend introduces you to a different side of life that if you haven't seen you should.

About an hour later the four of us are walking around the park after we've ridden a few of the more exciting rides. Currently they're arguing whether we ride another ride or do we stop for food.

Mia yells at DK, "Food, damn it!"

"For a girl who eats so much it makes me wonder where it all goes," DK glances at her behind. "Found it."

She elbows him hard in his side while he's laughing making him yelp a bit from the pain. "Jackass."

"Can the two of you please focus?" I look back at them. Man, today was not a day made for walking. My feet are howling for us to hurry up and sit down.

"Food. We're going to eat," Mia stops in the middle of the walkway.

"Who made you queen of all the land?" DK growls out.

"Who made you lord of the underworld?" She growls back.

Shoving his hands into his pocket he rolls his eyes, "Why you gotta be so damn difficult?"

"Why you gotta be so damn ug—

"Excuse me," a tall, tan, thin guy taps her on the shoulder. He looks like he belongs in a teenage version on the Real World. "I've seen you around the park a couple of times, and I was just wondering … maybe you wanted to … I don't know, ride a ride or something with me. Maybe get something to eat?" The preppy khaki shorts, the light green collared shirt, and flip-flops, will turn Mia off, or the stuttering 'because I'm too afraid to talk to you' act will.

What could have possibly attracted him to her? Is it her deceivingly short shorts or her purple spaghetti strap shirt that reveals a bit of cleavage?

"I—

DK interrupts him, "She can't."

Mia glares and slowly purrs out, "Excuse me?"

"You her boyfriend?" The guy asks DK. Billy and me stop our flirting to witness the confrontation.

"Naw foo'. I'm her big brother," DK lower his voice to sound like an ex-convict. I roll my eyes. He was born a pure genius. She looks Hispanic without questions and DK could never be mistaken for anything other than what he is.

I lean over and whisper in Billy's ear, "Your friend's an idiot."

Quickly he nods, "I know."

He continues his pitiful act, "That's right. Our skin is different, but we still blood. And I don't want my lil' sis goin' out wit' no preppy collared, lime green shirt havin', Abercrombie and Fitch wearin' nerd."

"Well I just—

"Bounce befo' I get the heat cuz," DK jumps in his face striking fear into him.

"Sorry," the guy mumbles and backs off going back the direction he came from. Bye bye you surfer boy look alike.

DK laughs evilly when the poor guy is clearly out of sight. As Mia debates whether to choke him now or later he continues to point and laugh. Just to let you know she will throw down in public especially after being embarrassed.

"What the hell was that?" She restrains herself from any action she's come up with.

We start walking again and he nonchalantly shrugs, "Nothin'."

Through gritted teeth she asks, "The purpose of that was?"

"Fun."

"Fun? You think that was fun?" her voice is still low and threatening. "Oh I'll show you fun."

Preparing himself for a cocky comeback, he looks at Mia whose expression I know only arises in extreme cases of revenge. Nervously DK scratches the back of his neck and keeps walking. "I ain't scared."

"You will be," she mummers growing a grin.

And I thought Billy and me were bad. It's like east coast verses west coast with them. Every time you think you have a truce all you're really getting is a small break to reload. I wonder what she's going to do to him. Maybe she'll make him cry. Man, I hope she makes him cry.

"Where the hell are we going?" Mia gripes again, this time directly at me.

Noticing the answer to this situation I quickly give it, "You and the world's worst actor can stop and get something to eat while Billy and I take pictures in the photo booth."

"Sounds good to me," Mia smiles calmingly at me. "Have fun," she parts away from me kicking DK in the calf before passing him.

Shrugging off the pain I hear him mumble, "Was that what I was supposed to be scared of," as he disappears from my sight.

"So you wanna click click?" Billy approaches the booth at my side.

I will go ahead and admit I'm camera hungry. Fame, when it arrives, will help soothe it. Until then, things like this booth will have to do.

Gazing at the unopened curtain, which plays as the door to the booth, I sigh, "Yeah."

He looks at it up and down as if afraid to go in, "Ya sure?"

"Yeah," I answer with slight attitude. I sure hope someone's not camera shy because otherwise we have an obvious problem.

Billy swallows deeply and starts to reach into his back pocket mumbling something really softly.

"And now where the rest of the world can hear you."

"Nothin'. It's jus' … nothin'."

Leaning against it accidentally covering up samples that are posted, I taunt, "You're not camera shy are ya?"

"A little," his nervous fidgeting states otherwise. "No biggie."

"The expression on your face reveals another message."

"I'm jus' worried I won't take a good picture," he slides a ten into the machine. "That's all."

"Well I'll make sure you take perfect ones," I wink. How a boy so fine can be so insecure I will never know. "Now hurry up."

"So demanding," he shakes waiting for his change. "I like that," Billy chuckles to himself. That was probably some poor perverted laugh about me in bed. Does he ever think of anything else?

"I bet you do," I mumble as he climbs in onto the red plastic cushion.

Climbing in next to him, I plop down as I notice the plain black background. My attention is suddenly swept away by the screen with all the options that seem to bewilder Billy. Shutting the curtain I wonder does he have trouble reading.

"What do I press?"

"Can you not read?"

"I can …" he adjusts his t-shirt. "I jus' don't know which package you want."

"Oh well we want …" I scan my finger over the monitor. "Double sets of five," I press the buttons and go to the next screen. "Plain background," I press the button again. Feeling the need to make Billy feel included in the decision-making, I read the next question out loud. "How long between pictures one, three, five, ten, twenty, thirty or sixty seconds?"

"Twenty seconds," his first choice is a good choice.

"All right," I press the button and the timer begins. "Twenty seconds."

"Are we jus' smilin' or what?"

"We'll alternate the first four, normal, goofy ... the last one will be a surprise," I mumble and strike a pose.

Billy turns his head to face the camera. I feel him wrap his arms around my waist as I lay my head on his chest and look at the camera. It snaps one picture, and while it reloads I simply twist to the side to capture a different angle. After the second one is taken I stick out my tongue to the side and try to look cross-eyed while Billy opens his mouth to the side bites his bottom lip and squints one eye. As soon as the flash is over we burst into laughter. Getting prepared for the next goofy picture I pull my ears, puff my cheeks, and stick out my tongue. Yes this is my sad attempt to be a monkey, which is funny because he has the exact same idea. Flash.

We continue giggling, and I run my hands up his chest, "You having fun?"

Leaning in he sighs, "Of course. What's more fun than bein' wit' you?"

"This," I move my lips up to touch his giving me more than enough time to kiss him before the flash goes off. Cheap, corny, and very predictable, I know. Sometimes that's just life.

Feeling his grip tighten I slowly push my tongue against his. Even though the flash is long gone by now, our tongues continue to stay together. Now I didn't come in here to make out, that just so happened to strictly be a bonus. Ha-ha. We are milking the supposed bonus for all its worth. Conjuring up the nerve I casually pull my lips away. Damn I wish I didn't have to listen to my conscious that feels bad for going at it in a booth while people are probably waiting.

"Come on," I pull back the curtain to see our pictures lying in the picture tray. Oh and what do you know? There's another couple waiting to go in.

We wiggle out and grab our pictures. Aw, we're so cute! Go figure we look like a real couple, which is a big achievement for the both of us.

"Here," I hand him his roll of five and look at mine again.

"That one's tigh'," he points to the very bottom one.

Playfully I ask, "And why's that?"

Billy smiles widely. "Amusement park tickets, seven dollars, bottle of water, two dollars, cost to take pictures in the photo booth, five dollars, to be able to see yo' tongue goin' into my mouth," he points to where it can barely be seen, "priceless."

Seeing me roll my eyes and shake my head only fuels his smile to get wider. You can only see it if you're staring at it extremely hard and very long. The only reason he knows it's happening is because he was there. Dick head. See if I ever kiss him like that again.

DK watches Mia slurp down her slushy, "Are you still mad 'bout that episode early?'

She continues to suck it down as she smiles to herself knowing her revenge is so close she can smell it. "Not really."

"Good. I was jus' fuckin' wit' you."

"Yeah," she slides her lips off the straw while watching a long legged brunette girl giggle with one of her friends before preparing to approach DK. "I'll be right back."

"A'ight," he admires her ass as she strolls away towards the ice cream stall.

The girl Mia was watching slips onto the bench beside him, "Hey."

Smiling he moves towards her a little, "Sup baby."

"I'm hopin' ..." she twirls the bottom of her hair around her finger and glances at his crotch.

Mia does a sexy hair toss and approaches the ice cream worker. If his white outfit and newspaper looking hat don't signal he's perfect for deception, than his head full of curly hair, stubble face, and goofy expression sure do. She decides to let the small factors of him being short and chubby not play a role in her choice making. "Excuse me?"

"Yeah," his smile widens as his eyes wander down her shirt.

"Will you do me a favor?" she innocently leans forward on the counter giving him a better view. Ironic they can be used as a weapon outside the bedroom huh?

"Anything," the ice cream worker quickly surrenders.

"I'm sitting over there, and my friend doesn't know who I'm talking about when I say that really hot guy," playing him like a fiddle she carries on creating him into her own song, "so can u just wave and smile every time I point to you. Who knows ... maybe blow me a kiss?"

Making a desperate attempt to be smooth he tries to pop his towel and accidentally pops himself in the face. Mia fights the urge to roll her eyes. The ice cream nerd winks, "Sure baby."

"Thanks," she plants a kiss on his oily cheek.

"No problem," he chuckles like a hyena while watching her butt as she walks away.

"Sucker," she mumbles shuddering away the thought of him.

The girl is pressed up against DK with a hand planted firmly on his inner thigh. She licks her lips slowly as Mia reaches the table, "So how about it?"

"How about what?" Mia asks looking at DK who's all ready decided to sleep with her.

"Kickin' it wit' her and a few of her friends at the beach tomorrow," he smirks hoping to make her jealous.

"Why?" her snobbish rich girl attitude comes out in attack mode, "Are you his girlfriend?"

"Girlfriend?" her laughter begins, "Honey no. He doesn't have a girlfriend," the girl smiles back at him once more. "But I'm pretty sure his boyfriend over there might be a bit upset," she points to the ice cream booth guy.

"Boyfriend?" DK barely lets the word come out of his mouth in full context.

"You're gay?!" she squeals, her hands pop off of him, and she jumps up.

"No!" DK shrieks while Mia giggles behind her hand that's covering her mouth. "There's no muthafuckin' way I'm gay!"

"Then why's your boyfriend standing over there waiting for you," Mia points again to see him blow a little kiss.

"That's not my boyfriend!" DK pleas as the girl folds her arms. "I ain't neva' met that white boy a day in my life!" he continues to scream at her. What a wise way to keep the girl around. Yell at her. Girls love that. "I'm not gay."

"I don't think Chuck would like to hear you say that all loud," Mia pretends to stand up for him. "You have been with chunk, I mean Chuck way too long to try to go back in the closet now."

"I'm not gay damn it!" DK yells at Mia. Turning back to the snobby girl he yells, "I'm not gay!"

Disappointed the snobby girl sighs, "Look, I'm sorry. I didn't know."

"But—

"No. Really it's ok. It's just such a shame, but tell your boyfriend I didn't know," she shakes her head. "Please," she glances at Mia who's trying to look sympathetic. "It's a shame that all the good prospects are always gay." The girl strolls away with her friend who looks just as let down.

"I'm not gay!" he yells again making her laugh under her breath. Although she can no longer hear him he continues, "I can prove it to you!" DK slowly turns around to glare at Mia who's laughing evilly. "You bitch."

She slowly catches her breath. Mia licks her lips slowly and strolls up to him, "Never thought me fucking you would hurt this much huh?" Glancing around at the park guests who are staring at him she speaks low, "Or make you look this stupid in front of this many people."

He clenches his fists, "I can't believe you."

"Told you to be scared," she waves to the guy who's still standing there with a grin on his face. Mia lowers her eyes and taps DK on the chest, "Don't play games unless you play them well."

"I knew yo' ass was nothin' but a—

"Be careful what you say. Never know what I might do to get you back," she glides around him to repay the ice cream guy with her phone number.

"Bitch!" he slams his fist on the table. Turning around she makes tears down her cheek with her finger.

The two of us sit at the picnic table with DK who's sitting down red faced. My guess is she got him back.

"What's wrong DK?" I ask as Billy wraps an arm around my side.

"I'm not gay," DK says calmly, exhaling hard.

Leaning into his embrace I ask, "This is a newsflash?"

"It needs to be," he looks around at a few people. "I'm not fuckin' gay. I'm not a—

"Watch it," I point at him. I know what he was about to say, and I don't want that kind of hate in my presence. You feel how you feel about the situation, but if you can't present it nicely or civilized than don't speak about it in front of me. Discriminating is very high on the list of things I hate.

Intensely he yells at me, "Well I ain't!"

"Calm down," Billy rests his elbows on the table. "What happened?"

"She-then I-she-bitch," DK manages to get out.

Mia strolls back over after throwing her slushy cup away. "Talking about me again?"

"You," he points evilly at her, "have ruined my Austin pimp card!" I'm going to go out on a limb here and am assuming an Austin pimp card is a metaphor for his ability to 'spit game' on girls here.

"Good. I don't need more of a reason for you to appear more often than you already do," she sits on the edge of the table beside me.

With a glare he grumbles, "I hate you."

"Boo-fucking-hoo," she wipes away an imaginary tear.

Leaning over I whisper in Billy's ear, "I guess the honeymoon stage is over." Casually I redirect my attention at Mia, "What happened?"

"Oh," she says like she forgot we weren't here to witness it. "This girl started hitting on him, and I told her he was gay. I told this guy to wave at me whenever I pointed at him and called him DK's boyfriend. The girl got freaked out, apologized, and bailed."

"That's all?" I glance at him.

"What do you mean that's all? That's a lot."

"It could have been worse. Just be thankful you're not the guy she tarred and feathered."

"You tarred and feather a nigga?" Billy's eyebrows rise.

Innocently she shrugs, "I don't really like to talk about it."

Terrified but refusing to show it, he leans in towards her, "Yeah well, I got a reputation to protect, and I worked too hard to get it to let a lil' big mouthed bitch like you fuck it up."

Billy tries not to laugh at my coughing. Yeah ok. What reputation does he have to be proud?

"DK," she tilts her head to side, "You're kind a sexy when you're mad." Standing up she sees him look hopeful. "Or maybe it's when you're gay."

DK's jaw drops to argue back, but thankfully she cuts him off.

With a tug at my shirt she quickly says, "Let's go get some'n to eat and ride the tilt a whirl. We'll let them eat and have a few moments to themselves."

"Need money?" Billy turns around watching me get up.

"Naw. I'm good," I kiss him on the lips quickly. "You be good. Make sure DK stops having outbursts of aggression … oh and doesn't cheat on his boyfriend again."

"I'm not a homosexual!" I hear him yell his first more than five letter word as we stroll off laughing. I didn't know he knew politically correct words.

"Nigga let it go," Billy mumbles shaking his head. "Jus' let it go."

"Worse part 'bout this whole thing," he shakes his head. "I still wanna tap that ass."

After Mia and I grab something to eat we sit on a bench within ear distance of the guys. We're not trying to be noisy it just so happens that Mia gets a phone call she insists she must take. Of course that leaves me alone on the bench with a thing of nachos all to myself.

"Why you still after her?" Billy twirls his thumbs around.

"Mia," DK laughs munching on a chip loudly. "I need to hit it."

"Nigga you ain't neva' gonna hit that," he laughs dipping his spoon back in his ice cream.

"Oh and like Kie's jus' waitin' to ride yo' pony?" DK shakes his head. "You neva' gonna get a piece of that. I mean she's the kind of girl who won't have sex even *after* she's married."

Billy shakes his head. "That's fucked up."

"You know I'm righ'. How can you be wit' a chick wit' an ass like that and know you'll neva' get all up in it?"

"Simple. I am," he licks the ice cream off his spoon.

DK stuffs a potato chip in his mouth. "Come on. Be real wit' me. You know it bothers you that you won't ever get that chance."

I know better than to listen to this. It's only going to give me a motive to commit a double homicide or damage my self-esteem. Come on. There's not a single thing I can hear that will do me any good. I shouldn't listen. I can't listen. I won't listen. Not being able to control myself I slip another chip into my mouth as I continue to listen.

"Man ..."

"You know," DK munches on another chip. Damn. I can hear him all the way over here. "There are only two possible outcomes fo' this situation. A. You'll cheat on her or B. you'll get wise and find a way to get her into bed."

"How 'bout secret option C? None of the above." Now that's a good man.

"You mean to tell me sex is not important to you?"

"I didn't say that," Billy points the spoon at him peeking my interest. "Why is it SO important to you?"

"'Cause it's good, and I love it. Sex makes relationships what they are today. Obviously it tells us some'n 'bout our culture. 'Bout the way we roll. It's made the world a better place."

"Explain."

"Every time we go through dramatic changes in the world sex is involved. Like in the fifties, they had separate beds and shit, but then once king size beds got invented, women started to do things they hadn't ever done befo'," he starts to explain watching Billy laugh. "Then there was that whole sex era where it was nothin' but that and weed. That had to be the BEST FUCKING TIME TO LIVE!" DK shakes Billy as he continues to laugh while shaking his head.

Shrugging DK off he tries to interject, "Wait—

"SEX and WEED man! It was the thing to do, and what came from that period? The best weed, no war, and some of the bes' black music," he munches another chip. I believe he has idiot engraved on his forehead. Does he really believe everything he says? Does he ever listen to what he says? He could write a book called Weed and Sex for the Insane and Criminally Minded.

Billy shakes his head and laughs, "Are you done yet?"

"Look at like this, if the whole world jus' got laid again like that, there would be no war right now 'cause everyone would be high and fuckin' like rabbits. The best things come from sex. If you sleep wit' certain people money, other's jobs, and if you fuck jus' the right person anything you want," he rambles on crumbling the chip bag.

Still laughing Billy swallows more ice cream. Sarcastically he encourages him, "Yeah DK."

"I think it would even remove that stick stuck up Kie's ass leavin' her wit' a whole new, environment slash people friendly attitude," DK sips his soda as Billy rolls his eyes again. "Nigga come on, tell the truth."

Shoving his spoon in his empty cup he sighs, "Alright. Yes I wanna eventually have sex wit' her—

"I knew it!" DK points at him grinning. We all knew that you scientific genius you. If he didn't ever want to have sex with me I would be a bit concerned he was really the gay one.

"But, if she don't give it up, she don't give it up, it ain't no deal."

See respectable ... understanding ...

"Besides, ya know, I'm sure she's jus' like all the other 'waitin' fo' the right guy' girls. We'll be datin' a lil' less than a year, and we'll be messin' 'round when she'll jus' magically be ready to give herself to me and be glad she did. So I'm not worried," Billy pushes the cup away from him.

I drop my empty plate.

"I knew you had real reasonin'," DK nods. "And you're righ'. She'll probably give it up at prom or some'n if the two of you las' that long."

Clenching the bench, I dig my foot into the ground and scream in my head as loud as possible. How ... why did he lie to me? Why did he LIE and make it seem like he was cool with it? How dare he accuse me of being like every other girl! What if I did give it up at prom? How is that funny? Better yet why does DK care so much? Are they gonna share details? Methods? Styles? Oh god I think I'm going to be sick. I try to calm myself down with relaxing breaths.

"Can we jus' drop it now?" Billy uncomfortably scratches the back of his neck.

Surrendering, he slightly raises his hands. "Ya know we made three grand off that x last week?"

"Damn."

"I was thinkin' befo' we bounce tomorrow we could hit up A.J.'s and see if he's got some clients fo' us."

"Is x always good money?"

DK nods proudly, "Yup. I mean as long as you push enough to the righ' crowd. And I've got this hook-up that can get us more fast."

So not only did he lie about wanting to get me into bed, but he lied about no longer selling drugs. In fact he upped his dosage. Good thing I found out what a liar he is early on. At least now I won't have to put up with his lying, no good ass much longer.

"Come on," Mia stuffs her phone into her pocket. "I think I want to ride one more ride."

"Nice call?" I ask glancing off at the sky to the see the sun finally starting to disappear.

"I've got a date Tuesday night, so I'd say so."

"Good," I rise up. You've got a date, and I'll be throwing a funeral.

Half an hour later we stroll up to the table, Mia a bit worn out, me angrier than ever. I've had an extra amount of time to dwell on the two wonderful facts I had to learn about my boyfriend, scratch that ex-boyfriend, by eavesdropping.

"Everyone fine and dandy at the table?" Mia asks looking at DK with a smirk.

DK smiles wide at her, getting up, "Yup."

"You girls have fun?" Billy looks at me with a pleasant smile. I should just smack him silly right now.

I resist the urge to sneer by clearing my throat, "Yeah."

"Good. Mia got to spend all that time wit' you," he puts his arm around me. I feel repulsed. "I'm ready to have some time wit' you." There's an all too familiar queasiness in my stomach.

"Yeah," I try to smile again but struggle.

Dropping his arm from around me he sincerely asks, "What's wrong?"

"Nothing," I shrug him off and glance at Mia who doesn't understand my behavior. Don't worry she will, very soon in fact.

"Kie," he reaches out towards me.

"Nothing," I tuck one arm underneath the other. Nothing except the fact my boyfriend is a lying two-faced bastard.

"So what did you guys do?" Mia asks trying to drag the focus in a different direction. "Not make out right? 'Cause I don't think Kie would appreciate it."

"Funny," he mumbles letting her know it still bothers him. Boo-hoo she called him gay like an hour ago. It's so sad their nonexistent relationship is *so* difficult.

"Where are we going?" Mia asks me since I seem to be strolling ahead of everyone.

I slow down trying to keep my cool. Pointing up ahead I say, "That cheesy boat ride thing,"

"Why?" She asks more without them realizing.

"Just because," I give her my evil eye she knows with an innocent smile.

"All right …" Mia reads in between the lines and slips her hands into her back pockets.

"What did you girls do?" Billy moves closer to me again. He better be lucky I have a better idea than cussing him out and smacking him in front of all these people.

"Eat," I answer.

"Flirt with some guys," Mia answers playfully elbowing me knowing the most action I saw was the semi-cute nacho guy who's sad attempt to hit on me was undercharging me fifty cents.

"Damn nigga you ain't even had a chance to prove what you can do yet, and she already out tryin' to find some'n new," DK jokes. Shut up you gorilla, odd head shaped, sex craved, history confused, retard.

Billy makes some joke as I ask the guy who operates the ride, "Is that water deep enough to stand in?"

"Yeah," he looks me up in down with his blue eyes. If I wasn't completely repulsed by the male species right now I'd say he's pretty cute.

I smile and lick my lips slowly while still looking at him. Eye flirting is the best way to make your boyfriend jealous without having to take it too far or start a confrontation.

Billy clears his throat and looks at me making me turn around. He glares at the guy as he shakes his head. What's he getting all green for? Afraid he won't get the chance to deflower me? Well no need to be afraid. He won't.

Mia, surprised, tugs at my sleeve. Is she trying to correct my behavior because I'm clearly aware of what I was doing.

The four of us get into the small two person swan boats. The seats are a little wet, but that's ok. I get in first letting Billy sit next to the side closest to railing. Shockingly they don't get in separate boats. At least there's enough space to fit a cow between them.

"Kie are you feelin' ok?" Billy asks putting a hand on my thigh. I glance down at his hand having the urge just to cut it off to slap him with it.

"I'm fine," I clear my throat once more.

"Ok," he moves his hand to his own thigh. Intuition kicking in?

Around half way through the ride I decide to make my move. I'm about sick of seeing his head next to the fake painted walls with all the crappy pretend romantic music. I swear the ride has make out for teens written all over, yet here I am with no urge whatsoever to kiss my dickweed of a boyfriend. Excuse me, ex-boyfriend. This stupid swan, my bad, rip off duck thing with a missing eye, makes me feel like I'm stuck in a floatable box. Oh yeah. It's definitely time to swing the plan into action.

I gently rub up against Billy a little grabbing his attention. He was talking about something. I don't know what. I don't care either. All I know is the annoying sound of his voice was making my stomach do gymnastics. Turning around to look at me I moisten my lips and get that I wanna be kissed look in my eye. He smiles assuming he said something kiss worthy and leans down towards me. I lean in towards him running my hands up his chest only to shove him right out the swan into the wide shallow water. Oh don't worry he didn't hit his head. He just made a giant splash and got a little water on me and I assume Mia, who's covering her mouth like she didn't expect I would do this. I'm friends with her for heaven's sake. She should know better. DK on the other hand points and laughs holding his stomach. Boy better shut up before he ends up right where his best friend is.

I fold my arms and sit in the middle of the swan. The wrath of Kie has only begun. Hell hath no fury like a woman's scorn, and he's about to breathe that phrase. Cringing at the music, which by the way is worse than elevator music, I focus straight ahead.

I step off the ride and onto the platform flipping my hair again. Quickly I turn and wait for Mia who is for some reason taking an awful long time. I eye the cute ride guy, but this time he reveals his sweet smile.

Mia, who is shocked, quickly catches up, and follows me over to a table where I plop down and rest my arms. She sits across from me while DK sits on top of the table at the end, continuing to laugh.

"Kie …" she diverts my attention away from the corn dogs that were calling my name.

I look back and wait for her to say something.

"Why—

"Why the fuck did you do that?" Billy screams at me rounding the corner completely drenched.

I turn and look at him expressionless. If he thinks that was bad he might die by the time I'm done with him.

"I'm fuckin' drenched," he comes over towards me again taking another step. "Why did you shove me in that water?"

Obviously it isn't clear to him that yelling at me gets him nowhere. I mean come on, I haven't answered him once since he started; shouldn't that ring some sort of bell informing him that that method isn't working?

Not saying anything I just lean forward putting my folded arms on the table.

"Damn it answer me!" his attempt to yell at me only creates more giggles out of our friends.

Mia lightly places her hands on his chest, "Calm down Billy."

"How you gon' tell me to calm down? My girlfriend jus' shoved into a river of dirty water fo' no reason! I'm fuckin' wet from top to bottom! Explain to me how I am supposed to calm down!" he shakes off some water like a dog. Oh like it's a stretch.

Mia shakes her head knowing she doesn't know what to say. "Why don't you go change and take a few minutes to cool off then come back. I'm sure she'll be ready to talk by then."

"Yeah," DK laughs helping him away from us.

"Fine," Billy backs up. He better back up because I'm at the point where I could just pop him one good. "Let's go."

I sigh and run my hands through my hair trying to calm down myself. All right so pushing him out of the swan wasn't *exactly* the best way to handle my frustration and furry, but it was one way. It was effective, and the second he gets back it'll be time for round two.

With my hands halfway through my hair, my eyes shut tight, and frustration boiling in my blood I let out a short scream. It gets a few glances, but no one stares. Mia knows what that sounds means. Quickly she leaves my side to gather what we call recuperation food.

Another plate of nachos and half a funnel cake later, the two of them are seen strolling back our direction. Mia tried prying information out of me, but

I was locked like a chastity belt. No one's getting a word out of me except a lawyer, a jury, and judge when I get charged with attempted murder.

Calmly Billy sits down across the table from me and clears his throat, "All right," with another deep breath he continues, "Why did you push me in the water?"

I ignore him and direct my attention towards Mia, "Let's get on the Ferris Wheel."

"Um ..." Mia looks at DK and Billy. "Sure?"

"Good," I pop up and throw my plate in the trash.

"Kie," Billy calls following behind me towards the ride.

"Just give me a sec," she whispers in his ear where I can't hear.

Once we're in line, Mia quickly lets Billy cut in front of her so that we have to end up together.

"Next two," the man calls to us.

I turn around and then back at the man, "Can I ride alone?"

"Sorry young lady," he apologizes. "Pairs only."

"Well I don't have a pair," I cross my arms. "I'm single. Guess I won't ride."

"Oh no," Billy argues. "I'll ride wit' her."

"There you go," the ride operator smiles. "Bands?"

We flash them before I angrily get on the ride knowing this is exactly the way I want it to go. I always have to throw a fit and pretend I don't want what I really do. It's childlike I know, but it never fails.

Billy climbs in across from me and just stares as the guy fastens us in. We slowly start up in silence. I know what he's thinking. If he knew that I was planning to dangle him over the edge I'm sure those thoughts would quickly change.

"Why won't you talk to me?" he asks leaning in, "What did I do to you? What did I do wrong now?"

I motion my finger towards me. Sadly Billy does as instructed, leans forward, and waits for me to say something. Pointing over the edge, I lean to look down at nothing, having him follow my actions. I quickly wrap my hands around his neck and toss his head over. Billy bounces his head out of my grip and sits back down.

"Tryin' to throw me over the edge?" he rubs his neck.

Glaring I sneer, "If at first you don't succeed try, try again."

"What did I do to be thrown over the edge?" he asks before mumbling what a good grip I had on him.

I shrug and look below me at Mia who's beginning to get a little less angry with DK. Ugh not that again.

"Kie," he reaches out and tries to touch my arm.

Hostilely I snatch it away and growl, "Don't touch me."

With a lick of his lips he leans over the edge of the rail, bracing it with his life. "Mia," he calls to her. "How do I get her to talk to me?"

Like a snitch she replies, "Ask Kie yes or no questions until you find the real root of the problem. Once you're there she'll talk." I don't appreciate her helping him break through my barriers. See this is exactly why your best friend should never get mixed up in your love life.

"No," he rejects her proposal like the moron he is. Directing his attention to me he shakes his head, "I refuse to play childish games wit' you."

"Don't ask for help if you're not going to use it," she snaps.

After lounging in the silence once again as we continue up, he gives in. "I guess I'll start wit' some'n easy and obvious. Are you mad at me?"

I nod sarcastically and roll my eyes. Didn't think he'd go for the most obvious.

"A lil' mad?"

I shake my head from side to side.

"A lot mad?"

I nod slowly.

"Was it some'n I said?"

Immediately I nod.

"It's gotta be pretty bad since you tried to throw me over the edge of a Ferris wheel," he attempts to lighten the mood. Crash and burn. "Did I say it to you?"

"No," I clear my throat.

"Mia?"

"Nope."

"DK?" he questions as we almost reach the top.

I nod slowly again. That cocky bastard should have been thrown in the water too.

"I was talkin' to DK 'bout ..." he mumbles off, "You. I was talkin' to DK 'bout you?"

"Very good Scooby-Doo, can you solve the mystery?"

Ignoring my sarcasm he questions, "We were talkin' 'bout ... yo' looks?"

I shake my head.

"Yo' smart mouth?"

Glaring I shake my head slowly.

"Uh ..." he stumbles around. "Damn it Kie! This isn't a game. This is our relationship, and ya know what? You're supposed to be my girlfriend who talks to me when we have a problem, but here you are actin' like you twelve in junior high," he insults me. Again, this guy has a way with words. "You said you trust me. Trustin' me means talkin' to me," he turns my face towards his at his own risk. "Talk to me."

"Why?" I push his hand away. "What's the point of talking to you if it means nothing? No matter what I say, no matter what I do, it's going to mean nothing to you unless you get me into bed. It's all matters to you."

"That's the stupidest thing I've heard you say yet ..."

"I guess I'm just that stupid. Stupid enough to be a girl who gives it up at prom or ends up going too far when we fool around? Yeah, let me just say you're looking at the stroke of the stupidest girl ever, but what makes me really stupid is ever believing you were different."

With a deep sigh as we finally reach the top, he feels his stomach turn, "Wait. You heard that?"

"No dick wad. I took a wild guess," I sarcastically remark.

"It's jus' talk," he tries to blow it off like it's no big deal.

"Just talk? No Billy it's really not. How dare you sit there and be two faced. You say one thing to my face and the complete opposite to DK's. Do you remember why I didn't like to date? It's because I know there are guys who just wanna nail me, dump me, talk about me, and be done, but you were suppose to be different. You told me on our first date you would wait forever, and now I overhear you saying magically I'll end up like everyone else," I yank his attention at me by his shirt. "I'm not gonna be in a relationship knowing that any minute my boyfriend's going to dump me to go get laid, and then wanna come back because 'he made a horrible mistake.' High school boys play those sick games, and I will be damned if I sit by and get caught up in them. I trusted you, and this is what you say about me when you think I'm not listening?"

"But I—

"You lied to me. To think you lied to me about how you feel about us, sex, as well as you're going to stop selling drugs." I release him.

Billy pulls the wrinkles out as we come closer to getting off the ride. "But I am—

"Don't even try to bullshit me anymore. Ecstasy? You upped from selling one drug to two, and that's stopping? Do you get stopping and multiplying confused?" I glance and notice we're not far from getting off.

"But—

"Shut up before I knee you in balls!" I yell at him. "I don't want to hear anything you have to say. I'm done with you. We're over."

Billy opens his mouth to respond, but doesn't. Good. I didn't feel the need to hear him try to weasel his way out of this. And to think I thought we'd last longer than this. My point is proven now that no guy is worth this much stress and agony even if at one time I felt like this could have been it for me and my bitter ways.

The ride makes its way to the base where we're expected to get off when Billy who hasn't said a word to me since I said I was done with him speaks up. "Wait," he says to the operator. "We're ridin' again. We've got bracelets, and there's no line, so I don't see why we can't."

Shrugging, finding no reason to argue back, he doesn't even open the door.

"Wait I—

The ride doesn't let me or Mia out. I didn't want to ride again, but now it's too late to get off. Jerk.

"Excuse you. I—

"Hush," he commands me. My jaw drops. Who the hell is he to tell me to hush? Does he want to get popped in the mouth? "You had yo' turn now it's mine."

Swallowing I fold my arms and roll my eyes. Good thing I learned how to tune people out a long time ago.

"Kiara," Billy leans forward and gently turns my face the way he did before. "I'm sorry. I know sorry doesn't make anything right, but I am. I was jus' talkin' noise like niggas do. If for a second I thought it would have hurt you, I wouldn't have."

"That—

"That don't justify what I've said, but don't let it go unknown that I'm sorry. You know I don't want anything from you that you ain't willin' to give. I've never pressured you. I've never as so much questioned you or your feelings about me or sex. It doesn't matter to me what people think Kie, especially DK. You are what matters to me, and I will be damned if I sit back and let you give up on us," he plants his foot down. There's a first. "I made a mistake. I'm human baby. I can't sit here and even try to pretend I'm perfect, but I asked for you to understand that and trust that any time I do wrong I'm a try to make it up and do right. You jus' gotta stick by me. Bein' in a relationship ain't some'n I'm used too. I jus' gotta work at it, and believe me … I am."

My head tries to sink and he lifts it back up. Staring into his eyes something tells me that this isn't one of those say what I wanna hear situations. I thought all I'd hear is I'm sorry, and I was a complete jackass. Maybe I was wrong for reacting so harshly. It was just guy talk, which is something a girl is never meant to hear. I knew I shouldn't have eavesdropped. Time out. What about the other issue?

"And lying about the drugs?"

"I told DK I wasn't down wit' sellin' that x, but somehow he convinced me that once would be enough. You jus' gotta believe me when I say I'm tryin' Kie. I need you in my life right now. Don't give up yet. Please jus' don't give up," Billy begs, his hands now rubbing my thighs.

As we creep towards the top I feel something I'm not used to feeling. Oh it stings. The burning feeling is what people have come to call compassion. It's not that I'm so cold hearted that I never feel it; it's just that I usually only give guys one chance to screw me over, yet here I am sticking by his side through every dickhead move he pulls.

I touch his cheek and rub it a little. How can I not forgive him? I'm starting to think I need him just as much as he needs me. I lean in and whisper, "All right."

"I mean it Kie," he leans in pressing his forehead against mine. "I can't let you go. Whatever it takes to keep you I'm gonna do," he whispers. "I promise."

That's a lot of work. More than he realizes, but hey he's the one who made the decision to pursue this head on. Pulling his forehead away from mine when we reach the top, he gently kisses me a little on the lips.

"They're not arguing," Mia whispers to DK. "I didn't see her throw him over the edge, so my hope is they've made up and not that he's lying dead waiting to be stashed."

DK rocks back and fourth attempting to try to see something, but clearly fails.

"Is everything fixed?" Mia calls up to us.

With a sigh I yell back, "Yeah ..."

"Either you're getting soft or Billy has a hell of a way with words," she giggles happily. She hates us fighting as much as we do.

"A bit of both," Billy mutters kissing my hand. I must be getting soft to let him woo me over again and again.

"What do you say we kiss and make up?" DK tries to sweet talk Mia.

Leaning in Billy plants a soft kiss on my lips, just as Mia gives him a smart remark back. As I fall into the kiss I sigh at the thought of how selfish I am. I hold a grudge, an unneeded grudge, against a good guy who drives miles to spend a few hours with me. Forgiveness isn't as painful as I expected. Hm. At least not yet.

CHAPTER 9

School Stuff

Tap. Tap. Tap. I watch the round clock on the wall switch hands as the tapping of my pencil continues. Time seems to drag itself out when you're in class listening to things that have happened in the past. There's something about how my teacher's monotone voice never manages to reach an interesting note.

Sighing, I look over at Mia who's doodling on her notebook while smacking on a piece of Winter Fresh gum. Where'd she get gum? I thought people share gum.

Tap. Tap. Just another minute and a half and I'm out of here. I stuff my pencil in my bag and zip it back up. Impatiently, I pull my hair to one side and let it rest on my bare shoulder. Buzz. That sound makes me feel like I've won a one-way trip to Hawaii.

"Kie," Mia calls to me as she stuffs her notebook in her backpack. "Practice?"

I forgot we had to practice. This weekend is our very first performance in front of our peers. A very good friend of mine, Casey, has a giant mansion out in the hills, with a pool and lots of space. We asked would it be ok if we threw a party where we perform and what not, and she was so excited that she nearly hugged me until I passed out. One of her favorite things is to throw parties, so to throw one for me was absolutely easy and perfect. She gets credit for throwing dope parties, and we get the publicity we need.

"Food first," I mumble and stand up pulling down my knee-length brown skirt. As much as I like skirts, I hate where all male eyes wander.

"I'm all for that," she giggles pulling down her short red skirt. It's cute how all the girls in the group are wearing skirts. Andrea wore a white one while Nat wore khaki. We accidentally match sometimes, but this time was planned so people could maybe distinguish who's in our group.

The two of us start strolling down the crowded hallways when the unexpected tosses his arm around me.

"Well, well, well," Daniel Forester casually says as his arm pulls me into him. His eyes gaze at our butts and he smiles wide, "Look at you girls lookin' all fine and shit. Damn Kie," he looks down my slightly low cut white tank top, "when you gon' let me hit that?" If I didn't have to try my best to keep the peace around here, I would knock him somethin' silly.

While Daniel has an infatuation with the idea of getting me into bed, no matter how many times I say no, something else makes him stick around to annoy me. I have a dirty little secret about him. It just so happens before Daniel became the "popular stud" he is, he was nearly a loner with no friends, and I was one of the only girls to ever say more than "move" to him. One day he let it slip he was still a virgin and had never so much as kissed a girl, which is something you never slip to a girl, especially one who could spread the information like wildfire if she wanted to. However, being the sweet girl I am, I swore I'd keep his secret.

I guess he feels like he owes me for being good to him before he was something. Though he sadly, underneath it all, has a good heart. Unfortunately he masks it like so many with cocky talk and the sexual advances. Once Danny got popular, built himself an ego by nailing every girl he's ever wanted, except for me, and made sure he had money to back it all up, he became an idol almost over night. Sometimes you can see it in his eyes that he wishes he could escape. Too bad once you're in, you're in.

"Sup baby," he tries to pull me in tighter.

"What do you want Danny?" I push his arm off my shoulder while Mia chuckles.

"You," he winks touching my hand a little.

Rolling my eyes I run my hand through my hair, "Let's skip the nauseating passes, and get straight to the point. What do you want?"

"This weekend," he slides his arm around me again until I give him a look to strike the fear of God in him.

Mia rolls her eyes and shakes her head. She must know what he's going to ask me. Too bad, I know too. He's going to ask me out just like he does every other weekend. If only he would give up or turn back into that good guy I used to know as freshman.

"Yes Danny that starts today unless you have Saturday school like you always do."

Ignoring the comment he licks his lips, "I hear you're performing at Casey's party this weekend ... I hear you're getting some crowd participation, so I was thinkin'—

"No," I shake my head. Smiling proudly I say, "My boyfriend is going to be my crowd participation."

"Boyfriend?" he holds the exit doors open for us.

Innocently I gasp, "Didn't I tell you?" He shakes his head slowly. "I have a boyfriend."

"I haven't seen you 'round campus with no one," he unhappily slips his hands into his khaki shorts pockets.

"That's because he lives in Ft. Worth and is nineteen," I smirk proudly. Mia's beside me smiling just as happily. It feels good to throw something like that in his face. "He's coming. He's going to be my crowd participation."

Quickly in denial he says, "You're lying."

"She is not. He's picking us up from school today," Mia ruins what was supposed to be a surprise.

"He is?" The two of us say at the same time. See I think this is why I don't tell her stuff. She lets things slip when she shouldn't.

"Oops. My bad," she bites the side of her bottom lip. Staring me down, she demands, "Act surprised or I swear—

"Don't worry. I will," I cut her off giggling.

"I don't believe either of you," Danny shakes his head.

"Denial is the medication for people who don't like reality," I mouth off as we walk across the courtyard towards the school parking lot and parent pick-up area.

My school is separated into four different buildings that are placed around the courtyard. There's an academic building, an arts building, a science building, and one that's half the cafeteria and half athletics' building. It's huge, but overcrowded regardless.

Continuing to stroll beside me he mumbles, "I'll believe it when I see this guy."

With a shrug, I smirk, "Ok."

"No one could tame the wild bitch," Danny quickly cocks a grin at my glare, "I mean beast."

"I never said I was tamed. Besides he's closer to it than you'll ever be," I wink as I ruffle my hair again, this time making sure it looks decent for Billy.

"Yeah like he has a real good chance of breaking into that chastity belt," he sadly snickers at his own pathetic joke. I flip him off as before he says, "I've got a better chance of winning a gold medal in the high jump."

"Better start practicin'," I flip my hair to the side as I see him approach us. "Look!"

Everyone's attention turns towards him as I dramatically shed my backpack a few feet before reaching him. I need all the surprise effects possible. Rushing over to him as quickly as I can in my low heels, I throw my arms around his neck as he does around my waist. I squeeze tightly while smiling genuinely. Although I'm acting surprised, the obvious parts of me don't really have to pretend.

In my surprised voice I ask, "What on earth are you doing here?"

Pulling away from me to look in my eyes he says, "Mia told you didn't she?"

"By accident a few minutes ago," I don't stop smiling. Wouldn't want to scare them off.

He smiles as he shakes his head.

"Please don't tell her," I mumble still smiling. "But seriously what are you doing here?"

"Came a day early. Thought it would score me some points to pick you up from school," he links hands with me as we go towards where I threw my stuff down in front of Mia and Danny.

"Well it did," I smirk.

Eventually we reach my bag, which is when I feel like I've entered a boxing ring. Tension is instantly raised as I pick it up.

Clearing my throat I introduce them, "Danny this is Billy my boyfriend. Billy meet Danny."

"Sup," Billy let's go of my hand and stretches it out to Danny's.

Shaking, Danny tries to play cool, "Sup."

"Danny is my uh …" I search for the right phrase. Guess I can't dignify it by saying he's a goodhearted guy turned jackass who continuously hits on me though I've only offered my friendship, so I'll simply say, "Friend. Sometimes."

Billy and Danny eyeball each other up and down while Mia and I smirk proudly. Let's match up the opponents shall we? I mean there's no real competition because I'm with Billy and would never be caught dead dating Danny as he is now, but let's just compare credentials. Billy is tall, dark, handsome, built and currently showing that off in a pair of jeans and a black wife beater with a baseball cap to casually match. He works two legal jobs, sells drugs illegally, owns a very hot car, and is expecting a nice set of inherence money from his late folks. Danny on the other hand is tall, tans at the booth as much as the girls do, built from playing almost every 'cool sport' our school has to offer, and is currently keeping the top of him covered by a striped green and orange collared shirt. To my knowledge he doesn't know the value of a dollar, but is a very experienced credit card user, whose parents bought him a Porsche. I believe he is a trust fund kid.

"Keys please," I stick out my hand. "I would like to put my stuff in the car." Not really. I just want them to beef it out for a moment over me. Girls love it too when two guys, especially two with such worth, fight over them.

Not breaking eye contact with him, he slides the keys out of his pocket, "Here."

"Thank you," I plant a small kiss on his cheek before strolling away.

"You drive a Benz?" Danny questions.

"Yeah," he starts smiling about my kiss. "How you roll?"

"Porsche," he grins widely because he *thinks* his car is better.

Glancing him up and down before sticking his hands into his pockets he shrugs, "Not all of us have to make up fo' things we lack."

"And some of us just have money to afford the best," Danny tries to low blow Billy.

"Oh it's real safe to leave the two of them alone," Mia mutters stuffing our stuff in the trunk.

"I know. If I'm lucky Billy will finally rid me of the curse known as Daniel," we giggle as I lock the trunk.

Billy sneers at a remark that Danny must have said intentionally to annoy him.

"Let's go," I say tugging at the side of his shirt. Quickly he slips his arm around me, "I'm hungry sweetie. Can we stop and get something to eat?"

"Of course." He cockily grins at Danny, "Nice talkin' to you."

"Yeah," he licks his bottom lip as we start to walk off.

"See you tomorrow Danny," I wave over my shoulder as I walk with Billy towards the car.

"I can't wait," he mumbles under his breath strolling towards his own car in the student parking lot.

It doesn't look like Billy enjoys the idea of rivalry for me. Heaven knows he'd beat Danny at every task thrown his way, but it doesn't seem like that's enough for him. He actually looks a little over protective and down right envious. Come on now? What does Danny have that Billy doesn't other than a gold medal in assholeness.

Fifteen minutes later we're sitting in Dairy Queen waiting for our number to be called.

"Did you have a good day at school?" He asks rubbing the back of my hand.

"Eh, I guess so," I shrug. "Did you have a good day?"

"It was ok," he shrugs as well. "What 'bout you Mia?"

"Wonderful," she smirks at him. Wonderful? What the hell made her day wonderful, but mine mingle at OK?

"I'm going to the bathroom. I'll be right back," I get up and stroll off towards the restroom.

Waiting until I'm clear out of sight Billy quickly asks, "What's wit' this Danny guy?"

After a sip of her soda she asks, "What do you mean?"

"Does … she …" he seems not to be able to say it, "have … a … thing … fo' him?"

Mia starts to laugh a little and then breaks out into a full all out laughter. A few tears come to her eyes as she keeps laughing at him.

"What the hell is so funny?" he slouches down as he feels stupid because of the strange looks coming from onlookers.

"I'm sorry," she apologizes covering her mouth laughing again. "That's just too funny."

"Why's that funny?"

Catching her breath she tries not to shout, "Did you see Danny?"

"Yeah. Did YOU see Danny?" he repeats. "He's tall, tan, athletic, he's got that-that white boy nice cut hair plus he drives a Porsche."

"And what are you, writing a personal ad for him? Come on, he's fake tanned, he's Mr. Popular so he has to play every sport, he keeps his hair cut that way because it's the only thing that doesn't make his head look funny shaped, and that Porsche thing … well let's just say he can afford to make up for things he lacks," she gives that look to Billy that makes him laugh.

"So she doesn't like him at all? Like there's nothin' there?" He questions again trying to double check seeing me walk out of the bathroom.

"They're friends, but let's just say DK's got a greater chance of getting me into bed then they ever have of dating," Mia smiles as she hears our number called over the intercom.

He slowly lets the word, "great," slip out as he goes to get our food

Plopping down across from her I ask, "What's he so happy about?"

"You," she sighs in a happy soft voice.

You would think by now she would know how to lie better. "Surprise, surprise."

Billy slides in next to me still smirking. Ok. Now he's suspicious happy.

"Why so happy?" I ask reaching out for a fry.

He shrugs and hands Mia her fries and shake. "Nothin'."

"Where's my favorite friend?" Mia asks munching on a French fry letting some pieces fall out. She has the table manners of a three year old sometimes.

"Workin'," he unwraps his hamburger. That looks so good. I lick my lips.

"Working?" she asks confused.

"Yeah," he nods sipping on his soda just letting that delicious burger linger in the air. I take a giant whiff trying to remember the last time I tasted a giant juicy hunk of beef, and I do mean the burger. Billy bites deep into his burger not noticing I'm drooling over it, "Austin makes good money."

"Oh," she exclaims dipping her fry in her shake.

"Don't worry though. Believe me baby I'm tryin' to quit," he munches on a fry directing his attention at me.

Lying I mumble, "I believe you." Believe him? Please, if he really wanted out he'd be done by now. Besides, right now my attention is not on him or his lie, it's on that delicious hamburger and grease crazed fry I'm dying for.

Finally noticing my absolute hunger he offers me a piece, "Want a bite?"

I listen to my stomach rumble. Now if she can have a shake, a little bite of a burger won't kill me. Everyone cheats on their diet a tad right? An itty bitty bite won't ruin the months I've spent dieting.

"Go ahead. I won't tell nobody," Mia promises in a low whisper.

Still debating, I nibble on my bottom lip and stare at the burger. I don't know. It would be so wrong for me to eat the littlest bite. Sighing I see Billy push it towards my face. Geez he's not helping.

"You know you want to," he tries tempting me.

I lean forward and nibble a little bite. Slowly I chew the small portion savoring every single morsel. That's the best thing I've had all week. Licking the small amount of mustard off of my mouth I keep eyeing Billy's burger.

"See everything's all—

I snatch the burger out of his hand and take a giant bite out of it.

"Good …" he mumbles watching me dive into it.

Chewing the mouthful of burger I let my shoulders slouch basking in the wonderful moments of hamburger bliss. How could anyone be a vegetarian with food like this being so good?

"Someone's been deprived," he watches me devour his burger.

"Here," I try to hand it back now that it's half gone.

Billy starts to take the burger but finds himself struggling to pry it out of my hands. When he realizes it's not going anywhere, he gives up and offers me a fry drenched in ketchup.

"Damn, this diet better be worth it," he mumbles eating another one of his own fries.

"Oh it is," Mia mumbles at him. "You'll see …" she drifts off sucking up her shake.

He will see that my body may not have appreciated the diet while it was in progress, but its basking in the glorious results.

I don't want to go out there. Not in this. I can't believe I have to wear this. Why this? I mean out of all the things we could have worn, why this? A better question is why do I have to wear the most revealing thing? Why couldn't Mia have done it? Our figures are similar.

"Come on Kie," Natalie pounds on the bathroom door, not sounding as sweet as normal. "Please come out."

"Get your whinny ass out here," Mia yells through the door standing next to Natalie. "If you don't come out here right now I'm gonna kick your ass."

"No!" I yell tying my see-through wrap around me. Sighing, I look at myself in the red bikini. I can't wear this. I can't do this. Why don't I remember it looking this revealing when I bought it? Did someone shrink it without me knowing; because it sure feels tighter than I remember.

"Hey Kie," I hear Andrea call me through the door. "Just let us see, and then we'll talk about other options."

I unlock the door and slowly crack it open, "Promise?"

Slowly she nods, "Yes. We will discuss other options." That's something I love about Andrea. She always tries to find middle ground and not just demand everything one way.

Hesitating, I open up the door all the way revealing the sexy two piece red swimsuit. I watch their faces light up in pure excitement. That's not good.

"What the hell is wrong with you?" Mia yells hitting my arm.

As I rub the sting I ask confused, "What?"

"You look killer girl," Andrea tries to flatter me.

"Yeah. What's the problem?" Natalie chimes in.

I shrug and tug at my red triangle top that ties around my neck and around my back. My string bikini bottoms tie on each side. Now I don't know why they gave me the outfit that ties everywhere. Everyone knows strings confuse me. "I guess I look ok."

"Yes you do. We all look good," Mia pulls up her red tube top. It's got a heart cut out of the center and a pair of bottoms to match. There's a heart cut near her hipbone. Tall, tanned, and fit, she stands gorgeously next to me gawking at herself in the mirror.

Andrea sighs, "I think I did a good job picking them out." She slides into the bathroom checking out the red one-piece tube top with the sides missing. Just a strand of material covers her belly button.

"Sure did," Natalie pushes her way through so she's in front of me to check out her half shoulder top, that match her shorts bottoms. The two of them didn't have much work to do. They were in so much better shape than me and Mia. Guess that's what happens when mommy and daddy can afford gym memberships.

I soon notice everyone conveniently has a red rose in their hair. Mia's is down with it next to her ear, Natalie is in two braids with baby roses on the ends near the rubber bands, and Andrea's is an up do with it so sweetly placed in there. Where will mine go?

"How's my hair supposed to go?" I start to pout, "And where's my flower?"

"Here," Natalie pulls it out as if from nowhere. She snatches the brush and starts on my hair. Gently she pulls part of it up, leaving some down to do as it wants. Adjusting my ponytail she pulls me by the hand, "Let's go to Casey's bathroom and put some curls in it."

While I'm being curled and later have my makeup readjusted, the girls giggle and talk with Casey as guests start to arrive. We're not allowed out until our first song, so I don't even get to see Billy and have him wish me good luck.

"Where'd Casey go?" Mia asks Andrea who continuously tugs at her suit.

"Here I am," she perkily pops her head in.

Casey decided she needed to use her parents' money, who are out of town oddly enough, to treat herself to a back to school party swim suit. It's a white, see-through bikini. While it ties at the top like mine, its triangles barely cover her average size boobs, which she might end up paying for her's soon to get bigger. The bottoms are like mine except they come much easier undone; oh and her swimsuits made by Prada.

Checking the bathroom clock Andrea tugs one last time and asks, "What time do we go on?"

"Seven," Casey answers tossing her fake died blonde hair from side to side like she's doing a hair commercial.

Her voice a bit shaky Mia says, "Thirty minutes."

"Nervous?" Casey asks still in a high-pitched tone.

Mia leans against the counter, "A little."

Natalie, quicker than I thought, finishes my hair, and we arrive back in the bathroom to hear Casey asking why Mia is nervous.

"Good question. Why?" I ask preparing to shake my curls out when Natalie pops me to stop.

"I don't know," she shrugs. "I guess it's because these are people we actually know."

"Point being? If they don't like how we perform then that's on them. Not everyone's going to like us, so it's not like that can be helped," I fold my hands. "Just breathe and chill out. You usually don't give a damn what people think, don't let this be any different. Imagine it like a room full of DK's." It gets a smile out of her.

"Oh yeah, we finally get to meet DK," Andrea jumps in moving out of our way letting us see ourselves again.

Casey layers on another pound of make up stopping Natalie dead in her tracks.

If this doesn't prove I get along with everyone, I don't know what does. Casey is your typical party-hardy girl with no limit on Daddy's money to spend. She believes the 'populars' aren't good enough for her, so she chooses very carefully who to associate with. You're probably wondering how we ended up in contact with each other. Let's just say Danny wasn't the only one lonely and had a secret to share.

Brushing off the fact Casey's make-up habit is pathetic in her eyes she says, "They're still coming right?"

Billy. I almost forgot he was coming. Talk about a stressful day. I have to worry about my friends and my bf mingling nicely, my classmates liking us as a group, our songs, and our dancing. Why do I have to worry so much about everything? I swear if I keep stressing out, my hair will just fall right out of my head.

"If I miss her first performance of the night 'cause you jus' 'had' to make this deal I'm gonna beat the hell out of you," Billy threatens pressing the gas pedal down.

"Shut the hell up," DK starts to count the money over. "Let me count this shit and then you can finish bitchin'."

Billy glances at the time. Six forty-five. Clutching the steering wheel in anger he says a prayer that they arrive on time.

"Two G's," he nods proudly handing Billy half the stack. "Not bad. We should make another two tomorrow befo' we leave."

Not saying anything he speeds up trying to ignore DK. He had told me that he'd quit hustling, yet he still hasn't, and every time he takes the money, it just reminds him that he's not trying nearly as hard as he leads on.

"Almost ready?" Mia asks watching me slip on my easy to tear open white t-shirt. On top of our suits are these incredibly flimsy shirts we plan to rip off like strippers. I'm totally picking the next outfits we wear.

"Yeah," I sigh slipping my manicured toes into my red open toe two inch heels. Fastening the strap around my ankle I pray I don't slip, trip, or fall in them.

Billy looks around for a place to park. Cars are lined up from her house on down each side of the road. "See what the hell you did!" He points at the cars. "There's nowhere to park!"

"Suck it up and park nigga," DK turns down the radio.

Speeding down to the end of the road Billy turns the corner and parks his car quickly. After he unbuckles his seatbelt, he yanks the keys out of the ignition and grumbles, "I can't believe we have to walk that fuckin' far."

"Stop actin' like a bitch," DK remarks following Billy down the road.

Stuffing his keys in his jean shorts pockets he snaps, "You wanna walk home?"

"Please," DK rolls his eyes and pulls down on his red A-town hat.

"Ready?" Casey opens her back yard door peeping in at us.

"Just give us a sec to adjust our microphones," Andrea fidgets with hers.

"OK," she squeals excitedly and closes the door. Why is she more excited than the performers?

"Remember," Andrea turns to look at us as she takes place first in line. "There are tons of people out there, make sure to please the whole crowd not just the ones up close."

We all nod, as Natalie gets ready to put her two cents in.

"Remember," She adjusts her earpiece, taking her spot behind Andrea, "Have fun and smile."

As we all nod Mia lines up next. "Remember," she presses her lips together. "Just let it flow."

I'm already in line so there's no need for me to go anywhere. Sighing, they wait for me to add something on to our traditional train of thought. "Remember," I make sure the earpiece is stuck in my ear comfortably, "To remember everything."

Making them giggle relieves much needed anxiety and helps the transition into focus mode.

"God is great, God is good, lord help us do this good, Amen," we all say together before whispering, "One for all, all for GFL."

Billy squeezes his way through a few people with DK slowly moving behind him checking out the girls lounging around in their swimsuits.

"Hurry up," he yells while DK just twirls his lollypop in his mouth.

"We ain't gon' miss shit," he gripes back as they stop by the end edge of the pool, which happens to be in the center of the yard, not close enough for Billy.

Before Billy can even attempt to move closer he notices Casey has taken the stage, giving the obvious sign we're about to start. There are four guys waiting on the stage, and one of them happens to be Danny. Last minute idea Casey came up with. I wanted Billy and decided I'll just have to find a way to get to him.

"Hey," she says into the microphone at people in her huge backyard.

Her backyard can fit up to 300 people comfortably. Half of the space is taken up, but the parties just beginning. She's got a giant rectangle pool where there are already people lounging around on floats.

"This is my Welcome Back party. I know a lot of you came here just for the free alcohol and to see these girls perform, so why don't we go ahead and bring them out," she giggles at her own joke. "Put your hands together for GFL," she screams as the crowd goes wild. Showtime.

DJ Sizzle puts on the beginning beat of our first song. DJ Sizzle produces all of our beats and spins them wherever we perform. We consider him one of the group members. He's Andrea's cousin and is only twenty-one, so it's not like he's that far away from us. When he's not working on beats for us, he's a waiter at a downtown restaurant, and then occasionally DJ's a club a few streets around the corner from it.

"Give it up," he says into his mic.

"Hey you guys," I say into my microphone making Billy smile at the sound of my voice.

"That's her," he elbows DK like a teenybopper excited to see her pop star.

DK pops the lollypop out of his mouth and gives him a sarcastic look, "Yea."

"I think it's time we introduce ourselves," I say again licking my lips, as Andrea cracks the door. "Andrea go ahead, bring 'em in." Now how I got the job of being the announcer, I'll never really know.

"Andrea's my name and I'm the queen of games," she strolls out onto the deck slowly swishing her hips when she walks. "I hear girls complain, it's a got damn shame," she sings spinning herself around once and leans against the DJ booth to flirt with him. With a lick of her lips at Sizzle she purrs, "How I swish my hips and I work my thang, but I'm not the same as them other girls." She pushes herself away from him before stepping down to the next step. "Put your mind in a whirl when you watch my hips swirl," she rolls her hips around in a circle at the guy standing on the step closest to the crowd. Slowly she starts to rip her shirt open, "Make your heart skip a beat when you watch me freak." Andrea tosses her shirt to the side after the word freak leaving the guy speechless. She's always had a little thing for him. Sliding her body in front of him she says to the crowd, "Learn not to hate but appreciate."

"We're all you'll want," we sing in unison. "We'll be all ya need. Just give us that one shot," Andrea starts to melt against him. He runs his hand across her waist and pulls her into him, which is when they freeze, "And we'll make ya hot."

"Now she's hot," DK whispers in Billy's ear.

"She's a'ight," he shrugs. "Not really a blond kinda guy."

"Natalie show 'em what you can do," I say as DJ Sizzle scratches the beat a little.

"Everyone says 'Oh Natalie, so young and sweet, she's the kindest girl that you'll ever meet," she slowly walks out facing the crowd with an innocent face. "So cute and innocent like a yummy peppermint.'" Pausing, still innocently smiling, she whips her head to DJ Sizzle she starts to sing it towards him, "If they only knew, what I really do," she body rolls down. Taking a moment, she strolls over to the guy made for her. He's one of her exes, but their still friends. "The naughty things would blow their mind," she quickly licks her lips at him, and turns to the crowd, "make them press rewind, to rewatch me grind." They're on the step behind Andrea and her man, on the opposite side. "Now let me tell you what they'll soon learn too. I've got the curves that'll make you turn, that'll give you heart burn," she innocently rips her shirt down the middle like Andrea, while he slides his hands up her legs, "and the sexual drive that you already yearn." After she tosses it out in the crowd she blows a kiss to the audience.

With her back pressed against him she sings, "We're all you'll want. We'll be all ya need. Just give us that one shot," Natalie slowly runs her hands across her body and wraps them around his neck freezing in that pose, "And we'll make ya hot."

"I wouldn't mind her givin' me heart burn," DK mumbles in Billy's ear still sucking on his lollypop.

Billy rolls his eyes and sighs, "She's got a nice voice."

"She's got a nice ass," he licks his lips.

"Yo Mia go give 'em some'n real," I sigh leaning against the kitchen counter. "Some'n they can really feel."

"Mia, Mia, oh god Mia," she runs her hand through her loose hair and slides her body down the doorframe like a stripper. "Is what I'm a hear your man sayin' so watch out bia bia." After picking herself back up, she sings while strutting towards the middle of the stage, "I ain't afraid to throw them bows, at you hoes. That includes you fools too," she looks at DJ Sizzle who smirks. "And if I offend you, then jigga boo-hoo," she steps down a step and tosses a glance at the cocky guy waiting for her. "I ain't got time for lames," she moves her hand across her neck like she was cutting it and continues to walk with her attitude down to the next step behind Natalie, but on Andrea's side. Pointing to Andrea she sings, "I ain't got time for games," then pops it at Natalie, "And I damn sure can't be tamed." She moistens her lips and prepares to rip her shirt while singing at the guy looking at her. "Make you go insane, and make you miss the rain, 'cause I'm just that damn hot," Mia rips her shirt quickly on the word hot and the guy slides his hand down her curves before winking at the crowd. They cheer gladly and loudly.

Billy leans back knowing DK's going to say something.

"Yeah she was a'ight," he puts up a front folding his arms.

Laughing, he shakes his head knowing I'm coming up next.

"We're all you'll want," Mia's legs are slightly apart and her hand is planted firmly on her hip. He plants a hand on her inner thigh and freezes. "We'll be all ya need. Just give us that one shot." She shoots DK a quick wink and sings, "And we'll make ya hot."

"Ya'll havin' a good time?" Sizzle asks. The crowd cheers and I take a deep breath. "You ready for this next hot little mama?" The crowd screams again.

"Who's that guy fo' Kie?" DK asks sliding the lollypop back into his mouth. Billy tries not to glare at Danny who's waiting for me. "A friend of hers."

DK passes on the chance to take a stab at him.

The crowd screams for me, and I try to remember everything I had to. "I don't think they ready DJ Sizzle," I say hearing him scratch the beat. Actually I'm not ready, but same thing.

"You ain't ready to see the things I can do," I rush out on the stage smoothly. I quickly approach Danny who's cockily waiting for me in his navy swim trunks with no shirt. Shooting him a look I sneer, "I'll make you get down on all fours just to embarrass you. And you'll do everything I tell you too, just for the thought of you getting a screw," I say hearing the crowd say 'oh' like they're impressed. "Baby boy I run this shit, I'm the world's biggest misfit, with a banging body and a quick wit," I flow pushing him a little. "You think you can handle it, think you can deal with what I spit?" I pause giving him a look like I want him, and he nods. "Newsflash foo' you've got the wrong chick, because this one will call you out if you have a small dick," I point to him, the crowd 'ohs', and I walk away. Moving my way around the girls, I head to the crowd, continuing my flow, "I don't give a damn what you've been told before, no respectable girl is a whore. Jigga I don't steal from the rich and give to the poor, I keep it for myself, got more ice than Santa and his head elf," I smile myself partying for the crowd. Good think I spotted Billy early on; otherwise this could be pretty hard. "I've been naughty, but I damn sure ain't been nice, and if you're lookin' for that girl here, you better look twice," I decide to give myself a better chance by stopping the DJ. "Sizzle stop for a moment." He cuts the beat, but unexpectedly. "Let me find a real man," I sneer making Danny huff angrily at me.

Finding Billy I stop in front him, "DJ rewind ..." and he spins the record back. I start it again, "You think you can handle it, think you can deal with what I spit?" I pause giving Billy a question look. Surprised I came to him after all he nods and I continue, "I'll make you, I'll break you, you'll be beggin' me to take you," I start in his face. "To taste me," I rip my shirt sexually and toss it aside him, "and hold me, tellin' me you can guarantee you'll be all I need," I wink and swing my body around. Body rolling against him I say, "You can have your chance, and try to advance," I glance over my shoulder, "but in your trance, don't forget what they call me, K I sexual E."

I can tell I've made Billy really impressed as well as nervous, but hey. He knew what kind of girl he signed up for. We sing the chorus a couple more times through, groping and rubbing against our designated men. Poor Danny is standing on stage alone, and I don't even feel bad about it. Every so often the girls sing his way to make sure he doesn't feel isolated. The crowd goes wild, and I quickly bounce my way back on the stage before their done cheering.

"That was ...," DK searches for the words.

"Fuckin' hot," he says nearly speechless as Casey gets back on the microphone.

"One more time," she giggles into the microphone. "Give it up for Andrea, Natalie, Mia, and Kie along with DJ Sizzle."

There are more people then when we first arrived. I'd guess about two hundred or so now. Great, two hundred people judging us, but from the sound of their screams it sounds like they enjoyed us.

Sizzle starts the music for some song as we pick up our things off the stage. I have to find Billy all over again when we can head into the crowd. Great. Something deep inside me has a feeling I will receive praise from him and criticism from his homeboy.

I follow behind Andrea back in the house to take off our microphones.

Once in the house I get what I expected. Andrea snaps, "Why did you change the show up like that?"

"Yeah. Why'd you leave Danny high and dry *and* change your words?" Natalie jumps in.

Mia thankfully swings to my rescue, "She told you she didn't want to be with Danny. You guys know she wanted her boyfriend, not Danny. Come on, besides they seemed to like it and I'm sure she won't change anything else will you?"

I quickly shake my head.

"Well," Andrea sighs. "She has a point. I guess that's ok ..."

Natalie quickly agrees, "Yeah. That was an awesome free style though."

"Thanks," I say as they disappear into the house to reapply and readjust before they go out to see the people we know. As soon as they're gone I turn to Mia, "Thank you."

"Mmhm," she ruffles her hair and gets ready to go out without redoing everything like the other two. "Come on."

A few minutes later Mia and I are trying to find DK and Billy.

The second he's in my vision he call's out my name like I don't see him, "Kie."

"Hey," I walk around a few people before reaching him. Tossing my arms around his neck I left my nearly bare chest press up against his. My chest touching him like this is probably more exciting than watching me perform.

"You were ..." he pulls away from me giving me moment enough to kiss him. This kiss isn't about just a kiss, but proving I have a boyfriend. I rush my tongue at his and quickly lock it tight, so he can't get away from me. Rolling my tongue around his, I slowly draw back nibbling his bottom lip a little before completely pulling away.

"Now," I run my hands down his chest to fold hands with his. "What were you saying?"

"Uh," he sighs licking his lips slowly trying really hard to remember. "Uh ..."

"'Bout her performance nigga," DK yells at him pulling the lollypop out of his mouth. "You were gonna tell her 'bout her performance."

"Oh yeah," Billy slowly nods as I turn my back to him to face Mia. I just want him to hold me from behind, which he'll do. "You were hot," he wraps his arms around me from behind. Told you. "Way to make the crowd feel a part of the show. I was very impressed."

"Yeah that's 'cause you were the part she used," DK mutters.

"Excuse me?" I quickly snap.

"I'm jus' sayin' I doubt he would have liked it as much if you would have cuddled yo'self on that pretty white boy," DK slides the lollypop out of his mouth.

I smirk, "And how did you like it?"

"Ya'll were hot," he nods and cocks a grin. "That whole rippin' the shirts off thing was classy yet slutty. I have to say everything you did was pretty on point. Yo' flow was a lil' off though, but you did ok fo' a girl from the 'burbs.'"

"Well thanks DK. I appreciate your honesty." I really do like the fact what DK had to say wasn't what I wanted to hear. Although I expected it from him, it still feels good to have someone say your work wasn't perfect, but it was fairly decent.

"When's the next set?" Mia asks watching DK out of the corner of her eye check her out.

Shrugging as Billy snuggles his face next to mine I ask, "Good thirty, forty minutes."

"Oh ok," she nods and rolls her head around to DK. "My swimsuit isn't going to magically disappear no matter how hard you stare, so you might as well quit wastin' your time."

As we make chat among each other, we're soon accompanied by the other two girls.

"Hey," they say in unison to us.

Billy says hey back, and DK merely checks out fresh merchandise in his head.

"Nice to see you again," Natalie politely says to Billy, using a non-flirty tone.

"Like the show?" Andrea asks folding her hands, blocking DK from staring at her chest.

"Yeah," he nods. "You two looked great."

"Look great, sound great, and mus' taste great," DK chimes in sleazily. "I'm DK."

"Dickhead?" Andrea pretends she didn't understand what he said.

"DK," he says it again over pronouncing it.

"Oh," Natalie giggles. "Well, nice to meet you."

"Yeah," he grazes his tongue across his lips. "Feelin's definitely mutual."

"What do you think?" Mia asks them.

They give DK another wince over and Natalie decides, "Doable."

"I second that motion," Andrea elbows her playfully.

"Not exactly my type, but doable," Natalie shrugs folding her arms as Mia starts giggling.

"You think I'm doable?" DK says proudly. "Why don't we test that out?"

"Ew," they shake their heads and dismiss themselves, but Mia goes into uncontrollable laughter.

Confused he asks, "Why you laughin'? They said I was doable, that's a good thing. They think I'm hot."

Mia tries to stop laughing for a minute but finds it harder than ever before. It wasn't that funny even though I know why she's laughing.

"What?" DK asks now annoyed.

"Doable means," she tries to stop giggling. "You're ok. You're not hot just because you're doable." Mia attempts to regain her breath, "That's like a notch right above loser."

"Fuck you," he gives Mia a snobby tone.

"No you're not fuckable," she starts laughing again. "You're just doable."

DK opens his trap to bite back, but I cut them off, "How about we go get something to eat?"

We mingle our way over to the BBQ area. DK and Mia spend most of their time downing food while Billy and I just flirt away.

Eventually Mia and I dismiss ourselves to take a few moments to regain our composure before taking the stage for a few more songs.

That set is about another thirty minutes, which is nice because that's when the sun slowly starts to fade. After the crowd cheers we go back into the house to refresh ourselves and take a break before rejoining the party.

I hop myself on the counter while the other girls gather in front of me.

"You know Crystal's out there ..." Mia hands me a cup of water as she joins me on the counter.

"So," I shrug.

"Come on," Natalie strolls towards me. "We all know you hate her."

"And?" I say sipping my water.

"And it's a known fact she's determined to make your life a living hell anyway she can," Andrea jumps in downing a bottle of water.

She has a point. Crystal has had it in for me since we were five years old, and I got the first edition of some Barbie doll that her parents couldn't find. Ever since that moment, that very moment when she saw me with that stupid doll, it's been her life mission to destroy me every chance she's gotten, so why would today be any different? You would think the girl would learn to let go already.

"True, but what is she going to do? Tell me I can't sing, and my flow was weak?" I laugh a little to lighten the mood, "What can that do to me other than make me reach my hand up and backhand her?"

Slyly Mia mumbles out as she puts her lips to her cup, "What about Billy?"

"What *about* Billy?" I shoot her a quick harsh glance.

"She'll take a stab at him," Natalie says like it's a sure thing.

Andrea so sweetly adds, "More like a grab. That girl has pushed up on every man who's ever entered your life."

Another point well proven. I can't recall the last time she hasn't went after a guy I've wanted. Hell, she's continuously after Danny, who plays her on again and off again, sex buddy. Crystal goes after losers like him, so I know she'll go after my dear sweet Billy. He's a good man, and everyone knows skanks go after good men.

"I'm Crystal," she sticks out her hand to introduce herself to Billy who looks preoccupied with waiting for me.

He shakes her hand politely and takes it back, "I'm Billy."

"Mm," she hums out flipping her blonde hair that has thick brunette highlights. I guess a highlight for every moment of revenge she's tried to take on. Crystal slides her hand along her stick figure body that's being covered by a tiny white see through tube top, and a pair of similar string bikini bottoms. What is it with rich girls and white swim suits? "Very nice to meet you. Would you like to dance?"

Looking around for me Billy nicely declines, "Thanks, but I'm waitin' fo' my girlfriend."

"Oh," she says in a high-pitched pout pretending she doesn't know it's me. Seductively she touches his chest with the tip of her finger, "She's got to be a lucky girl to end up with a hot guy like you."

I hop down off the counter and start out the kitchen.

"Where are you going?" Andrea asks watching Mia follow behind me.

"To make sure history quits repeating itself," I answer opening the door, leaving it for Mia. I know exactly where Billy is. He's in the same spot I left him thirty minutes ago, but now he's not alone. I recognize the slut even from behind. Letting out a growl I calmly walk towards them.

Crystal flirty laughs at something Billy says and casually touches him the way all girls do when they flirt. I've pulled that move before! On him! I'm going to rip out every strand of her fake hair if she keeps on.

"You know Billy," she innocently slides herself against him in the 'too friendly' manner. "I would love to be so lucky to have a great guy like you for a boyfriend." Her eyes are trying to seduce him as one of her hands slowly, but surely makes it way up his back.

Pushing my way through the crowd I said loudly, "Excuse me!"

Billy says with a smile, "This is my girlfriend Kie."

"The bitch knows me," I fold my arms across my chest with Mia standing behind me strong, and ready to throw down. "Crystal, I'm only gonna say this once. Keep your needy eyes and greedy hands off my man."

She rolls her eyes and steps up in my face. "If I want him I'll get him so don't even start with me," she tries to dismiss me by placing a finger in my face.

Oh no, this heifer did not just put her nasty two-timing finger in my face. She better move it before I break it off.

"Look you Britney wanna be," I take one more step forward. "You will never have my man so don't waste your time. Now don't make me get ugly."

"A little too late for that don't you think," she sneers in my face. This bitch wants to be hit.

"Watch it," I warn her again as she gets in my face.

"Look, you're boyfriend already wants me, and there's nothing you can do to stop him. After all why would he want a talentless bitch like you when he could have a pure bred beauty," she barks grazing her bottom lip with her tongue.

I pull back my fist and shatter her jaw like glass. A good portion of the crowd watches as her toothpick body falls to the cold hard deck. I can't feel my right hand, not a single finger, but it's worth the glory of finally getting to hit that noisy trash-talking whore in the mouth.

"Pure bred beauty my ass," I growl out as Mia cheers me on from behind. Something tells me here in the next few minutes I will regret that, and not just because of the fingers I can't feel.

After laughing and expressing happy "ohs" the crowd goes back among themselves. Billy and I are just staring at each other when DK finally comes from wherever it is he was hiding.

"Damn Kie! That girl went down hard!" he yells a bit looking at me and then Mia whose shaking her head at him.

Turning I snap at DK, "The time I want you to cock block is the time you ain't even around!"

"Cock block?" the two guys say together.

"Who did he need to block?" Billy looks at me. "You think I was flirtin' with her?"

"Sure looked like it with her nasty body all pressed up on yours while you buy into her every nasty two-timing word," I growl as Mia snatches a cup of ice from a passing person.

"But Kie—

"Save it," I put a hand up. "My hand needs some ice. Come on Mia."

"No," Billy stops Mia by the arm. "I'll go wit' her fo' some ice."

Rolling my eyes I start to storm off. He has a lot of nerve to want to come with me. I swear he better be lucky I can't feel my fingers otherwise I would sock him a fist too.

Once we're in the kitchen I hop onto the kitchen counter while he searches for a towel to make me an ice wrap. He doesn't look too happy with me, but what right does he have to look pissed at me? Which one of us was flirting with the girl who's been around the block?

"Look Kie," he dumps chunks of ice into a cloth and wraps it closed. "You didn't have to hit that girl fo' speakin' to me."

Again I roll as I correct him, "Flirting with you. Flirting …"

"I wasn't flirtin'," he brings it over to me.

"Oh I beg to differ," I snatch it from him. "That girl was all on you like a fat kid on a Popsicle in one-hundred degree weather, and you were just eating it up with a spoon."

Billy gives me a long glare into my eyes angrier than before, "Watch yo'self. You're on thin ice."

"Thin ice? Who the hell says thin ice any more? And how am I on thin ice when you're the one who was all up on the upclass trailer park trash—

"Shut up Kiara," he bluntly remarks. I raise my eyebrows, but he doesn't budge. "Don't come at me like that any more. I don't appreciate you tellin' me I was flirtin' wit' that trick when I know damn well I wasn't. So shut up about it."

Swallowing hard I roll the ice around against my fingers.

"You know I have never shown interest in any other female, so you ain't got no reason to come at me crooked. I've never seen you flip out over a trick like that ..."

"Maybe that's because it's bigger than just you," I quickly sneer out.

"And what's that supposed to mean?"

"Nothing," I look down at my plump throbbing fingers that have turned into slender plums.

He lifts my chin up and demands, "Tell me."

"The girl has had it out for me since we were in elementary school. Everything I've ever wanted or had she's gone after it, and for the most part got it. If I was a superhero, she'd be the villain who won't sleep until I no longer exist."

Billy snickers underneath his breath.

I'm glad my life's amusing to him. "Then the one thing that means the most to me right now besides my career she goes after. And what do you do? Just let her start a conversation and start to—

"Slow yo' roll," he abruptly stops me. "I was jus' bein' polite. She approached me, started a conversation, and I kept throwin' you in it. That girl was well aware I'm wit' you."

"And?" I sigh.

"And she knew she wasn't getting anywhere wit' me. I told her that, yet you flipped shit on me fo' no reason. I think I deserve an apology."

Sighing again I look down. That's something I don't really like to do. As much as I like to flip out on him I don't like to apologize for it. That has to be because I'm hardly ever wrong. In fact my motives are usually well thought out and very well supported, but this one was foul on my part.

"Kie," he lifts my chin up once more. "I know you care a lot about me ..." Nodding he continues, "You said you trust me, and I'd like to think that, even though you had a minor lapse of judgment. I know the only reason you did that was 'cause it's instinct. I would know," he starts to smile. "I nearly went haywire on yo' friend Danny."

I giggle a little, "I'm sorry. I didn't mean to come at you like that."

"It's all good," he kisses my cheek. "Trust me Kie. You're not gonna loose me to any other female. I promise."

I smile and look down at my semi-swollen fingers. Wow I guess I underestimated just how understanding he is. He's much better than I was when he knocked that dude out, but now that I think about it his circumstances were more justified than mine. I guess I know what people mean when they do some crazy things out of ... well out of having an abundance of any sort of overly affectionate feelings for someone.

CHAPTER 10

Homecoming

It's that magical time of year again where people are full of school spirit. Football season means I'm forced to sit through Pep Rallies against my will to watch cheerleaders scream enthusiastically about our loosing team, while I'm pretending like I actually have pride in our over confident school.

Now football season is dealt with until it reaches its peak … homecoming. Most people love homecoming. It's the one game our football team actually wins, it's the one game even those you believe have no ounce of school spirit whither out a tint of green somewhere on the body, and it's the one dance that somehow or another all of our school ends up showing up to.

I believe I hold our schools worst date record to this day. For the past two years my dates have ditched me for my best friend. While it wasn't the same best friend, and neither of them asked for it, it managed to happen the same way, and hurt just as bad. Who wants to relive their nightmare three years in a row? I mean sure I have boyfriend now, but that doesn't mean I won't get ditched. Do you know what that can do to a person? It's like having your heart ripped out of you, handed to you in a lame ass punch glass, and being asked 'would you like some ice in that?'

"You don't even need a date to go!" a half brained cell homecoming endorser shouts over the announcements. I may not be a big morning person, but one thing is for sure, having the announcements moved to the part of the morning where everyone is awake really is a pain in the ass.

Mia glances over to see that I'm twirling my gum around my index finger. "Hey," she whispers to me. Why does she whisper when it really doesn't matter either way?

"What?" I stop twirling.

"Are you going to homecoming?"

"Didn't plan on it," I mumble with a bit of hostility in my voice since she was the one who I was ditched for last year.

"Stop playin'. You know Billy's gonna wanna take you."

Ok, first of all, why would a young man who's thankfully kissed his high school career goodbye drive four hours to engage in the very activity he wanted to escape? I wouldn't seriously consider making him suffer through a lame dance unless I find it deep inside me to want to go badly. And let's face it. I don't see that happening.

I make a sarcastic face, roll my eyes, and twirl my gum at her. "So?"

"So you're going then?"

"Probably not," I stuff the gum back in my mouth.

Annoyed she sighs, "Ok. Why not?"

"If my recollection is correct, I've been dumped the two previous years, which would lead me to a year in which I refuse to give history the chance to repeat itself."

Mia almost let's out a growl, "You have the world's worst problem getting off stuff, you know that?"

"So because life is traumatizing to me I'm a bad person? If that's the case then I'm guilty, a very guilty person who's still not going to homecoming."

"What does it take for you have some faith in life? I've been right about the past few situations I've gotten you in—

"You were lucky."

"Oh come on. Can't you just trust me on this one?"

Stubbornly I shake my head.

With a glare she changes tones quickly, "Look I'll level with you. I know you're going to spend the next five to seven minutes trying to convince me you're not going when we both know that you are." I open my mouth to object, but she cuts me off promptly, "Now I'm not going to give into you and your mind game. I'm simply going to say you have a boyfriend who adores you so much that he's going to want to take you, a mom who expects you to go, and three best friends who will be *very* angry for a *very* long time if you ruin this by not going."

Sighing, I lean back in my chair. I hate it when she's right. Nonchalantly I sarcastically nod at her before I roll my head back to the front of the room where our teacher's struggling to get our attention.

A few hours later I'm reading a magazine on my bed while listening to the radio. I'm resisting the urge to call because I know that he's going to call me very soon, but obviously not soon enough.

Ring, ring, my cell phone goes like an angel calling. Eager, I roll over and answer it.

Sitting up I answer, "Hello."

"Hey baby," I hear Billy say smirking to himself.

"How are you doing?" I ask turning the page slowly.

"I'm better now that I'm talkin' to my girl," he taps his fingers on the bar counter. "How are you?"

"I'm doing all right," I shrug continuing to look at the magazine. "How's your day?"

"So so," he shrugs to himself. A smile creeps across her face, "Jus' tryin' to make a livin' and missin' you of course." Corny line, but it still makes me smile. "What about you?"

With another turn of a page, not really reading any more, I reply, "Oh I've had better."

"Why? What's goin' on?" He asks sounding concerned, which I hate. When he sounds all genuine and what not, it makes me feel like crap for dumping my teenage drama queen problems on him.

"Nothing," I sigh looking down at another 'is he interested in you' quiz. God people, if he sends you 'be gone' signals it probably means he's not going to ask you to dinner.

"Kie ..." he says slowly feeding into my silly teenage mind game.

I decide to make an attempt to humor myself by taking the quiz even though reality already revealed his signals to take me to dinner meant he wanted to take me to dinner, "Really, my friends and me were just talking about homecoming today."

Quickly he questions, "And?"

Forgetting instantly that I want to take a shot at the quiz I begin a nervous doodle. I hope he catches on to where I'm going with this, "They all want to go, and they want me to go ..."

"Oh," the cheerfulness leaks from his voice. That's not a good sign.

"I said I'd talk to you about it," I nervously chew on top lip. "So what do you think about us going and making a little bit of an appearance next weekend?"

Silence. Good thing my mom pays for air to play ping-pong back and fourth through the phone. I know it doesn't take this long to answer yes or no, especially considering this isn't a life and death situation about his reputation or social status, which isn't everything, but it is something.

I scratch through the picture for the quiz I mumble, "Any day now."

"No," he says without considering my feelings, unless it was done during the five minute grace period, which I highly doubt.

Positive I misheard I blurt out, "What?" I know he didn't say no after all the bull he put me through as not wanting to appear to be his girlfriend.

"No. I don't wanna go," he says so quickly I feel like he didn't even take the time to rethink his feelings.

"But," I slowly start off growing a very strong urge to want to go. By far I am one of those people who when you tell them they can't have something they instantly want it. I know. I know. I can't help all my childish impulses. "I do. Besides, you're my boyfriend, and you're supposed to go with me."

Taking another moment he says in a laid-back attitude, "Well. I'm not. It's not a big deal."

"To hell if it isn't," I snap back. "It's a very big deal. It's a social appearance I have to make—

"Ten seconds ago you didn't even wanna go!"

"That's not the point. Look I have to go and I would like you to be there with me." Now maybe he's forgotten high school is about status, being liked, and the social appearances you do and do not make. I've got a great amount of friends and people who I adore that are expecting me to be there. If I didn't show up it would be like committing social suicide.

"I'm not that kinda guy Kie. I've never been the guy to be into anything school related besides the basketball games, which I played in, and an occasional football game—

Promptly I interrupt, "Let this be the occasional football game!"

"No."

"But Billy—

"I don't have to have those occasional games any more because I'm not still in fuckin' high school," he snaps at me with so much bite I feel like I need a Band-Aid. "I refuse to sit through some high school bullshit dance where the music's whack and you gotta be patrolled by teachers."

"But—

He reinforces one more time that he won't go, "I ain't doin' that shit fo' no one, not even you." Oh I know this fool is not raising his voice at me like he's lost his damn mind. I think he has lost whatever commonsense he once gained.

"Excuse me," I say in a slow rude tone back at him. Tossing my pen down I say, "Suddenly it's asking too much from you to attend a harmless football game and a little dance?"

"Yeah," he quickly answers without actually taking time to think about it. "I don't even know if I'm gonna be able to get off work next weekend. Besides, even if I do I damn sure don't wanna sacrifice my weekend and the few hours I get wit' you, on some worthless bullshit."

"Sacrifice?" I say surprised to hear *him* use that word. "What happened to it doesn't matter what we do as long as you're with me? Oh I guess you meant ALMOST anything?" With a deep breath I continue, "I guess I haven't sacrificed enough for you huh? Heaven knows getting shot at, deadly driving, time with my best friend, and the open honest relationship I use to have with my mom before you, aren't enough sacrifice on my part. I'm sorry," I fake apologize. "I am so sorry for being un-thoughtful, Mr. Sacrifice. I guess I'm just being selfish all of sudden, so let's do all the things that YOU wanna do!"

"You're being ridiculous."

"You're being ridiculous!"

"Kie you're really bein' over dramatic I—

"I am not being over dramatic," I huff.

Billy rolls his eyes finally fed up, "Look I'm not goin', so grow up and get over it."

Did he just say grow up? I want to go to a little bitty dance, and he throws a hissy fit, yet I'm the one who needs to grow up? Slowly I form the words, "Grow up?"

"Yeah," he slouches against the barstool. "You're actin' like a child, and you know it."

"How's this for childish?" I hang up. Fuck him for calling me childish. The only person who can call me childish is my mother, and that's because she gave birth to me.

Who does he think he is? I don't know who kicked his asshole switch on, but if he's not careful I'm gonna switch it back off with my knee in his balls. Am I seriously asking too much from him? I mean I can understand not wanting to go, but he could have at least thought about how I felt, or how it came out when he said no. He should never be so rude to his girlfriend. Jackass.

Billy looks at the phone seeing the ended call. Tossing it on the bar he rolls his eyes again.

He opens where his pictures are to share the

His boss slings the dry rag over his shoulder, "You look a little distressed."

Shrugging it off and he rests his elbows on the bar, "Hunnie problems."

"Oh," he nods. "I feel ya on those. What's the deal?"

"She wants me to go do some'n wit' her that I don't wanna do, and she threw a temper-tantrum, like always, when I said no. It's not like I was tellin' her I don't wanna marry her or some'n," he shakes his head. "I don't know what the big fuckin' deal is. I have my reasons; are they not good enough?"

His boss looks at him while continuing to smack on his gum. After a moment he leans down on the bar, "Look kid. If it's one thing I've learned about women it's that you end up giving up a lot more for them than the other way around. Besides it pleases them, making the relationship a whole lot more enjoyable for the both of you. Ka-peesh?"

Billy shrugs, "So I should do what she wants? Like I'm fuckin' whipped? Like I'm a dog?"

"Naw. I never said play lap puppy," he shakes his head. "Let me ask you this. Do you love this girl?"

"Well ... I ... um—

"Let me rephrase that. Do see yourself loving her?" After getting a nod out him he continues. "Is she worth anything in this world? Is there something you WOULDN'T give up to see her smile? Honestly IF she's the best thing going for you why wouldn't you do what you can to keep her?" His boss gives him a stern almost fatherly look, something very unfamiliar to him.

Billy looks down at the bar again and over at his phone. He was right. There's nothing he wouldn't give up to see me happy. What was wrong with him? Why did he react the way he did?

Slowly he rests his head down, "Well she doesn't wanna talk to me now."

Taking the dry rag to start shinning the bar again he questions, "What makes you say that?"

"She hung up on me. That's a clear sign to leave her alone."

"Are you sure? I mean some girls expect you to call back and show you care and all that."

"Not my Kie," he licks his lips. "If she hung up on me, I'll be lucky to talk to her befo' tomorrow at the earliest."

"Mmhm. You got a picture of this girl?"

As he pulls out his wallet he explains, "She's the reason I went out and got this job. Had to be a better man." He opens where his pictures are to share the carnival pictures, "That's her."

"Damn. She is a PYT," he nods. "I see what the fuss is over."

Billy chuckles a bit of a sigh, "Yeah."

"She looks like a keeper, but it's you who has to date her."

Billy starts drifting off into the picture as his boss leaves him to answer the phone.

"Did he really?" Mia questions me as I yell into my cell phone while I pace around the room.

"The nerve of him calling me childish! Oh and then to tell me I don't sacrifice? Who does he think he is Mary Teresa?" I growl.

"It's Mother Teresa," Mia giggles cutting me off.

I sneer, "Ugh you know what I meant."

"Calm down," she smiles. "I think you need a little break away from all of this, so why don't you come have dinner with me and a friend of mine?"

"Which friend?" I put my movement on pause.

"You don't know him," she pulls up to a stoplight. Before I can object she says, "Change. I'm seven minutes away."

I hang up and quickly squeeze myself into a graphic tee that shows a little midriff. Staring at myself in my full length mirror as I slip into the jeans I wore to school, I know Mia's going to accuse me of trying to look cute to spite Billy. I'm not sure if that's true or not, but I don't think I need to decide right now.

Quickly grabbing my purse I toss my cell phone into it. I scribble a note on the fridge's dry erase board letting my parents know I went out.

"Hurry up," she leans her head out the window. Oh I know this heifer isn't rushing me after the day I've had.

I climb in her mini SUV and toss her a scold.

"What?" She pleads innocently. I continue looking at her like she's crazy. "Oh all right. I'm sorry for rushing your whinny ass."

As she backs up out of my driveway I mumble, "Uh-huh."

"So Billy really pushed a nerve with you huh?"

Buckling my seatbelt I snap, "A nerve? Try all of them. I don't know what he's trippin' on but he needs to get over it fast before I—"

"Calm down," she looks at me after switching lanes. "There's no need to be so hostile."

No she didn't tell me to calm down. Of all the un-calm and irrational people I know, who threaten to rip out hair and break bones every other day, she has no room to try to tell me to calm down.

"Don't get me wrong though. If he would have been here and said those things to my face I would have took my shoe off and done some serious damage. But," Mia turns and looks at me, "instead you have to do what females do best." Turning back towards the front she steps on the gas, "Make him feel guilty and jealous."

I shake my head. I said I was done playing these games with guys. No male is worth that much hassle, not even the boy I was considering my prince charming. That's just too much work for me. "Nah. No more games Mia."

"Not games," she insists. "Think of it as activities that must be completed in order to put him back in check."

"Mmhm big difference," I look out the window. Feeling my phone start to vibrate I hear his special ringer. I pull out my cell phone to stare at it blankly. No. Oh hell no. Kie is currently unavailable.

"Don't you answer that," she snatches and tosses it in the backseat. It continues ring as we pull up to a small Chinese food restaurant. This must be where we're meeting her friend. Her friend? Who the hell are we meeting?

"Who are we meeting here?" I ask again preparing to get out.

She smiles pulling her mirror down to fix her lip gloss, "Just wait." After she's done she grabs her bag and my cell phone.

I follow her into the place where the guy is already sitting down at a booth looking at a menu.

Clearing her throat she states, "Ryan. I'd like you to meet Kie. Kie meet Ryan from my chemistry class," she licks her lips as he looks up and smiles.

Damn! Now that's one fine ass looking white boy. His sleeveless shirt is clinging to his tan built chest revealing some very eye catching arms. Tilting my head I start to imagine what the rest of him looks like, until Ryan stands up to shake hands with me. In my head I let out a deep sigh. No need to wonder any more. It's even better than I thought. Where the hell has this boy been hiding? I know most of all the jackasses who attend our school, and I have never seen this wonderful piece of art a day in my life.

"Hey," I politely say shaking his hand.

"Hi," his crooked smirk is making me bite my bottom lip a little. Damn.

"Nice to meet you," I say still holding his hand.

"You too," he smiles fully, this time making my knees weak. Looking this fine should be some sort of crime against humanity. And why am I still holding his hand?

"Ryan just moved here a couple of weeks ago," she smiles to herself proudly. "He doesn't have many friends, so I thought we could help him along." Mia gives me a look like I should start messing with him even though I'm already with Billy.

"Oh," I nod managing to pry my hand away from his. Politely I sit down across from him, "That explains why I haven't seen you around."

"Yeah," he nods licking his lips softly drawing my attention to those delicious looking things.

What has Mia done? You are not supposed to lead me to temptation. You're supposed to lead me AWAY! I'm not a cheater in any way, but from the way Billy's acting and the looks of this fine boy have me rethinking my scruples.

Smirking again she sits next to me, "Ryan moved from Rome. His family moves around the world for his dad's company, but they moved back to the U.S., so that he could graduate with friends."

"Rome?" No wonder the fine boy came back with a tan and an accent.

"Yeah." With a heart warming smile that he explains himself, "I lived there for a few years. I … uh … know plenty of Italian still." Continuing to struggle with his speech he says, "English has always been … how you say …"

"Difficult?" Mia finishes his statement for him.

"Yes, yes," he nods.

"Wow. You have a girlfriend back home?" I ask trying not to be too forward. I don't care for my own personal reasons. I'm just trying to be friendly.

"Um …" he starts stuttering trying to find the right words again. "We … um … have taken what you call a …" all the struggling just makes the boy more attractive, "Time … out …?"

Enthusiastically Mia questions, "A break?"

"Yes."

"Oh," we both say together like there's something we would like to do about it. I know there's something she would love to about it, but not me. Ironic the first decent looking guy comes around when I'm finally taken.

"How do you like the United States?" I stuff my phone deep in my purse.

"It's …" he starts struggling again driving Mia and me crazy. "Different. But … the women here are … beautiful."

Mia and me giggle as we look at each other.

"Like you ladies," he compliments us. I shouldn't let him hit on me like this, maybe he doesn't even realize it. Let's go with that idea. With a smile he sighs, "You … are … how we say in Italy … sexy oltre credenza."

I lean over and whisper in her ear, "What does that mean?"

She shrugs as she whispers back in my ear, "Beats the hell out of me."

"Could you two help me … or … order," he smiles again making me just fall back against the booth. God is testing me. All I have to do is get through dinner without flirting, and I'll pass.

"The egg rolls or the orange chicken is good," I give my two cents.

"Or the sweet and sour shrimp," Mia points on his menu being flirty about it.

"I like shrimp," he looks up at her. "In Italy they say," he begins smiling once more. Shutting his menu he says, "Il gambero è un aphrodisiac per il sesso migliore."

We look at each other still confused. This boy is sexy and all, but it would be nice if he came with a human translator or subtitles.

"What does that mean?" I quickly question.

With a laugh he shakes his head, "Forgive me ... I ... forget that you don't know Italian much like me ..." he says in the most sincere voice I've ever heard any guy use. Now why can't Billy use that tone of voice with me? "It means ... shrimp is an ... aph ... aphro ... aphrodisiac for better sex."

We look at each other once more. To hear that boy say the word sex makes my heart skip like a scratched CD. Stop it Kie. I'm not supposed to be thinking about him this way. Why is it when your man makes you mad suddenly other guys become more appealing than ever?

"Oh," Mia gets excited in her seat as the waitress comes over to us to take our order.

"I wouldn't mind ..." he begins struggling again. "To ... have ... another date with you two ..."

"Wait Romeo," I say coming back to some of my senses. "This is not a date. We're just having a nice meal together as *friends*."

"I wouldn't mind being a little more than that," Mia mumbles under her breath. I shoot her a glance.

Shaking his head at us he pleas, "I ... didn't mean ... any disrespect."

"No disrespect here," Mia quickly says back sighing. Quickly she sings like a jailbird, "She has a boyfriend."

"My apologies bello," he says softly. Did he just call me Jell-O? "I did not mean to ... hit on you if you will ... I am not a man to ... break up a couple ..."

"Good to know," I smile as I feel my phone start to go off in my purse. Annoyed I sigh, "Damn it Mia order the sesame chicken for me." Picking up my phone I say rudely, "Hello."

"Kie," Billy's voice whimpers out on the other end.

"What?" I snap.

Still in an innocent voice he asks, "Do you not want to talk to me right now?"

"Would you want to talk to you?"

"No," he sheepishly says. "If I call you later tonight, will you talk to me then?"

Lowering my head I mumble, "Call then, and we'll see."

"Ok," he sounds like a hurt puppy dog, which serves him right for being so rude to me. "I'll try back then."

I hang up and look at Mia who's flirting with the hot foreign guy, making me just wish Billy weren't acting like such a prick right now. Maybe things will look up tonight, maybe not.

Mia snaps her fingers at me as I stare at her lunch, "Kie."

"Hm?" I look up from the bag of chips I've barely touched.

"It won't kill you to go ahead and buy Billy a ticket," she stuffs another fry in her mouth. "He said he was going to do his very best to try, so just go ahead and do it. If push comes to shove you will have just wasted twenty bucks, which I'm sure he'll give back to you if it matters that much."

Mia dips more fries into the ketchup and just lets it run down onto the plate. I roll my eyes at her eating habits. Must she leave a mess? It's like watching the lions prey on zebra bodies on the Discovery Channel. Sometimes I wonder where's the camera that's supposed to be zoomed in on her, and the announcer saying 'this small beast feeds on all sorts of things any time of the day and does not take no for answer.'

"Kiara I mean it," she points her ketchup finger at me. I wish she'd be careful. The last thing I need is ketchup on a white jacket.

I don't say anything to her still. Looking at my bottle of water that has water half way in it I ponder. Why is it someone always wants to know if the bottle is half empty or full? Why does it matter, and on top of that does it have to be one or the other all the time? Doesn't everyone have both days? If it's half empty you're a negative person who only sees the worst part of everything, who only plans for the nastiest outcomes in life. If you see it as half full, then everything is positive and you're just so optimistic that everything in your life just has to be the best thing to ever happen to you. Screw that. No one always has good days and no one always sees things the worst they can, or at least I don't. The glass is neither for me. The glass is just half. Half.

"I'm sure you do sparky," I get ready to bite into a chip when Danny plops down next to me. Now I know I'm being taped on the Discovery Channel.

"Hello," Danny licks his lips at me.

Mia sneers in disgust, "Didn't know they let the puppies out of the pound to play."

"Always a pleasure to be in the presence of television stars," he looks her up and down.

Confused, she stops mid bite of another fry, "Excuse me?"

"Yeah, ya know a lot more people watch the Animal Planet now a days," he smirks rudely at her. Ouch. Mia opens her mouth to snap back, but Danny turns and looks back at me. "Anyway …"

I look at Mia and shake my head, letting her know to just let it go. On a normal day I wouldn't mind watching the lion destroy the gladiator, but I'm far from in the mood today. Understanding how I'm feeling, Mia resists the urge to whack him.

He checks me out in the most obvious way possible, "I was wondering are you going to homecoming."

"Why?" Mia quickly asks wiping off the ketchup from the side of her lip thats been there since the first fry she ate.

Annoyed he rolls his eyes and ignores her, "I was hoping that I'd get a chance to dance with the most beautiful girl that will be arriving that night."

I try not to smile at being flattered. Although he is repulsive most of the time, I know when he pays a compliment he means it. He's not just one to throw out words like that and not mean it. Surprising I know.

Licking his lips slowly he slides closer to me, "After all, wouldn't you like to dance with one of the star players from the winning game?"

"I'm sure that would be nice, but one of them hasn't asked her yet," Mia rudely intrudes.

"Funny. Good to know they're finally going to add a comedy section to the Discovery Channel. Maybe they can call it when 'Animals talk back'."

Is the constant bloodshed really needed? Can't they take the hate they have for each other and the very nerve racking animosity elsewhere?

"I'm going to homecoming," I toss the chip aside feeling my appetite disappear.

"With her boyfriend," she quickly reminds him that I am taken. "You met him remember?"

"Oh yeah, mini Tupac," he sarcastically says. Who does he think he is? I didn't open the door for sarcasm.

"As opposed to Brad Pitt's stunt double?" She tears back.

Wasn't this conversation supposed to be directed towards me? What the hell happened? They find something new to argue about every six seconds.

"You know what," he starts off getting defensive.

"Hey!" I announce grabbing my water bottle. "I don't mean to interrupt the never ending war between beauty and the jock, but I'm not really in the mood for the fighting, so is there a point either of you are coming to any time soon?"

Danny slowly looks back at me. "Sorry," he apologizes. Good boy, just like man's best friend. "I was just hoping I could have the pleasure of getting a dance with you. Ever since Casey's party I've just had this craving to dance with you."

"Well we'll see …" I push the bag towards Mia. He opens his mouth to say something else, but I quickly interrupt him. "And that will be the best answer you can have as of this moment. Now Danny if that's all, you can go."

"Later Kie," he gets up and walks away to meet up with some of his friends that were rushing him to hurry up. I swear he's from one of those teenage movies. Sometimes I would love to do nothing more than shove him down a flight of stairs.

"Do you actually plan to dance with that dick for brains?" Mia snaps at me.

"Don't start," I point at her fiercely. Attempting to change the subject I casually ask, "Who's your victim?"

Mia takes out her compact disk to touch up her make up while continuing to talk to me. Rubbing her lip gloss across her lips she sighs, "Either the captain of the football team who plans to lead us to victory or the captain of the basketball team who will three point our school into a championship and possibly into my life."

I didn't know people actually said corny lines like that out loud. Shaking my head I sigh, "Why the captains? I know you know the only reason why they're going to ask you if they do."

"Yup," she nods closing the compact disk. With a smile she lets her eyes wonder to one of them, "To bag the one they can't. It's a fun game that never gets old."

"To you," I mumble and roll my eyes.

"What?" she snaps away from eye-fucking long enough to respond.

I clear my throat throwing away the bag of chips that's barely empty, "Nothing."

"What do you say we do a bit of dress shopping this weekend?"

Realizing it doesn't matter how much I don't want homecoming to arrive, it's coming, with me on board or without me. "Sure."

I don't want to dress shop, I don't want to keep fighting with my boyfriend about homecoming because nothing valuable comes out of it, and I don't want to be forced to dance with some scum sucking slime balls who just want to get me drunk at some after party so they can feel me up hoping to get farther the next time, although they'll tell they're friends they slept with me anyway. I don't want to dance around annoying preppy girls who aren't really dancing, as so to rocking back and fourth in place to a 'special rhythm' in their head. I don't want to do any of it, but of course it doesn't matter what I want. It's everyone else in the world I have to please. Just once I'd like for the attention and focus to all be on me. Just once I'd like everyone to go great lengths to please me, to make me feel special, to make me feel like more than I'm worth. Go figure that I always want what I can't have.

I struggle trying to zip up a dress as Mia talks on her cell phone outside waiting to see it. Lucky for her she fits so lovely in EVERYTHING and is the PERFECT size for all the marvelous dresses. I, on the other hand, actually have to search for things that fit all aspects of my body. I hate her.

"Mia," Billy pleads at her. "I can't make it."

Stomping her foot she pouts, "Why not?"

As he finishes tying his shoes he grunts, "I can't get of work Friday night … of either kind," he passes by DK who's on the couch switching channels. "My boss told me he'd give me Saturday night off—

"Which is perfect!" Mia exclaims not letting him finish.

"Not quite," Billy enters the kitchen. "I've got a deal that goes down that night, and I have to be here."

"Push it back," she argues.

"Can't."

"And why not? I thought you were done with that sort of thing?"

Grabbing a bottle of water from the fridge he snaps, "First off I don't appreciate the attitude. It's uncalled fo'. Second of all, do you 'member what happened the night you guys visited over here?"

Mia hesitantly answers, "How could I forget?"

"Let's jus' say we'd loose some customers causin' us to take from others, havin' a repeat offense like the one you two had on that marvelous evenin'," he says sarcastically. "I can't make it."

Trying to stay on her toes she quickly asks, "Why can't DK do it alone? Or why can't it wait another night?"

"DK could get jumped if he went alone to do our usual. Besides this isn't like a real job. Shit don't get pushed back at my convenience. Now look I'm sorry Mia, and let Kie know I'm sorry too," he sighs.

"Yeah."

"I tried …"

"Sure."

"I did."

"Jus' not hard enough," she mutters. "I hope you know you're letting her down again. She does nothing but give you chances to step up to the plate and be the man she's looking for. I'm warning you. If you don't start to change you're going to loose a great girl and kill yourself later for it."

Billy doesn't say anything. He just fiddles with the lid on his water bottle, "Look just send me my ticket and pass in the mail a'ight?"

"Yeah," Mia rolls her eyes. "Whatever."

"Great. You're mad at me too?"

"Yeah," she bluntly remarks. "I have to go though; your girlfriend's trying on dresses to impress no one. Bye."

Billy pounds his fist on the counter making DK mute the TV and turn around.

"What's wrong wit' you now?"

Angrily Billy asks, "Why can't this deal jus go down on Sunday?"

"'Cause we're suppliers and have money to make when it's time to make it."

"I don't give a damn DK," he plants his hand firmly on the bar leaning over. "This shit is fuckin' up my life! I'm tired of havin' to blow off my girl, so I can help you make paper I don't need. I've got real responsibilities, a real job DK." Under his breath he mumbles, "You should get one."

"Nigga this is a real job," he gets up off the couch. "What, 'cause you got yo'self a lil' nine to five you think you hot shit? You need to get a hold of yo'self, and realize this shit is what's really taken care of you and will be the only thing here fo' you when that bitch of yours and job fuckin' fail. Me and this job are all you ever had and all you ever will, so stop complainin' and suck it up."

He looks down at the sink. After letting it sink in he looks back up, "Look DK … we've been boys since we were young, but I ain't cut out fo' this. I've got more important things to do in my life."

"Like what? Play love struck boyfriend every other weekend? You really think this girl is different than every other girl you been wit'? I let you pretend long enough that bitch makes a different. Well I've got news fo' you," DK takes a step closer to him. "She's not yo' fuckin' fairy godmother. She's nothin' more than yo' every day hunnie coded wit' morals and values. She can't do nothin' new fo' you, and she damn sure can't change you. And you know why?" With another step he reiterates, "You know why? 'Cause thugs don't change. You can change their surroundins, you can change they place of business, and you can even change the women they fool 'round wit', but you can't change a thug. You of all people know that."

Billy looks down again as DK continues.

"Don't act like you forgot who you are. It's time you stop frontin' and look in the mirror playboy. You ain't nothin' more than the average thug. You'll never be nothin' more or nothin' less."

Looking hard at him Billy feels a lump in his throat. The sort of lump that comes when you're trying to swallow the truth and just can't get it down.

A week later I'm over at Mia's house pouting on her bed while looking at my black dress that's staring at me in a taunting manner. It sucks having a very sexy, very flirty dress with no one to enjoy it.

Falling backwards onto Mia's in between bed, you know the stupid bed who's sick of being a twin, but isn't quite ready to be a queen yet, I let out a deep sigh.

"Kiara," she walks out of her bathroom in a tight red tube top dress that stops right below her knee with so much sparkle it looks like a bottle of glitter threw up on her. It's like something out of a Jennifer Lopez reject magazine. She calls my name again. And then again. Can't she dance the night away with a back up dancer and just leave me here to wallow in my own misery? "Kiara!" Guess not.

"Yeah," I pop open an eye to see her peering down over me with half of her hair done.

"Why aren't you dressed yet?" I give her hair a wince over noticing its straight down the very ends where all the curls lie, like she's from an Herbal Essence commercial.

"Because I'm not going," I close my eyes again and yawn.

Kicking her bed, which makes me bounce up and down, she quickly growls, "Oh you're going."

"Is that because my boyfriend is going to be there? Or is it because the music is going to suck? Or maybe I'm going for the jackass who thinks it cute to play cat and mouse?" I sit up with my shoulders slumped, my eyes a bit droopy, and frown imprinted on my face.

"Good," she smiles sarcastically. "I'm glad you've got the right homecoming spirit." Mia treads back into her bathroom to finish curling her hair.

"Sorry for being selfish," I yell falling backwards.

"I forgive you. Just get off your lazy ass and get dressed," Mia yells back.

A couple hours later we're dressed, full from dinner, and at the dance with the other people who have decided to waste a Saturday for a school related function.

I feel like I'm a marshmallow roasting on an open fire. If I didn't look so hot in my black halter top dress that hugs my curves in the right way, I wouldn't force myself to stay here. While my cute up do compliments my outfit, I like to think my jewelry does it better.

Danny so casually slides an arm around my waist and spins me around, "Hey gorgeous."

"Hey," I say back trying to smile.

"A dance?" He asks, as the song is getting ready to change. "Please?"

I sigh and look at Mia whose grinding so hard it looks like she's trying screw a nail into the ground. That makes me miss Billy even more knowing I can't grind with my boyfriend like she does with her plaything. Glancing at Danny again I feel my stomach turn because he's not an adequate replacement, not even for a second.

"Sure," I let him lead me to the center where the other couples are dancing. I can't believe this was once my sanctuary, and now it's a miserable place I would be forced to wallow in alone if Danny wasn't after me like a dog in heat.

How ironic is it that the first important event where a boyfriend should be shown off Billy is busy? We haven't talked in almost a week, and I don't even know how he feels about me anymore. I wonder at times is it all worth it? Was the wonderful night we had in Ft. Worth worth all the trouble we have to go through to make this relationship work? I mean I know relationships are about work and struggles, but only when two people put everything into it. I guess you could say I feel like I'm in a relationship by myself, working for myself, and trying to make myself happy.

Danny and I begin dancing together; leaving enough space between us to make sure he doesn't think he's getting any closer to me than necessary. Although I admit I enjoy a good grind, I have a boyfriend and know he wouldn't appreciate it if I was closer to him than I needed to be.

We dance through a fast song and right into another. During our dance session I hear girls start to whisper and awe about something. Taking a moment I look at Danny and realize all of his attention is directed at me. Wow. I haven't seen a guy look at me like that in a while. As sweet as it is for him to pour all of his thoughts into me, mine are still wondering how Billy could just leave me deserted on something that's really important to me.

I hear the fast song fade so that the DJ can make an announcement.

"This next song is dedicated to a special girl whose man wants her to know that she means everything in the world to him, and that he doesn't know where he'd be without her," the DJ announces making some girls awe. Lucky bitch. "Kiara, this one is to you," he says my name making me turn around to see what the hell he's talking about. Now I know I'm not the only Kiara that goes to this school, but the thought peaks my interest.

The DJ puts on a classic R&B song I love, making me cringe at the thought of having to dance with Danny to it.

Slowly the crowd parts as someone walks towards the center of the dance floor where I am. I really hate when movie moments happen in the real world. Ignoring whoever's glory moment it's supposed to be, I look down to see if my shoes are still clean since I paid so much money for them.

"Kie," I hear what sounds like Billy's voice. Afraid to look up I don't move. "Kiara," he says again this time I force myself to. Holy mother of god, it is Billy.

What … how … why … I … Wait. Is my mind playing a sick game with me? Is this all just a dreamt up moment I'll later regret for having. Giving him another glance over I casually pinch myself to make sure I'm not dreaming. Yup. He's really here … with a damn rose in his hand. Ugh. And it's red. In a very sweet tone he asks, "Can I have this dance?"

I've got girls who are dying for me to say no, so that they can jump at the chance to get after him, and all the guys waiting for me to say yes, so that they can have their girls' attention back. Even in a romantic situation I can't say no even if I wanted to. Splendid.

"Yes," I place my hand in his that's been dangling there and just waiting for me to accept it. Slipping the rose into my free hand I casually toss both arms around his neck and begin to slowly sway to the music.

As we begin to dance I see Mia jumping around like a kangaroo on speed. I wish someone would calm her happy ass down before she gets hurt jumping around in those heels.

I pull back to look Billy in his eyes that look like they've been crying. What does he have to cry about? A little upset his big bad girlfriend hasn't talked to him in a week?

"I'm sorry Kie," he starts to apologize as we continue dancing. An apology? Did Porky grow wings? "I—

"Later," I put my finger to his lips. Finding it somewhere in me to smile, I simply say, "Right now, just dance with me."

Billy holds me the closest I think he's ever held me before. I hold him closer as I rest my head on his shoulder listening to him sing softly under his breath. His fingers lightly rub my back in a very soothing way.

The DJ ends up playing two romantic songs in a row, which turns out to be the most romantic six minutes I've experienced with Billy since our first date.

When the song is over Billy lifts my head off of his shoulder and meets eyes with me. I've missed staring into his hazel brown eyes like this.

"Are you ready to go?" He asks still talking to me in the sweet tone he use to when he first started going after me.

"Are you?" I ask back feeling him fold his hand with mine.

"Whenever you are baby," he smiles softly. "This night is all about you."

Those are strange words that I don't understand.

I'm fairly certain my social appearance has be set and completed. "Let's go then," I say allowing him to lead me to the exit. Walking faster than I expected I point back towards Mia, "Don't we need to tell—

"Naw," he shakes his head walking slowly with me. Leaning over, he whispers in my ear with a smile on his face, "She already knows." Billy puts his hand on my back helping me through the crowd.

Once we're in his car we drive in silence to wherever it is he's taking me. My hand is on his thigh and his hand is on top of mine rubbing it softly with most the tender touch.

You know what? Now I'm scared. At first I thought maybe he was trying to live up to the prince charming image he set for himself, but now I think he's trying to set me up for some sort of deeper blow. Like one that's going to hurt a lot worse than I ever thought possible and I know I won't be able to handle it. What if he breaks up with me? Seriously I mean what if that's what this is all about? What if all this sweet talk and moves are just to soften the blow of telling me he's finally ready to move on to something better? Better than me though? What happened to all that talk about me being the best for him? What happened to me changing his life? He wouldn't do that to me would he? On my homecoming?

After a forty-five minute drive we arrive in front of the lake where Billy backs in so that his trunk is facing the lake. Does he have like a dead body in the trunk that he wants to dump, but doesn't want me to tell anyone about? Am I dating like a murder? What dating a thug wasn't enough, now you're dating a killer too? Great Kie, a drug-dealing killer. Your mother would be proud.

Billy looks over at me, turns off his car, turns up his radio, and gives me the nod to get out of the car. I smile and get out as well, walking around towards the back leaving the red rose sitting so nicely in my seat. Once I meet with him around at the back I simply look at him. He hops up on the trunk and offers a hand to help me up, which I take.

I forgot just how beautiful the lake looks at nighttime with the moon shinning so beautifully down on it. It's like one of those romantic moments you dream about as a kid never believing you'll actually see it.

"It's a beautiful night," I say trying to break the strange tension that's dividing us right now.

"It doesn't compare to you," he smiles scooting a little closer to me. Classically appropriate line.

With a smile I lean over to give a small kiss, but see him move away from me. Now he won't even let me kiss him? Great. He *is* breaking up with me.

"What's wrong?" I ask folding my hands in my lap.

He takes a long stare at me see and then out at the lake. Bringing me to the lake to break my heart sounds a bit un-thoughtful doesn't it?

"Kie," he starts off licking his lips slowly. After a deep breath he says, "There's some things I need to tell you."

This isn't good. See I knew I shouldn't get mixed up with guys. All they bring is heartache and pain. I always get my hopes up with them. It really is a pointless conquest.

"And I don't know," he begins to struggle thinking about it. "But I know that you need to you know 'em 'cause it's been killin' me not tellin' you."

"Ok ..." I ponder out loud still looking at him.

"I know I've been actin' a bit shady lately," he starts off like guys who have cheated start. Did he cheat on me? It's one thing to make me think that he's killed someone, but I know if this fool's cheated on me it will be his body they find in that lake. "I've hurt you, and I never wanted to do that."

"What's her name?" I hop down off the trunk of his car.

Looking at me confused Billy asks, "What?"

"Monique? Jackie? Shantel?" I tap my foot impatiently.

"Wait I—

"I will not hesitate to find her, drown the both of you, and leave you to float in your watery tombs," I raise my voice at him making it all the more harder for him to talk to me. "How could you cheat on me?"

"No Kie," he shakes his head immediately, reaching for me to bring me closer. "That's not how I get down. You know that."

"Then what's this all about?" I rush him.

He slips his hand into mine and looks deep into my eyes. "Lately I haven't exactly been the best boyfriend," he begins to look me in my eyes. That's a good start. Maybe I should sit down for this. I hop back on the hood of the car and snuggle next to him.

"Not really …"

Smiling at me trying to be modest for him he continues, "Far from the best. I'm not exactly the guy who I thought I was." So is this the part of the conversation where he rips off his face and reveals his actual identity? "For the longest time I believed I could have any female I wanted, when I wanted, how I wanted," cocky much? "But then I met you. It was like the strangest wake up call. Some'n hit me tellin' me I couldn't run game on you the same way I did on every girl before."

I nod to help him along in his struggle.

"So I started feeding you what you wanted to hear. I would be a better man, I would get a job, I would change and all that other shit. I wasn't sayin' it to you to try to get you in bed, rather than just to get wit' you to prove to you, as well as myself, I still had it. But I didn't. Suddenly I was bein' who you wanted me to be, not who I knew I was," he licks his lips. That's nice to know I made him live in some false image I created. "Next thing I knew I was feeding into it. I couldn't tell the difference between who I wanted to be, and who you wanted me to be 'cause finally we were on the same page. Everything you ever dreamed of me to be was who I really wanted to be, but was just to busy fuckin' up my life to see. You know once I realized the truth about myself and the fact I was destined to be some'n I never thought I could be I got scared."

"Scared of?"

"Scared that changes would occur that were long over due, scared you'd see I was just pretendin' all along, and am really just now becomin' who I should be. Worst of all I was scared you'd leave." And the exit would be where? I never saw an excuse to leave. Do I tell him? "So I figured I'd punk out and push you away from me like every guy does. That's the way it works. A guy gets scared of commitment and change that's what he does. He punks out. He pushes the good out of his life and replaces it with his old ways of life," Billy continues staring into my eyes. Well at least he knows he does it.

"So is that …" I lead my hands to finish my sentence for me.

"That's exactly what I did. I didn't stop hustlin', bein' around chicken heads, followin' in DK's shadow once again, but that's when it hit me what I was doin'. I was hurting the girl who I had done everything to get. I was hurting the one girl I worked and put my life into gear for. I couldn't bring myself to say it or see it 'cause it just didn't seem possible. I had been sayin' it as a way of runnin' game on you, but I woke up and realized I was really fallin' in love with you." I feel his grip with my hand get tighter.

Oh no. It's bigger than dead bodies, break ups, and cheaters. The boy believes he might be in love. This is the part of life where they would flash across the screen in big red letters: This just in! Thugs can fall in love!

"When a guy can look in the mirror and see a changed man, he knows that it's time for him to man up and be real to himself. I was told that all I would ever be was a thug, and then you walk into my life and make me figure out that I'm way more than that. I literally can be whoever I wanna be. I should've been thankin' you wit' everything I have in me, but instead what do I do? Drive you away from me, hurt you, and make you feel like you've done a world of shit wrong when you've done everything right. I under estimated you from the straight up, and I was wrong for that," he apologizes softly to me. Talk about inner self struggle coming to surrender. "I've come to a point in my life where I realized you're the most important thing to me. Not weed, not my job, not DK, not even myself."

"Really?"

"Yeah. Everything I've been doin' to make myself a better person I did for you and just recently myself. You're the reason I smile during the day and have strength to go work. You're the reason I don't go to the club every other night. And you're the reason I really am a better person. Kie," he places his hand on my face ever so tenderly sending chills down my spine. "I'm not there yet, but I want you to know I'm on my way to loving you the way you want *and* need. Just pray you can bear with me on the way there 'cause I really do care about you. I just ..." he sighs, "don't know how to show you."

Not knowing exactly the right words to say I take my best shot with, "It's ok." I rub the back of his hand. "I feel ya."

"Tonight," he begins on what I assume will be another speech. "I had a deal to do, but I basically told DK to fuck off."

"You told him to what?" You mean to tell me they didn't box about that?

"I said if he wanted me to be there we had to do that shit on my time, and we beefed about it, but the deal went down early this afternoon. Afterwards I went out to buy some'n to wear and then drove however long it takes to get here just so I could give you the homecoming I never had," he kisses the back of my hand softly. "I'm sorry Kiara for not bein' here for you when you needed me. I'm sorry for overreactin' over stupid shit, and I'm sorry for not bein' the man you want." His head lowers, "I'm sorry for ... everything."

Isn't he cute? He's all worked up and upset because he's been a bad guy. Hey, at least he stepped up and realized it before it was too late.

I lift his chin up so his eyes meet mine. "Billy. It's ok. It doesn't matter any more. All that matters now is that you're here with me and do everything you can from here on out to make sure I don't go anywhere. You told me once upon a time you needed me and not to give up on you. I'm not going to give up on you, but I'm asking you not to either," I lift his falling chin once more. "Please."

He nods and hugs me. I hug back tightly feeling his body relief itself of tension.

"You're my everything Kie," he whispers as he pulls me in even closer. "I can't loose you."

I know how he feels. Some days it's the thought of him that helps me through everything. Even independent women need someone too. The most independent people are sometimes weaker than the most dependent. We're really one in the same. I didn't want to admit it, but I'm falling for him just as much as he is for me. The only difference is I'm afraid I'll hit it before he does.

"I don't wanna say I love you and let it be just another few words said between us. Now a days so many people say it without meaning it. When I do, it's gonna mean more than it ever has to me," he kisses my cheek. "No rushin' anything between us."

I nod and smile softly at him, "No rushing."

As he holds me in his arms I close my eyes and wonder what I did to inspire the prince to come out of him. Something I learned though is don't question what doesn't need to be answered.

His body slides away from mine, "Kie, are you ready to start your homecoming with me?"

"Yeah ..." I say slowly not exactly sure of what he means.

Billy hops down and holds his hand out for me to take. I place my hand in his, and he helps me down. Wrapping it around his neck, I feel him place his hands around my waist.

After everything is said and done, I know that this is guy for me. There's no need to look for anything better or set my hopes on anything higher because I really do have my prince who came and swept me off my feet. Now that I think about it, there will never be a day here after that I regret letting him into my life. Sure we have our good days and our bad, but in the end I can't see anyone else I rather make the journey with. I always thought I'd be the one to give him life, teach him what he needed to be taught, and then set him free like a dove. Little did I know that wasn't a one way street, and I wouldn't be willing to let him go for anything in the end.

PART III

HOLIDAYS

CHAPTER 11

Thanksgiving

Everyone has something to be thankful for on Thanksgiving. Whether or not it's that you simply have a roof over your head or the fact you have someone in your life that cares about you, you have something to be thankful for. Now that that is said, let me say this: I don't like Thanksgiving. Hey, all I said was everyone has something to be thankful for, not that you have to like the holiday.

Let's go over the criteria that makes up Thanksgiving and look for something to like. You sit around with relatives who only drag themselves out to eat unidentifiable dishes. I mean suddenly everything is a 'casserole' because it's put in one of those long travel pans. To make the matter of the side dishes worse, secretly in the back of your mind your thinking 'I have to clean those dishes out', which will take an eternity to do by yourself.

If the dishes aren't enough to frown about, there's that big smelly roasted bird that just sits on the table as people pry into it like hungry lions on an episode of Wild Kingdom. It's a damn roasted bird! It's not like it's anything good. It's just some once upon a time feathered friend who ate bugs and other crap for its life until it could be killed and served for the holiday set aside to be thankful for things and people, which brings me to my next point.

Why is one day set aside to thank God for everything in your life? Shouldn't you be thanking him every day of the year for letting you live another day? Tomorrow isn't promised to anyone, so why wait for that one day of the year to thank the man upstairs for blessing you with what he has?

While I admit I don't like this holiday and tend to cringe at the family gatherings, this year I plan to make more of an effort because my mom told me

Billy could come. Sure he's dragging along the one person I would be thankful not to see on this day or any other, but at least he'll be here. I guess suffering won't feel as bad as it does every other year.

"Kie," my mom peeks her head into my very neat and organized room. That's right. I took the time to make the natural disaster area look socially presentable just in case Billy gets the chance to enter. "When are the boys supposed to arrive?"

I shrug with a polite smile pulling up my khaki Capris. One of the things Billy neglected to tell me was the time he planned to arrive for the festivities. I sure hope it's soon considering the fact almost everyone else is here.

"Well your aunt and uncle just got here, so we'll be in there. I'm sure you'll look into it," she points a finger at me.

"I sure will," I zip them up and smile at her. She thinks I'm fake smiling because I have to, when I'm really smiling because I have hope that this holiday will turn itself around for once.

She leaves, making me more than thrilled to have her out of my space putting pressure on me. My poor nerves are already in overdrive, and she was really just making it worse. Billy has to pass the family test today or our relationship will definitely be in trouble.

"Cuz I'm thug baby," DK sings along with his own song.

Billy shoots him an annoyed look, "Don't you ever get tired of listenin' to the song that landed you your deal?"

"Hell naw," he shakes his head as Billy speeds up. "This song goes hard."

Rolling his eyes at DK, he just lets him go back to rapping along with the CD.

"So when are you free to come make a million dollar track?" DK turns the radio down when the next song on the CD starts.

"I don't know, but I doubt it'll make millions right away," Billy shakes his head.

"What?" DK snaps. "Since when did you start doubt'n yo' talent?"

"I haven't started doubt'n my talent. It's just that it takes awhile for things to really start to happen in this business."

"So what? What's the problem with that? You know we gon' blow up and be bigger than anything else to hit the planet," DK boasts them.

"Could," he corrects him. In an unfamiliar voice to DK he sighs, "COULD be bigger. Nothin's guaranteed in this world, especially not in this business."

DK takes a moment before he asks, "What the hell is goin' through that thick head of yours?"

"Look, I've just been thinkin' about it lately and decided I have to have a back up plan incase this music shit don't work out. I'm gonna want a fall back career."

"Alright at firs' I jus' thought you were trippin' and would faze through it, but now you're messin' me up wit' this bullshit. What happened to you? Oh wait I know what happened. You let Kie get all up in yo' head and fuck up yo' vision on life."

"She didn't fuck it up. If anything she cleared it wit'out havin' to say anything to me at all. I just realized that growin' up means facin' the real world and the demands, like the bills, the stress, and the work. As much fun as it is to dream about livin' in a million dollar crib, I can't base life on that hope alone."

"You got a female in yo' head that's doin' nothin' but damagin' you. Let me ask you this then Mr. Grown Up, what are you gonna do? Go back to school and get some degree to be some sort of doctor or some shit? Go spend money you ain't got on books and money fo' some white dude to lecture you on shit that ain't never gonna apply to you?"

"Maybe," he looks at him. "I don't know DK. Not knowin' what the world's gonna hand you is half the damn battle of life. Sure I wanna go to college one day. Who knows, I might get a business degree. You know what else?" Billy takes a deep breath gaining courage in his lungs. "I don't wanna live in D-town fo' the res' of my life."

"What?" DK asks as if not understanding. "Where you think you gonna go? The 'burbs? Go live in Austin wit' them rich motherfuckers lookin' down on yo' black ass? You wanna move there so you can be closer to this hunnie that you migh' las' a lil' while wit'? Man I can't wait 'til you let this ho' go, so you can finally come back to yo' senses."

Billy licks his lips slowly, "I might move to Austin 'cause my boss wants to relocate and has been lookin' to do it in Austin. Yeah. I wanna move 'cause my girl's there, but I can really make some'n of myself there. And you know what else DK? Kie ain't goin' nowhere. As long as Kie will have me, I'm hers. There's no other girl who can do what she can do fo' me. So this lil' beef you've got wit' her ... needs to end now. I can't have my boy fo' life beefin' wit' the girl I want forever in my life."

DK is takes many deep breaths trying to maintain his composure. "Marry this girl? This ain't the Billy that was once my boy. This is some punk ass bitch who wants to be a family man, a schoolboy, and a sell out. You want this bitch to be in yo' life forever and us to be coo' then you make sure to let her know that this hate thing is a two way street. You need to stop pointin' that finger one way. You know you've changed a lot on me? I use to know the real Billy. The nigga I risked my neck and my life fo' day in and day out. That's the nigga that's my boy. Not this foo' sittin' next to me."

Billy looks like he's ready to just pull the car over to box with him, "That's right. I've changed. I admit it. I grew up. I'm fuckin' nineteen years old with the whole world just waitin' fo' me to fail because I was raised a lil' thug boy. Well guess what DK? I didn't choose that life it was handed to me! But I'm about to choose the one I can live now. I faced it. I ain't perfect. I owe you for keepin' me alive this far, but I've got to make it alone without you. You're my boy and always will be. Thick and thin, but DK it's time fo' you to make some changes too 'cause the way you livin' now man," Billy shakes his head. "Will either land you dead or in the pen," he reassures him.

"Billy—

"I'm not lecturin' you. I'm watchin' out for you like you've done for me, and maybe you don't see it now, but one day it'll hit you that I ain't always gonna be around, and you've got to know how to handle everything in life and better yourself like I'm tryin'."

I flip my hair out of my shirt before I adjust my lip-gloss once more. As I put the finishing touches on my lips, Mia's special ringer on my cell phone begins to go off.

"Yeah," I flip it open and answer it.

"Happy Thanksgiving!" She says the most excited I've ever heard her on this holiday. I wonder what meal they're planning on serving her to make her squeal this much.

"Is it?" I say not embracing the holiday cheer like I should.

With a deep sigh Mia says, "I'm sorry I forgot I had called the Grouch who beat-up Thanksgiving." We take a moment and snicker under our breaths at the joke. "So what's up?"

"Nothin' much," I say slowly. Heading towards the front door I smirk, "I know you just called to make sure I saved you some food."

"Well … you know …" she begins to giggle. "Did you make me a plate?"

Going out the front door I close it behind me, "Yeah I did, and some peach cobbler as well as a big ass piece of chocolate cake for you when you get here."

"Good. You know a girl like to eat," she says in a voice that reminds me of DK. Gross. "Anyway, have you found a reason to have spirit this year?"

I smirk to myself trying not to gloat. "I guess I should be excited because I'm a girl who gets to see her man this year."

After her gasp she snaps, "Then you need to have a more pleasant attitude! Does he have to bring his faithful servant along with him?"

"When doesn't he?" I grumble.

"I guess that explains the snippiness."

"If you want to pin it on him, then that's fine, but I'm sure DK's presence will be appreciated by you as usual."

Mia sighs, "Sure. He gets to meet Ryan though."

Ironically enough Ryan hasn't started to fade from her world yet. Last time a guy didn't fade I was stuck dating his best friend. "Excuse me?"

"Oh yeah," she starts like she magically forgot to tell me. She didn't forget! She knew she didn't want to say anything until there was no way I could object. "Ryan's parents had to travel for the holidays, and he didn't want to go, so I invited him to come to spend it with me. My parents were happy of course. They seem to really like him." That's not a good thing. She doesn't really like it when her parents approve. Guess that's his first strike.

"They like him huh?"

"A lot. Whatever. I'm sure we'll end up having a little kissing session. Ya know, everyone needs love on the holidays."

"True," I start to smile.

Her mother starts yelling her name making her say, "Well I have to go. Mom wants me, but I'll hit the phone before I come."

Hanging up I decide I don't feel like waiting forever and a day for my boyfriend and his no good trouble making friend to arrive, especially not with it being as hot as it is. Texas won't even give cool weather a break on the holiday. Damn.

As I prepare to open the front door to enter the house I notice a Benz turns the corner towards the direction of my house. Well if it isn't prince charming in his over prized chariot. Slowly I stroll towards the curb he's going to park next to.

Billy mouths the word, damn as he bites down on his fist. Strolling towards me he sighs, "Damn. You tryin' to kill a brotha' on a holiday?"

After his arms are wrapped around my waist I innocently ask, "And what's that supposed to mean?"

"That you gon' give me a heart attack in that outfit," he shakes his head looking me up and down. Billy slowly licks his lips and starts to struggle with his words, "You look ..." he deep sighs at me.

"I look …"

"Let's just say I have even more to be thankful for this holiday." I'm just wearing a pair of khaki Capri's, a dark green tube top, with a khaki zip up vest that's unzipped over it, and a pair of flip-flops to match. I'm sure it's just because he hasn't seen me in a while. "I've missed you."

I embrace him as he does me. The sweet smell of his cologne makes me smile as I say back, "I've missed you."

"Damn. Could you two break it up?" DK gets out of the car on the sly. There's what I'm not thankful for. Shutting the door he shakes his head and groans, "I swear you two hug and kiss more than them damn magnetic bears."

"Don't be jealous 'cause nobody wants to magnet up with you," I playfully joke.

"Right," he rolls his eyes. "Heaven knows I wanna live like the two of you."

Opening my mouth to fight back I feel Billy's lips on top of mine being more tender and caring than the last time he kissed me.

"Mm," I pull away from him forgetting about the need to insult DK back. With a smirk I ask, "You drive three hours for that don't you?"

Innocently shrugging he mutters, "Among other things." He kisses me once more quickly making DK roll his eyes. This is one of those cases where the more the merrier doesn't apply.

"Can we go in already?" DK whines. "I feel like I'm roastin' like I'm the turkey."

Biting my tongue at the obvious joke I divert my attention to Billy, "Remember no hand holding, hugging, kissing, or rubbing. Nothing."

"I know the definition of nothin'," he tries to lighten the situation.

"Why not?" DK buts in again. Did we invite him into this conversation?

"Because no one knows we're actually dating. They all think we became just friends after that one date in Ft. Worth," I say still attached to him, not quite ready to let go.

I see DK's grin slowly grow into a full fledged smile, "You mean to tell me mommy and daddy dearest don't know their princess is datin' a thug?"

Does he ever listen to the questions he asks? I want to see him try telling my parents that I've fallen for a thug and have it go over real well. They only want 'what's best for me' which everyone knows is code for what *they* think is best for me. You know once they know they have no reason to object, well at least my mother doesn't. She *pushed* me to date this boy! She tried to manipulate me into dating him, and when that didn't work she *forced* me to, so she cannot complain even a little bit. If she pleas insanity for those few days she was encouraging me date him then I'm going to say that's too bad because now she's stuck with him.

"No," Billy turns around. "And we're keepin' it that way. Got it?"

"I mean if it slips ..." he begins to grin.

"How would you like my fist to slip into your face?" I make a move towards DK, but feel Billy pull me back.

He opens to argue back, but Billy cuts him off, "Look DK, on the real, don't say nothin' about it."

"Don't worry 'bout it man, but you need to talk to her befo' I put her in check," DK looks me up and down and heads towards my front door. Check me? If anyone is doing the checking it's going to be me. I'm a check my knee in his nuts if he isn't careful.

I open my mouth to say something smart back, but Billy stops me with a finger to my lips. What's this sudden need to keep cutting me off? Yeah and um, since when is it ok for him to be sticking his finger all up on lips like that? I don't know where it's been. I mean yeah he's my boyfriend, and I trust him, but I know for a fact many men don't enjoy washing they're hands.

Quickly I remove his finger and gripe, "What was that about?"

"I told DK that I'm tired of you two goin' at it all the time like Chinese fighting fish." Lame metaphor. "So DK will lay off if you do." I think my life would be perfectly fine if I never made a pack to play nicely with the devil, but for Billy I guess I can make an exception.

"I'll try," I smile at him to only receive a stern look in exchange. "What? I really will!" To seal the truth I lean up and kiss him on the lips.

"All right," he hugs me once more and plants a kiss on the cheek. Slipping his hands into his pocket he sighs, "Let's go do this."

As nice as it is to have him, I have to admit it would be nicer if we could engage in the actions of a normal couple. I guess I'll deal with what I'm given.

We walk into my house hearing them laugh hysterically about something.

With a deep breath I announce his arrival, "Mom Billy's here."

I watch her get off the couch still laughing the way she does when she's tipsy.

"Hey," she greets him in an overly friendly manner. "Glad you could come."

"Me too," he politely hugs her back trying to avoid the awkwardness in the situation.

"You kids be good in here. We're going to hang in the garage," she giggles heading for the door.

Our garage is set up like an extra living room. It's got chairs, a television, and a couch. Usually it's where my dad avoids my mom, but on holidays it's where they prefer to socialize. Stopping, she points the direction of the kitchen, "By the way, DK is already eating something in the kitchen."

Rolling my eyes I shake my head.

"Billy," my dad sticks his hand out for Billy to shake it.

"Hello sir," he smiles his gentlemen smile. Good, win them all over for a second time.

My father peeks into the kitchen a little and chuckles, "DK."

"Hey," DK nibbles on a spoonful of potato salad.

Once the last person closes the door I look over expecting to see Billy there, but instead I just see our grandfather-clock staring back at me. I walk back towards the kitchen to see him looking at DK who's piling everything in sight on his plate.

Shaking my head again, I stroll over to Billy and attach myself to his lips for a second. I gently slip my tongue into his mouth, leaning him in the corner of the kitchen where our counter meets that's hidden from eye view. I feel Billy place a hand on my face as DK stuffs a dinner roll into his mouth to drown out his grumbling. We lightly touch tongues once more before I pull away from him.

He deep sighs in satisfaction.

"Hungry?" I ask innocently removing my hands from him.

Pulling me back into him he says, "For more of that."

"Thought you guys weren't gonna be doin' that stuff," DK complains putting his plate in the microwave.

"Yeah, well no ones around," I press my body back against his.

He argues back pressing the start button, "Someone could walk in."

"Then be a good friend and play look out," Billy says quickly pressing his lips feverishly against mine. I suck his bottom lip into my mouth this time, sucking on it softly occasionally grazing my tongue against it making his wobble against me.

"Do ya'll have to do that 'round the food?" he points to the dishes surrounding us. "That's contamination."

Ignoring him, Billy struggles to with stand the pleasure of having me play prisoner with his bottom lip. I can feel Billy slowly run his hands down to my lower back right above my behind. Now I can't get too wrapped up into this myself because the second I do I will just completely forget all about the fact someone could catch us. After all, we all know DK has to be the worst lookout alive. Good thing this isn't war because we'd probably all be captured thanks to him. I slowly graze my tongue teasingly against his once more and pull away.

Trying his best to make words he only lets air out first. "Are there seconds?"

"Maybe later," I shrug and slide out of his grip. "But now it's movie time."

Following behind me into the den area, he flops down on the couch. "I don't know how you think that you can kiss me like that and expect me to focus on a movie."

As I continue to smile deviously, I scan our collection of DVDs for something to watch. I simply shrug playfully, turn around to give him a wink, and go back to searching. Grabbing some random comedy movie from our cabinet I prepare to put in when my uncle and dad stagger into the den in a hurry.

"Kie go watch whatever it is you want in your room," my dad holds his hand out for the remote.

"But—

"We're gonna watch the game." I stand in front of the TV remoteless with a confused look on my face. It's clear from the expression on my face I don't understand so he quickly says, "You, Billy, and DK go watch whatever in your room."

"Naw I'm a watch the game," DK says still shoving his first bites of real food into his oversized mouth. I don't know if he's trying to be nice on the sly by letting us be alone or if he actually wants to watch the game, but it doesn't matter either way because we get to be alone!

Deciding I should make the attempt to look like it bothers me I start, "But dad—

"Look Kie, either watch the game or go in your room," he demands sternly. "No more discussion."

"Ugh fine." Fighting every urge in me to smile, I sigh, "Let's go Billy."

Without hesitation he follows me into my room. My walls are plastered in music and movie star posters. Around on any sort of stand where a frame can be, there are framed pictures of my friends. Smiling I proudly admire how clean everything is. My bed, which takes up most of the room, is the dead center draped in stuffed animals, I have a bedside table on the right side full of jewelry and other girly products, a lounge chair on the left side, my dresser is right next to you when you walk in, which is what my TV rests on. On the other side of it is my small entertainment area where my stereo, CDs, DVDs, and video games are. I often hear I've got more stuff then I have space for. Good thing I shoved a lot of my stuff in my closet.

Once he closes the door behind him I pounce on his lips again. Billy doesn't fight me. He merely wraps his arms around my waist and kisses back intensely. It probably isn't the wisest thing to make out with my dad in the next room, but what can I say? After letting our kiss linger for a moment, I pull away to look at my boyfriend who is now panting.

"You gotta stop doing that!" he snaps at me in a loud whisper. "You can't just turn me on, and then once I'm off get me all worked up again knowin' damn well we can't do anything!"

I giggle, "Sexually frustrated?" He gives me a sarcastic look. Bad question? Trying not to giggle any louder I slip the DVD in the player, hit the light, and crawl in bed next to him.

We relax against all of my pillows that are there to prop us up. Snuggling under a blanket together we leave space between us, but start holding hands in the center under the blanket.

About twenty minutes into the movie I look over at him to see him not paying attention to it. Wonder why he's staring at me? "What are you thinking about?"

"You," he smiles softly. Kiss ass. "How beautiful you are." Why does he still feel the need to suck up when he already has me? Billy places a hand on my cheek, "Ya know, I thank God every day for you, but today you're the thing that I am *most* thankful for?"

He knows just what to say to get a kiss out of me. Our lips press against each others, falling slowly into one another forgetting anyone could walk in. These kisses are a very bad idea. They're trouble.

Unexpectedly my sister opens my door to be surprised by our lip lock. Gasping she quickly closes the door behind her and turns on the light.

"What ..." she slowly strolls towards Billy's side of the bed. "What the fuck was your tongue doing in my little sister's mouth?" She grabs his throat tightly forcing him to rely on the small amount of air he was able to rob before her hand got there.

"Chenille let him go!" I yell at her and try to pry her death grip off him. What did she do, take Death Grip 101 in college?

After getting an extra squeeze in she lets him go and looks at me like I've killed someone.

"Calm down," Billy heaves.

"Don't you start with me little boy. I will slice and dice your ass turning *you* into a side dish at this feast," she points a finger at him.

Billy looks at me as if to tell me to get a hold of my crazy sister.

"'Nell it's ok," I rub his back comforting him. "Billy's my boyfriend."

As I watch the look of terror strike her once again I simply roll my head. Must she be so dramatic?

"I'm sorry. Your what?"

"Boyfriend …"

She takes a deep breath and looks at him, "Is that true?"

"Yeah," he nods clearing his throat.

Like a lawyer, which she is studying to be, she darts her head and voice into hostile witness mode, "For how long?"

"We've been together since that trip we took as a family back in June," I answer just like a witness in the biggest case of the year would say. Petrified.

"June!" She squeals like she's feeding off a jury's reaction.

"Shh," I put my finger to my lips. "They don't know yet!"

She opens her mouth to say something again, but stops letting the words process first. Chenille takes a deep breath, regains her calm composure, and folds her hands together, "Mom and Dad don't know you're dating the thug next door?" I grit my teeth. This constant reminder of his "status" is really unfair. The poor boy's not even getting credit for trying to better himself.

"No, and I'd like you to keep it to yourself if you don't mind," I continue rubbing his back until he stops me to hold his hand.

Tossing Billy the look that he is the most disgusting thing on this earth, she quickly asks me, "And why not? Don't you think they deserve to know who and what there youngest born is dating?"

"Yes 'Nell," I sigh. "Just give me time to tell them."

"Oh you need time?"

"Yes your honor."

"How much time?"

"Enough. I plan to tell them soon."

Nodding slowly she asks, "Soon? When exactly is soon?"

I shoot him a quick glance and bite my bottom lip. "Before Christmas."

"Christmas? That's almost a month away!"

"Maybe she wants to ease them into it," Billy makes an effort like an outspoken watcher in the courtroom.

"Did I ask you thugarella? Don't act like I forgot how you use to treat my baby sis," she snaps rudely.

"I—

"Shut it junior." Chenille takes another deep breath like this information, the information she's hounding me for, is killing her. Making a judges ruling she announces, "Now look, you will tell them soon, and I do mean soon Kiara. As for you," she bangs her gavel at him. "I don't play when it comes to baby sis. You hurt her; we'll be playin' cops and wind."

Like an idiot prisoner who was just sentenced he asks, "What's cops and wind?"

"I'm the cop and your ass better run like the wind," Chenille licks her lips evilly at him. He shouldn't have asked. "Got it?"

"Yeah," he nods scooting a little closer to me on the sly. If I didn't know any better I would say Billy is afraid of my big bad sister. How hard are you really if my five foot one sister scared the daylights out of you?

"Now you two quit all that kissing before someone else walks in," she heads back towards the door and puts on a fake smile as if court has been adjourned. Before walking out the door she sighs, "Happy Thanksgiving."

Billy gradually turns his head to look at me. "Yo' family is crazy."

"You don't even know the half of it," I reaching on my bedside table for my ringing phone. "Hello."

"Let me in. You know a girl hungry!" Mia says into the phone in a very excited voice.

"Be there in a second," I say flipping my phone close. "You wanna come meet her with me or wait here?"

He rubs his throat nervously, "I think I'll wait here." After a pause he asks, "Does yo' sister take some sort self defense class or some'n, 'cause her grip is lethal."

"No," I slide my flip-flops back on.

"Steroids?" he rubs his neck again. Poor guy. It's not normal for a girl to put a guy in so much pain, and we all know Billy is not some little sissy boy whose mouth is bigger than anything else on him. He can take more than most of the guys I know when it comes to pain, so if he's complaining she must have really done something worth groaning about. "Tryin' out for the NFL?"

Giggling, I peck a kiss on his cheek and go to get Mia. When I return I've got not only Mia, but DK and Ryan.

"Hey Billy," Mia says, happy to see him for some strange reason.

"Hey," he smiles back. "Good to see you."

"You too," she leans against the front of the bed.

"This is Ryan," Mia introduces him to Billy.

"Hello," Ryan says in his adorable Italian accent.

"Sup," Billy gives him the nod.

Pointing to me, Ryan asks, "That is your bello?"

"Yeah that's his whale," DK laughs to himself.

"Excuse me asshole, but bello means beautiful," I snap at him. "He was asking him am I his girlfriend."

"Gotcha," Billy says understanding now. "Yeah that's my girlfriend."

"Oh," Ryan says looking at Mia. "She's ... how you say ... has ... sweet ... heart," he looks at me and smiles. "It ... is ... a ... priv ... privilege to be in the presence of such a bello and out ... outstanding woman." Now Mia smiles at me. No wonder she is excited to be here. She's created our very own big game.

"She is huh?" Billy looks at me with a smile.

"You guys can come out here and eat," my mom opens my door. "Everyone's back in the garage."

"Ok," I reply and shoot Mia a glare. She brought him here so someone could throw down, which is really the last thing I need.

A few minutes later we're all at the dining room table eating. Well I'm not eating because I never eat with everyone else. I always eat alone after everyone has had all they can eat, after everyone has packed away how much they want, and after I have cleaned the dishes. Usually there's nothing for me to eat or much of anything left, but that's ok because I don't like Thanksgiving food, so why not let everyone else eat their hearts out because they actually love it.

"This is so good," Mia says in a mumble letting breadcrumbs fall from her mouth. "I love your mom's cooking."

"I know," I nod watching her eat while sitting next to Billy who has his arm wrapped around my waist while he eats.

"Yeah, on the real though," DK nods while eating his third helping. Chewing with his mouth wide open he smacks, "Yo' mama can throw down."

"Your mom's cooking ... is ... how you say ... fan ... fantastic," he puts a forkful of dressing in his mouth. "She ... can cook ... better than many of the ... women in my country ..." Aw.

"Wow your English is really improving," I say crossing my legs and leaning back.

"Yes," he nods smiling at me again.

I better stop drooling in my head over him. After all, my boyfriend is right next to me and probably wouldn't appreciate knowing how his smile and accent are making me whimper.

With a wink he sighs, "You and Mia have ... helped me ... a lot."

"You guys hang out a lot?" Billy asks me curiously before stuffing part of a roll in his mouth.

"Yeah," I shift around uncomfortably. "We hang out pretty often. I mean we're trying to help him settle down here. Is that wrong?"

"No," he says in between chews.

Ryan starts again, "Kie … she treats me …" he struggles to find the right words. "Like no other … She … is really won … wonderful and you're … a very … lucky man."

Did he have to say that? I mean yeah that's really sweet to say, but does he realize what trouble he just set himself up for? Seriously that's not what you say to a girl's boyfriend in this or any other country.

"Yeah I am pretty lucky," he pulls me closer to him in a more protective way.

"If you weren't … together … I wouldn't regret … hitting on her … so much …" he grabs everyone's attention.

I hear Mia choke with DK and Billy. Nice. Just what I needed. Frustrated, I slide my hand onto my forehead.

Somehow Billy manages to say one word. "What?"

"Did you jus' say you hit on her a lot?" DK asks trying not to smirk to himself. "Please tell me that's what you said."

"Yes," he shrugs. "I feel bad … because she's taken … but not because … she's such a wonderful girl," his eyes meet me again. Ryan sighs eating the last of his sweet potatoes, "Her and Mia both are … two … perfect … bellos."

DK tries not to laugh to himself as Billy slowly turns his head around slowly in my direction letting go of me.

"So you jus' let him hit on you?" He asks in the angry expected tone.

"No," I quickly answer. Innocently I plea, "I tell him not to. He does it without realizing it."

"True," Mia points her fork at him before licking it. At least she's trying to help me since she brought this trouble to the table.

"You didn't feel the need to share wit' yo' boyfriend," Billy points to himself, "that you've got guys chasin' you right and left?"

I hate the way he wants to pull at dangerous strings like this. "Oh and like you're telling me about every girl that steps to you?"

Mia and DK start snickering under their breath. Neither of them knows how to deal with the complications of a relationship because neither can be in one for very long, which sometimes makes me believe that they are perfect for each other.

"Please, there ain't time fo' 'em to step to me. I bus' my ass at that hotel durin' the day and at the club every night. When I'm not at work I'm sleepin', layin' tracks wit' DK or tryin' to talk to you on the phone," he snaps at me again.

DK chimes in, "It's true. He spends every wakin' moment playing pussy whipped boyfriend."

I can't fight the urge to throw sticks into this hellish fire, "Are you trying to tell me there aren't girls who try to get with you and free drinks at the club? Besides we all know that DK's dirty ass has hoes of a feather flock on him like no other."

"True," Mia says again nibbling on a piece of a ham, watching us like we're a movie.

Suddenly DK stops smiling to but in, "I ain't dirty."

"False," she points her fork at him while Ryan sits back just watching us like we're insane.

"That's beside the point!" Billy yells at me.

"No! That's exactly the point!" I raise my voice as well.

"You weren't up front 'bout this dude whose been pushin' up on you for how long?"

"Billy I—

"Don't Billy me you—

"You what?" I growl under my breath.

He takes a moment to regain his composure, "Nothin'. Look, keepin' that shit from me is foul, and you know it."

Leaning back I cross my arms, "Really? I'm the foul one? Since you wanna start shit, let's talk about the females chasing you day in and day out or about all your ex girlfriends who want your ass back."

"Ouch," Mia mumbles drinking some of her Kool-Aid. "Point Kie."

"You know what? That's not even righ," he gets up and grabs his plate.

"Right? You know what's not right?"

"You actin' like a trick."

My jaw hits the table in disbelief. Did my sister remove the common sense he had left from his brain when she choked him?

Mia's fork slips from her hand, "A trick?"

"Oh now he agrees with me," DK mumbles getting a quick look from all of us.

Slowly I repeat the word using it to push myself up, "A trick?"

"What's a trick?" Ryan leans over to DK.

"A slut," he clarifies it for him folding his arms.

"I'm a trick now?"

"Yeah."

"You know what? That's fine, but let this trick tell you something," I grab him by the collar of his shirt. "If you don't lay off this bullshit, you're gonna need an oxygen tank for you to breathe."

He attempts to say something, but decides it's best not to waste his only air.

I grip tighter around his collar and shake him a bit, "You know maybe it wasn't the best thing for me not to tell your ass to avoid this very situation, and maybe it was wrong for me to bring up your business in front of mixed company, but it was so uncalled for you to call me a trick." After a dead stare into his eyes I let go of his shirt, "Now whose foul?"

Billy doesn't break eye contact for as long as he can stand it. I think it's sad how strong he tries to be compared to how strong he actually is, especially when it comes to going toe to toe with me.

DK licks his lips hoping it'll help him stop laughing while Mia and Ryan just stare at us.

"Excuse me," I say expecting him to move out of my way, which he does. I calmly escort myself into the kitchen.

"Let's go hang out in the garage," Billy says moving around the table to throw his plate away.

DK nods and follows him out the door making a heart with his hands to quickly make it break while mouthing the word, "Finally."

She shakes her head and mouths, "I don't think so."

Ryan looks at Mia who looks back at him licking her fork again. Finally her plate is clean. Her separate dessert plate isn't, but she's already decided to take it with her. A couple of minutes later Mia and Ryan walk into the kitchen where I'm pouring the food into smaller containers.

"I think we're gonna leave before World War III breaks out," Mia pats me on my back as I stop moving around to look at them.

"I'm sorry ... I didn't mean to—

"It's not your fault Ryan," I quickly stop him, put a smile on my face for him, and move my hair out of my eyes. "You didn't do anything wrong." I mean he really didn't. He didn't know any better, so you can't blame him for that. Where he's from it's a compliment to tell another man that about his woman, but because American's are so uptight about relationships he doesn't understand why that's bad. I'm sure Mia will clarify that in the car.

"Billy's just being over dramatic," she shakes her head.

I smack my gums, "Yea."

"Don't worry about it. Everything will be just fine." She hugs me, "Anyway I'll call you later. Love you."

"Love you," I hug back quickly. Pulling away I glance at Ryan whose looking innocently at me. "Don't worry it really wasn't your fault."

"My apologies once more bello," he kisses my hand.

"Happy Thanksgiving ya'll," I wave goodbye to them.

"You too," they say waving goodbye back. I watch them walk down the hall together. Mia hands him her plate threatening him not to touch her dessert while she looks for her keys.

I turn on the radio in the living room and go back to cleaning the dishes. The nerve of that boy to call me a trick! I am not some hoodrat who sleeps around with different guys every night, who uses her body to get money and jewelry as well as other things. Asshole.

Once I have all the dishes emptied I begin to wash them. You know I don't appreciate the fact how everyone 'hates to eat and run', but does. They leave all the dishes for me to clean. You know I understand guests aren't supposed to do dishes, but they're family, they could at least *offer* to help me. Is that so hard? Would it kill someone to say 'hey Kie do you need some help?' or 'need a hand?' Even on Thanksgiving, the time when you're supposed to be more thankful for everything and more helpful, it still doesn't trigger in their mind that *I* would like some help.

"Need a hand?" I hear a familiar voice come into the kitchen.

Turning around to see Billy leaning against the counter I roll my eyes and turn back around to finish washing the pot I was scrubbing so hard that I almost forgot I was mad. "Sorry. I'm an independent trick."

"Kie," he calls to me as he comes my direction.

"Maybe I'll change my name and go by something sluttier."

"Kie—

"No I was thinking more like Special K."

With a heavy sigh he tries again, "Kie—

"Oh and if I'm such a trick why are with me? I mean you're all grown up now right? Everyone knows tricks are for kids," I rinse the pot under the hot water and toss it in the drainer with a bit more anger than before. "I wonder how many ways I can make my body twist before I'm considered a hooker."

"Stop it Kiara," he says grabbing a dry towel to start to dry the pile of dishes in the drainer.

Rinsing another dish I sigh, "Sorry this trick doesn't take commands, but I guess being a trick I do take requests if you drive the right car or have enough money in the bank right?" I know he doesn't expect me to just forgive him in an instant like nothing happened.

"I'm sorry," Billy says as he dries his first dish.

Not letting it go I ask, "Are you just trying to get a freebee?"

Glancing at me he sighs, "I'm really sorry. I didn't mean it Kie. You aren't a trick and you know that."

"I know I'm not a trick, and I damn sure don't appreciate being called one."

"I know I—

"Then why'd you call me that?

With a simple shrug he sighs, "There's something inside me that goes off in an instant when I hear someone's been trying to get with you. The last things I want are to get hurt and me to be replaced. I feel that's what's going to happen when they step to you, so I figure if I push you away first it'll hurt less if its true."

"But it's not. Just because another guy hits on me doesn't mean I'm going to rush off into his arms. Have a little faith."

After nodding and having a moment of silence he starts up again, "You know I don't mean to say the hurtful things I do sometimes. I need you to believe me when I say I'm trying to change," he dries his hands and wraps his arms around me. I don't recall sending a mental memo to him saying it was ok for him to touch me. "Be mad if you want, just don't leave me."

With a confused look on my face I turn my head to face him. "You think because you say something rude to me out of anger that I'm going to leave you? You always think because we have some little dispute that I'm just gonna get up and go out of this relationship. Why?"

"I thought that's the way relationships work …"

"No sweetheart. If that was true then you'd never date anyone longer than," he raises his eyebrows at me. "Oh …"

"Wait so you're not so mad at me that you're ready to leave me? I mean as much as I make you mad you don't wanna jus' get up and go?"

I shake my head not being able to help the smile from creeping onto my face. Tossing my arms around his waist I hug him close to me. "No honey. That's not how relationships work. You fight, you have your throw downs, but you get pass them and move on."

"I mean I know that, but all the shit I put you through—

"Don't worry about it," I look up at him. "I'm not going anywhere, so let that thought go, but if you really want to me to stay here then you need to treat me the best you can at all times. I'm a lady, so treat me like one. These little things like temper-tantrums need to stop. All they do is pull us apart. I know you're trying to be a good man."

"I really am."

Smiling softly at him I drape my arms around his neck, "I know, and I'm here for you babe. Just watch your tongue before I have to cut it out."

After I place a kiss in the middle of his forehead, he lets out a sigh of relief, "Alright." Billy pulls me closer to him and whispers, "I'm sorry Kie."

"It's ok," I look up at him.

How he got me to just let it go so quickly is beyond me. I have never let someone calling me names go by so easily. Holy crap am I changing too? I mean yeah I know I'm growing up, but I never thought I'd out grow getting mad over being called names. When your boyfriend calls you a trick you're supposed to be mad for awhile, but I think knowing and understanding why he is the way he is helps me forgive him quicker and see the bigger picture. Great. Mia's right. I am going soft.

Suddenly he places a kiss on my cheek, "Let's do these dishes so DK and I can head back."

Drowning my hands in the warm soapy water I say, "You don't have to help if you don't want."

"I want to," he grabs the dish towel. "More time with you."

With a smile I go back to washing dishes. Playfully I blow bubbles at Billy here and there while he fights them off as he dries the dishes. I'm glad to know that if we were to ever live together he'd help with the dishes rather than lay around like a lazy idiot.

About an hour later my kitchen looks back to normal. Everyone is heading out so they're in the garage saying goodbye to my parents. Everyone except Billy that is. He's right here holding me in his arms soaking up the last few minutes he gets with me.

"I don't wanna leave you," he holds me close to him, head resting on top of mine. "Ya know this is the first Thanksgiving since my parents died that I felt like I was apart of a family again?"

I look surprised as I break free of his arms and hop on the counter in front of him. "Really?"

He nods at me putting his hands on each side of me. "I remember the first Thanksgiving after they died ..."

❀　　　❀　　　❀

"And what are you thankful for?" Big Mama asks Billy as he places his napkin in his lap before reaching for the sweet potatoes.

"Nothin," he bluntly remarks dropping a chunk full on his plate.

"Come on. There has to be something you are thankful for," she encourages him. "So what is it?"

Looking around the table at a few of Big Mama's children with their own kids, he simply turns to her and says, "No parents. No house. No love. I jus' can't find nothin' to thank God fo'."

With a deep sigh she places a hand over her heart, "One day someone will come into your life and show you exactly the point of Thanksgiving. It may not be this year, it may not be next year, and it may not be while you still here in this house, but some year, someone will."

❧   ❧   ❧

Pushing a strand of hair out of my face he smiles, "She was right. You made me understand the true meanin' of Thanksgiving," he says. I swear sometimes he sounds like those corny after school specials. "Today I felt more thankful for havin' you in my life more than any other day, and instead of showin' you my gratefulness like a good guy I treated you like shit."

I open my mouth when he cuts me off determined to finish his speech before I can say anything.

"Once you looked into my eyes and forgave me, I realized just how much more thankful I am to God for you. For you and him helping me to shape into a better man to keep you. I know I have a long way to go, but now I know I don't have to worry about fuckin' up so bad that you leave, any more," he runs his hand up to my face to make sure my eyes are still on his. "This Thanksgiving Kie, I'm grateful for God blessing me with someone to care for me like I thought only my parents could," he leans in. "Thank you."

Aw! I'm such a wimp when it comes to guys who say sappy things. I almost feel a tear coming. When someone can look you in the eyes and tell you you're the reason their faith in God is restored and when you're the reason they have something to be thankful for, to not want to cry would be heartless.

Billy plants a small kiss on my lips and then lets his forehead rest against mine. "You're the reason for me," he sighs. "And I just hope you never forget that."

I lift his chin up and kiss him softly on his lips. Slowly I part his lips with my tongue and press against his, feeling something more deep inside me relieved.

Hearing someone open the door I quickly pull away from him acting as innocent as possible. Billy slides away from me leaning against counter looking around the corner to see DK come in. Damn, it's just the untrained chimp.

"Let's go," he whines to him.

"Alright," Billy sighs, helping me off my counter to give me a giant hug goodbye since we can't hug in front of my parents. We hold each other tightly with eyes closed and secret prayers being said to God about how thankful we are.

I whisper in his ear, "Get home safely."

"I will."

"Don't get into any trouble."

"I won't."

"Maybe you can come back for Christmas and my birthday," I snuggle my head on his shoulder.

"I'm sure I will."

"I'll miss you."

"I know baby. I'm gonna miss you too," he kisses my cheek before he lifts my chin up. "I'll be comin' back to you, so don't sweat it."

"Could you two nip the lovey dovey shit in the bud so we can bounce?" DK interrupts.

I shoot DK an evil glare and quickly look back into Billy's eyes, "No sweat." Our lips touch briefly again.

"Let's go," he holds my hand until we reach the doorway where he sees my parents.

Smiling a bit drunk my mom says loudly, "It was a pleasure having you."

"Yeah it was," my dad nods a little tipsy himself, which is odd because he rarely ever drinks.

"Thank you guys for havin' us," Billy slips his hands in his pocket.

My mom leans against the door to stop from stumbling around, "Feel free to come up for a visit any time, hell you two should come up for Christmas."

Shooting me a glance Billy tries not to smirk to wide, "Sounds good."

"Great," DK mumbles under his breath.

"You drive safely," my mom puts an arm around me for balance.

"We will," Billy strolls towards his car.

"Bye," both of my parents wave in unison.

"Later," DK says giving them a nod.

"Bye," Billy says like a gentleman. You know I think DK could learn a lesson from Billy on how to act towards people's parents.

We watch them get into the car as a family. I think it's the first time in a long time we've stood together like a family, minus my sister who left much earlier I'm going to assume.

"Billy's such a nice boy," my mom pats my shoulder.

"Yeah I guess," I nod trying not to be too enthusiastic about him.

"DK's a pretty bad thug," my dad places his cigarette between his lips.

"I would never want you to date anything like DK," my mother shakes her head in disgust. "Never."

"Don't worry about that," I shake my head shuddering at that thought. Never have I once considered dating DK or anything remotely close. Even when I first started hanging out with him and Billy, you could tell they really weren't one in the same.

"I guess I wouldn't mind you bringing home a guy like Billy," my dad takes a puff of his cigarette. Notice the words 'Like Billy'? What was the key word there? Like. Not Billy, but a guy *like* Billy. See what I mean. See. But that's ok. It's a mental note made that Billy's type is acceptable, meaning Billy is acceptable.

My mom agrees, "Me neither."

I simply smile and nod like the innocent teenager role I'm supposed to be playing.

"Dishes done?" my mom asks me watching them drive away down the street.

"Yeah Billy helped me do them," I slip my hands in my pocket.

"See look at that. He even does dishes. You might want to lock him up Kie," my mom strolls into the house with my dad as I continue to watch the day fade away.

I'm gonna hold her to that because when they have a heart attack at Christmas because of who I'm dating I can remind them of this very moment we just shared.

As I cross my arms and lick my lips softly I let out a sigh. I must admit something. As much as I've helped him change, that river really does flow both ways. I mean look at me. I'm learning to let grudges go and things not bother me so much, as well as be more forgiving. It's like when God was playing matchmaker in Heaven he knew which flaws we both had that the other could help fix and grow from.

I think I get Thanksgiving now. It's not about setting aside one day to just be more thankful about the things in your life but to really open your eyes and be aware of everything he has given you. Not just your family and the things you need on a daily basis, but what you are unaware of sometimes. Thanksgiving is about learning the differences between people, and why you should be thankful for them rather than letting them be the reason you're not together. It's not about the food, the dishes, or the annoyance of having to be around people you could careless about, but getting past all that to see how God works in everything he does. I am thankful for learning that. I guess Billy wasn't the only one whose eyes were finally opened to what Thanksgiving is all about.

CHAPTER 12

'Tis the Season to get Caught

Who hates Christmas? I mean seriously who hates the time of year where you give gifts to the people you love, the time of year where adults rack up high credit card bills, and the time of year where everyone believes it's how much you spend rather than where it comes from? I know I don't. I guess that's because for me it's double the fun because my birthday is two days before Christmas, which means I get twice as many gifts.

Now don't get me wrong; I am not a materialistic person. I just happen to like presents. That probably sounds really shallow, but there's something I love about knowing someone took the time and effort out of their busy schedule and personal life to either buy or make me something. That's right. I said it. Make me something. I love homemade things.

Last year because money was so tight around my friends and me, we decided to do secret Santa among us where we gave homemade gifts. It was so awesome. Mia, ironically enough, made me a big poster full of pictures from the year of all of us. It was really detailed, and you could tell that Mia put more time and effort into it than she knew possible. She hates artsy things, and she also gets frustrated really easily, so to have a piece of artwork she made meant a lot to me.

We all have money this year, so exchanging presents with them isn't what I'm excited about. My mother told me Billy could come stay with us during the Christmas holidays while he's off of work, so he gets to spend four or five whole days with me! What could be better than that? I'll tell you; if he got to be here for my birthday. But no, instead he gets to stay the day *after,* also known as

Christmas Eve. It just shows that sometimes work will have to come before the girlfriend, though I just never thought it would be as often as it is. I don't mean to sound bitter, but he can work any other day of the year. I have only one birthday. To add to that, it's not until the end of year right by Christmas, which is a pain in the ass because it's rare that I get to spent it with my friends.

I guess you could say that the best gift will be a delayed birthday present and an early Christmas present. I can't wait for him to be back in my arms.

"Have fun," my mom says to me as I leave out the front door. "You and Mia be careful."

"We'll be fine. We're just going to get something to eat and catch a movie with the girls," I zip up my jacket and put my hands in my pockets.

"Happy birthday honey," she waves as I start towards Mia car.

"Thanks," I say sighing.

Hey I got nice gifts. I got money for new clothes and a gift certificate for me one of my friends to go out to eat, more than likely Mia though she could eat the whole amount on her own.

I get into Mia's car to see her smirking like crazy. I know her ass isn't that excited about *my* birthday.

In a squeal she claps, "Happy birthday!!!"

"Thanks," I smile putting my seatbelt on with a suspicious look. She's more excited than me. Is she on a cake high? Did she make me a 'special' birthday cake and have the first slice?

"How's it been so far?" she backs out of the driveway in her mom's 2003 white Ford Mustang convertible.

"Normal," I shrug unzipping my jacket.

"Oh," she sounds a little hurt. Smirking to herself she sighs, "I'm sure it'll get better."

"If you let me drive it'll make it better."

Shaking her head she sighs, "Sorry sis. Any other day, but unfortunately I am playing chauffeur today."

"Why? I mean I want to drive. Shouldn't you be giving into my birthday wishes?"

With a laugh she rolls her eyes, "Don't let this birthday thing go to your head. I mean yeah it's your birthday, so you get some rights, but don't push it."

The way she sounds you'd think I asked to fly a jet for my birthday. Oh well, it was worth a try. It has not really been an eventful birthday. Let's see; I sat at home most of the day sleeping, watching my favorite movies waiting for Mia to call to let me know where the girls are taking me, and then I got dressed to leave. My parents didn't even buy me a damn birthday cake. Hell, I think I'll be lucky to get the restaurant people to sing happy birthday to me.

"We're gonna hit this club for your birthday first ok?" she announces rather than asks me.

"We're not even 18 yet, so how does that work?"

"I've got the hook up, don't sweat it."

"Who are you? DK now?"

Fighting the urge to let her face sneer she snaps, "Um no. Can we leave him off our lips for the moment?"

I roll my eyes, "Ok. Well, what happened to dinner and a movie?"

"We'll do that later. Restaurants are open late, and we'll catch a late movie. I just think for your birthday you should check out this club, plus you get free birthday drinks," she nods as she speeds towards wherever this 'hot club' is.

"You can't drink," I point at her.

"I know because I'm driving," she answers in a mocking tone.

"Are the other girls meeting us there?"

"Yeah. Now no more questions. Just sit back, enjoy the ride, and chill to the radio," she turns it up as I just look at her.

I roll my eyes again and look down at my phone. Ya know, I haven't received a birthday call, voicemail, or text message from Billy. I feel neglected by my boyfriend on my own birthday. Am I just not worth that few extra seconds of his precious time? Is it being selfish to want a little attention from him on *my birthday*?

Nearly half an hour later we're outside some club where there's no line or anything. How hot can this club be if no one is dying to get in? The bouncer doesn't even look like he could do any damage if his best friend slept with his wife on their wedding night.

"Why are we here again?" I look over at her as I zip my jacket back up.

"To celebrate your birthday!"

"No seriously."

"I am serious."

"Yeah ok, why are we here again?"

"We're here to celebrate your birthday at one of the hottest clubs around."

Looking blankly at the bare building in front of us, I turn to face her again. "Hottest clubs around? Where's the crowd dying to get in? Where's the bouncer who you have to flirt with just to get him to even let us wait in line? Where's the music that's so loud it's destroying our ear drums from outside?"

"Well—

"This isn't a club. It's more like a funeral home."

"Sh. Stop complaining," she points a mean finger at me. "Try to have a good time."

Complaining? It's my damn birthday! I should be allowed to complain, whine, groan or whatever it is I want to do.

"Let's go," she unlocks her doors and grabs the keys. Where's her purse? And why is she all covered up if we're going to a club? Besides those two strange facts why didn't she let me know so I could look cute going out? This doesn't add up.

I follow her over to the bouncer who looks like he was rejected off the Real World casting calls. He doesn't even say a word he just moves the rope and lets us go through like we're regulars. I slip my hands in my back pockets and look at Mia before she opens the door.

"Now remember it's your birthday, so try to have fun," she says gently touching my arm as if preparing me for someone's funeral.

With darted eyebrows, I simply nod.

She opens the door to a pitch-black place. Now I know I'm not supposed to be saying negative things or whatever, but last time I checked nightclubs were supposed to have what they call lights and music … oh yeah and people!

Quickly she claps her hands together and big lights come on revealing there are people along with decorations.

"Surprise!!" They all yell in their most enthusiastic voices. If I didn't know any better I'd say this was a surprise party. Now wouldn't it be a bitch if it were for someone else on my birthday?

Shaking my head I smile as I look around the room at all my friends and acquaintances from school as well as some I know from elsewhere. I see some of Mia's cousins I'm tight with as well as some of Natalie's and Andrea's. It's a room full of all sorts of people I like and love, except Billy of course. Hey this means tons of presents!

"You threw me a surprise party?" I look at Mia who's slipping out of her jacket revealing a red tube top to match her extremely tight jeans and red cute heels I hadn't noticed before.

"Yeah," she nods as I take off my jacket to reveal my loose gray t-shirt and faded jeans. Is it fair that I look worse than everyone else here? "You know you're one of the hardest people to surprise. You wanna ask tons of questions, whine, and if that's not enough you wanna complain." With a clap of her hands three times club lights and music start.

"Shut up," I roll my eyes as two built guys in tight black t-shirts take our jackets.

"Now," she takes my arm and starts to lead me towards the stairs. Pointing out the directions around the room she grins, "This is called the princess palace." It looks like one giant castle with blue lights and baby blue decorations. I love how she picked my favorite colors.

"It's pretty."

"I know. Since it's your birthday, you're the princess," she says as we walk up the stairs. "This kingdom is yours to do as you wish. I know you don't look like a princess right now and probably don't feel like one, but if you go into that room right there labeled 'The Princess Chambers', I'm sure you'll find some things to change that." Mia stops right on the top stair as I scan the second level.

I see a throne next to the upstairs bar where a pretty cute bartender is waiting to serve me.

Leaning over she whispers with a smirk, "Courtesy of your sister." I join her in the smiling fest before she says, "Now hurry up we've got things to do."

Taking a moment I read, "The Princess Chambers," out loud. With an even bigger smile I open the door to see a white leather couch where a sexy dress is laid, a pair of heels, and some fake diamond jewelry. Off to the side there's a stand with make up and perfume. Looking around I notice a mini bar behind the couch, a vertical fish tank, and high class art on the walls.

I slip on the baby blue halter-top dress that acts as a push up bra to my boobs and stops a few inches below my butt. As I slide my feet into my silver heeled shoes that really do remind me of Cinderella's, I wonder what possessed my sister to buy this for me knowing damn well she's always complaining about how much skin I show.

As I stare at the fake tear drop ear rings and necklace my sister has always dubbed tacky I wonder if she even picked this outfit out for me. Maybe Mia did and just convinced my sister I would like it. Quickly I fasten the jewelry on, change eye shadow colors, my blush, and of course my lip gloss. My rule on make up: natural is sexiest.

After smiling at my reflection I grab my cell phone to check for a message from Billy one last time before I leave it behind. Nope. Nothing. Guess everyone cares, but him.

Walking out to see a crowd of people surrounding my throne while Mia dances by herself in the same place I left her, I clear my throat causing her to cut the music. I sit down in my throne chair and cross my legs feeling like actual royalty.

"Now," Mia comes to stand right by my side. "You have your court, your throne …" she looks around. "Where's your crown?"

Andrea strolls over and places a tiara on my head. "Your majesty." She moves beside Mia on the other side.

I giggle and shake my head.

"Yes, yes," Mia nods and squeals to herself. "Well every castle isn't complete without a fairy godmother, and we all know I don't look like nobody's grandma let alone mama, so your ass gets a fairy god sister," she winks at me making me giggle again.

"Fair enough."

"Now where's my wand thingy?" she looks around lost as can be until the sexy bartender hands it to her. Giving him a flirty wink she whispers, "Thanks."

With a pleased sigh I ask, "What more could you possibly have for me?"

"Be patient," she points her wand at me. Putting a finger on her nose she continues, "Every birthday girl needs a cake, but since you're a princess it can't be just any cake." Mia waves her magic wand in circles as the two guys who took our coats come up the stairs holding a big beautiful cake with my face on it. They place the cake on the bar next to me. As she taps her foot she recites, "See you've even got people ready to do stuff at your command. Let's see, cake, peasants, court, fairy god sister, crown, throne, dress … what am I missing?"

"Music?"

She puts her hands on her waist, "No." Her attempt to be cute and clumsy isn't going to waste, but it is going to get old eventually. Mia yells, "Oh yeah a birthday present!" Everyone starts to chuckle at her causing her to say, "Hey don't be laughin'. This job is harder than it looks!"

"It is," I try to calm Mia down.

"Thank you. Anyway," she licks her lips, "what does every kingdom need? What's that person called who sits next to the princess? He's tall, usually handsome, very sweet in most cases … damn what's his name?"

"Prince Charming!" Natalie squeals out as she migrates her way next to Andrea, who's now a bit more behind Mia than beside her. You can tell when they've rehearsed this skit. We'll work on their acting skills another day, but right now I need to know who's prince charming?

"Bingo!" Mia says slyly. She starts waving her magic wand around towards the stairs where I begin to hear humming. What's wrong with her? Has she already been drinking?

"Happy birthday to you," I hear a voice coming from the direction of the stairs.

Slowly I divert my attention there, where I see Billy coming up them dressed in a nice pair of khaki pants and a long sleeve black shirt. He's got a fresh new hair cut, he's clean shaven, and looks even more filled out than he did before. God I love how he gets hotter as time goes on.

"Happy birthday to you," he sings passionately slow into the microphone strolling towards me.

Some girl next to Mia reaches out for Billy, which is when she slaps her with her magic wand and gives her a glare.

"Happy birthday my baby Kie," he sings taking my hand into his hand. "Happy birthday to you," Billy finishes off real slow just swooning every girl especially me.

I've got one hand cupped over my mouth, and the other one in his hand. His beautiful voice just wows me more and more every time.

The crowd claps and goes wild for his voice as he leans down and kisses me on my cheek. "Happy birthday baby."

Before I can hug or even touch him Mia cuts me off with one more thing. "You're damn right I'm good," she says to some girl who screamed at her. Deviously she giggles, "No castle would be complete without a jester, so let's see him." I already know who she would make a jester. "DJ serve some'n hot."

The DJ puts on a beat none of us know as DK takes the stage downstairs. All of us upstairs turn our heads to the big screen.

"Yo birthday girl," DK gives me a shout out from the stage as I watch him on the screen. "This one's fo' you. Kie is hot as can be. She's got style, grace, wit' a sexy little face ..."

I stop paying attention to him and go back to looking at a Billy who's beaming down at me. Crossing my legs the other direction, I innocently whisper, "Hey ..."

"Hey," he leans closer allowing me to get lost in the sweet smell of his cologne.

"I'll take my thank yous later," Mia snaps her fingers, "but my piece of cake now."

"You can cut it yourself," I hint for her to leave me alone.

"Mmhm," she walks away sticking her wand in her pocket.

Wasting no time I toss my arms around his neck and allow him to pull me up. As I hug him I loose myself again in the tight grasp. I never wanna let him go again.

"It's ok Kie," he rubs the bare part of my upper back. In a whisper he reassures me, "I'm not leavin' any time soon."

Slowly I pull away and look at him. Sometimes I forget just how much I miss him until he's standing back in front of me. After taking a second to absorb him all in, I nail my fist in his stomach in a playful yet slightly painful way. "How dare you not call me!"

Billy grabs his stomach with a confused look. "What?"

"It's my birthday! You lied and told me you were working," I hit him again this time in his arm before I assume the pout position. I mean I see the big picture being he sang for me and is here now, but he could have called me despite if he had plans of seeing me or not.

"I was!" he pleas. "I was workin' on this for you," he rubs his arm. "I've been here since five in the mornin' settin' up for this with Mia. Gettin' bartenders, decorations, and a freakin' throne!"

"I'm sorry," I say hugging him again. "I would've preferred a simple phone call ya know? You can do all this, but can't call to say happy birthday?"

He holds me close to him still, "Sorry. I'm so sorry." A kiss lands on my forehead. "Forgive me for not callin'?"

I probably sound selfish like no other, but hey it's my birthday! Don't build the princess monster if you can't handle its wrath. In a high pitch, perky voice I say, "This time."

With another kiss on my forehead he smiles, "Good. Now I think the birthday presents should be given throughout the evenin', so how about we start by dancin'?" He takes my hand and places a kiss on it, "If you'll have me."

"Of course I will," I follow him down the stairs where everyone else has left to go watch DK rap on and off.

Billy and I dance for over an hour. Fast and slow, grinding and holding, just everything I could ask for on my birthday. I mean seriously, could this have been a better birthday? My best friend and boyfriend arranged for me to feel like a princess on my seventeenth birthday all night long, probably into the early morning. I don't think I even need presents any more as long as I get Billy. I mean gifts would be a fabulous bonus, but I don't need them so much any more.

"All right Kie," Billy pulls away from me. Leading me back towards the stairs he says, "Time for yo' first present. Go up there, and sit in yo' throne."

"Why?" I whine.

"Don't worry. Please just go sit down," he says walking away from me. I storm up the stairs and quickly sit in my throne. I'm here now; what's *his* next wish? Isn't this my birthday? Aren't they supposed to be fulfilling *my* commands? Wow this princess thing has gone to my head.

I watch Billy on the screen take the stage as the bartender fixes me a margarita with the little umbrella. Now most people probably wonder how we get hooked up with alcohol on a regular. There are some things that you just shouldn't question. We all have connections, and that's all that needs to be said.

"Hey," Billy pulls a stool to the middle of the stage. DK turns around to him, "Mic."

DK tosses it to him walking off the stage as the DJ continues playing the beat to some mainstream song. I begin to sip on my drink while waiting for him to do whatever it is he left me to do.

"Party people," Billy says into the microphone, as the DJ gets ready to play the next song. In his performer voice he says, "I need you guys to calm down now. This song I wrote for my girl Kie, I want everyone on the dance floor to find someone to dance to this song with. No one can be alone for this song a'ight? I'll give you guys a second." As he fiddles with his shoes and pant leg I pout wondering why I don't get to dance with him.

Did he write me a special birthday song? Finally I get a first hand taste of what his lyrics are like. Yay. Ya know, it's amazing just how much he's grown from when I made him karaoke. That was one interesting night.

Ryan strolls up to Mia who sees DK slowly but surely coming her way. "Would you like to dance with me?" he asks making DK stop dead in his tracks and just stare at her.

Mia looks at DK once more and back at Ryan who's looking hopeful. "As much as I want to, my dance is set for someone else," she pats his back. "Sorry."

Arriving in front of DK he gives her a sarcastic look and grunts, "Why you turn down Romeo?"

"Felt like I wanted to dance with someone else," she licks her lips hinting all she can through her body language.

"Well better go find that nigga befo'"—

"Do you want to dance with me or not?" she folds her arms.

Caught in the mist of trying to front he glances away at a lost for words. "What makes you think I wanna dance wit' you?"

Mia shakes her head fed up. "Look DK if you wanna act like you weren't on your way to come ask me to dance then fine, but I know you were. I'm so sick of your games."

"Nobody's playin' games wit' you."

"God, for once why don't you step to me real and tell me what you want."

DK looks over at Billy who's telling him to 'step up to the plate and do it' with a look. "Mia," he rubs his chin and look her square in her eyes. "Dance wit' me?"

She smirks to herself and takes his hand going to the middle of dance floor where Billy and I can both see. I squeal to myself. Oh it's about time. Some things are so obvious despite how bad we don't want to see them. Honestly I don't want her dating a dog, but I know something about the two of them fits whether or not I want it too. Besides, no one said they're going to hook up from one dance.

"Now," Billy licks his lips as a smooth R&B rhythm begins to play. As couples slowly begin to sway the beat he sighs, "I know every guy has wanted a girl you thought you couldn't have."

DK meets eyes with Mia who moves a little closer to him.

"Thought she was too good for you whether or not you would admit it," he puts a hand on his thigh. Billy looks directly at Mia and DK before glancing at the camera for me, "What would you do to get her? Better yet what would you do to keep her?"

I lean back and cross my legs anxiously waiting to hear him sing. This should be interesting.

"You heard about my past, things I use to do, the things I use to say," he looks out at the crowd. Before he gets up he points at DK singing, "the twisted games I'd play. You knew better than, than to mess wit' me." Pointing to his head he walks down the front stage steps, "Unless I could be," he slides by DK and Mia, "more than whatchu see." Slowly gliding to another couple he sings, "You drove me crazy girl, wit' yo' sexy days, plus yo' sassy ways."

Yeah so I'm a bit sassy. That's not a newsflash to this crowd. I should've known he'd throw that into the mix.

"Had my mind in a daze, had no clue jus' what to do," he shakes his head confused making his way back to the middle of the circle. "I wanna be wit' you," he says pointing to a couple making them move closer to each other, "baby believe it's true." Billy starts his way to the edge of the stage where he plans to sit down. "You're about to see the better man, I became fo' you," he points at the camera making me giggle to myself. "Jus' listen girl, I wouldn't lie to you. I jus' need you to hear me."

Hear him, what does he think I've been doing so far? Playing pick up sticks?

A bit more of the beat plays, and he starts again on what I assume will be the chorus. "I'm a better man, I'm a treat you right," he nods closing his eyes. "Kiss you slow while I hold you tight. Do things only you deserve, call you my queen fo' only you I serve. I can be more than whatchu dream, I can do a lot more than what I seem," he looks back out at the crowd. "I jus' want to love you."

He just wanted to love me all along? Why couldn't he have been up front from the start and told me though I probably wouldn't believe him.

I see him get up as the song goes on. "People are sayin', I'm more trouble than I'm worth," he heads back down into the crowd towards the stairs. "There're more men on this earth, he's been a playa since birth." That was cute. "None of 'em can judge, they don't know me like you do, they haven't seen how I've grew, or how I just don't wanna screw."

It's nice to know he's willing to pledge to the entire world that he isn't all about sex any more.

Casually he starts up the stairs. "I need you more than you know, right here in my life, there'd be no need to strife, one day I'll make you my wife."

Did he say that he has plans to make me his wife? Is this assuming I'd marry him? Who would wanna marry a man who does nothing, but screw up all the time? Seriously who would wanna marry a man like … Oh please, who am I kidding? I would marry that boy in heartbeat. Look at all he's done for me, not to marry him after all the changes he's made for me, and how much he's grown to meet my standards, would be ridiculous.

Billy reaches the top, "I was completely lost, just a broken a man, needed a new plan, with you my life really began." FINALLY he comes up here to be with the birthday girl. "You're about to see the better man, I became for you, jus' listen girl, I wouldn't lie to you," he sits down on the side of my throne. "I jus' need you to hear me."

With an unstoppable grin on my face I lean closer to him in admiration. I love how this song is so reflecting of our relationship.

"I'm a better man, I'm a treat you right," he takes my hand into his and rubs it softly. "Kiss you slow while I hold you tight. Do things only you deserve, call you my queen for only you I serve." Putting our hands to his heart he continues, "I can be more than whatchu dream, I can do a lot more than what I seem." He leans down to look me one on one in my eyes, "I jus' want to love you."

I swallow a bit nervous. So does he plan to tell me that he loves me tonight? Big step. Very big. "I'm a better man, I'm a treat you right," he lets my hand go going over to the bar. Where's he going? "Kiss you slow while I hold you tight," Billy takes a red rose from the bartender and leans back around to hand it to me. "Do things only you deserve, call you my queen for only you I serve. I can be more than whatchu dream, I can do a lot more than what I seem," he licks his lips slowly as the red rose slips into my fingers. "I just want to love you."

After I take it I hold it to my chest as Billy gets on his knees in front of me. The beat changes up once more for what I assume will be the last verse. Everyone is holding each other so close down there that it looks like the room is full of nothing but couples. It's amazing what a love song can do huh?

"There's no other girl, who can compare to you," I cup my mouth. "No matter what they do, it's to you I'll stay true. Baby be wit' me, I'll give you the key, to my heart to keep, just realize my love for you is forever deep," he sings still on his knees looking me in my eyes that are now filled with a few tears. In a low romantic tone he sings out, "I jus' need you to love me."

As the chorus continues Mia and DK maintain only looking into each other's eyes. He's being gentle, treating her preciously, something neither of them expected.

When Billy finishes the song he looks me in my eyes in absolute awe. He turns off his microphone as the crowd claps before the DJ puts on the next song. Billy takes my hand and leads me back into the room where I changed as I let tears run down my face. Why am I crying?! I am not a crier!

"Kie," he says closing the door as I sit down on the couch. "Aw babygurl it's ok."

Trying to regain my composure I cry out, "It was just so pretty."

With a smile Billy asks, "Do you remember when we were in my room, and you saw that locket draped around my parent's picture?" Slipping beside me Billy wipes away the tears on my cheek as continues, "Do you remember what my dad told my mom when he gave it to her?"

I choke on my sniffles as I whimper, "Yeah."

He moves closer and takes a small box from his pants pocket. As he opens it he says, "It's a circle 'cause my love for you will never end and without you I don't have life. Kie I've never been more scared of lettin' some'n go," a sniffle escapes him.

Like an idiot I chirp out, "Don't be scared. I won't break your locket."

Billy shakes his head, "I don't mean the locket. I mean my heart."

"Oh," I sigh. I won't break that either though.

"But I'm not really lettin' my heart go. I'm just givin' it to you to keep safe. Just like my dad said to my mom. I don't wanna ever loose you. I'm gonna be the best man I can for you every second of my life, and I want you to know I will never let you go." After placing the open box on his thigh, he uses one of his hands to remove mine from my mouth and then places his hand on my face. "I promise you that. I love you Kiara." He takes one long deep breath and repeats himself. "I love you."

I look back into his teary browns eyes and whisper back, "I love you."

Billy takes off the necklace that's around my neck and replaces it with the locket. "I know you'll take care of it Kie, and if you don't feel like I love you or that I'm not here for you, look down and remember this day, this very moment." It fragilely lays itself against my chest. Before pressing his lips to mine he whispers again, "I love you."

After an endless night of fun we stumble into my house around seven thirty. Turns out Mia had already told my parents I'd end up crashing over there. Although we didn't crash anywhere, we just partied all night.

Right now I'm only half sober, but you can't tell unless you know me really well. As for Billy, he is almost completely soberly cuddling in the guest bed with me while DK is passed out on the floor. That's where he landed five minutes after being in here. I'm not certain how much exactly he drank, but I'm certain he tried to take on Mia who had two margaritas, three vodka shots, two wine coolers, and a beer.

My parents are both sleeping in their room; after all it's a little early in the morning for them to be up, but I know they'll probably get up soon.

For the next thirty minutes or so I'm in an unforgettable bliss. I'm wrapped up sleeping in Billy's arms under a blanket. Ironic the birthday I'll never forget is the one that people usually just pass right over.

"Oh my god!" I hear my mother yell in the room.

We all rush to get up to see what she's yelling about when it hits me I'm the reason for the yelling. You know you've never really heard your mother scream in anger until she's caught you sleeping with your boyfriend in his bed, not knowing you're together. I honestly think she could take the yelling down just a notch. It can't be good for my headache that's coming. Besides it's not like she walked in on us having sex.

"What?" my dad comes stumbling in half awake.

"They were sleeping together!" she says sounding nearly ridiculous. "In his bed under the covers!" My mom screams like it's the biggest sin ever committed. We must alert the church elders. "I think they had sex!" With our clothes on?

My dad turns on the light. Oh how bright the light is. I feel like it would be less painful to rip my eyes out and hand them over to me.

"You had sex in my house? With my daughter?!" My dad yells balling up his fist. Good thing my parents just think I'm that STUPID *and* EASY.

"Timeout," I step in between him and Billy who's leaning shirtless against the bed. We spilt a little bit of liquor on it … or maybe it was frosting. I don't actually remember what; I just remember him taking it off before a stain set. "No one had sex. Why would I have sex with him here? With you guys right across the house? With DK in the room?" I point to him half awake on the floor. That's just not smart. My parents lack on dishing out credits on intelligence. Relaxing on the bed next to him I stuff my hands into my jean pockets. "I wasn't having sex. I haven't had sex with Billy or any other guy for that matter."

"Thank god," my mom puts a hand over her heart sounding relieved.

"Wow," I mouth out and look down at the ground.

"Then what's going on?" My dad looks at us sternly. "Why were you sleeping in his bed with him?"

"In his arms?" my mother adds like she needs to draw me a map of where I was sleeping.

"Well," I look at Billy who looks more anxious than ever for me to tell them. "Mom … Dad … Billy and I are dating." I wait for the fiery gates of hell to open and unleash the flames.

My mom gasps and covers her mouth as my dad looks like he doesn't understand. This would be where our over dramatic skills come from.

"What?" she whispers.

"We—

"How?"

"Well we—

"Since when?" My mom asks what I hope will be her last question for this series.

After maintaining my silence long enough to realize it's my turn I answer, "Since around the time we were in Ft. Worth, and we went out on that date."

"Ft. Worth?!" they yell in unison.

"Yeah," I nod slowly still half awake and half sober. You know I don't think if I was sober that my reaction would be any different. I don't care if they approve or not because I love him and that's all that matters.

"I told you not to let them go out," my father instantly blames my mother.

Distraught she replies, "I figured they would just be … ya know hang out like they never did as kids."

"They're walking hormones! They don't just hang out now-a-days. It's all about finding a quick hook up and getting some action." I feel my stomach turn hearing my father say that.

"Well I didn't know any better!" She stomps her foot and look at me, "Why him?"

"Why not?" I shrug finally having a say in this conversation I envisioned going differently. "You're the one who forced me to hang out with him, and then go on a date with him—

"I just said I figured—

"I heard you mom, but what about at Thanksgiving? You told me you wished I would date some guy like Billy."

Shaking my head my mother objects, "I had been doing my holiday drinking. You shouldn't have been listening to me."

"Well you said it, so instead of some guy I'm dating better. I'm dating him. Come on now would you two really rather have me date the 'one hitter quitter'," I point behind me at DK who's on the floor half listening.

"Hey!" He objects.

"Seriously DK," I shoot him a glance.

Curling back up he mumbles, "Even if it's true, you ain't gotta call me out like that."

My parents scrunch their nose at the thought of me dating DK as I continue, "Come on mom you love Billy. He's like the perfect gentleman you dreamed of me dating, and you've loved him since before I can remember. So why not love him now as my boyfriend?" Guilt card number one played.

"He has always been polite and very considerate," she gradually nods.

"As for you dad, correct me if I'm wrong, but aren't you the one who told me you like the way you and Billy talk?" Guilt card number two.

"Yeah, he is a good kid to talk about the game with," my dad lets a small grin creep on his face reflecting about the football game they watched on Thanksgiving.

"Isn't he better than anything I've ever brought home?" Now that my cards are on the table I'll play the let it sizzle card to seal the hand.

They simply turn to each other and in unison sigh disappointedly, "True."

Disregarding that statement I scoot closer to Billy, which causes him to wrap an arm around my waist, "Now can you two except this and get past the little picture of me not telling you to realize your daughter is the happiest she's ever been?" Don't you love the way how he is usually so charming, but when it comes to the two people who can keep me from him he's mute?

My father begins "That may be true Kiara, but I do not like the fact he doesn't have job—

"He has two," I quickly correct him.

"I don't like that he's not in school—

"He doesn't know if that's right for him or not, but he is at least considering it."

"I don't like the fact his priorities aren't in order."

"Dad he works two jobs, has an interest in music which he is slightly pursuing, and is considering going back to school. He handles his, which more than I can say for some," I tilt my head DK's direction.

Taking a step closer staring him in the eyes he asks me, "Is he faithful?"

"Like my shadow," I playfully nudge Billy in side not getting a smile.

"Does he love you?" the question rolls off his tongue and before I can respond he directs it at him, "Do you love my daughter?"

"Yes sir," Billy's voice trembles. I'd be afraid of an ex military man who grills you like he is the highest ranking officer in the house, but that's just me.

"What?" DK pops up confused. "You love her?"

I turn and look at him nodding with a smirk showing him my locket. Despite what DK wants Billy to do, he loves me, and there's nothing that idiot can do to stop him. Oh I love making DK unhappy; it makes me feel even better about myself.

My father's voice sounds like we're in an army court, "Are you good to her?"

"Always sir."

"Do not hurt her," my dad coldly says before leaning in, "Trust me. I know the right people if that does happen."

"Darryl," my mother hits his arm.

Clearing his throat my father does as told, "I guess all I have left to say is welcome to our family."

My mother forces a smile on her face as she gives Billy a slight hug before she says, "No more sleeping together like this. No more keeping things from us about this relationship or anything. Got it?"

Yes captain or whatever the highest ranking position is. In this house the military man is not the absolute word; she is. "Yeah."

"You go to your room, and go to bed. And no late night rendezvous in the bathroom just because your room connects to it," she points a stern finger at me. I'm glad my parents think I'm a sneaky whore who'll do anything to get some from her boyfriend.

"Ok," I say to them as they stroll off back towards their room talking about us.

I look at Billy whose grinning. I toss my arms around his neck hugging him tightly as he does the same back. "Goodnight."

"Goodnight baby I love you," he whispers back in my ear.

"I love you," I peck him with a kiss on the cheek.

"See you in a couple of hours," he says letting me slip away. "Wake me up when you get up?"

"Yeah. Bye Billy," I wave to him as he waves back hesitating to let me go. Once I'm in the bathroom with the door closed I relax the back of my head against the door and sigh. I don't know if I can sleep after the night I've had. Even though I'm worn out, the excitement in my body doesn't seem to be dying down. I really should get some rest so that he doesn't have to deal with cranky Kie, because she's not a pretty person.

We end up sleeping away the entire afternoon until it's time for us to get ready for church. I always go to church on Christmas Eve. For the past few years it's been with Mia, whose family goes at separate times. Her mother, father, and younger sister go to the evening service at six while Mia and I go to the one at ten, but before we go we have our annual Christmas Eve dinner of pizza at my house.

Billy, me and DK get up around six thirty, which is just enough time to get up, stretch, and eat pizza before getting ready for church. Mia shows up a bit later than normal due to last night's lack of time to rest.

We talk and eat together before I go off and get dressed as she lounges around in my room talking to me about the killer party she and Billy threw for me.

She tells me how he has some big news besides the fact he loves me to reveal, but quickly forgets about it when she's given permission to open her Christmas present. It's a gift certificate to a full spa treatment. It does her nails, feet, gives a full body massage, facial, the whole works. I know she loves it by the way she screams and hugs me. What can I say? Every girl needs a day of pampering.

"Have a nice time at church," my mother says as we walk out all dressed up for the service. I'm in a black skirt and read sweater while Billy is dressed up in his best pair of dress pants and white collar shirt.

"We will," I say being the last one out of the house.

"How about you ride with Mia?" Billy suggest to DK hoping he can ride alone with me.

"Yeah," Mia smiles back at him knowing she wants us to be alone as well. She understands we like to grasp as many moments alone as we can and hopes now will be when he reveals the big news to me.

After DK hesitates and debates internally he strolls over to Mia's car, "Fine."

Billy opens my side of the car as my mother watches him act more like a gentleman than she's ever seen before. I get in and smile politely as he walks around to his side getting in. He starts the car, letting me fiddle with the radio station as he begins down the road following Mia.

Once I'm done I place my hand on his thigh as he drives. Without looking away from the road he slips his hand so that he's cradling mine in his and just rubs the back of it softly. It drives me crazy how he does innocent things to let me know I'm still the girl of his dream. This far into the relationship most people forget they have to keep those things there to keep the relationship healthy.

"So how'd you pull off the party?" I ask crossing my ankles.

"The owner of the club I work for is movin' his club from there to here in Austin," Billy looks at me smiling. "And I'm transferrin'," he says making my eyes widen. He's movin' to Austin? Meaning I can see him every day? Meaning he'll be here every time I need him? Grinning to himself he explains, "So I asked him could I test his club out by throwin' my girlfriend a birthday party. I talk a lot about you, so he was more than willin' to let his best worker try it out."

"You're gonna live here in town?"

"Yeah. I'm changin' all kinds of other things. Why not change this too when there's the opportunity?"

"What about Ft. Worth? That's your home. And what about DK? Your deals? The music recording?" Why am I pushing him to stay there? Am I completely stupid?

"I don't really deal any more. I just watch DK's back. Besides he's thinkin' about movin' in with me, but if not I'm fine on my own. I can support myself," he stops at the stoplight. "I've learned to do that. As for that bein' my home ... you know how they say your home is where your heart is? Well my hearts with you here in Austin, so that's where I'm gonna be too."

With a smile I place a kiss on his lips. Leaning back I continue looking at him with a small smile. He's moving for me now. If getting a job, stop selling weed and whatever other crime he commits, as well as becoming a presentable person breaking the thug shell DK built for him wasn't enough, now he's moving.

"Unless of course you have a problem with me movin' here. Afraid I'm gonna invade some sort of space you enjoy us havin'," he says sarcastically to me.

Stupid thing for him to say. Stupid. Almost a mood killer in fact. "Of course I don't mind you moving here. I love the idea."

"Mm," he smirks to himself. "Good."

There's some silence between us as the radio plays a song we both love. At one point and time, I see Billy turn and look at me waiting to get my attention. I turn and give him the answering face.

"You know what else?" He asks pulling into the parking lot behind Mia.

Digging through my purse I mumble, "What?"

"You have to look at me," he parks behind her and turns off the car. I look over at him awaiting an answer. Billy leans in and places one hand on my face as he strokes my cheek. "I think you're beautiful." Softly he places a kiss on my lips.

Ya know I never hate to hear that from him. Sometimes it's nice to just have him stop whatever I'm doing to let me know he still thinks I'm attractive.

"Thank you," I grin as Mia taps on our window to go.

"Let me get the door," he gets out of the car as I quickly look at my face in the mirror. Billy moves Mia out of the way to open the door for me. His hand is being held out for me take.

"Thank you," I say again holding his hand walking next to Mia while DK's on the other side of Billy trying to talk to him about something.

"Not now DK, for god's sake it's Christmas. Jesus' birthday is tomorrow, lay off about it," Billy snaps. I wonder what they're talking about. I know they're not discussing selling weed or doing anything else illegal on Christ's birthday. DK's not that inconsiderate is he?

"We're going to go to the bathroom," Mia says grabbing my arm pulling me off towards the bathroom leaving the two of them waiting in the lobby. I follow her knowing I might as well pee, so I don't have to in the middle of service.

As soon as I'm done I lean against the sink and wait for Mia to come out. Once she comes out she heads straight to wash her hands and reapply her make up.

Curiously I ask, "So what the deal with you and DK?"

"Excuse me?" she plays innocent turning on the faucet.

"Yesterday … at my birthday …" I refresh her memory. "You two were dancing awfully close and looked as if, heaven forbid, a spark of some sort occurred. So tell me."

She dries her hands before answering me. "Last night he stepped to me real for the first time, and we danced to that song Billy sang for you."

"Did you guys make out at my party?"

"Do you really wanna know?"

"Yeah … no … well yeah … no wait no! Yeah I do … come on and tell me, wait on second thought," I argue with myself.

"Kie," she looks at me before reapplying her lip gloss.

"Yeah give it to me straight."

"Yes we made out here and there."

I shudder a little. How could she do it? "Did you hold hands? Hold each other?"

"We held hands through out the night. We didn't hold each other though, but he didn't talk or hit on any other girl the whole night. He was just into me."

"That doesn't sound like DK. Maybe he was drunk, but even if he was drunk that still doesn't sound like DK. Are you sure you were with DK?"

She gives me a sarcastic look in the mirror before focusing on her lips. "It was different last night. We were in a different state of mind. There's something about being half drunk and watching you and Billy be in the state you are that makes us crave that some so …" she shrugs. "I mean it's not we're about to start anything. It was just sort of a way to soothe the urges we get from wanting to be a couple like you two even if neither of us will admit it to the other there's something about each other that satisfies us especially when it comes to wishing we could be like you and your man deep inside."

"Mm," I manage to say and fold my hands as she digs through her purse for her eye shadow.

"Besides, like I always say," she presses her lips together again. "Everyone needs love on the holidays.

I giggle a little.

"And how did you enjoy your party? I mean after Billy sang to you I didn't see much of either of you."

I smirk to myself and hold my locket. "It was great. After he sang to me he took me into that room and gave me this locket that his dad gave his mother before they died. He said some really sweet things to me, and then he told me he loved me," I start to head off towards the door after witnessing Mia stab herself in the eye.

"Ouch! What?" She turns to look at me sneaking off. "Come back in here!"

"What?" I ask harmlessly.

"He told you he loved you?"

"Yeah."

"He said the words I love you?"

"Yup."

"In that exact order?"

"Uh-huh."

"Directed at you?"

"Yes."

"He said I love you, in that exact order directed at you, and was completely sober?"

"Geez Mia you make it sound like he's incapable of that emotion." With a deep sigh I nod slowly, "Yes. He admitted to me he loved me last night."

"The boy who had no idea what it was or how it felt suddenly after around six months of being with you and all the changes he went through for you confessed that he loved you?"

"Yes," I beam. "The locket has our picture on one side and just his on the other."

"Wow," she undoes what I accidentally made her do. "I'm happy for you, which is of course if you said it back. I mean I know you said it back because you wouldn't be dumb enough not to right?" Slowly she turns around, "Kie please tell me you said it back."

"Of course," I sigh.

"Aw my little Kie is all grown up," she puts an arm around me. "I'm happy for you sissy, but remember just because he loves you, does not mean you have to make love."

I look at her like she's been smoking something. How dare she try to give me the minor relationship sex talk! Better yet, how dare she do it on Christmas Eve, in a church! It's amazing how she feels the need to wag a finger at me about *my* morals.

"I know," I nod as we open the door to see Billy and DK impatiently waiting.

"Damn you females take a long ass time," DK whines. Mia gasps and hits him twice in his arm with her heavy purse.

"Shit! What was that for?" He holds his arm as she whacks him in his stomach this time.

"This is God's house," she scowls him. "You don't cuss in his house, especially not on the eve of his only son's birthday!"

"Damn my bad," he shakes his head and she whacks him one good this time in his head. In pain he corrects, "I mean dang."

"Better."

DK mumbles, "They ain't gon' be too many more hits."

"Excuse me? Speak at the level where not only god can hear you," Mia says to him with her hands on her hips. "If you dare."

He shakes his head and follows in behind her. I wonder is he just too tired to fight with her, or does he think if he keeps up with this 'I'll obey you' charade long enough she'll give him some. What a horrible thing for him to be thinking on Christmas Eve. No wonder he'll receive coal in his stocking.

We sit down together towards the back a little. Mia and I sit next to each other between the guys. Billy without even thinking slips his arm around me while holding my other one making sure we're comfortable to listen to the minister. I watch DK on the sly reach over a little and slip fingertips with Mia. I try not to laugh at how unobvious they try to be as well as keep their boundaries while they're together.

The four of us listen intently to the story of the birth of Christ. No matter how many times you hear it, it still manages to wow you every time. There's something about understanding the story and seeing just the other miracles god can bless you with, which makes you want to break down in tears in thankfulness.

I wake up early Christmas morning to turn over and see the clock read 6:15. My mom is up making coffee and hot chocolate for me. I wonder if I should wake Billy up or not. I mean would it be wrong to wake him up to open presents like a family? Like he misses? He told me yesterday to wake him up when I got up, so why should today be any different?

Quietly I get out of my bed, creek open his side of the bathroom door, and tiptoe over to where he's sleeping. It's cute how he's sleeping on the side closet to the door just in case I do choose to wake him up.

Leaning down I give him a little shake. "Billy," I whisper in his ear to hear him groan. "Wake up."

He groans once more and opens an eye to see me looking at him. "Yeah?"

"It's time to open Christmas presents," I whisper to him trying not to wake DK up.

"What time is it?"

"About 6:15," I whisper kneeling beside his bed.

"Wow," he yawns. "Early."

"You can sleep if you want, and me, mom, dad, and 'Nell will open presents."

"No, no," Billy insists. "I'll get up."

I smirk to myself. He has trouble telling me no. Billy groans some more as he gets up. Sneaking back around to my room I come out the front door yawning and stretching as if I just got up to fool my mom. Nonchalantly I stroll over to Billy's door where he's doing the same.

We link hands and go into the kitchen where my mom is sipping her coffee with my dad.

"Good morning love birds," she says smiling putting her cup down.

"Morning," we yawn together.

My dad gives Billy a wince over, "She wake you up?"

"Yeah," he nods adjusting his white t-shirt that he barely had time to put on.

"Same here," my father looks at my mom. "You get use to them."

Billy smirks as my mom, and I give my dad a sarcastic look. We head towards the living room where the Christmas tree is gushing with presents. I mean there is almost no room to walk. Don't worry, all the gifts aren't for just my immediate family.

As we enter the living room where the tree is Billy admires the white leather couches that surround a coffee table with an opening where the tree blocks. It's cold and pretty well lit by a chandelier, but not very welcoming because we never spend much time in here. It's to look at more than to actually be in. We have a few nice stands with pictures and portraits on them.

"Should we wake 'Nell?" I ask looking at my mom as we sit down on the couches opposite from each other.

"Nah," my dad shakes his head. "We've woken her up every year since you were five. We'll give her a year off."

I nod as Billy sips on his hot chocolate next to me. Why didn't he hand me a cup, or at least offer me some of his.

"Want some babe?" he offers it towards me. Aw. I spoke too soon.

"Sure," I take the mug and get a drink. I lick my lips and hand it back as I pass gifts around. "This ones for mom, dad," I hand them to them. "Billy …" I turn to him. "It's from my parents."

Billy looks confused as well as sad for not getting them anything more than cards. He rips open the first gift revealing a basketball. You're kidding me right?

My parents got him a basketball? I try not to laugh. Ironic? Billy smiles and then opens the card where a fifty-dollar bill falls out. Oh there's the real gift.

"Thanks," Billy sighs looking at them. "You didn't have to do this."

"Sure we did," my mom shakes her head. "You're our daughter's boyfriend, and you've been a great friend to this family, so merry Christmas."

"Merry Christmas," my dad echoes.

Looking touched he says back, "Thank you. Merry Christmas."

I can't help feeling warm inside. My parents and boyfriend are bonding for the first time and to make matters even better on a holiday that I have not once ever disliked. It's the holiday that just gets better with age rather than worse. I love this holiday even more now. It's not about gifts, but about the feelings you get when you give them, and the feeling you receive just knowing that someone else cares about you.

After I've opened all the presents from my parents and sister they leave so that Billy and I can exchange presents in peace.

"You wanna go first?" He asks putting his hot chocolate down on the table.

"Yeah," I nod knowing his gift will probably top mine because after all this boy is just full of wonders left and right. I could buy him a ticket to Disney Land to ride all the rides he wanted from dawn until dusk, but his gift would still be better if it was a macaroni card. That just proves it's not about the cost, but the thought.

I hand him a big box. If only he knew everything in it was wrapped separately.

Billy opens it up to see that there are different things wrapped within it. "Oh you did it ol' school. Make me work for the gifts," he smiles to himself as he unwraps the first one, which is another Lakers' jersey.

"I know how much you like 'em," I say watching him grin. "Can never have too many huh?"

He shakes his head and kisses my forehead. "What can I say I'm a Lakers' guy," he shrugs and looks at me. He opens the next present, which is a Lakers' hat to match the jersey. Billy smiles even wider. "Nice."

"Glad you like it," I feel him kiss me on the cheek.

"Very thoughtful," he pulls out another gift that he doesn't waste time unwrapping. He slowly gets another grin across his face.

"It's a journal for you to write your songs in," I smile. "That is if you keep writing them about me."

He laughs a little and kisses my lips. "Of course," he nods. "You're the only brown suga' mama I'll ever write about."

"Better be."

Pulling out the envelope, which happens to be the last item in the box, he pulls a ticket out from it. "What's this? What is The Show Case?"

"Remember how I told you we plan to compete to win that competition of a record deal, and the whole nine yards? Well each person who competes gets two tickets to give to family members to see them. Neither my mom or dad can come, so I figured who would wanna see me more than my boyfriend who's very supportive."

He nods and twists the ticket around.

"Will you be there?"

"Of course baby," he takes my hand and leans in. "I promise."

I kiss him quickly not wanting my parents to catch us in the middle of a kiss. He pulls away from me to reach over and get my gift.

Billy smiles as he hands me my present. "Unlike you I didn't go the ol' school route. I just straight up wrapped it once. Neat though righ'?"

Inspecting the box I nod, "Very good. You wrapped this all alone?"

"Yeah. I had to practice on Mia's present though. I kinda messed hers up and got yours right."

"Good," I wink and rip off the paper and quickly open the box where there's a burned CD, a receipt of some sort, and a hundred dollar bill. "What—

"The money," he points to it, "is so you can go shoppin' and pamper yourself." With a wider smile he continues, "The CD is a copy of the song I sang to you the other night, so you can listen to it any second you choose as well as play it for your friends. The receipt is for studio time."

"Studio time? Studio time for what?" I ask dumbly. What else do you use studio time for? How stupid did that sound?

"I figured that you girls would like to be in the studio and record some songs just in case for some reason you don't win. This way you still have some'n to work with as well as your own personal studio time to lay beats, mix, and do whatever it is you want in there. Who knows maybe do a duet with me," he leans in towards me once more.

"Thank you," I smile and touch his cheek.

How sweet. He makes sure to take care of my dream as well as me by myself.

Is there anything he doesn't do right? Ok a better question. Is there anything he can't give to me emotionally or financially? With him it's the whole nine yards. The entire package. It's like no one could ever be placed above me in his eyes.

For some reason he chose me to give his life to. All of it. Every single memory, the amounts of money, all of his love, just everything he has to me. Sometimes I lay awake in bed at night and ask did God drag us together to make us realize that there's more to life than our egos and pride? Did he want us to understand that sending his only son wasn't the only miracle he was capable of?

I never thought of Christmas as more than a time to focus just on Jesus and that blessing god gave us. It's his son's birthday, but it's more than that. You have to realize what he did while he was here and that if you love someone there should never be a sacrifice too big for that person. God gave everything he had to us and for that we're forever grateful. So while we're here shouldn't we follow in his light to make the best of our time here and give what we can for other people, whether it's presents or love?

I think all Billy wanted was to be loved again on Christmas. When you grow up without your family, there's a bit of love missing from your heart. At this moment, this year, this Christmas, I think he finally felt it back. As for me, I know what it's like to have people love you and feel that love, but I've never known what it's like to be *in* love at this time. I want to be in love every Christmas and get to experience this joy.

My greatest gift wasn't the presents he just handed me, not the fact he gets to spend the night here, and not the fact he threw me a wonderful party. The best gift is being in love with a wonderful person and somehow I know that Billy feels the same.

CHAPTER 13

Cupid's Free

Who really likes Valentine's Day? It's a holiday created by the greeting card companies who hooked up with the chocolate companies in a great scheme to sell more products than any time of the year. Just label it the world's best marketing idea. The day is made to make people who don't have a significant other wallow in their own pity while downing chocolate they had to buy for themselves. They are forced to watch couples of all sorts show off their love with expensive presents and signs of affection, secretly wishing that they could be them. Either way chocolate is being consumed or presents are being bought. The things people do to place themselves above other people in corporate America.

I don't like most holidays or events that take place in my life, but this one in particular, irks me more than the others. See at least all the others have some point to them, Thanksgiving for blessings, homecoming for school pride, but what does Valentine's Day really bring to the table? All right, so I have a boyfriend. Big whoop! Having a boyfriend ONE out of all the other years doesn't make a significant difference. When you're one of those single lonely people every other year, having a boyfriend doesn't really register as a big change.

I hate Valentine's Day more than any other time of the year. Yes. This is the day I hate most. I know you're thinking yeah well that's going to change Kie look at the rest of your life. Billy's worked wonders for you, and you're going to be so happy. News flash, this holiday doesn't change. Every year I end up sad and miserable about something. Every year.

"No idea Mia," I say walking around my room desperately searching for my English book.

"Come on," she whines. "You've planned something for this weekend right?"

"No," I shake my head tossing around some stuffed animals. "I don't even know why you're trying to make plans with me for that Satan created holiday when you know damn well you ditch me every year." Oh yeah that makes it better too. My best friend says she'll hang out with me almost every year, and it always changes. Some hot dude will want to hook up and hang out with her so being the selfless friend I am I just let her go.

"I swear Kie," she pledges. "I will not ditch you this year."

"Mia you—

"Double dating! Let's double date."

I stop mid motion of picking up my book I finally found underneath a pile of blankets. "Who?"

"You, Billy, me … DK," she mumbles under her breath. I knew it. Of course she'd wanna spend the devil's holiday with none other than the devil's first born.

"Aw man," I whine picking my book up.

Trying to convince me she whimpers, "Come on Kie."

"Um," I flop on my bed with the book. "No."

"Kie!" She yells into the phone. "Why not?"

"Why so?"

"I like hanging out with DK. I mean sure he has a few bad qualities—

"A few?"

"Some—

"Some?"

"Ok sure he's got bad qualities, but we get along really well some times, particularly on holidays. Come on Kie … please," she says in a child like voice. "Please …"

"I'll see," I roll my eyes flipping open the book. "I don't even know what Billy has planned for us."

"I'm sure he'll call you sooner or later," she says twisting her hair around her finger.

As soon I glance over at my cell phone it begins to ring. What is she, a mind reader now? What if Mia could predict the future and know all the need to know before hand? Wouldn't you fear for your life?

"Speaking of the boyfriend," I lean over and grab my phone. "It's him. I'll call you later ok?"

"Yeah," she sighs and hangs up as I do.

"Hello," I answer my cell phone.

Softly he says, "Hi baby."

"What's going on?"

"Nothin'. Just got off of work."

"The hotel?"

"Yeah," he sighs kicking off his shoes. "What about you?"

"Trying to do my damn English homework. What kind of teacher assigns twenty three pages to read *and* a four page essay to write?"

"The bad kind," he chuckles slightly. "Doin' anything else?"

"I was talking to Mia about this weekend," I say slowly.

"What's this weekend?"

I laugh at him like he doesn't know. Sometimes playing that innocent thing is cute. It usually just means he's got something pretty big planned. "Valentine's Day."

"Oh yeah. What do you girls have planned?"

"Well … double dating with you and DK was hopefully the plan."

I hear silence on the other end. It's not the good kind of surprise silence. It's the 'I have no idea what you're talking about' sort. "I don't think so."

"Well if you want it to just be the two of us that's cool too," I say wondering why he wouldn't want his homeboy to roll with him now, as he does every other time of the year.

"No. That's not it," he says slowly. "I can't see you."

I open my mouth trying to figure out is he kidding with me or not. He has to be kidding. He better be kidding. "Stop playin' Billy."

Explaining he says, "I'm not. I can't come down there. I have to work both Friday and Saturday all day. It's a really important time of year. I took off Thanksgiving and Christmas, so to be fair I said I'd work the next two holidays."

"You all ready missed New Years with me, and now you have to miss Valentine's Day too?"

"I'm sorry. I figured the other two were more important times to take off."

"I mean they were, but you don't get to see me at all?"

"The places get really busy, especially the club. You know they need me there in order to make 'em a few extra. A lot of couples go out on Valentine's Day so know I'm gonna be bringing in a lot of cash."

"I wanna be one of those couples," I mumble under my breath.

"What?"

"Nothing," I grumble. See. Even with a boyfriend things are still going to suck.

"I'm sorry Kie. I really am," he apologizes again like it's really going to help. "I'm sure Mia and you can find some'n to do."

"Mia sure can. Ryan asked her out for Saturday all ready," I sigh. "But she had her hopes set on being with you and DK just like I did. I guess we could go out with Ryan and Danny—

"Danny?" He cuts me off. "That punk ass white boy who's been after you since long before we were datin'."

"We're just friends," I reassure him. "You know I don't even like him like that."

"Wait, you don't get to spend this weekend with me, and you've already got a back up plan?"

"Back up plan? It's not like that. Billy—

"So what is he like, yo' back up boyfriend?"

"Back up boyfriend that's ridic—

"I'm not in reach, so you go out wit' him?"

"What's your problem?"

"I don't know. I guess there's some'n 'bout hearin' yo' girlfriend is gonna go out wit' some other nigga on the mos' romantic day of the year that pisses me off," he snaps at me in the phone.

He really gets on my nerves with all the drama. It's not like I said I was about to marry the boy or something, and if he would have let me finished I would have said that I don't want to go so she can just go with Ryan, but of course my boyfriend stops me before I get that far.

"Billy—

"Ya know what Kie? You have fun wit' yo' preppy boy this weekend and holla at me Monday to tell me all the fuck about it," he overreacts one last time before he hangs up in my face.

I look at the phone in confusion. I know that nigga did not just hang up on me. You know I could say a lot of things to him about the way he acts when I mention another guy. I really get tired of this male testosterone territory issue. It's really a pain in the ass.

Instantly I call Mia back on my house phone still baffled.

"Yeah," she says turning down her radio.

"Billy has lost his damn mind," I say still in shock.

"Why? What happened?"

"That boy hung up on me!"

"I don't understand. He did what?"

"He hung up on me!! He told me he couldn't come down here. After I attempt to throw a minor fit, I tell him we were invited to hang out with Danny and Ryan. Next thing I know he goes off and hangs up," I explain still trying to let it process.

"No-huh."

"Yeah," I shake my head. "I have no idea what's wrong with him. It's like any time he hears another guys name it hits his crazy 'let me act like a jerk for no reason' switch."

"So I've noticed."

Sliding off my bed I begin to pace back and fourth. Sometimes I wonder does he think that I don't do enough for him. I mean he makes all these trips down here along with all sorts of other little things to show me he cares, yet I sound selfish because he's throwing a fit if I spend Valentine's Day with another guy. Maybe I didn't see the big picture. Maybe he wants me to do something big and different for once. Maybe he wants—

"Mia …"

"Yeah," she pauses in the middle of turning a page in her magazine.

"Let's go to Ft. Worth."

I hear her laugh on the other side of the phone, "I didn't know you were in a joking mood."

"I'm serious," I smirk myself. "Let's go this weekend."

"And tell our parents what? That we're going to spend the weekend with two thugs to bring the romantic side out of them on the holiday?"

I thought when you used sarcasm it was supposed to amuse someone other than yourself. "We'll tell them that we're going down there to use our recording studio time. We'll say that this was one of the only free weekends before competition. Besides while we're down there we can actually go early Sunday morning."

Mia is silent on the other end of the phone for what feels like a class period, "You're serious aren't you?"

"Yeah. I mean why not? We have the perfect alibi and on top of that don't you think I should show him for once that I can make sacrifices to come see him?"

"I guess," she hesitates to agree. Her philosophy is to always have them show you, never the other way around. "How are we going though? I mean whose going to drive?"

I feel myself smile as it hits her that she's the one doing the driving.

"Oh no," she shakes her head. "No. No. No."

"You owe me! You owe me for every Valentine's Day you ditched me. It's time to pay up Mia."

"Can't I pay in blood or somethin'?"

Ignoring her I move on, "Besides if you want to hang out with DK, for only god knows why, then you have to get to him. He may not be worth the drive, but you know me and Billy are." Guilt trip 101.

I wait for her response. I know she's debating the best she can in her head weighing the good with the bad. There's not really any bad unless we can't get a hold of DK to tell him, then we're kind of screwed.

"Are you sure there's no other way?"

"None."

She sighs, "Then I guess let's do this."

"Yay!" I scream into the phone. "Just call DK and let him know the plan. I'm going to secretly surprise Billy, and he can't tell him."

"Hints the word secret."

"All right smart ass just call him ok?"

"What make you think I have his number?"

I give the phone a sarcastic look. "Who you tryin' to fool?"

"Girl I don't know," she reaches for her cell phone. "So we'll leave Saturday afternoon then? Around three or so and be back Sunday evening?"

"Yeah. Don't forget to run it by your parents. I'm sure they'll let you, for your career and all ..."

"I never knew pursuing this music thing could have hidden perks like this."

I giggle and shake my head, "Call me back ok?"

Well I still have to run it by my parents, and we all know that they'll put up a hell of a fight before even thinking about letting me ride all the way to Ft. Worth with Mia and stay with Billy and DK, no matter how much they may like him.

"Yeah. Bye," she clicks off.

Glancing over at my English book and then at my bedroom door I debate homework or fight? Finish boring things for school or go ask my parents now? Time to myself or an argument battle with two of America's hardest unofficial lawyers known as parents? Homework it is.

I stare out the side window as Mia sings along to the radio. So our parents, after hours of lecturing and precautions, they let us go. Nothing is better than being away from our parents. Just the open highway, the loud radio, Mia's chips, and us.

You know she's driving calmly, there's little to no traffic, and the radio's playing everything we want to hear. Strangely enough everything is going our way, which is usually a sign something is going to go wrong soon. Sorry if that sound pessimistic, but let's be realistic here.

"So now let me get this straight," she turns down the radio and pops another chip in her mouth. "We get there and DK is waiting to meet us at Big Mama's while Billy is home changing to go to the club. DK will take us to their place, you'll set up his room, and I'm going to chill with DK in the meantime. Billy will come home dead tired, go in his room, and see his sexy girlfriend waiting on his bed for him?"

"Doesn't that sound perfect?" I happily sigh.

"Yeah, but you really haven't talked to Billy in two days? Like no text messages or voicemails?"

"Not a word. I've left him so many messages and still nothing."

"Brotha' must be pissed," she shakes her head. "I don't understand how he can be this mad for no reason. He's probably hiding something from you."

Why she gotta put that thought in my mind? I mean she didn't have to add that to the mix. "I don't think so."

"Hey it's just a thought."

"A bad thought, but thanks."

She rolls her eyes at me, "Don't be gettin' all upset at me. I wasn't the one who hung up on you, and who hasn't returned your phone calls or messages."

"Why you gotta bring that back up? You know that just makes me want to ring his neck."

"I'm sorry. Damn. Why don't you give me a script on what I can say that won't make you mad?"

"What's with all the attitude? Why are you of all people being bitter today?"

"Why can't I be bitter? I ain't got a man. I'm not driving nearly four hours to go see some guy I love. No, I'm driving four hours to go see some guy *you* love who has a tendency to have a bad temper despite his cool outer presence."

Shaking my head at her I argue back, "You know all of this is unnecessary. It's not like your ass is about to be left all cold and lonely with no one to love you, so stop trippin.'"

"How come when I want to vent about not liking this day I get it thrown in my face that I have always had someone on this holiday? I ain't really ever have somebody who's in love with me, just a bunch of little horny boys all lookin' to get some."

"Boo-hoo," I mumble at her.

"Really," she pleas.

"Yeah. My heart bleeds for you."

"Ya know what? Let me just toss your ass out my car."

"Throw me out then," I play back with her. Sometimes when she drives for long hours of time she gets cranky and needs some laughter.

"Don't make me pull my ass over."

In a playful fighting mode I yell, "Pull over. Pull this car the fuck over!"

"Where you want me to pull over?" She glances around.

"Let me out by the mother fucking cows!" I scream and point at them.

She gives me one long glare before she starts to laugh. We start cracking up and just can't stop. There's something about play fighting with your best friend that relieves some sort of stress. Now Mia can drive with a smile and I can relax about Billy keeping something from me.

The drive has to be quicker because I'm driving with my best friend, but longer because I actually have to stay awake to navigate.

After a couple more hours of driving we arrive in front of Big Mama's where we see DK leaning against the back of his car, looking at his watch as if being impatient. He should know how long that ride from there to here is and should understand before I use my fist to make him. Mia pulls up right in front of him not getting out the car, but merely rolling down her window.

"Sup," she gives him the nod on the cool. What is the need to be incognito about the love affair you two share?

"Waitin' on you," he doesn't even attempt to come over our way. Yeah he's changed *a lot* Mia.

"I bet," she looks him up and down. "How long we gotta wait 'til we leave?"

DK looks down at his watch, "Well Billy left for the club 'bout ten minutes ago, so if we go the back way we should miss him."

"And where does he think you are?"

"Where I always am," he says with a cocky grin.

Rolling her eyes Mia sighs, "Strip club chasing ho's?"

Smoothly he says, "What do I need to go the strip club fo' when I've got a beauty like you to look at?"

Shocked yet disgusted at that comment I lean over a little to ask, "What time does he get off?"

"Around midnight or so," he shrugs. "Since he'll probably be missin' you, he'll come home right away."

I smile to myself. Good to know when he's miserable without me he drags himself home to bury his sorrow in his sleep like normal people.

"That's kind of sweet."

"I guess so."

"Do you know why he hasn't called?"

Taking a breath he shrugs, "Naw …"

"Excuse me. Can we speed this adventure up before a car decides to come from behind me and hit me?" Mia asks looking at the two of us like we're keeping her from moving her mini SUV.

"Yeah," DK misses a perfectly good opportunity to say something smart back to her. Not taking an easy set up shot like that? What's his world coming to? First the un-need compliment now passing the opportunity to make a smart ass comment? Maybe he has changed a little for Mia.

Mia reverses so DK can back his way out of the driveway. As soon as he steps on the gas she's on him like a cop on a loose criminal.

I look out over the dashboard to see DK smirking wildly in his review mirror. What is he smiling about? I haven't seen that boy grin so much since that day Mia kissed him way back when we first went to their place nearly eight months ago. I look over to see her smiling crazy as well. Great. I've got two psychopath lovebirds that would probably kill each other in the process of falling in love.

Thirty minutes later we're outside their place waiting for DK to let us in.

"Could you be any faster with the door?" I ask knowing all the stuff I have is heavy.

"I don't know, but I damn sure know I could be slower," he turns around and looks at me. "Watch I can pull some slow motion on ya," DK puts the key in the lock and begins to turn it slow as possible.

Mia and me look at each other and nod. We each grab one of his ears and yank.

With a bit of an evil smirk, I lean forward and whisper in his ear, "Do you wanna go a bit fast now?"

DK quickly jingles the keys and lets us in.

I let go of his ear and move past him sighing, "Thank you."

"Very good," Mia pats him on the shoulder passing by too.

"Fuckin' females," he mumbles under his breath.

"I heard that," Mia calls back to him.

"I did too," I say walking back towards Billy's room where I drop off everything I have.

Tossing his keys on the glass table he groans, "Of course. You women hear everything."

"You're damn right we do," Mia walks around the leather couch in confusion. "Where do I put my stuff?"

DK licks his lips and leans over the couch with a small grin. "You could always sleep in my room ..."

After she gives him a sarcastic look she drops her bag to lean over the couch. "Let's get something straight," she points at him. "We are not a couple. We do not do couple things and even though it's Valentine's Day that doesn't change those facts."

DK can't help but continue smiling at her.

"Why are you still smiling?"

He hesitates to say anything. His tongue grazes his lips once more as he continues staring at her.

With attitude she snaps, "I'm waiting ..."

"It's jus' ..." he tries not to laugh. "You even hotter when you in charge."

Rolling her eyes in an annoyed way she starts away, but is stopped by DK's hand that grabs her arm.

"Look I understand we're not a couple. I don't want a girlfriend, and you clearly don't want a boyfriend, but it's Valentine's Day. I didn't wanna be wit' no other girl on this holiday."

Taken off guard she stumbles to say, "And wh-wh-why not?"

In one clean motion he tilts her chin up, "Maybe 'cause fo' the firs' time I knew who I wanted to be my valentine."

Her eyes widen as she swallows nervously, "Well if you're gonna ask me to be your valentine, we need to set boundaries. First of all I will not have sex with you. I'm sure you're use to that, but you will not be having sex with me tonight or any other night for that matter.

Curiously he asks, "Can we make out?"

"Of course."

"Then no problem. What are the other rules?"

"I demand I am talked to like a lady not a chicken head—

"Like Mia I think you look gorgeous today?"

As she tries to fight her smile she continues, "That I get respect—

"Proper talk, romance ..."

"You just remember that I can still whoop your ass if you cross any line with me."

"So bein' my valentine means I can do this and not get in trouble right?" He leans in and kisses Mia softly. "Or is that a line I shouldn't be crossin'?"

Mia doesn't know how to make her mouth to say no to that. She shakes her head and licks her lips.

Slyly he questions, "Anything else?"

"We don't make anything more of this weekend no matter how we may feel momentarily."

"No," he promptly disagrees.

"No?"

"Look Mia I can't promise you that I won't wanna be wit' you after this and damn sure can't promise you that I will. So how 'bout we jus' do what we do and what happens happens?

Completely stunned she answers in an airy voice, "Deal."

"Now, Mia," he takes her hand as I peek my head out from around the corner. "Will you be my valentine?"

She smirks and nods. "Yeah ..."

He leans in to kiss her again this time wrapping his arms around her waist. As sickening as this display is, it makes me want to say aw. It makes me miss Billy even more than I already do. I wish he were here now, hugging me, holding on to me, asking me what DK just did.

She pulls away and winks at him.

"Do you wanna sleep in my room by yo'self, and I'll sleep on the couch?" he offers her his bed, something I never thought he'd do. Ya know being selfish and all.

"We'll play your part by ear, but as for mine," she smirks. "Yeah, take me to your room," she grabs her bag, takes his hand, and starts towards my direction. I quickly dart back into Billy's room where my stuff is already dropped off to hear her say, "It better be clean."

The thoughts of what sort of germs will be eating her alive tonight is mind blowing. I don't know what sorts of hideous creatures have spawned from in there, the last time that boy cleaned his room, or washed his sheets. I've never been in there and really don't want to go in there now or ever.

An hour or so later I'm on Billy's bed trying to write a song, but am struggling to focus.

"We're going out to get something to eat," Mia comes into the doorway dressed in a tight black skirt and red halter-top, with her hair done nicely and her make up very sexy. Aw! Date moment. "We might head to a movie or something too."

"You look good. Very sheik."

"Thank you," she pops her knee out and poses. After a smile 'you're welcome' she in a paranoid tone asks, "Do you want or need anything? Do you need me to be here? Will you be ok?"

"I'm sure she'll be fine," DK comes over and drapes an arm around her waist.

If I didn't know any better I would say that they've got more feelings than their letting on. I just hope they don't fall in love, not that DK can spell the word let alone understand it.

With a wink he chuckles, "She's a trooper."

"Yeah Mia, I'll be ok. I know where everything is," I nod. "I have your cell if I need anything before you two get back or Billy gets here. Now go out and have a good time. Enjoy Valentine's Day."

"We will. Now call if you need *anything*," she points at me.

I give thumbs up.

"Bye," Mia waves slowly.

"Later," I call to them as they leave.

I roll back over onto my stomach reopening my notebook. It's so hard to concentrate while I'm anticipating his arrival. I miss him so much right now. He's probably at work just moping around missing me too, which makes this surprise even better.

After a couple more hours of writing it's somewhere close to eleven. I should probably start getting everything ready. Closing my notebook I get started on his bed. Now I know I made a bit of a mess on it, but it's not like it's about to make much of a difference anyway.

After I toss the journal on the floor I begin to fix his covers. I remember the first time I saw these sheets. I never knew we liked the same type or colors, and I damn sure didn't know I'd be back in his room, on his bed, about to sleep in them.

Glancing up, I notice the windows are fixed. With a smirk I straighten up his pillows and pull out my container of rose petals to sprinkle. Did you know they sell these already pulled apart so that you don't have to fight to rip them off their stem properly?

I set up the red, white, and pink candles on the windowsill, his nightstand, and his dresser. They're in groups of four, with the tall ones in the back.

Checking the time, I'm surprised that it's 11:30. Maybe I should start moving faster. I start to move quicker pulling everything else out of my bag. I set his stuffed animal with the card and candy in the middle of the bed, and I set the chocolate covered cherries with the homemade brownies on a tray that I sit on his dresser.

With a squeal to myself, I take out his big present putting it on the side where his empty dirty hamper is. He'll love it. I know he will.

I look around the room wondering if I'm forgetting something, which is when I look down at my outfit with my make up that's spread on the floor seeing the other present I got for him. Ah. I knew I forgot something.

After hiding it underneath his pillow I eyeball my lingerie on the floor.

It's the most covered up lingerie they had. I know that if I wear it it'll get his mind wondering which is what I want, but please believe sex is not on tonight's agenda. My virginity will be kept nice and safely on this holiday as well as all the others that follow. That's not a gift you give just because most people do it, but I will definitely look hot in this tonight.

Mia watches DK slip his hand with hers that's sitting on her lap causing her to look over at him. They're sitting in the back row of a movie they've both seen with couples making out all over the place. He hasn't even tried to kiss her yet making her wonder maybe she should join the party and kiss him. After all he took her to a somewhat upscale restaurant, more upscale than she expected, and paid for her movie. He also bought her a teddy bear and some candy to try to make her feel more special like she was hoping. This is the first girl he had ever showed respect to. He has to work for Mia. She's a challenge, a conquest, but most of all, his motor mouth match. Leaning over she plants a small kiss on his lips not meaning to start an intense kiss, but does.

I adjust my red low cut lacey bra along with the lacey shorts underwear. Once I slip on the see through jacket that goes over it I flip my curled ends out from it. I feel so pretty yet almost naked.

Quickly I turn on the radio, putting in one of my favorite R&B CDs. After I look at the clock I lay down in the middle of the rose petals. Maybe I'll just take a little nap while I wait for him, since I am tired.

Billy turns the doorknob to his door gasping a little when he sees me lying on his bed. I can understand why he wouldn't want to wake me up since I look so peaceful sleeping.

He places a gentle kiss on my lips waking me up the way I would love to be woken up every morning. The next thing I know he's laying on top of me, and we're making out. I can tell he's been daydreaming about this all day at how anxious his tongue is to touch mine. I love to kiss him, and I can only imagine how wonderful it would feel to have his bare body pressed against mine. I start to pull off his shirt as he runs his hand up under the pillow behind me finding the little box I slipped under there.

He pulls away and looks down at me. "What's this?"

"A gift."

"You didn't have to get me a gift. You were enough." He kisses me passionately once again running his hands so smoothly over my body.

The next thing I know I hear loud music and lots of voices. I slowly open my eyes realizing it was just a dream. Damn. Yawning widely and stretching, I sit up on the bed. What is all of that racket? DK wouldn't have the nerve to bring a party to this house knowing it's supposed to be a romantic night would he? Come on, Mia wouldn't let him do that.

I sneak out of the room to the corner of the hall to see lots of people grinding against each other. Glaring, I search the crowd for DK, but can't seem to find him. Where is that jerk at? Wait. That looks like ... it can't be. It couldn't. It wouldn't. He wouldn't do this to me. I cup a hand over my mouth as I see Billy spank another girl from behind.

"Yeah! Bring it home to daddy," he says running his hands all over her body, landing them on her inner thigh to bring her closer him. Shaking my head in disgust as well as disbelief, I continue watching their interaction.

She twirls around to push her boobs against his chest while moving his hands to her behind that's barely covered by some skintight leather shorts. The girl starts nibbling on his ear lobe.

I can't believe he's just letting her do that. He yells at me for a friend wanting to take me out, but he can have some pigeon head, who by the way looks awfully familiar, all up on his neck kissing away? Not a cheater? Well from the looks of it he sure seems to be going down that path at a very fast pace.

I turn around and rush into his room where I lock the door. As I let the tears fall from my eyes I bury my face in a pillow. I can't believe he would do this to me! And on Valentine's Day! This is the day where you're supposed to show the person you love and care about just how much they really mean to you. And what does he do? He brings a party to his house and starts freak dancing with some girl he probably barely knows. I bet if I weren't in here on his bed he'd have her in here so he could … so he could … I let more tears fall from my eyes at the thought I can barely complete.

DK laughs wrapping his arm around Mia as they head towards the car from the movie, "Tonight was fun."

"It was," she giggles rubbing his hand that's around her waist.

Exchanging romantic glances he says, "You actually pretty tigh' to hang wit'."

"You only say that 'cause you liked my tongue in your mouth."

"Naw. I like the cute lil' way you laugh and the fact you yell at the screen wit' me."

Playfully she says, "Well you ain't too bad yourself."

"Ya know I bet they're home havin' fun too," DK smirks unlocking her door and opening it.

"Probably at home just making out and doing all sorts of other things," Mia giggles getting in.

"Stuff we ain't gotta do," he states as if it's a fact.

Mia tugs the end of his shirt to make him come down to her. "But stuff we probably will do," she winks making him smirk again.

"Oh it's like that?"

"It's like that baby," she licks her lips as he closes the door.

DK licks his lip as strolls around to his side of the car.

Hearing the music get louder causes more tears to fall. I thought I had prince charming not a dud. He's not supposed to be in there doing that. Billy was supposed to come home missing me so bad that all he wanted to do was sleep and find me here, in his bed, waiting for him. Instead he's having a wild time with some bimbo. Happy Valentine's Day Kie. You've had another one of those memorable years of sorrow.

"Come on baby," Billy pulls the girl by her hand towards the direction of his room. "Let's go do that lil' twirly thing I like."

"Got protection?" She drunkenly giggles throwing her cup down the hall.

"Fuck yeah," he places a hand on the knob to his door as I listen to the conversation.

"Yo' Billy!" one of his friends calls to him.

"What nigga?" he calls back.

"Come here playa' I got some'n fo' ya," he lures Billy back the direction he came with the girl still attached to him.

DK pulls into the parking lot of the apartments to see a lot of cars surrounding their place.

"What's goin' on?" He asks pulling up pissed about the fact there's no where to park.

"Uh … yo' crib, you tell me," Mia flips the mirror back up.

He circles around the corner and parks it an annoying distance away from his place. "I didn't plan to throw no party."

"Don't lie," Mia scolds him.

"Why I'm a throw a party if I knew you guys were comin'? If I knew I wanted to spend Valentine's Day wit' you alone?"

"Good point," she looks at him confused. "Well I thought Billy was coming home after work … alone …"

"That's what he told me," DK pleas innocently. "He said he got off at twelve and was comin' home to go to bed."

"So then why are all those people at your place?"

"I don't know," he shrugs. "How 'bout we go find out?"

"Yeah that sounds like a good idea to me," Mia agrees getting out of the car.

The two of them hold hands as they walk to the apartment. Music continues blaring loudly as DK opens the door to reveal to them a party, a cloud of smoke thick enough to cover the block, and an alcohol stench so strong it smells like an alcoholic who drowned himself in a liquor cabinet. His jaw drops open a little as he spots Billy across the crowd. Mia moves closer to DK in a scared manner at the way a few of the guys are looking at her.

"DK," she whispers in his ear. "Where's Billy?"

He points in Billy's general direction, and they start that way when one of the guys calls to Mia.

Some guy takes a swig from his plastic cup and says to Mia, "Let me hit that sweet ass."

Before Mia even has time to respond to what he said, DK turns around. Taking a step in his face he growls, "You say some'n to my girl?"

The guy shakes his head and walks away. DK turns around to see Mia who's staring at him like he's a superhero. She leans over kissing him on the cheek for doing something she could have handled on her own, but is thankful he stepped up first.

They maneuver their way around the crowd until they reach Billy who's smacking the same girl on her butt with one hand and using the other as a cup holder, DK rushes towards him letting Mia's hand go in the process, although she's right behind him.

"What the fuck are you doing?" DK shoves him a little.

Billy looks at him and shrugs him off. "Partyin'. What the fuck does it look like I'm doin'? Havin' tea and crackers wit' grandma?"

DK looks back at Mia knowing Billy only gets that rude when he's intoxicated.

"Have you been drinking?" Mia leans over and asks.

"Yeah so," he shrugs taking a sip from his cup again watching the girl still dance for him. "What are you doin' here anyway?"

"We'll worry about that later," DK says stopping her from saying anything else. Taking a moment he looks into Billy's eyes to notice their red, "Are you high too?"

"Why? Why you sweatin' me?" Billy asks drinking from his cup again.

"'Cause you don' gon' and lost yo' head," DK shoves him again. "All up on yo' ex girl," he shakes his head and looks at her. "Jackie."

She turns around looks him up and down, "DK."

Scratching the back of his neck he sighs, "I think it's time fo' you to go."

"I don't think Billy's ready for me to leave," she wraps her arms around his waist.

"Oh hell no trick," Mia moves DK out of the way. She points her finger at her, "Get off my best friend's man before I do damage to you."

"Bring it on ho," Jackie says back in Mia's face.

"Oh I know that bitch didn't just call me a ho," Mia turns around and looks at DK. "I KNOW that bitch did no just call me a ho," she says taking off her hoop ear rings handing them to him. Mia snatches the girl by her weave as hard as possible and twists her arm behind her back with the other one. "I know *you* didn't just call me a ho."

DK goes over to the radio behind him and shuts it off. "Everybody get the hell out!" he yells at the top of his lungs. Everyone awes and whines, but that doesn't stop him from continuing to kick them out. "Get the hell up out of my crib. I don't care if you don't wanna leave. Yo' ass is grass if you ain't gon' in thirty seconds!"

"I'm a take the trash out," Mia says as Jackie begins to wiggle. "Be right back."

DK smirks to himself and looks back at Billy who looks annoyed by him.

Billy mumbles under his breath, "Cock blocker."

"What the hell happened to you?" he asks slowly leaning against the table.

"Nothin' happened to me," he looks around for another drink.

"Oh some'n happened to you," Mia joins DK's side. "You stopped drinking, and you stopped smoking, yet here you are in front of us high as hell and drunk off your ass."

"Get off my dick," Billy sneers.

Through the middle of my sniffles I notice the music is gone. Wiping away the tears I open the door to hear Mia's voice. Great, *now* they're back.

Before Mia can say anything back DK cuts her off.

"Man up," he folds his arms. "What happened?"

"Man," Billy shrugs him off again. "I was at work and next thing I know Jackie shows up, and I realize I'm jus' wastin' my time on worryin' 'bout that female. I figured she was off at home wit' you on a date wit' some nigga who wants to bang her. I wasn't 'bout to sit at home and mope while she has fun, so Jackie asked did I wanna dance next thing I know I'm gettin' drunk and throwin' us a party," he reaches for the cup next to DK which Mia quickly moves.

"Us?"

"Yeah nigga. There was plenty of beer and bitches fo' the both of us 'til you ran 'em off."

"Naw this wasn't 'bout us. There is no us in this situation. This was 'bout *you*. YOU and some dumb idea to get drunk and fuck yo' ex girl—

"Which I didn't get the chance to 'cause you fuckin' ruined it."

"I'm glad. 'Cause you were jus' doin' it to get even wit' yo' current girl who didn't do nothin' wrong," DK shakes his head. He has a point. I didn't do anything wrong. Hold on. The girl he was dancing with is his ex girlfriend? I know she looked familiar. "You foul Billy."

Mia nods slowly moving closer to DK who's showing a side of him she's never seen. "Wait that was your ex-girlfriend?

"One 'em," he rolls his eyes. "Easy lay."

"Easiest lay," DK quickly corrects him.

"Why you makin' such a big deal out of this fo' no reason?" Billy gets ready to move.

Mia steps in, "No reason? Now your one and only girl is not a reason? I thought you were a changed man."

"Mia," he shakes his head at her. "Thugs don't change." Coldly after shooting his friend a glance he says, "Jus' ask DK."

Slowly she glances at DK who glances back at her. He remembers saying that, but he never thought it would come back to bite him. "You know what? I was wrong Billy. Thugs can change. Thugs who wanna change like you can change, but there are some who can't. Don't try to pin yo' fucked up mistake on what I said," he points to him intensely. "You know what else? For once, even I was convinced this girl was 'bout to change you and turn you into some'n you had been dreamin' 'bout since I don't know how long. This girl did nothin' but good things fo' you and all you've done is fuck up," he shakes his head. "I hope she leaves you fo' bein' a dog."

"If I'm a dog I learned it from you," he snaps back. I've never heard him sound so cold. Tossing Mia another cold glance he asks, "What are you doin' here anyway?"

"I … uh …" she shakes her head more annoyed with him than DK. "Brought a special present for you from Kie. It's in your room. Why don't you go check it out?"

"Naw. I'm not really in the gift mood."

"No I really think you should," he insists. "Maybe you'll realize what an asshole you've been this lovely Valentine's Day evening."

Billy rolls his eyes and starts towards his bedroom where I am back to balling on his bed. He opens his bedroom door to see me crying. I look up into his glazed over eyes that have now sulked. He can't even find the words to say anything as Mia and DK join his side.

"Happy Valentine's Day," she whispers sarcastically in his ear.

"Comprehend yo' level of asshole?" DK asks him. "No? Why don't you step into yo' room and see what she set up befo' you join Mia and me fo' some cleanin'," he strolls off. "Come on Mia."

"Aw I don't wanna clean," she whines following him into the living room.

Billy walks into his room to see the candles glowing and the present on the side of his bed along with the homemade desserts on his dresser. He runs his fingers over his fade.

He doesn't have anything to say to me? You mean to tell me he does all that awful shit that I have to sit and watch, was about to willingly cheat on me, as in would have if someone wouldn't have distracted him, and snaps at me for being merely asked out, yet he still has nothing to say to me.

"Kie," he starts towards me.

I shake my head at him wiping away more tears. "Don't talk to me." I mean I don't want him to talk to me, but I want him to at least try.

Continuing to try to talk he takes another step towards me, "Kie I'm so sorry."

"Don't say anything to me!"

"I—

"Not another word," I point at him like his mother would. "You have the nerve to yell at me for being asked out while you're in there spanking one of your ex girlfriends. You were going to sleep with her Billy."

"That's not true I—

"Don't lie to me! I heard you say you wanted to fuck her! Jackie, Billy? Jackie? The one girl you dated the longest before me. The girl you almost got pregnant."

"Kie I—

"Ya know I didn't say yes to Danny because I wanted to spend my Valentine's Day with my boyfriend who supposedly loves me more than anything else. I convinced Mia to drive me all the way up here after hours of begging followed by days of lecturing from our parents, just to come see you."

"Baby—

"I thought I didn't sacrifice enough for you, and now I realize I sacrifice plenty of my heart for you. I've had nothing, but shitty valentines, and the one year, THE ONE YEAR, I think things will be different it turns out I was wrong. Of course I'm wrong. When it comes to matters of the heart about me, I'm always wrong," I stand up to be in his face. "You know what I learned? It doesn't matter if you tell me you love me a 101 times unless you've got a 101 times to prove it. And guess what Billy?"

The only thing I let him say is, "What?"

"You come up a bit short," I swallow the lump in my throat. "You don't love me like you say you do. In fact, as far I'm considered, after seeing what I just saw, and hearing what I just heard, you don't love me at all. The only person you love is yourself." I take the necklace from around my neck and hand it to him.

Billy looks down at the necklace in his trembling hand. His jaw slightly opens to argue back.

"Get out," I point to the hall. "I don't care if this is your room. Just leave me alone. I never want to see you again."

"Kie—

"We're over Billy."

"Come on Kie. You … you don't mean that."

Before shutting the door in his face I sigh, "I really do."

He rests his head against it for a second letting it marinate in his mind he just lost the best thing he ever had.

Billy strolls into the living room where he sees Mia cleaning up plastic cups by herself.

Flopping down on the couch he asks, "Where's DK?"

"He went to the store," she shoves more cups in a trash bag. "Feel any better yet?"

With a deep sigh Billy feels his eyes tear up. His head begins to hang as his hands reach his face where they act as shield from the outside world.

"Guess not," Mia says sarcastically continuing to pick up cups.

He continues crying by himself for another few minutes as she keeps picking up trash.

Eventually she drops the bag and plops herself down next to him, "Take that as a no … Billy why are you crying? Shelled out the pain, but can't take it?"

"She doesn't think I love her," he manages to say between groups of sniffles. He pulls out the locket from his pocket. "She broke up with me."

In disbelief I went that far Mia denies, "She did not."

"She did," he whimpers out.

"Well she's probably just really angry and doesn't mean it …"

"No Mia," he looks over at her. "She told me I didn't love her. I feel like my heart is broken. I feel like it's shattered to a million pieces. I feel—

"You? Why's it always about you? She catches you fooling around with your ex girlfriend that you were going to sleep with when she drove only god only knows how many miles to surprise you, and all you're worried about is how you feel? How selfish can you get Billy?"

He stares at Mia until she becomes a blur of tears. He slides his face in the palms of his hands again as DK strolls in.

"Oh he must have sobered up and come to his senses," DK says with a small plastic grocery bag in his hand.

"Yeah," Mia leaps off the couch in a desperate attempt to see in DK's bag. Quickly she snitches, "She broke up with him."

"I'd break up wit' him too," he growls loud enough for Billy to hear.

Changing the subject Mia asks, "What did you go get?"

"Come here," he says going back towards the bedrooms, but not past Billy's. He pulls out a lollypop and a card. "For Kie. Go give 'em to her."

"What? No. I all ready gave her a present. You give her the gift," she says pushing the gifts at him. "Trust me. It could even be a peace treaty between the two of you though word is, your not gonna need it after your boy's stunt."

DK silently protests, groans and eventually walks into Billy's bedroom where I am still balling. I look up, make up smeared all over my face, and let out a deep sigh. Slowly strolling towards me I notice something in his hand.

"Happy Valentine's Day Kie," he holds out a lollypop with a card.

He had the nerve to go out and buy me something when my own boyfriend nearly cheats on me. His best friend who I have the worst history with can show me more compassion than him. Now isn't that fucked up? I get up and toss my arms around his neck to give him a hug.

"Thank you," I sniffle.

Hesitating at first to hug me back, he puts his arms around me. "You're welcome."

I pull away from him and look him deep in his eyes for the first time. Why is it I never noticed how soft his eyes were before?

With a smile he walks out shutting the door behind him. I lock it and begin to blow out the candles one by one, saying goodbye to my relationship with Billy.

As soon as it's completely dark, I crawl into his bed and curl up in a ball. While the moonlight desperately attempts to peak itself through the curtains, I feel my eyes begin to fill up with tears again.

Every year cupid makes me feel like shit, and this has to be the final straw. I will not be celebrating this greeting card, candy created, corporate America worshipped holiday.

How is it I can't even catch a break the one year I swear I have Prince Charming? Ha. Prince Charming. He's more like an ugly frog I kissed with the hope he'd turn into something better. Ironic how the only princesses that get stories are the one's with happy endings. If we recorded the ones without children would be traumatized from an early age and would have no faith in love or the good in life. I guess that's when you know you've grown up. The moment you can say to yourself love hurts and there isn't nearly as much good in everyone as you think, you've finally left your childhood fantasies behind.

The next morning Billy wakes up on the couch with a headache strong enough to take down a giant and eyes so puffy you would think they were marshmallows. After helping clean up the mess he made, he sprawled himself out on the couch and just let himself go.

Looking around, he checks the time on the cable box noticing it's almost ten in the morning. It's a little too quiet for it to be ten in the morning, unless no ones home or everyone is still asleep.

Billy drags himself off the couch and down the hall to his bedroom door. Seeing it's cracked, he knocks before peeking his head in to realize it's empty. Everything from last night is still in its place, except me.

"Thanks for breakfast DK," I say tossing the bag in the trash as we approach the studio building.

"Yeah," Mia sips the last of her orange juice. I told her not to drink that. She doesn't realize that orange juice is bad for her voice in the morning. She's not going to like it when I forced her to chug a bottle of water before her vocal exercises.

"No thang," DK strolls in the building with us behind him. "Dolores," he stops at the front desk. To the older woman who's on the phone behind it he says, "You're lookin' mighty good this mornin'."

"What did I tell you about coming into the studio high?" She scolds him.

"I'm not high," he innocently snaps.

Annoyed she covers the receiver, "Then why are you acting funny?"

"I'm not actin' funny. I'm jus' a lil' more cheerful."

With a deep heavy sigh she says, "Same thing. What can I do for you today Mr. Happy Go Lucky?"

Leaning down in a sly manner he asks, "Which studio will these lovely ladies and myself be workin' in?"

"B," she pushes his elbow off the desk and returns to her phone call.

"Follow me," he says taking a left after leaving Dolores with a wink. This weekend I've met the better side of DK and actually like him. The saddest thing is I will probably never see it again.

Billy sighs and flops down on his bed accidentally lying on an envelope. Sliding it from underneath him he reads his name on the outside of it. He sits up, scoots to the edge of his bed, and rests his arms on his thighs as he rips it open to reveal a letter.

Billy—

Last night was one of the worst nights of my life. I gave this night so much thought with the hope of being the one to get to show YOU how much you mean to me. I can't believe you were going to cheat on me because you were angry. I didn't know that we found ways to hurt the other when we're upset. I didn't know we played those games. I thought we were better than that, but I guess I was wrong. If it were games we were into playing then we wouldn't have made it this far. You know you say all these things about wanting to be with me now and always and never want to leave me, and then you turn around pull a stunt like this. Does that make any sense to you? I hope you know how it killed me to watch you not give a damn about me like that. Are you curious to what I had planned for you last night? Do you see those brownies on your dresser? There are nine. One for every month we've been involved in something. Do you see those strawberries? There are 12. One for every hardship we've overcome. The candles were just for the romantic effect, the CD was full of songs that reminded me of you, and the rose petals because I heard they bring the sensual side out of people. Guess I was wrong again. Oh yeah and the present next to your bed, that really big one, I spent a couple of hours looking for it. I hope you like it. There's a note to read after you open it. There's another gift under your pillow that I wanted to say something really ... important with, but oh well. It wasn't supposed to be about you receiving the gifts. It was supposed to be about me GIVING them. Saying those special words to you make you feel the wonderful things you made me feel. You love me? You really love me? I didn't know you treated people you love so lowly. I don't know why I took the time to write this because it doesn't really matter any more since we're through. We've had our end so what's done is done. Well if you're wondering where I am I went with Mia and DK to the studio, what I told my parents I was coming up here for. If for some reason you want to say goodbye to me we'll be back around five or so. I don't know if we can be friends because I don't even let my friends treat me that shitty, but I'll think about it. I've got my cell, but I'm not answering it. I just have one question I want you to think about. How does it feel to be all alone?

~Kiara

The paper is shaking in his hands as a couple of tears stain his cheek. Looking around at the beautiful setting I created for him last night he feels his chest to start burn. Billy lets out a deep sigh and closes his eyes.

"I get it DK," I say annoyed at being told the same thing repeatedly. "That makes the volume go up, and that makes the beat go up. Click. Click. And we go. I'm not stupid. I get it," I nod rapidly. "I know what I'm doing."

"Forty five minutes of bein' taught how to work this and you think you've perfected it. Fine, jus' don't fuck up the equipment," he points at me. "It's pricey."

"I think she knows that," Mia snaps drinking more water.

"Can we start now?" I whine at him.

"Yeah," he sighs. "Do what you do."

I begin to play with the beats finding what fits best and what matches, what clashes, and most of all what I think will sell to the judges. A couple of hours later we've got the first song sung by Mia featuring DK, and it's a master piece if I do say so myself.

Coming out of the booth I see DK slip his hand into his pocket to answer more than likely a ringing cell phone. Mia shakes her head at him as he answers it.

"That was hot," I say with a smirk. "You make a good team. Play it back and find any spots you think might need tweaking. I'm going to pee before I go in there ok," I get up and head towards the door on my right. The bathrooms down that hall while the front is through the door on the left. It's a very strange studio, but hey a studios a studio.

"Ok," Mia flops down into the leather chair I was sitting in.

Pulling into a studio parking space Billy asks, "Where are you?"

"At the studio," DK answers leaning next to Mia. "Why?"

As he parks his car quickly he asks, "Which studio A or B?"

"Why?" He repeats again snapping at him.

Nearly tripping over his own feet he rushes towards the building, "Fuck DK jus' tell me!"

"B," DK calmly says as I come back into the room. "But I'm not lettin' you in."

"Go into the booth and warm up," Mia instructs me under the impression of who DK is talking to.

"Don't push," I take a long drink before I let myself into the booth.

"Why?" Billy rushes into the building passing Dolores barely waving to her.

"'Cause Kie's 'bout to be in the booth, and you can't come in while someone's recordin'."

Appearing in the window he demands, "Let me in now."

Mia glances over surprised to see him.

"No," he says firmly as Mia stares blankly at Billy in the window. "She doesn't wanna see you."

"I'm beggin' you to let me hear her voice. I swear I'll leave before she even notices I was in there. DK jus' do this fo' me," he pleads in the window with a hand over his heart.

"No."

"DK. Please."

He sighs and looks at Mia for approval. She nods and quickly rushes to open the door while I'm fiddling around with my back to them.

Billy slides in beside the door where I can't see no matter how far I lean in or around.

"Let's go Kie," Mia smirks. "Whenever you're ready."

After a deep breath Billy rests his head as Mia begins to play the beat.

I put the headphones on covering my left ear. You always leave your good ear open so you can hear yourself better. Sure you can hear it in the headphones, but you have to hear yourself from the heart, which always takes your good ear to do.

Hearing the beat come in I hum. "Yeah ..." I sing softly. My beat is much slower and smoother than Mia's. "Every girl dreams of her prince. The man who came straight from her dreams, who gives her everything, so she feels like she's supreme. Finally, she's a queen. He's done things she's never seen. Life is now so serene ... I'm that **girl** whose got that man, I'm that girl whose livin' that plan, they say my life's just began, but there's some'n they don't understan'," I sing shaking my head knowing no one is prepared for this punch I'm about to throw. "I thought you gave me all the love I needed, but you haven't quite succeeded. You've still got a ways to go. My prince isn't everything he seemed. Some how I feel as if I got schemed. This isn't my fairy tale love ..."

DK and Mia glance over at Billy who feel worse than he did when he walked in.

"They say, I've got a good man to keep, his love for me runs deep. I should be so thankful. He's also hurt me bad. Made me more than burning mad, I thought the story wasn't supposed to be sad ... Sometimes his words hurt, I've even had to watch him flirt ..." I close my eyes hoping not to cry, "do his dirt ... I'm that girl whose got that man, I'm that girl whose livin' that plan, they say my life's just began, but there's some'n they don't understan'," I sing. "Whoa ... I need more," I sing in the background. "So so far to go. Whooaaaa," I shake my head. "Not real love."

Billy runs his fingers through his hair frustrated. He knows that he never wanted to be the person to hurt me, he never wanted to be the person who I wished was someone else, and worst of all he never wanted to be the inspiration for a sad love song.

"Cinderella had her perfect dance, the mermaid got her chance, snow white had her romance, and even sleeping beauty lived out her trance. So when does this princess get her true love? Where's my love sent from above? When do I get everything I've dream of? I'm still waiting for my happily ever after," I hold the last notes as the chorus comes in. I add lib here and there as the chorus continues.

DK never expected that my voice could do what he just heard, and Mia never knew I could write the things I did. Neither of them expected the song to be a sad one about wanting more than Billy, but that's what sells. Sadness sells.

DK leans over and whispers something to Mia.

"Go," she says to Billy. "Leave now, before she comes out."

"But—

"Just go. Call DK from outside. Leave before Kie comes," she instructs him to leave as I hang my head lost in the beat.

"That was hot," DK presses the intercom button as Billy peeks around the corner to catch a glimpse of my face. "Real R&B right there."

"Thanks," I smile and hang the headphones catching eye contact with Billy. Quickly I exit the booth, looking around for him, "Was Billy just in here?"

Clearing her throat Mia denies, "No."

I continue to look around the small area for a second swearing, "I thought I saw him."

Mia raises her eyes at DK who's on his cell phone with him as I speak. "You didn't Kie. It was just me and DK. I guess you got so deep into it you imagined you did."

With a pout I say, "I guess so. Well what do you think of the song?"

"That he really did mess up," she mumbles under her breath. With a smile she answers, "Beautiful Kie. Very impressive. If you sing that for your solo the judges at comp will love you."

"I sure hope so because I really do love that song." I take another sip of water, "Who's he talking to?"

"I don't know," she says quickly trying to over power DK's voice who's talking on the phone to someone I hope is not Billy. "When you'd write it?"

"This morning when I woke up," I roll my eyes. "When I couldn't get back to sleep."

She nods slowly and looks back at DK who gets off the phone.

"Who was that?" I ask biting my bottom lip.

"Uh … my buddy J-Rock," he swallows his lie. "We've got a few more minutes in the booth then I'm gonna take you back home Kie, so me and Mia can have a lil' more time together alone befo' she has to go back," he licks his lips like he's up to something. Either he's plotting something for Mia or trying to get Billy and me back together, either way I don't like it.

An hour later I'm opening their front door by myself. You know if I wasn't such a good friend I would be cock blocking right now and would have insisted on DK taking me with them so I wouldn't have to be around Billy. Oh well, I will just spend this time packing carefully rather than in a rush like I'm use to.

I walk in to see him on the couch with the notebook I bought him for Christmas sitting on the table and him singing from it. Without looking over at him I just walk straight to his room to begin to pack my stuff.

The second he realizes I've walked into the house he comes into his room where I'm on the floor folding what I wore here yesterday.

"Kie," he says slowly coming in.

You know everything is in the exact spot I left it except for the big present. Go figure the only thing he moves is a gift. If that doesn't look selfish I don't know what does.

Sitting on his bed next to where I am packing he says, "Kie please talk to me."

"And say what to you Billy?" I turn around. "I forgive you for being a jerk to me? I forgive you for basically cheating on me last night? I forgive you for destroying our relationship? Is that what you wanna hear? I forgive you for being an asshole," I turn back around to begin packing once more. "Better?"

"No Kie it's not better. That's not what I wanna hear," he shakes his head. "I want us to talk. I want us to be together again."

"Well I don't. God, it's always about what you want. Do you ever consider what I want?"

"Obviously not enough," he mumbles. Billy takes my arm to stop me from moving. "Please Kie jus' talk to me."

Slowly I look down at his arm that's touching me. I wonder has he showered since the last time he touched that dirty girl. As I shudder he removes his arm from me. The sooner he feels like he's gotten a fair trial the sooner he can stop pestering me.

"Are you gonna talk to me?"

"No. I'm gonna listen. As far as I'm concerned I've said all I need to say."

"All right," he nods and leans towards me. "When I heard you say that Danny asked you out the first thing that came to mind was to be defensive. That's what I know bes' Kie. I've been cheated on so many times that at some point and time I came to the conclusion of hurtin' someone befo' they got that chance."

Angrily I interject, "So wait, I'm supposed to just sit back and pay for your ex-girlfriends mistakes? That's bullshit."

"No. Look my judgment isn't always correct for the situation. I didn't have parents to learn from as I grew up. All I have are the faded memories of how love's supposed to be. And in all the gaps, I have to fill in what I've learned from watchin' relationships around me. I've never seen a successful one like my parents, so they're not my main example no matter how much I want them to be. I don't enjoy bein' this person Kie, but this is how I grew up. You have to know and understand I'm changin' the best I can as fast as I can. You have to be patient wit' me and my messed up ways. Everyone back tracks, but it's the steps they move forwards that count. I've always begged you not to give up on me, and you said you wouldn't, which means understanding what a complicated person I am."

"Yeah well that was before you tried to fuck your ex-girlfriend last night."

"I know what I did las' night was beyond wrong. It was inexcusable. Some'n came over me from my old ways, and I had every intent to hurt you befo' you could me. I did everything I knew would upset you not even wonderin' if you would find out or not. All I could think of was another guy in your arms," he runs his finger up my arm, "feelin' your touch," he outlines my face, and then softly places it on my lips, "and yo' kiss. It drove me to a point of insanity."

Swallowing any sympathy I begin to feel I say, "What if I was in another guy's arms, holding him, grinding on him, letting him feel in places I swore I'd only let you. Would you forgive me? If the table was turned would you just let it all go?"

"Yeah because I love you."

With a disgusted voice I roll my eyes, "Ugh. Whatever."

"Look I'm sorry I'm not the fairy tale prince everyone made you believe I was. I have my flaws too. I'm not perfect. No matter how hard I try to be the perfect man fo' you I'm gonna fall short. I'm gonna fall short 'cause no one's perfect."

We all have flaws. I'm not perfect whatsoever. Geez, I have a worse temper than him, but I've managed to learn to control it. Not everyone can do that though.

"All I can do is try Kie, and I know las' night I wasn't tryin', but I will *never* do some'n like that again. I can't live knowin' I ruined some'n so wonderful wit' you. If you give me one more chance I swear I'll leave befo' puttin' you in that pain ever again."

"Billy I can't—

Getting down on one knee he tears up, "I'm beggin' you wit' every inch of my body, wit' everything I have left in this world, to give me back that chance to be that man you dreamed of, to be that man you want in yo' life, and to be everything you need," he lifts my chin up. "Please."

"But—

"Baby come back to me."

"How do I know you really mean it this time? You always say shit like this and sure enough hurt me again. I'm so tired of this Billy. I really don't think I have the strength to keep try—

"Wait," he cuts me off before I can finish. "No matter what I say right now nothing can prove to you how sorry I am and how much I wanna be wit' you. Jus' give me the chance to show you my love wit' every breath I take."

"I—

"Please," he comes closer. "Baby," he takes my hand and kisses the back of it. "Please. I need you so much."

I feel like one of those girls who accepts her cheating man over and over again. He may not have cheated on me, but the pain of his actions has all the equivalents. I feel like I'm being such a pushover. If this was any other guy I wouldn't dare to think twice. Was it about him? Does god just want us to be together so bad he robbed me of the ice in me that once upon a time made me so cold. Who knows though. I'm beginning to believe what doesn't kill us only makes us strong, which would make me superwoman.

"Ok Billy," I look him in his eyes. "But this is it. No more chances. I understand you're not perfect, you're still learning, and you've still got a few more stumbles to go, but I will not sit back and let you break my heart ever again. You will never try to cheat on me again. You will never treat me less than I deserve. I know you're doing the best you can, just know that this is it. I'll take you back, but any more mess ups and we're done forever. No apologies, no fourth chances, nothing. Got it?"

"Yeah. I got it. I swear baby, this is it. No more," he slowly wraps his arms around me. In a whisper he says, "I love you."

I enjoy the first embrace I've had since I've been here before pulling away and sighing, "I love you too."

Dangling the necklace in front of me, he asks with hopeful eyes will I wear it. I nod and let him fasten it around my neck. Afterwards he places the softest kiss on my cheek and looks me back in my eyes.

Billy takes out the small box still wrapped so nicely in its paper.

"I want you to give this to me on a day you feel I deserve it. I don't care if it's a holiday or not. I don't even care if it's three days or three years from now. Jus' give it to me when you feel like you can really mean everything you wanted to tell me when you give it to me," he places it in my hand.

I smile and wrap my fingers around the small box. At least he understands it's about me giving it. Honestly, it's a surprise he didn't open this one first.

"Now what do you say I make the same breakfast I made you the last time you were here befo' you had to leave fo' home? I mean wit' you in bed of course and me usin' my brand new cookin' supplies my girlfriend bought because she knows how much I secretly love to cook," he winks at me.

I try not to laugh under my breath. Of course he opened the big box. He's human. I hate to admit if I were in the same situation I probably would have opened it too. Nodding I tilt my head to the side, "Sounds like a good start to me."

"Ok," he smiles helping me get up with him. Billy leans down and ever so slowly kisses me on the lips.

I really don't know why I just did that. I'm better than a man who does nothing but screw up unintentionally. I mean, sure everyone messes up in life, but their held accountable. Yeah, I know he's had a messed up past and that's why his futures so hard for him change.

You know, I wasn't brought up to be so forgiving to people's mistakes and wrongful doings especially towards me, but there's something about Billy that changes that about me. I mean I always thought I was the one changing him, accepting all of his imperfections, but in reality I've done my fair share of wrong. The difference is I learned from my mistakes. I know deep inside he's slowly but surely learning from the things he does wrong.

Ok so he doesn't just love himself. If he loved only him he wouldn't work so damn hard to make me see how much he cares about me, how much he's devoted to me, and how much he adores me. I've heard people say when you're in love you'll do some crazy things, forget about certain unacceptable behavior, and just face the fact that love is blind.

I think that's because it's about the connection only you can feel. I feel that connection and no matter how much wrong he causes, it doesn't nearly compare to how much right he's done. It doesn't matter how much I shouldn't love him, I am. He's determined to give me what I need, so I can't let him go. No. It's not that I can't, it's that I won't. Stunts like this will be punished and we will move on because I understand there are going to be rough points in our relationship, as well as life. You feel pain at times, but that's the sacrifice you make for love.

PART IV

CHANGES

CHAPTER 14

A Time for Firsts

What is it about growing up that makes you start questioning the choices you make? After all, the choices you make will affect the rest of your life so you should be very careful about the littlest thing right? I guess this is making prom sound more intense than it should, but this could be the only year I go. We might win the competition, which means we won't be in an actual high school. With that in mind I'm going to make this prom as fantastic as possible.

As exciting as getting dressed up and making everyone else jealous with my prize-winning boyfriend is, I have to say it's not what I'm looking forward to. After prom Mia and I are staying at a hotel in a room right next door to Billy and DK with parental consent. Yes. You heard correctly. With parental consent. I don't know how or what exactly we said to convince them this was a good decision. All I know is they *trust* us to make *responsible* choices. What does that mean you ask? Right now, I'm pretty sure it's open to interpretations.

Moving a dress I wouldn't wear unless you paid me to I ask annoyed, "Well who do you want to go with?"

Mia doesn't say anything as she weaves away from me in between racks.

Why did I ask a question I already know the answer to? "Come on Mia you can tell me who it is," I lean against the mirror watching her search continue, knowing I ended mine a long time ago. Even though I know the right answer I dumbly ask, "Is it Ryan?"

"Ugh," she rolls her eyes.

"What's wrong with him?"

"I'm done messing with him," she shrugs. "Once you get past the whole hot foreign guy who doesn't speak English thing, he's really not that different from all my other toys."

"Ah …" I nod in acknowledgement.

"Ya know though, I've always had my eye on …" she drifts off and begins to grin.

"Yeah I know."

In a whine she pleads, "I can't help it! Sure he is without a doubt one of the rudest people I have ever met, sure he has one of the worst problems with authority I've ever seen, and fine, yes, I know he really just wants me for my body, but come on Kie. You know I have a weakness for bad boys with hearts. I know you know he has a heart. You saw it."

"Yeah, I think he rented it though."

"Kie," she snaps.

"Fine, he must have seen the wizard."

"Kie …" she growls.

"I'm sorry. I meant Christmas came early."

"Kiara if you say one more—

Cutting her off, I sigh, "Ok. Ok. Did you ask him yet?"

"No," she returns to her pattern of moving every two dresses to look at the third. "I'm gonna tonight."

"You think he'll say yes?"

"Billy's going." she glances at me. "He'll go."

With a shake of my head I glance off to the side where I see the foreign toy himself. Ryan casually strolls towards us and I slyly move away to leave the heart shattering between the two of them.

"Mia," Ryan says in an accented voice trying to be debonair. Slipping my hands in my front pockets I groan at his lost efforts. How is it all the guys I wish she would give an actual chance fail and the *one* I want to bomb out is the one who will most likely succeed?

She reluctantly turns around forcing a smile on her face. "Hey." Quickly she starts looking for me. I've all ready hidden behind a rack of clothes so she's forced to tell him without using me as an excuse to get away.

Folding his arms nervously he asks, "Whatcha doing?"

"Shopping for a prom dress," she answers with her fake flirting. Wouldn't it just be easier to NOT flirt with him so maybe he got the picture a bit faster?

"Oh," he clears his throat. "Speaking of prom. I was wondering ..." shyly he looks down making it all the more harder for Mia to say no. "If you would like to go as my date?"

She clears her throat looking around again for me, knowing I've hidden from her for just that reason. "I have plans on going with someone else." she places a hand on his shoulder and sighs, "I'm sorry."

"Oh," he sounds as if she ripped out of his heart, shattered it with a sledge hammer, and used the pieces as a bread trail to find her way back to him in case she ever got lost. "Oh ok," Ryan lets the awkward moment sizzle for a second before he gets the hint to leave. "I'm going to go catch up with my friends."

Nodding she smiles, "Ok."

"See you around," he strolls away from her for what will probably be the last time.

Biting my bottom lip I give the whole DK thing another thought. Maybe DK's not such a bad idea for her. He could give her love life hope. Yeah sometimes they clash like two Chinese fighting fish, but other times he's the cherry on her ice cream sundae. So basically they need each other's attitudes to stay grounded and remember there are still challenges out there.

I pop up from around the corner with a perky smile knowing she was expecting me to show up after he was gone.

"Ironic timing," she shoves the dress violently back on the rack.

With a deceitful smile I say, "Sorry. Thought I saw something I might like."

"Of course you did," she rolls her eyes. Growling a little bit she reiterates a point she's all ready made at least six times today alone. "We have to pick dresses this weekend. Prom's next weekend."

"I don't want my dress looking like anyone else's," I lean against the rack across from her.

"Me neither," she gives me a funny look. "What makes you think I wanna look like a carbon copy of Barbie?"

"Or apart of the school prom patrol," I make her giggle. Taking a moment I let a grin creep across my face, "Let's go. I know where we'll find some'n for sure."

"Take us there then," Mia follows me towards the door as her cell phone begins to ring. "Hello," she quickly answers it barely giving it any time to ring. Way to be desperate for a phone call.

"Sup," DK says slyly into the phone.

Smirking she responds, "Shopping." Gross. I know exactly what trouble she's talking to.

"Sounds fun," he licks his lips. "You lef' me a holla on my phone, what'd you need?"

"I didn't *need* anything," she starts twirling a strand of her hair. I think I just felt my stomach turn. "I just wanted to ask you some'n."

"Ask then," he says with an attitude laughing under his breath.

"Don't rush me."

Continuing his smirk he says, "Sorry."

"I was going to ask you … did you maybe wanna … or possibly might wanna …"

"Mia are you tryin' to ask me to go to prom?"

She shakes her head still in disbelief herself that she's asking him to go with her. "Yeah. Do you wanna go to prom with me next weekend?"

He nods to himself as Billy gets back in the car, "Yeah. That sounds tigh' to me."

"All right then," she folds her arms as I unlock her car. It doesn't take all day for the two of them to set up a date they both know is to going happen next weekend.

"I'll see you next weekend then."

"Bye DK," she hangs up after what had to be the longest but shortest conversation they've had on the phone yet.

Billy starts the car asking, "So now you've gotta go prom shoppin' too?"

"Might as well. Have a little extra cash now," he takes the grip from his pockets to finger the bills. "I can't believe you tryin' to leave this money makin' life style behind."

"Don't worry about me. Worry about you and how much this is about to cost," he fastens his seat belt and takes off.

"Figured he'd say yes," I mumble under my breath.

Tossing her hair to one side she puts on her sunglasses, "Of course. You and I both know he can't resist this."

A few days later, Tuesday afternoon, we're at the shoe store searching for the perfect shoes.

"I need sassy and sexy," Mia looks through the shoes hoping to find her dream heels.

"And I need something softer, but with a similar point," I look around the corner on a different isle.

"Don't crowd me! Get up out of my space before I make you," she growls under her breath to a fellow shopper that's a little too close to her. Mia is like those animals on TV who are protecting their territory from invaders. It's best to give her at least five feet when it comes to shoe shopping.

"Damn I look good," DK poses in the mirror in his tux. He pops his cap and then leans against his cane.

Billy strolls out in his tux straightening it out. "Yeah. You do pull off the pimp tux nicely," he grins as the worker at the moment comes over to help them. "I must admit."

"Well ya know I graduated from playa to pimp," he cockily chuckles popping his cap once more.

"Those look really good on you guys," says the female worker pulling her strawberry blonde hair to one side moving her way to into between them.

"Thanks," DK nods adjusting himself.

Billy struggles with his tie when she turns towards him to help.

"Let me help you," she runs her creamy hands up his chest while staring in his eyes as she slowly, seductively begins to tie it.

Grumbling at DK he snaps, "I can't believe yo' punk ass can tie a tie, but I can't."

"Yeah well," he glides his tongue across his lips, "that's them pimp skills."

After rolling his eyes at DK he smiles down at her to politely sigh, "Thanks."

"This is one of the best tuxes we have," she says slowly never pulling her eyes away from his. "It's usually only used for weddings. Ya know. Real men."

Billy swallows and glances at DK whose shaking his head.

"In fact," she finishes tying his tie. With a press of her pout pink lips she continues, "You're the sexiest man I've seen in it yet."

"Thanks," he nods and steps back away from her.

Moving her hand slowly across her low cut white blouse to play with her dangling chain she says softly, "Are ... *you* getting married?"

"Yeah he is," DK buts in before Billy can answer. Clearing his throat as he fixes his own tie he backs her off, "And I'm sure his future wife wouldn't appreciate you pushin' all up on him."

Her hands attach themselves onto her size three hips, "Excuse me."

Leaning over he tries to read her name tag, "Look Barbie—

"It's Brandy," she corrects him. "And I was just trying to be friendly and help him with his tie."

"No. You were tryin' to hit on him on the sly," he pops his collar. "Look we don't need any more help Brenda, so you can go."

She rolls her eyes at DK, innocently smiles at Billy, and walks away wiggling her hips hoping to capture Billy's attention.

"Chicken head," he mumbles glancing at Billy's reflection in the mirror. "You need to check them females befo' they start on you like that. Ain't gon' have me bein' all up in the middle of ya'll mess. Tryin' to keep yo' ass in check."

Modeling his own tux he protests, "I was gonna tell her to step."

"Uh-huh," DK twirls his cane around.

When Saturday finally arrives you would think that maybe I would be allowed to sleep in so that I wouldn't be cranky the rest of the day. Not as long the prom Nazi is running the event.

"Mmm," Mia sips enjoying her morning coffee. "As soon as the nail place opens we're in! I mean we're first on the list for heaven sake."

Her excitement is nauseating. My half open eyelids form to that of a glare as I sip my cold frozen frappachino. I don't care if we're first. In fact, I don't care about anything except for the fact it's eight in the morning, and I can't figure out why I'm up against my will. If it were up to me, our day wouldn't start until noon.

Poking my side she demands, "Look livelier."

I open my mouth to yawn in her face and begin sipping my coffee again.

"Come on Kie," she urges. "It's a very important day."

"You know you've said that so many times that I no longer believe it's an important day. As a matter of fact I think today is going to go miserably and all the hard work and effort you put into this is going to waste. The only way today can be saved is if you let me linger in my morning grouch so that it doesn't carry on into the rest of the day," I give her a fake smirk. Mia's mouth slightly parts, but immediately shuts it. And to think I didn't actually believe that would work. If only she knew I didn't mean a word of that, except for the grouchy part.

Around nine we've got our fingers and toes being soaked like we're celebrities in there for our regular appointment. Do you ever wonder what they're saying in another language? They're Asian women who don't speak English too well but manage to speak their language perfectly fine. Don't misunderstand me. I'm not trying to make any sort of racist judgment or anything. I'm just saying if you could speak another language that only your co-workers understood; wouldn't you be doggin' people's feet? Hell I know I would be saying all sorts of nasty things about peoples crusty, worn down, flaky, ain't been cleaned since they were born feet.

"So what are you and Billy gonna do tonight?" Mia asks glancing up from her fashion magazine.

"After prom? Probably watch a movie, snuggle, make out, you know the good stuff."

"That's it? Are you gonna hit an after party with us or not?" She waits for the lady to allow her to turn the page.

"I don't know yet. I haven't talked to him today."

"You know I haven't talked to DK either."

Shaking my head I wonder what they're up to. Probably still sleeping, not stressing or giving a real thought about tonight. Lucky bastards.

DK watches the girl braid his hair in the mirror, as the guy gets ready to fix Billy's fade.

"So what you got goin' on after the adventure?" DK asks noticing she's almost done.

Billy shrugs as the guy finishes up his fade.

"You have to know some'n. Are you goin' to an after party wit' Mia and me?"

He simply shrugs again knowing in his head what his real plans are.

"Oh I see. You gon' stay in and keep the tradition alive," he winks as the girl finishes the last braid on his head.

"What are you talkin' about?" He asks as the guy begins to trim him up.

"Deflowering ..." he checks himself out.

Checking himself out as well and he asks, "What?"

"Nigga you know what I'm sayin'. Are you gonna stick yo' key in the ignition and give the car its firs' ride?"

Billy blinks blankly at him.

"Give the CD its firs' spin?" Receiving no reaction he tries again, "Take the baby on her first pony?" With a final deep sigh he asks, "Play house?"

He knows exactly what DK is talking about, but he doesn't believe he's actually asking him these things.

"Are you gonna sleep wit' Kie or not?"

Running his fingers over his hair he snaps, "Uh I think you got them braids rolled a little too tight. They cuttin' off the circulation to yo' head, and we all know it needs all the circulation it can get."

DK shrugs him off as he hands the girl a fifty telling her to keep the change. He's in the mood to tip nicely.

"Well I know I'm a get me some kind of action tonight. Might not fuck the girl, but believe me ..." he drifts off. "I'm a get me some'n."

"Unlike you," Billy hands the guy thirty knowing it was only twenty for it. "The only plan I have for tonight is to make Kie understand how much I really love her."

"Aw," a female who's over listening mutters.

They turn around and look at her.

"My bad. It's just nice to hear a guy finally give a damn about a girl like that," she puts down the magazine.

Billy smiles politely at her as they get up to walk out the front door.

"My names Candy," she sticks her hand out.

Courteously shaking back he smiles, "Billy."

DK just watches like a hawk from behind, curious if she'll hit on him or not.

"Your girlfriend sure has to be wonderful if she can land a guy who cares so much about her," she blushes pushing her chestnut brown hair behind her ear.

"She's more than wonderful. She's perfect," he brags getting ready to open the door. "She's wifey."

Later that evening we're all dressed and ready to go. The guys are supposed to meet us as the restaurant. The limo will come get us, drop us off, pick up the guys and bring them back to us. I can't believe that all the hard work and days of preparation are about to pay off. That is if we can make it past the castle guards. Mommy and Daddy.

Blinding us with another flash my mom gushes, "You girls look so beautiful!" Talk about feeling like I'm on the red carpet. She hasn't removed her eye from the camera since the moment we walked out of my room.

"Thanks," Mia says proudly sucking up most of the poses. She's a bit camera hungry, but rather her being snapped the hell out of than me. Hey, the more pictures of me they get, the more shots there are to show off to my annoying family members.

"Now you two remember everything we said?" my dad asks leaning against the wall far behind my mother.

"Yes," we say in unison noticing the limo that's pulled up.

Pointing a stern finger at us he demands, "And you swear to be careful?"

"Yes," we say again smiling politely at him.

"Ok," he sighs. "Cells?"

"Yes dad," I look him right in his eyes. "Everything will be fine."

"Promise me you'll make responsible choices."

"I will dad."

"Promise me you won't—

"Calm down dad. I know how to handle myself."

You know you never really appreciate how much your parents worry about you until that second when they really let you be the adult you're trying to grow into. It never registers in your mind until you can see it in their eyes that they really are just looking out for you, hoping to see you succeed, and not make any of the same horrible mistakes they did.

"Ok you girls have a good time," my mom says as we start towards the door to grab our bags. Turning around to give him an evil glare to get them she reassures, "Don't worry about your bags your father will get them."

My dad groans under his breath as he rushes in front of us to grab our bags. While I'm still in disbelief this whole thing is actually happening to me, I know that sooner or later it'll all set in, and I will be too happy for words.

He walks ahead of us with our bags, while my mom walks behind us with the camera still glued to her hand like she's the paparazzi.

"One more by the limo," she sighs trying not to get teary eyed. "Please."

We sigh as my dad puts our bags in the trunk while the limo driver waits on the opposite side of the car.

"I haven't taken this many pictures since I was born and my mom felt the need to alert every single member in our family," Mia leans over and whispers in my ear.

Through gritted teeth I whisper back, "Yeah well I've never taken this many pictures a day in my life. The only day that even compares close is my sixth birthday party where they took me to the Pizza Palace, and I kicked the big peace of cheese."

"Smile!" She squeals snapping away.

It's scary how many rolls of film she used on her own. Mia and I have six cameras between us, but my mom had at least six on her own. I'm sure she'll force my dad to go up the store as soon as we leave to get them developed.

"You'll call us when you wake up?" She says upset that she has no more film.

Absolutely annoyed behind my safe point I sigh, "Yes."

The limo driver politely comes around to open the door for us. I bet he hates his job. Having to drive noisy, rowdy, irritating, unappreciative teenagers around on prom night has to be the least enjoyable thing you can do on a Saturday night, but let's just say he makes a hefty chunk of change.

"I'm Sam," he sticks his hand out to shake ours. "I'll be your driver for the evening."

"You remember how everything was discussed on the phone?" Mia questions letting his hand fall away from hers.

"Yes madam," he nods. "Everything will go according to plan."

"Good," she smiles excited about something. When my best friend keeps secrets from me on a night like prom it makes me a little more than nervous.

"Have a good time girls," she says leaning forward for us to kiss her on the cheek. We do a kiss on each cheek and smile as she backs away. "Love you."

"You too mom," we both say together.

Sam opens the door letting Mia get in first knowing she'll have the least amount of trouble. After I'm in, he closes the door leaving Mia and me in the most beautiful limo we've ever been in. Hell it's better than the inside of some houses I've seen.

"Damn," I say loudly as Sam gets in the driver seat.

After giggling at some of the discoveries like the beautiful champagne flutes, expensive ashtrays, and a secret candy stash Mia dove into the second she spotted it, I ask, "How do you work the radio?"

Forty-five minutes later we arrive at a closed restaurant. Why the hell would she drag me to a closed restaurant on prom? I know I said I don't want to wait in a line, but damn I didn't mean I didn't want to see people at all.

Sam opens the door helping us out. I look down at the rocks under my heels and over at Mia whose still smirking like she knows something I don't.

"Not to sound … curious," I start off sarcastically. "But why the hell are we at a closed restaurant?"

"This is where we're having dinner," she says waving to Sam who tips his hat and returns himself to the vehicle.

"Excuse me? I didn't sign up to eat rocks outside a nice looking place," I point to the ground.

"You know you haven't made one part of this day easy?" With a big huff she mutters, "All I've done is try to give us a nice day, and all you do is bitch. Bitch. Bitch. Bitch." In a voice directed at me she snaps as we head up the stairs, "Look, quit bitching about everything and relax."

"Fine," I throw my hands in the air surrendering.

Mia quickly explains as we rapidly approach the last, "Now my uncle owns this place, and when I asked if he would close it down for one night to let us have our own PRIVATE dinner he agreed, saying he already owes my family one anyway."

After she knocks I smile hearing the locks turn, "Thoughtful."

"Sorry Mia I was just putting the finishing touches on your dinner area," her uncle apologizes politely letting us in to the most beautiful restaurant I have ever seen.

My jaw slightly parts as I take a long look around. I feel my body tense up as I become nervous to even look at something wrong. Why on earth would one clumsy person like Mia bring another just as clumsy person like me, to a beautiful upscale place like this? Survey says. That's not smart.

"Now it's very simple," her uncle strolls off towards the stairs alerting me that there is more than one level, although I could tell that from the shape on the outside. As we follow him up he begins, "On the top two levels there are dinners for two."

We continue on our path as he tells us how long he's had the place, how expensive it is, how it was his ultimate dream, and he's talking a mile a minute so it's a lot of information to receive at once.

Once we arrive on the fourth level, which must be the one before the very top since there's only one more set of stairs.

In this room there's plush red carpet to match the lacey cloth placed over the table for two, which is next to the window. Out of the window you can see the view of the beautiful lake. Can you imagine how beautiful that will be watching the sun go down? There is a small chandelier that is barely lit due to the fact there's a firing going on in the room. Towards the back of the room there's a black leather couch angled towards a fireplace where a famous piece of artwork is proudly being displaced. At the other end there's a chase lounge surrounded by other works of art as well as a miniature bar to serve yourself. Can we say wow?

"One of you will be seated in here," he proudly beams at his work of art.

"As for the other?" Mia asks curiously looking at me meaning she's already got dibs on this room. First she wants this to be utterly romantic for *me*, yet she claims the room with the romantic fire and view. Thanks.

Heading up towards the longest set of stairs he says, "Follow me."

"Thanks again Uncle Rob," she says. "We really appreciate it. You're making this something special."

"Anything for my favorite niece," he turns around and smiles at her. If she wasn't my best friend I'd totally call her a brat.

Once we reach the top my jaw lands on the ground. From the door there's a white carpet leading right to the table. It's a covered balcony area that looks directly over the lake. I knew I knew this lake! It's the same one Billy and I danced in front of at homecoming. Aw. The dinner for two is just as beautiful as the other one, except there are more candles than the one below as well as a swing that faces the lake. There are white roses in various places with white rose petals sprinkled on the ground. It's decked out in white everything along with soft music playing from some unobvious space. I hate music that plays as if from nowhere.

"This," her uncle begins. "Is the finest place we have. Only two couples have ever dined here, and they were two of the most beautiful singers I've ever seen. You two actually remind me of them."

"Who were they?" Mia quickly questions.

"Dezaray," he glances at me. I absolutely adore her. She's like who I would aspire to be if I had to be a current popular singer right now. "With her boyfriend Blaine."

"The Blaine Williamson?" I ask quickly. There's no way he's telling the truth.

"Yup," he nods. Smiling he states, "In fact he proposed to her here."

I can't even make words anymore because of the shock. They are the biggest power couple I have ever seen, and I would love if Billy and I could be like them. They dated for several years, got married, and have not once separated or had any tabloid slander. They're like America's favorite young couple.

"Who's the other?" Mia asks still very curious.

"Alyssia," he looks deep into her eyes.

Breath escapes her as she gasps, "The Alyssia?"

"Yup," he smiles to himself knowing how much she's always wanted to be like her.

"No way," she sighs looking at the seats like I am. These are sacred seats to us both. With my luck, I doubt these seats will go to me.

"You remind me so much of her."

"Uncle Rob …" she blushes.

"You look as amazing as she did that night," he winks at her. Before strolling off he sighs, "I'll let you two decide who gets what room while I go to kitchen to check on the chefs."

I look at Mia whose eyes are sparkling at the thought of getting to possibly sit where her music idle sat. I should probably let her have this knowing this'll mean more to her than me, and the fact it is her uncle who got us the hook up.

Clearing her throat after her uncle is gone, "This is for you."

"Excuse me?"

"I arranged for you to have the best seat in the house," she smiles at me. Beaming at me sweetly she continues, "I told you I'm about to give you you're perfect Cinderella dream, so just accept this with no argument."

I thought she was just joking around telling me how she was going to do a number of wonderful things for me tonight, but she's really come through. Talk about being the best friend she could possibly be. "Thanks."

With a deep sigh she leans on the balcony, "Now don't get too comfy like this. It's only my job to treat you like a princess until your man gets here, and that's when it becomes his duty."

"Let's hope so," I lean over it with her.

"I never thought the two of us would be in the presence of where glory once sat."

"Me neither, but one day we'll sit here being the great ones having teenagers faint over the fact they got to sit where we did," I make her smile.

"Yeah that's the dream," she looks down at the lake.

"Wrong," I look over at her grabbing her attention. "That's our life."

Smiling at me she nods knowing I'm right. Sometimes she gets a little doubtful on just how far we'll go, but there's no stopping us until we are exactly the people we have dreamed.

We continue staring out across the lake in silence until her uncle rushes up the stairs at us announcing they've arrived. Smiling at one another, we know this is the moment we spent so many hours preparing for.

Billy and DK wait impatiently at the bottom of the stairs for us.

"Quit bein' so anxious," DK scolds Billy as he rocks back and fourth in place.

"You quit being anxious," he snaps back.

"Oh I'm calm," he places his free hand on his chest. "But you makin' me edgy."

"Oh shut up," he growls.

"You know this is the reason why we didn't go to our own prom righ'?"

Billy nods making DK smirk, which lightens the mood.

Mia's aunt, who's there just to support her husband and help if she can, comes from around the corner to announce us. She clears her throat making them look over at her.

"Are *you* two ready?" She sighs to herself remembering her first prom.

They nod politely to her sighing under their breaths.

"Sandy!" Rob calls to her right as she gets ready to announce Mia.

Yelling back she declares, "Busy!"

"I need you!"

"Well I'll be there in a few!" Mia shakes her head waiting at the top of the steps in front of me. "Where was I?"

"About to announce the girls," Billy says innocently.

"Oh yeah," she giggles to herself. "I'd like to present you with my beautiful niece. Which is her date?"

DK raises his hand slightly, and she nods. Mia strolls down the stairs lifting her dress that sweeps the ground slightly. She slowly passes the second branch off finally reaching light where they can all see her.

She's wearing a lipstick colored, satin back crepe dress. It's a halter top, which crosses in the back. The sides of it meet in the middle in a bit of a slight scrunch. Her hair has slightly large curls pinned on the top with her bangs being left out to shape her face. On her feet are clear heels with rhinestones placed on the part of that that covers her toes. The shoes are about three inches high, so she's walking slower than she ever has, trying not to trip. Her earrings glisten in the light bringing even more attention to her perfectly painted face.

DK's jaw drops, trying to mouth words on how good she looks. No sounds can come out as she stops and poses like a sex kitten against the wall.

"You're right he is fine," her aunt whispers in her ear making her giggle. "You've got good taste."

"And what do you have to say?" She puts her hand on her hip as he glances one more time at her whole body. The dress hugs just the flattering curves, which on Mia is all there is.

"Damn!" he basically jumps when he says it. Shaking his head he exclaims again, "Jus' ... DAMN!"

Winking at him she strolls over to him slowly, "That's what I thought." She wraps her arms around him to give him a slight hug, "Hey."

"Hey sexy," he holds her close for a second.

"Quit staring at my ass," she whispers in his ear during the embrace.

As he pulls away he mumbles, "Can't help it."

"I know," she says cockily to him.

"This is fo' you," he hands her the single red rose making her smirk.

"Thanks," she nods knowing this gesture wasn't conjured all on his own.

DK hands her the red rose courage she's supposed to wear, "And this thing ... I don't know how it goes on or anything, but I know yo' ass better like it."

She looks at him like he's crazy. "I know you didn't just—

"I mean I hope you like it," he tries his gentlemen like charm on her.

"That's better." She opens it up then demands, "Now slip this on me, kiss me on the cheek, and pose next to me for a picture."

"Look at you tryin' to be in control," DK shakes his head. "You know that turns me on."

"Better be ready for a wild night," she winks before letting him slip around her wrist.

She leans over and poses for a picture with him, making Billy smile as he wonders just when exactly he will have his beauty in his arms.

"Now I know I look good," Mia starts.

"You do look hot," Billy nods and compliments her knowing she just wanted more to feed her ego.

"Thank you," she says letting her shoulders bounce a little with it. "But I know you're dying to see the number I did on Kie."

"Heaven forbids you let yo' homegurl look any uglier than she already does," DK mumbles.

They both shoot an evil glare at him.

"What?!" They respond together upset.

"Jus' playin'," he chuckles under his breath. "Damn."

"Don't play like that," Mia turns around and points at him. "Anyway where was I?"

Billy says even more nervous than before, "Introducing my girlfriend ..."

"Oh yeah. Go ahead Aunt Sandy," she squeals. Mia quickly points a stern finger at him, "Better be careful with this."

"Cinderella would envy this girl," she begins to introduce me.

With a deep sigh I start down the stairs holding up the bottom of my gown that has, what we've come to call, fluff. It's a halter top two piece gown that pushes up 'my ladies' and gives me a flatter stomach. There's a bit of shimmer across the design, and shimmer sprinkled on the bottom as well. My heels are two inches and clear. The straps criss-cross overlaps my foot and buckle around my ankle. My hair has curls around my head with two pieces of hair down on both sides to give my face a romantic look.

When I reach the first stair where I can become visible, I see Billy's jaw drop and his eyebrows raised as if in a moment of shock.

Unlike Mia, I stop in the middle of the stair rather than lean against the wall.

"Wow," Billy barely is able to mutter out of his mouth. Some how he manages to get out, "You look ..."

I give Mia props on being right about the look on his face being priceless.

Taking a final step onto the ground I stroll over to Billy, "Look like …"

"Beautiful," he compliments me breathing out deeply. Gently he touches my face, "Like an angel. Just so beautiful."

This is the most beautiful I have ever felt, and I have to admit seeing his reaction makes all the primping worth it. I smile softly being modest, "Thank you."

Billy just can't tear his eyes away from me. Not just my body, but my face as well, particularly my eyes that he's fallen into. He seems so caught up in them that he doesn't know where we are or the fact we have a whole night a head of us.

Mia clears her throat and mutters, "The flowers."

"Oh yeah," a part of him snaps back into reality. "This is for you," he hands me a white rose. He slightly wets his lips, "It's pure beauty just like you."

I smile wider as Mia tries not to awe.

"You know it wouldn't kill you to say sweet things like that ever so often," Mia mumbles at DK.

"The flower is jus' as beautiful as you," he tries to smile and come back on the cool.

She smacks him upside the head with the rose, "Jackass."

Billy slips the corsage around my wrist and places a small kiss on my cheek.

"Let me show you to your tables," Sandy says starting up the stairs. "Follow me."

Mia and DK immediately follow behind her with his arm around her waist as he checks her out from behind mouthing damn to himself, while Billy and I casually follow behind them hand in hand smiling widely at each other.

After a romantic dinner comes the actual dance. This is the night I waited for since I was a little girl to go and show off my boyfriend. That's right; I love the right to show off my man any chance I get because I know for a fact now that he's not going anywhere.

"Wow," Billy leans over and whispers in my ear. "I've never been to a prom before," he tells me something I obviously already know. I just hope that his, scratch that, DK's behavior doesn't make it apparent.

"Me either," I try to comfort him.

This is the biggest social event of the year for us. We've already imprinted our names and faces in their hearts. This is just a chance to make sure they save it there. It's a chance to prove we have just as much class and style as anyone else here.

We begin dancing to the music, and the entire time we are Billy's attention is focused on me. It's marvelous and very ego boosting when you're drop dead gorgeous boyfriend is in a room full of beautiful girls and only focuses on you.

The music cuts off a little sooner than it should have. I know for a fact that song wasn't over. What's the necessity to cut the song short? I'm sure whatever over-done dramatic event they cut it off for could have waited a few moments longer.

"Time to announce the prom king and queen," I hear someone say. Told ya.

Billy looks at me as if to ask if I was nominated. I look back at him like he's lost his damn mind, which if he's thinking that he has. How the hell would I be nominated for that social discrimination? Unless your parents are socialites you don't get a second thought. He simply shakes his head as Mia and DK move beside me.

"Alright," some woman begins to announce. I don't know who she is. She doesn't work for our school. In fact, I've never seen her before. She must be a volunteer chaperone. "And our prom king is …" she opens the envelope. "Danny!"

Everyone claps for the loser. There was no doubt in my mind that he was going to take home that shinny crown so that he could stare at himself in it. I've learned that if you give him something he can see his own reflection in, he'll leave you alone.

Danny smirks as he puts the crown on his head. He leans forward to give his thank you speech. "Thanks for this. This is really pimp to win king like this," he tilts his crown to the side a little. Cocky bastard.

"Did he really just say pimp?" Billy questions.

I simply nod as a response while snuggling closer to him.

"And the prom queen winner is," she opens another envelope.

As she prepares to announce it I lean up and ask him, "Are you ready to—

"Kie! Come on up here and get your crown," the lady says.

My jaw stops the word as I find myself frozen in my spot. My entire body is stuck. Are they joking? I was nominated? Is this not a mistake?

Mia looks at me slowly and asks, "You won?"

"I won?" I question back at her.

"Baby," I hear Billy whisper in my ear. "Go get your crown."

"Come on Kie," I hear peers urge me on. "We're glad it's you."

Touched, I slowly walk towards the stage making sure not to trip over my dress. In shock I continue to replay how this giant mistake happened in my head. Whose name could they have confused mine with? Maybe Kimberly?

The lady hands me the tiara, and I give it a nice long stare. I don't know why this is so exciting. Now that it's in my hands I can't fathom why people are heartbroken from not winning this piece of metal.

"Hey …" I start and get a little uproar from the crowd clueing me in that I am supposed to win. "I just would like to thank all of you who voted for me. I didn't ever think I would or could win something like this. It's flattering to know you think I deserve to win this tiara, but it's more flattering just to know you really like me that much. I'll be the first to admit that I'm not Ms. Popular, but I'm glad enough of you know me and love me to break the stereotypical tradition. Thank you."

The crowd claps for me and DK leans over to Mia, "Was she really supposed to win?"

Mia sighs happily, "I believe so."

"It's time for the tradition of the king to dance with the queen during a song of their choice," the woman announces. "What shall it be?"

Danny looks at me informing me I can request whatever song I like, so I pick one of the best love songs from my era. The two of us take the center to start the dance.

Within our first few steps Danny says, "You really look good. Very classy."

"Thank you," I say glancing over his shoulder at Billy who's patiently waiting for me next to DK. He's antsy especially considering the fact I have to dance with Danny, his arch-rival if you will. "You clean up well too."

"Thanks."

"Danny, can I ask you something?" I say as the first verse continues behind me.

"Anything baby," he says trying to be sly as he moves closer.

"Do you mind if we break tradition and dance with our own dates?" I ask hopeful.

He takes a long look in my eyes for the first time. For once he let's down his guard of Mr. Everything to think about how much I've done for him, and how much I really mean to him. He looks over his shoulder and calls Billy to the middle of the floor.

Billy looks at him in confusion, waits for the nod of approval, and then takes himself over to us.

"I think this princess belongs to you," Danny lets me slowly go.

"Fo' real?" Billy questions.

"Yeah."

"We straight?" he asks in a sincere voice.

"Yeah," Danny nods and looks me deep into my eyes again. "Yeah."

"Thanks Danny," I sigh as Billy wraps his arms around my waist.

Billy holds me close as I place my arms around his neck and embrace him closely. Inhaling the sweet smell of his cologne I get lost in his arms as everyone else takes the crowd with their date. He holds me gently and rests his head next to mine, singing the song softly in my ear much like he does every time we slow dance. Call it his trademark to let me know I'm in his arms.

About an hour and a half later we're outside our two hotel rooms right next to one another. Billy's jacket is draped around me while his arms are planted around my waist as he kisses my neck with the tips of his lips.

"So are you hitting some after parties with us?" Mia questions as DK lays an arm around her shoulder.

"Nah," I yawn a little. "I think we're going to just hang out here."

Billy smiles softly and looks up at Mia, "I've got something special for Kie, so it's no for now and later." He smirks as he starts fishing for his key, "But the two of you have fun."

"Don't do anything that you wouldn't see in a PG-13 movie," I point a finger at her and giggle as Billy leans against the doorframe.

"Talk to you guys in the morning," Mia grins the all-knowing smirk.

I turn and enter our room not ready for what I see. My jaw hits to the floor as I enter further in the room. Billy closes the door and locks it behind me as I ogle over the beautiful surroundings he set. There are candles lit around the entire room, rose petals scattered across the floor, desserts of all sorts on a table for two near the window, and soft music playing to top it off. Why … how … when did he do all this for me?

"I …" I stumble to find words. This is more beautiful than what I did for him for Valentine's Day. He really went out of his way, and what I don't get is why.

"You know Kie," he slides his arm around my waist as I feel like I stepped in super glue because my feet never move from their spot. "We've been through a lot of times together, good and bad, and every moment that should've been some'n great for you … I came up short." His other arm slides around my waist, "I promised myself after what I did to you on Valentine's Day that you deserved to know how much you truly mean to me, and what a great woman you are." I fold my hands on top of his. "So I figured what a better night than tonight to show you just that."

He plants a small kiss on my cheek as I discover new things around the room like vases full of white roses and a teddy bear in one of the chairs at the table. "But ..."

"I just want tonight to be special for you," he smiles and leans his head against mine. "I love you."

I hate being speechless. I hate it more than I hate watching bad pop music videos on television. I mean there's something about needing to find certain words in certain situations, and not being able to that just frustrates me. I wish I could just tell him something, anything, but my voice is like a ghost, it almost doesn't exist.

Somehow I whisper out, "I love you."

Billy turns me around casually and looks me in my eyes, "So do you wanna dance?"

"Mm," I hum out loud and look behind me once again. Nibbling on the bottom of his lip I say, "I've danced all night."

"True," he nods pulling me closer to him. "Do you have some'n in particular you would like to do? I mean we can do anything your heart desires."

"Can we go to the moon?" I ask in a playful voice.

"And have cheese while we collect moon rocks? Sure," he exclaims in the same playful tone.

Giggling a little more, I know the reason I made the joke. I've been fighting myself not to think about it all day, and after that last dance at prom, I'm sure. I want Billy in the only way I haven't had him yet.

"Billy," I start looking down terrified.

How do you let the man of your dreams know that you want to give yourself to him without coming out like one of those sissy virgin girls or those anxious first timers that are just looking to give it up to the first guy that wants it? Why is everything so complicated the older you get?

"Yeah baby," he lifts my chin to look him in his eyes.

"I ..." I start out again looking behind him at the door. I can do this right? I mean I'm a big girl I can let him know I'm ready for the next step in our relationship.

"Kie what's up?" he focuses my attention back on him by moving my chin over so that our eyes meet back up.

"Billy I love you so much," I feel my body start to tremble a tad.

His eyes try to comfort me, "I love you too."

"And lately I've been giving something a lot of thought," I swallow nervously. He waits patiently, obviously very unsure of what I'm going to say next.

"We are very closely connected. I mean we have an amazing relationship that I never dreamed possible, even with the pitfalls; this is still the most incredible thing to happen to me. You are the most incredible thing to ever happen to me."

"And you to me," he interjects even though I'm not finished yet.

"I know that I'm ready for the next step in our relationship ..." I say in a low whisper causing obvious confusion. Billy's eyes get a very unsure glaze over them. "Billy I want to make love with you," I manage to finally say.

I watch as Billy's grip becomes loose, and he looks like he's going to have a heart attack. Well damn I didn't know he was going to die of shock. I hope I don't have to call an ambulance.

My eyes never leave the panicking Billy. Great, now I've scared him, and he'll never want to do this with me.

"Uh ..." he stutters now to find the right words to say.

Wow you know I thought telling the guy who loves you that you want to show it in a new way would make him excited, happy even, but instead it makes him distant and almost scared. Great. Just great.

My jaw starts to bob as I begin to try to defend myself.

"Kie," he takes my hand and leads me to sit on the bed couch. The bed couch is this nice leather couch that sits at the foot of the bed. I was so busy admiring everything else that none of the furniture stuck out to me.

In an uneasy tone I say, "Yeah?"

"I know you love me, and I know that this is not some'n inconsequential to you."

Inconsequential? Has he been reading the dictionary again? Couldn't he have used a non-standardized test word? Especially in the situation right now, little words are best in moments like these.

"This is a *very big step* that I don't want you to make because you think you have to, or you feel pressure from me or anyone else," he says slipping his fingers with mine. "You're an amazing girlfriend, and you mean to me just as much if not more than I mean to you. I don't want you to do some'n you're going to regret for the rest of your life."

Way to call me dumb. What's the matter with him? Does he really think that I'm that stupid? That I just woke up one day and decided that I wanted to have sex? Does he think I'm some immature thirteen year old who wants to get down and dirty because I saw it on TV or because my closest friends are? How can he underestimate me like this?

"Billy … I've given this a lot of thought. I know there are certain risks just like with everything else you do in life, but I think this is good for us as a couple as well as individuals. I know that I don't have to do anything I'm not ready for, and I wouldn't. You know me sweetie. I'm a very strong independent person," I tighten my grip on his hand. "This decision I made on my own, and I know that you are ready to whenever I am."

"You're right Kie," he nods at me moving closer. "I'm ready whenever it is you are a 100% ready, whether that's today or fifty years from now. You're worth any amount of time baby." Titling his head to the side he continues, "If you're really ready to do this then I'm with you."

"Honey," I touch the side of his face. "I want you to make love to me tonight," I say without being the least bit frightened. There's something about having him look me in the eyes and say the types of things that he just said that creates a shield or builds a comfort level that I need.

Billy nods at me and smiles once more. "Ok," he says twisting a finger around a free floating strand. Deeply he sighs once more, "Ok." Why is he more nervous than me? Oh I hope he doesn't get performance anxiety.

He leans over and places a tender kiss on my lips. I kiss back capturing his bottom lip for only a split moment because he pulls away. Looking scared, I watch as Billy takes my hand to lead me to the bed.

He sits me down on the edge and moves away, "One sec, ok baby?"

"K," I respond back slipping out of my shoes slowly.

Wow I didn't realize just how much heels bite when you're on your feet all night long. Who knows how I'm going to dance in those. I think we'll call ourselves the flattops and wear nothing but flat shoes. I cross my ankles and wait impatiently for Billy to come back.

Billy comes out from the bathroom with his tux shirt undone a bit and a secure look in his eyes. I wonder what that was all about. Self pep talk maybe? He sits down on the bed next to me not looking at me, which makes me uneasy once again, that he might be changing his mind.

"Billy what's wrong?"

"Nothin'," he shakes his head. "Is there anything you want or need? Water? Candy? The air turned up or down? Better pillows? I mean I can run out and get you—

I can't help but giggle. With a wide smile I cut him off, "I'm fine. Trust me I'm fine."

"You're so beautiful," he smirks at me.

"Thanks."

He nods and looks back behind us at the bed that's still made. Getting up Billy pulls back the covers a bit. "Are you ready?"

I nod and swallow any last doubt or fear that this isn't right for us. Taking my hand, he sits me in the uncovered bed area and starts to kiss me slowly as he sits back down. Just relax Kie you're in good hands; you're in the best hands god could give you.

As we start kissing more intensely I feel Billy slip his jacket from around my shoulders and toss it onto the floor. His hand slithers its way around the curves of my hips then up to my face where it plants itself on my check ever so softly. I wrap my arms around his waist and continue kissing him. I'm glad our kisses right now are very soft and sensual. I don't think I could take the over-done, porn-like type where there's more tongue than passion.

Billy and I move to the middle of the bed where I lay back onto the feather pillows. He takes the tip of his fingers and traces the curves of my body once more as his lips inch their way over to my neck. I don't know if he can feel my body trembling, but it is. For a few moments he nibbles on my neck bringing back the memory of the first time his lips laid themselves on my body.

My eyes roll back into my head bringing back the butterflies of the first experience. They slide themselves back to mine, and he passionately wraps his arms around me holding me tightly. This has to the best feeling in the world. It feels like he'll never let me go, which I hope is right.

It's kind of funny because as I'm focused on the marvelous feeling of his strong sculpted arms holding me, he's ever so casually unzipping me. I don't even realize it until my dress starts to feel loose. Somehow I get lost between the touch and his kiss so easily. Billy slowly slips the dress off my chest revealing my black low cut bra.

I pull away a bit in between kisses undoing the buttons on his shirt to reveal his wife beater underneath. Ripping off his shirt I toss it on the ground on top of his jacket. After I capture his tongue with mine once more I begin to tug at his undershirt eventually shedding it with the rest.

Around the time kissing is kicked up a notch we've both managed to be out of our clothes and underneath the blanket. Billy lays his body on top of mine and stops kissing me for a moment.

"Are you sure?" He whispers leaning his forehead against mine.

I nod and swallow. I've never seen him naked, and let me just state for record if this guy failed at life he could still do porn because his body is that hot.

"You can tell me any time to stop, and I will ok?"

Nodding once more, he goes back to kissing me. Can he feel my heart racing like the street racer running from the cops? The butterflies in my stomach calm down for a sec as Billy gets ready himself to enter my uncharted body.

"It's gonna hurt baby," he says in a soft whisper. I nod and prepare myself for the pain I'm going to encounter.

He plants his lips on top of mine giving me the sweetest kisses he possibly can as he slowly enters me. I feel a slow sharp pain. It makes me whimper and pull my lips away from his. I begin to groan a little as the pain feels like it becomes more and more unbearable. A small tear trickles down my face and immediately Billy notices, striking fear into his heart.

"Baby do you want me to stop?" He questions wiping away the tear. I shake my head, and he kisses my forehead entering my body as far as he can.

I lift my lips back to touch his as his hips slowly move on top of me.

We begin to feel things neither of us has ever felt before. Our bodies are marsh-mellowed together, inseparable in every single way and our emotions are running high as there's an unspoken connection that only we can understand. I love every second, every moment, every inch of feeling him and knowing how much he loves and cares about me. Sure I know it by the way he says it to me every few minutes, but there's an unspoken level as well. The way he holds my body, and makes sure I'm alright really proves to me how much I mean to him, and how much he's grown since we've been together.

It feels like hours that we're in heaven. I swear that it's never going to end, but moments later the feeling of ecstasy reaches its highest point. My lips slip away, and I let out a moan in his name, at the same time he lets out one of mine. At that point our lips slip back together as our bodies' slump together. My tongue runs lazily around his before he pulls away from me.

Billy runs his fingers through my hair and starts planting kisses all over my body. With a deep sigh he places one final kiss on my lips before whispering, "I love you."

"I love you," I say as he curls up beside me locking his fingers with mine.

"Are you ok?" He asks wrapping one of his arms around me, pulling me closer to him.

"I'm a bit sore and exhausted, but I'm as fine as I can be," I snuggle up next to him resting my head on his chest.

"I'm sorry I hurt you," he apologizes again. "Is there anything I can get you?"

I simply close my eyes, "No."

"You're so wonderful," Billy kisses the side of my head. "Thank you for comin' into my life," he kisses me once more. I don't know if he's being all-sentimental because we just made love or because he genuinely feels like expressing himself, but either way I don't really mind because I love being flattered and feeling important.

"Thank you for coming into mine," I fold my fingers with his once again. I don't know if he realizes it, but I'm on my way to sleep whether he's on his way or not.

When I wake up, hours later, I realize that my warmth is gone. Where did Billy go? I know that fool didn't think this was a hit and run. Abruptly getting up, I raise my naked body that's wrapped in a sheet to see him at the table by the window in his boxers with the journal I bought him and a pencil in his hand completely absent minded.

"What are you doing? I ask in a weak voice.

"Oh," he drops them both. "I was just writin' a song." Moving his way towards the bed he grabs his tux shirt off the ground, "Nothing important."

"Song writing is important …"

"Not as important as you," he hands it to me climbing back in bed next to me. "Good morning."

"Mm good morning," I plant a soft kiss on top of his lips. Oh well if I have morning breath. It's not like it's the first time he's ever kissed me with morning breath, and I can guarantee it won't be the last.

"How are you sexy?" he asks as I put his shirt on over my body and ruffle my hair.

"I'm fantastic, how are you?"

Wrapping his arms around me cuddling me for a moment, he answers, "The happiest I've ever been."

"You just say that 'cause you got some," I playfully joke.

Smiling back he shakes his head, "No-huh."

I close my eyes again, "What time is it?"

"About 7:30."

"Wow it's early," I yawn feeling Billy get anxious behind me.

"We're supposed to meet Mia and DK for breakfast in thirty minutes," he gets up from behind me.

"We'll I'm glad I woke up then," I droop back over the pillows.

"Yeah me too," he gets that nervous look across his face again. "I need to do some'n before we leave."

"What's that?" I ask in a cheerful mood. It's very rare I wake up in such a marvelous mood, so he better take advantage of it.

"Hold on," he disappears into the bathroom. He's like a ghost sometimes, just appears to disappear. I close my eyes and don't even realize when he comes back. "Kie."

I roll over on my side to see him kneeling beside the bed, "Hm?"

"Last night was … indescribable," he starts what I feel like is going to be the beginning of a very important speech. "I mean making love was something I never really experienced until last night with you. I've had my fair share of girls and you know that, but you Kiara are some'n different," saving himself from a fit from me he continues. "You know for the longest time I had no idea who I was, what I was doing, where I was going and for that matter I didn't care, then you stroll into my life and become my spy glass to see all that I needed to. You made me a better man. I know I've told you that more times than you can remember, but it's true. I can't believe I almost threw it away because for one second I let it slip how much you mean to me, but that will never happen again. Kie I can't live without you in my life every moment of every day. I want to be you first, last, and only baby in everything," he takes my hand and scoots closer. "You already make me the happiest man alive, so make me the happiest man alive for the rest of my life and marry me," he pulls out a diamond princess cut ring from his other hand.

I feel my breath robbed from me. I can't believe he's asking me this. He can't be. This isn't happening to me. This can't be.

"I know Kie that you're only seventeen and have more than a bright future ahead of you. It's not like I wanna get married tomorrow and start a family right away or anything like that. I just wanna be the only man for you, I wanna be guaranteed a spot in your life, and I just wanna know at the end of the day you'll be all mine forever. So whether you marry me two years from now or twenty, I don't care, as long as you are willing to spend the rest of your life with me," he says so worried that it's cute.

Ya know, he's right, I am only seventeen. I could easily say no and dismiss him as crazy, but why do that? Isn't this the one guy I never want to go anywhere? Don't we want the same assuredness that the other one isn't going anywhere? What would be the damage and crime in pledging my life to my love right now?

"Yes," I whisper out. "Yes Billy I'll marry you." Poor guy probably would have died if I had shot him down. He slips the ring on my left finger and leans in to kiss me.

"I love you," he smiles at me more excited than I've ever seen him.

"I love you," I smile back watching his excitement continue to flourish.

"You know this isn't just because we made love right? I mean I was gonna ask you regardless of last night," he quickly says like I would think he did it only because we were intimate.

"Yeah," I lay back on the pillows.

"Good," he nods sitting down on the edge of the bed to kiss me. Before his lips reach mine he repeats himself, "Good."

As I replay the proposal over and over again in my head during breakfast, Mia somehow manages to continuously interrupt me with no remorse.

"You ok?" She questions flipping through her menu I swear for the fourth time.

"I'm fine," I smile softly adjusting the rock on my finger.

"So you said yes?"

"No. I just wear the ring to remind him how I shot him down."

Ignoring me she goes on, "Good to know you two had an enjoyable morning. What sort of night did you have?"

I look over at Billy and DK who are arguing over something on the menu. "It was like a dream. Like a good dream I could have for the rest of my life."

"Did you two ..." she raises her eyebrows.

"Yeah," I nod. "I'll give you the details later."

Demanding she growls, "Screw later. You'll tell me right after we order."

"Later," I snap as the waitress comes over.

We go around ordering different items, the waitress even makes eyes at Billy but his attention is so focused on me he never notices.

"DK can you go get my jacket from the car?" Mia asks politely trying to shoo them away.

"Yeah," he gets up.

"Billy why don't you go with him," I nudge him giving him the girl talk moment look.

"Alright," he gets up.

"I'm gonna have a cig while I'm out there," DK says to us.

"Ok," Mia says like she doesn't care.

"I love you," I whisper to Billy as he plants a kiss on my cheek.

"I love you," he whispers back before disappearing with DK.

While I start to spill my guts to Mia, DK is busy spilling his to Billy.

"Damn that girl's got some moves. I mean at the party all I wanted to do was jus' take her back to our room and—

"I get it," Billy cuts him off leaning against the side of the car.

Taking another drag of his cigarette he continues, "But I mean foolin' around was good enough I guess. One day I'm gonna see what she's like in bed."

"I'm sure you will. DK, do you even have feelings for Mia?" Billy continues staring off into the morning skylight.

"Yeah," he nods. "Feelings I've never had for a girl and never thought I would," he blows out smoke not even making Billy divert his attention back at him. "For the firs' time it's not all 'bout sex. I mean sex is involved, but there's more to it than that. She's a lot of fun to hang out wit', cause trouble wit', and jus' be wit'. I like her a lot."

"Good," Billy shrugs in a daze.

Confused that that's all he said he questions, "Good? Jus' good? No words of wisdom or advice? No judgments bein' made? What's up Billy? What's on yo' mind?"

"Nothin' man. I don't have a problem in the world. I literally am the happiest man alive."

"Why's that?"

He merely shrugs which annoys DK.

"Damn it Billy! You know you wanna tell me."

"Kie and I just had an unbelievable night last night. Let's leave it at that …" he sighs in ultimate satisfaction.

"So was he any good?" Mia questions me.

My jaw opens a bit in shock she'd ask me something like that. "Mia!"

"Well some guys are bad Kie, don't forget that," she points a finger at me. "I asked a legit question. Is he?"

Giggling, I roll my eyes refusing to answer that question.

"Come on Kie. For the love of god just tell me was it worth the wait?"

I nod repeatedly. Stirring my hot chocolate I sigh, "By far. Believe me by far."

"Wow I can't believe you're no longer a virgin and an engaged woman at that," she wiggles in her seat with a smile. "So you two are permanent huh?"

"I'd like to think so being engaged and all."

"This is where you say thank you to me for helping fate along," she gloats with her cocky grin that makes me want to reach across the table and smack her.

"Thanks Mia. I'll never be able to repay you," I sigh.

"Maid of Honor," she makes me giggle as the boys return to our sides.

There are moments in life that I swore would be the greatest; I just didn't know that they would happen to me so soon. I spent my childhood imagining that you were grown up at certain moments in life or that events had to happen at certain points, when the truth of the matter is it's gonna happen whenever it's right for you. I've never felt pressured to a damn thing in my life. Everything comes so natural, and I wouldn't have it any other way.

I dreamed that everything that happened to me last night and this morning would be just like you read in those fairy tale books as a kid. I guess in my own sick twisted way that's exactly how it is. I've got my prince, I've had my ball, I've been awoken by a kiss, I've been rescued, I've had my fairy godmother, and I've gotten my proposal. I guess you could say I've lived out every major moment you dream up as a kid, but the difference is that it's not exactly perfect. Part of growing up is realizing that life's not perfect, but there are perfect moments that you'll never forget.

I guess you could say crossing the line from childhood to adulthood is personally based. No one single event makes that transaction for you, but I would say that every experience with Billy has brought me closer to the growth and grown up woman I am trying to become. What can I say though? I guess for the first time I've accepted what sort of woman I'm destined to become without fear or anxiety.

CHAPTER 15

The Audition

The time has finally arrived. I've waited years for this to happen to me, and finally the time for us to shine has come. Well it hasn't quite arrived yet, but we're preparing for it. Most teenagers look forward to graduation, moving away from their parents, and living the crazy college life, but what I look forward to is simply two weeks where I push myself further than I ever have. We've spent the last couple of days torturing ourselves to make sure that when we step off that plane we are ready to be crowned the best of the best. It takes so much to make it to the finals.

I need this music deal, they need this music deal, and this is what we've set our hopes and goals on, this single week of auditions. It's probably not healthy to set everything you are on one single moment, but I'm doing it. We've sacrificed so much to just make it this far that I don't think there's anything I wouldn't give up to go a little farther for us.

You know some people are lucky enough to feel this way about sports, academics, drama even, but there's something different about doing it for the love and feel of the music. We're not in it to make the money; we're not in it to just make a name for ourselves, but to let the world know who we are as individuals as well as a team.

That's exactly what our group is, a team. I have this feeling that when we step up to the plate and look at all the other groups that they will just be that. A group. They'll blend and synchronize, but be about themselves, and it'll show, while we do what they do as well as take it the next step, really prove that we are one and how bad we really want this.

It's a struggle to the top that I spent my entire life preparing for; I just hope if I fall in the process that Billy will pick me back up.

"Finally a break," Mia drapes her towel around her neck trying to cool down.

"Yeah," I wipe the sweat that's dripping down my face. Trying to catch my breath I say, "I'm going to call Billy."

"You do that," she sneaks out a candy bar as I start off. With a shake of my head I snatch it from her, "What the—

"Don't play," I toss it in the trash. "You know damn well you can't eat that."

"I could've it if someone weren't busy playing candy tyrant," she mumbles grabbing her bottle of water from beside her. "I'll just chew this and PRE-TEND it taste like chocolate!"

Grabbing my cell phone from my purse, I head off outside to get some fresh air as well as have some privacy. As I slouch down against the wall, I hit Billy's number on speed dial.

Billy sketches another song line on his pad while DK fools around with the beats. Feeling his phone vibrate he slips it out of his jean pocket and with a smile answers, "Yeah baby?"

I love knowing he'll always answer the phone with a term of endearment. "Are you busy?"

"Kind of. I'm at the studio," he goes back to finishing the chorus he's been struggling with.

"You're always at the studio," I groan patting the sweat off my arms.

"Yeah well, you're always at practice."

"I've got competition."

"And he needs to lay his tracks, so they can hear his CD," he sighs back.

"But when you're not there you're at work," I whine again. As the cool wind wraps around me I continue my complaint, "It's one or the other. You get so busy I feel like you don't even have time for me."

"Kie don't start," he grumbles tossing his pencil down. "You know you're hella busy too."

"Still make time to call you every second I get don't I?" I say back like he hasn't been trying. Well if he has I wouldn't know, because it sure doesn't feel that way.

"Look I'm not in the mood to argue with you," he rolls his eyes. "If that's the reason you called you're wastin' your time."

Now he's telling me what I'm wasting? What's his problem? Who hit his jackass switch? "Nice to know I'm wasting my time on my boyfriend now. You know what? I'm just gonna go."

"Fine," he rolls his eyes.

"Bye," I hang up on him and toss my phone aside not caring if it gets scratched up. Is it supposed to be this hard to have a decent conversation with the man who wants to marry me?

My phone begins to ring.

With a bitter expression I answer, "Angry girlfriend 911, how may I help you?"

"I'm sorry baby," Billy sighs pushing away his note pad. "I'm just a little frustrated right now. I didn't mean to snap at you."

Saying nothing back to him, I merely sigh and relax against the wall once more.

"What did you need to talk about honey? I know you're at rehearsals, and I know it has to be important by the way you made a big deal out of me bein' in the studio."

"First of all I haven't talked to you in a couple of days …" I start.

"You just talked to me last night."

"Yeah for like five minutes so that you could tell me you made it home from work and were off to the studio then to bed. I mean I haven't held a decent conversation with you in a good couple of weeks, and you know what else Billy, I really miss you. I've had some things on my mind that I really needed to talk to you about, but haven't been able to because it seems like suddenly your life doesn't have room for me."

"Hold up," Billy stops me heading out of the studio so that he can have some privacy. "My life always has room for you. You know that."

"Not lately. I mean lately it feels like its work and music. Forgive me if I sound selfish or like a brat, but Billy this is the time of all times I really need you."

Scratching the back of his neck he begins to realize just how messed up things have gotten. "I'm sorry baby. I guess I didn't realize you felt neglected and needed me so much. Tell me what's been on your mind."

"I really need you with me next week."

"In Florida?"

"Yes. I need you out there cheering for me, pulling for me, and being my support system out there for the one day you can be out there."

"In Florida?" His voice rises. "I mean you need me to go all the way to Florida?"

"Yes Billy you promised. You said you'd be anywhere for me, do anything, and I need this. I need you to come see me compete in Florida. Tell me you'll come."

"You really need me there huh?" He takes out his palm pilot to check out his schedule. "I ..." he sees that it's the only week he doesn't have anything to record. "I can be there."

"Can or will?" I quickly question as Mia pops her head out the door and holds up five fingers, indicating five minutes until they need me back in there.

"Will. I will be there baby any days that I can."

Pushing for more I say, "That's not really what I wanted to hear ..."

"Look I will be there Tuesday ok? I can't make it Monday, but I will make it Tuesday."

"Well since there are only two days you can see me, and we don't audition until then I guess that's fine."

"So we're good. You can make it without me 'til Tuesday?"

"Yeah," I smile slightly getting up. "I miss you though."

"Baby I miss you too," he grins slightly. "I love you."

"I love you too," I sigh. "I've got to get back to practice, so I'll call you later right?"

"Yeah," he nods smiling too. "Bye."

"Bye," I quickly hang up the phone as Mia stares at me with a scolding look. "I'm coming," I growl as she looks annoyed.

It's official. Billy says he's going to be there, and so he'll be there.

When Monday rolls around I'm impatiently waiting to leave our room to take a tour of the audition site. I can't believe I'm in Florida away from my parents getting ready to possibly change my life forever, career wise at least.

"Come on Kie," Mia whines at me. "They're waiting."

"Hold on one sec I have to check if he's still coming," I put my hand in her face.

"Oh no she didn't put her hand in my face," Mia cocks her hip and places her hand on it.

Finally hearing the ringing stop, "Hello?"

"Yeah," Billy answers stumbling around to find his wallet.

"Are you heading off to work?"

"Yeah baby, why what's up?"

"I'm just calling to tell you I made it here safely and to see if you're still coming tomorrow ..." I innocently twist my leg back and fourth.

"Of course. I promise baby. I'll be there ok?" he snatches his wallet off his dresser. "I've gotta get to work though. I love you."

"I love you," I say excitedly. "See you tomorrow."

"Bye," he hangs up and stuffs the phone in his pocket scurrying out the door by passing DK, who's casually strolling in with a girl on his arm.

After going out to eat, hitting a few places to shop, it's finally our turn to take a tour of exactly what's going to happen these next couple of days.

I don't know whether to be excited or nervous with our tour guide, but one thing is for sure is that this is a test. I mean I'm not stupid. I doubt she's really a tour guide. She's more than likely one of the judges and is out already making her marks.

We tour the vicinity and have her explain that the only day out of this intense competition that we are allowed to hear or see family or friends is Tuesday during the open performance. The rest of the time we are basically out of service. No cell phones. No phone calls. No friends. Just each other which is ok for us, but something tells me that's what's going to break a lot of groups.

Billy comes home much earlier than he expected. His boss let him off early knowing he had things to do before he left to see his girlfriend in the nation wide competition.

"You home early," DK remarks from the couch with a beer in his hand.

"I gotta pack. I've got some'n to do before I leave tomorrow," he sighs tossing his jacket on the table.

"Well I need you to do some'n wit' me tomorrow," he simply changes the channel.

"I can't DK. I've gotta fly to Florida to see Kie, you know that."

"You have to help me wit' some'n Billy. You my boy, you can't jus' cas' me to the side fo' some—

"Some what?" he sternly leans against the kitchen table. DK doesn't say anything. "Ya know I've had this planned since last week. I promised her I would go. I've bought my fuckin' plane ticket, so whatever it is DK, you've got to do handle it by yourself."

Billy heads to his bedroom with DK in pursuit behind him, "Hold the fuck up."

"What now?"

"You wanna know some'n Billy? I've let it slide that you've been all wrapped in this new found love affair you have fo' the girl you've claimed you're gonna spend the res' of yo' life wit', but enough is a fuckin' 'nough. How can you stand here and call us boys, yet I need you to have my back, and you're ditchin' me fo' her *again*? You swore you'd never let anything, especially not a female, come in between us, and here you are breakin' that promise lyin' to yo' self."

"You're the one lyin' to yourself. I'm so fucking sick of you DK. I've been here for your ass. I've bailed you out of jail, I've stood behind you when you did shit you knew was wrong, and I even watch you play Mia like she's some fuckin' sex toy because I'm yo' boy, because I'm down for you like that, because I've spent every day of my fuckin' life tryin' to pay you back for savin' my ass from endin' up like you. But guess what DK? The day has come where you've got to handle your own bullshit because I'm through."

He leans against Billy's door, "Oh you through havin' my back? You sayin' you don't wanna be boys no mo'?"

"No," Billy opens his drawer to begin packing. "DK you're my brother. You were raised with me, you've stuck with me, and you've been down with me since we were kids, but we ain't kids no more. We can't play these stupid bullshit games you continue to play! We can't piddle through life on fuckin' hopes and dreams! I'm makin' some'n of myself, and you're makin' me out to seem like I've left your ass behind. The truth of the matter is you wanna stay behind."

"What the hell are you talkin' 'bout?"

"You sit in my face and tell me I'm neglectin' you, leavin' you behind, when you're the one choosin' that path. DK I've tried to help you all I can. Job interviews, helpin' your music career, hell I even told you I'd help you get back in school if you wanted. I'm breakin' my neck to try to help you, but yo' ass chooses to not move on with your life. You wanna live this thug mentality because you're too much of a pussy to let it go and grow the fuck up," Billy stops pulling out boxers to look at him. "Now you tell me what the fuck I'm supposed to do. You taught me to take care of myself, put me ahead in the game, and here I am doin' just that while you sit back and fuckin' complain I ain't there for you. So be real with me DK tell me how I ain't been yo' boy."

DK is left almost speechless. Staring Billy coldly in the eyes he mutters the words, "You've changed."

"Yeah," he nods. "I have changed. Sure we've grown apart DK, but that's only because you won't change with me. You don't have to live this way. Hustlin' every day to make what you think is ends meet plus a little extra. Let this go man, and become some'n better. Whether or not you admit it, it's in you, and you want it just as bad as I did, but some'ns holdin' you back. Whatever it is, let it go," Billy begins to pull out wife beaters from another drawer. "It just ain't worth it."

He knows Billy is right and just can't admit it to him. He needs to change even more than Billy did. To think he's almost twenty years old and still acting like he did when he first got into high school. Life is moving on with or without him, and it's time to move on to something more, something better.

DK simply nods and leaves Billy's room without saying a word. Billy doesn't know if it's because he's so pissed off or because he's finally realized that he's right. Either way it doesn't make a difference, because Billy still has to pack for the couple of day's he's going to be in Florida.

For the next few hours Billy is slaving away cleaning and packing. Time continues to pass by without a word said between the two of them. It's like the life long friendship they spent so long and worked so hard to keep suddenly didn't exist anymore. It's like they're strangers who lived under the same roof.

"Billy," DK's groggy voice breaks the silence atmosphere in Billy's room. "You right. I guess I didn't realize it wasn't all on you fo' our friendship fallin' apart. I know I've gotta change, and I will."

"Good. Ya know that I always knew you would come—

"Jus' one last favor fo' me man. I really need it."

Sighing, he stops stuffing his clothes in his bag. He doesn't even know why he tried to fool himself into believing DK would give up that easy, "What is it?"

"You know that nigga Dunk," he gets a sour grin across his face.

Billy knows who Dunk is. Dunk is the guy that got DK thrown in jail instead of Billy. He had got into a club fight with them, setting them up of course. He knew that they'd fight, and he wouldn't get in a lick of trouble because his cousin owned the place and wouldn't press charges. That night Dunk and his boys were going after Billy because he slept with Dunk's sister. DK bounced in right before the cops got there giving Billy just enough time to escape. There's always been a big beef, room of tension, boys against boys. It's always been an ongoing thing that seems like it'll never end.

"Yeah," he slowly answers knowing DK's got his attention now.

"A couple of days ago not only did he hit up my clients, he stole some money from a girl I had holdin' it fo' me," his fists clench up.

"How much?" Billy sits down on his bed.

"700 dollars."

"Damn. You let a female hold 700 bucks?" Billy questions in the utmost disbelief. "Why?"

"She's like my sis. I trust her."

"Charlotte?"

"Yeah. Anyway she was in the mall because she had to stop and pick up her younger sis when Dunk pulls a snatch and grab, takes my money, and tosses the shit aside laughing hysterically."

"You would think he'd let it go already."

"Maybe he would've if you wouldn't have slept wit' his sister twice," DK pins the blame on him.

"Maybe if you hadn't slept with her too."

"Look, I know that I have to end all this 'childish behavior', but this is important to me. It's *money*. I could understand if you turned me down fo' some'n less meaningful, but this is hard earned cash I could put to use fo' the new life style I've got to move on to. Come on Billy you can turn me down if you want, but you know how important this is to me ..."

Billy scratches the back of his neck and looks at the ground.

"Hey you don't have to decide righ' now, but at least think it over," DK nods starting out the room.

He simply gets up and closes the door to have some time to himself to actually think about the situation.

When we return from our tour, we divide into our separate rooms that connect by a bathroom. After we change we decide that some down time is a good idea.

I'm sitting on my bed reading a magazine about the latest in fashion, thinking of some possible costume ideas when Andrea and Natalie come strolling in wearing their pajamas.

"I think we should have a talk," Natalie flops down on my bed next to me invading my personal space in my personal time. This better be important.

"'Bout?" Mia stops brushing her hair long enough to switch sides.

"Our group," Andrea answers taking her place on the floor. Why couldn't Natalie have sat down there too?

Continuing her grooming Mia asks, "What about us?"

"I'm having some major doubts about tomorrow," Andrea admits. "And so is Natalie. I mean what if we don't make it? What if we're in over our heads?"

"Yeah what if the judges hate us, and we get nowhere?" Natalie chimes in.

"Think about it you guys, it's totally possible. We could mess up anywhere. One little thing and we could be out. That's all it takes. I don't know if I can do this," Andrea leans against the edge of Mia's bed. "It's a lot of pressure."

"I know how you girls feel. While we were taking that tour all I could think about was how bad we could get beat here, and how all of our hard work could've just been for nothing," Mia stops brushing.

I'm so sick of their talk. Sometimes I feel like I'm the only sane one. I just can't take it anymore. I mean I have my doubts, I have my fears, but they are taking it to the extreme. We haven't even started to compete yet and here they already doubt us.

Rubbing my head in frustration I quickly call, "Ok time out." All of their eyes focus on me. "You're all entitled to have your worries, but you do realize if you go to competition that way tomorrow we're going to loose," I look around the room. "We will loose without question if you walk in there thinking you're anything less than the best. We are a group and are only as strong as our weakest link." Yeah I know it's cliché, but there's a lot of truth behind it.

"Kie, I hear what you're saying, but I don't know if we have enough talent to make it," Natalie leans against me. "Those girls I've seen that are competing tomorrow are packed with a lot of power."

"First of all," I look at her. "Don't worry about them. Don't even think about them. They should be the furthest thing from your mind. You want to talk about talent? Do you girls really wanna talk about talent?"

"Yeah," Andrea nods. "Let's talk about it."

"Alright," I stand up. Around the room I go making sure everyone of them knows exactly what makes them winners, what makes them different, and what's so valuable about them that we're going to win. "We're different and that's exactly what they're looking for. They can make carbon copies, those are so easy to do, but to find a group with essence that's unique and has style that has never been discovered is something that they would take pride in. We are what they will love and take pride in. Us," I look around at them. "Us as group is exactly what will win us this competition."

The classic pep talk causes a soothing silence in the room. The encouraging words I've said are sinking into their brains like the Titanic, slowly, but surely. After waiting a few moments it's hit them just how I'm right about everything I've said so far.

"You're right Kie," Natalie leans her head on my shoulder. "We can do this."

"We can win this," Andrea backs her. "Those girls ain't got nothin' on us."

"Yeah," Mia nods. "The innocent, the classic, the rebel, and the leader," she licks her lips. "You're the leader. The only thing keeping us together Kie. Don't let that strength go, for the sake of us."

I nod knowing I've got my own insecurities to face, but I will lock them in a small tight box inside of me so that this group can flourish, so that nothing's holding me back, and so that everything will be ok.

"I feel better," Andrea grins.

"Me too," Natalie agrees.

"Good. Now off to bed," I nudge her off of me. Turning on my motherly voice I snap, "We've got to be up bright and early tomorrow, and I don't want to hear one single complaint from anyone."

"Yes mother," Andrea groans getting up off the ground.

"Night you two," Mia waves to them.

"Night," they say back in unison closing the bathroom door behind them.

"We should probably head off too," I look over at her as she begins to braid her hair into her nighttime braid.

"Yeah," Mia yawns watching me put my magazine away.

I hop up and head off towards our balcony, "I've gotta make a call first though."

"Hurry," she whines continuing to do her hair.

I hit his speed dial number expecting his voicemail. He should still be at work or on his way home, so I'll probably get his voicemail, which will just have to do until he gets here tomorrow.

Billy looks over at his phone that's lighting up on his nightstand. He knows it's me, but with so much on his mind he doesn't know if he can talk to me yet.

Licking his lips he makes a grab for it and quickly answers it, "Hello."

"Babe?" I question in disbelief.

"Yeah," he answers in a sigh.

"You're off of work early?"

Frustrated with everything he deeply sighs, "Yeah. My boss gave me off, so I could do some packing, take care of some things."

"Well that was nice of him. I was calling to get a good night, some words of encouragement, and to see when will your flight be in," I say pretending to be timid.

Billy slightly chuckles and strokes his jaw, "My flight will be in tomorrow evening, probably a little late."

"That blows," I pout. "Our performance is at nine or ten, maybe even eleven. Will you be here before then?"

"Yeah and if that's not good enough know I'm there in spirit with you every step of the way."

"Mm," I grumble leaning against the balcony.

"You're gonna do great. I've heard you sing and seen you dance. You'll bring the heat baby; just don't give up on yourself. Don't be worried about anything and know that you can do it. You'll be great some day whether it's through this competition or not, you will. I'd gamble my life on you achievin' greatness," he smiles closing his eyes. "Any day."

Flight time. Check. Words of encouragement. Check. "You always know just the right things to say."

"Yeah I remember when I used to talk to you, and everything I said got my foot in my mouth."

"You still do that," we laugh a bit together.

"Well you should get to bed, and get some sleep love," he says scratching his chest. "Good night, I hope you have a nice night, and I wish you the best of luck in the morning during rehearsals. I'll see you tomorrow night during the show. I love you so much. Never forget that," he says in a serious tone that I haven't heard him say in the longest time.

Perfect good night. Check. "I love you. Get a good night sleep too," I say back feeling the wind briskly lift up my hair. "Bye."

"Bye," his voice is gone that quickly.

Billy twiddles his phone around in his fingers knowing he has to make a choice. It's either go against everything he was working so hard for and help his best friend that helped him out of so much trouble, or loose a bond with his best friend just to keep true to himself. Couldn't he do both? Couldn't he still be true to himself even if he helped out his brother? DK had done everything he could to help him. He couldn't just abandon him like that. It was his responsibility to be true to his friend, besides it wasn't like he was changing his life again. It would be a one time thing. The last time. Billy nods as he closes his eyes knowing this will be the last time for helping DK out.

I look out at the city lights. I can't believe I'm here and that life is going like it is. A year ago I couldn't have pictured myself living in such a marvelous bliss, but now that I'm here I couldn't imagine trading in it for anything else. I thank god every day for every blessing he's put into my life. I mean look at it. I've got it all going for me and to be stupid and abuse it would be something I'd never be able to live with.

Ya know I just hope Billy's right. I just hope that what he said is true. I don't wanna fail tomorrow. The last thing I want and need is to have my dreams come crashing down even if he is there to catch me.

Laughing a little inside I sigh. I can't even imagine what it would be like if he wasn't there to catch me if anything ever happened to me. I'm glad I'll always have Billy, when I really don't know where I would be without him.

CHAPTER 16

Which Door?

It's a shame when you just can't have as much faith in yourself as you wish. I've never wanted anything so bad in my life other than to make it this far in my singing career, yet I am just not emotionally prepared as I would've hoped. It's almost like I spent my entire life preparing for this single moment, but once it's here, I don't know how to handle it. Why on earth is life so damn difficult when it comes to something you want so badly?

We go from dawn until dusk. Every aspect of the audition is worse than the next. I never realized just how intense and how harsh the judges were going to be on us, particularly me. Here I am supposed to be the rock of the group, and I'm the one they're beating on the most. Every ten minutes I feel like I'm ready to cry.

I just can't wait until Billy arrives. He's supposed to be here already yet he's been nowhere in sight. I wonder where he is. Too bad that's all I can do is wonder. I don't have my cell phone, which is the biggest bummer. What happens if Billy needs me or if I need another word of counseling?

Around five or so Billy is in the car beside DK debating whether or not he's in the right place doing the right thing.

"You ready?" DK pops his knuckles.

"This ain't righ' DK," he clenches his fist. "This don't feel righ.'"

"Look," he turns to him. "Everything's gonna be alrigh,'" he clears his throat. "It's a quick job. In, out, up, bounce."

"Some'ns not righ' here," he states again.

"Leave it 'lone," DK shakes his head. Getting out of the car he calls Billy with him, "Come on."

Billy hesitates for a moment. He always told himself that any time something didn't feel right you shouldn't do it. That night at the club it didn't feel right and look what happened. He shouldn't do this. He couldn't do this. He gets out and leans over the top of the car to protest once more.

"I can't do this DK."

"Yes you can," he says in a threatening tone. "Look, we'll go in there, get the money, come out, and I'll take you to the airport, so you can be on yo' flight to go see Kie."

Billy slams the door and takes his place next to DK. They stand together looking at the vacant house. It's got a fresh white coat of paint as well as new gutters.

"New house?" Billy questions while scoping it out.

He takes out a cigarette before he answers, "Brand new."

Pulling up his jeans he asks another question, "You sure it's empty?"

"Yup," DK responds. "Not home from work yet. Just gotta be quick. It'll be a piece of cake."

I turn and look at Mia who's sprawled on the couch in the waiting room. She looks like she's about to bite the dust she's so tired. I can see the drool begin to escape out of her mouth as she dreams about sugarplums and juicy hamburgers.

My attention turns to Andrea who's all curled up in a ball near Mia's feet as if afraid to be kicked. She's snoring away just like Mia. We've been up since four and working since five, so I don't really blame them for any tiredness they're experiencing.

As I smile to myself I wonder where Natalie is until I see her coiled underneath the coffee table by the girls.

Giggling, I shake my head yawning to try to keep my eyes open. It's hard to keep my eyes open. I can't survive like this. No phone, no sleep, no decent food. It's like I'm being punished before rewarded. Yawning once again I rest my head up against the arm of the couch. Oh, just a little shuteye won't kill me while I wait for the judges. Just a little shuteye and everything will be ok.

A couple of hours later we're awaken by one of the judge representatives.

"Excuse me," she tugs on my sleeve. Politely she clears her throat, "You're up."

"Like our group?" I question in a yawn.

"No. You. It's the individual round first," she says with her clipboard lingering between her hand and her hip.

"Wow," I rub the sleep out of my eyes. "Already?"

"Yes," she says in a rushed tone. "You have five minutes to prepare before you're expected on your mark."

I nod in understanding indicating that she can leave. Trying to breathe, I attempt to wake up the girls. How come I have to go first? Why is it that I randomly got selected to be first?

I haven't even talked to Billy yet. Where is he? The one time I absolutely need him the most, and he wants to do his disappearing act. He said he'd be here this evening, what time is it?

"Look I'm up first," I start downing water so I can begin vocal warm ups.

Mia looks in shock, but slightly happy even though she doesn't want to be. "Do you know which one of us is next?"

"Nope," I begin little vocal warm ups. "But I do know that you all need to wake up and start warming up. Can you do me a favor though?"

She yawns once again boxing the sandman, "What?"

In a concerned voice I say, "Find a phone and try to track down Billy." I don't remember what time his flight was going to get in, but it's getting dark. He really should have taken an earlier flight. Why is it guys can't do the logical thing when they should? I mean when it really matters.

I hurry down the hallway continuing to warm up my voice every inch of the way. Where could Billy be? I wish I could get him off my mind, but everyone knows I don't do well worrying about something, particularly him.

Approaching the wooden, windowless door to my fate, I take one more deep breath hoping to prepare myself.

I enter and see three judges sitting behind a long wooden table, paperwork ready, with pens of criticism in their hands. Great, just three people to determine my future in the music business. Three? Why is it just three measly people to always decide someone's fate? Ever notice that? It has to be the saddest way to be judged.

"Kie?" The male judge in the middle questions me in a solid frozen tone. Wow, I wonder would it kill him to have a bit more emotion in his voice.

My eyes meet the ice caveman. Wow, just when you think you couldn't get any colder than Simon here stands living proof otherwise.

"Yes," I manage to chisel my way through the ice.

"Are you prepared?" He asks folding his arms slowly bringing his pen to his clipboard. What's with all these damn people and clipboards?

"Yes," I respond once more not breaking eye contact. It's a sign of uncertainty in you. I may be very doubtful in myself, but the key is to never let it show.

"Music?"

"Yes."

"Any questions?"

"Yes," I sigh thankful that I get to finally ask him what I've been dying to know. "Am I allowed to move during my performance?"

"Yes," he answers. "But as a fair warning to you, I recommend you don't over do it ..."

"Thank you," I smile and nod politely.

Keep your manners, stay in line, and never forget that attitude needs to be shown through performance, not through speech to judges. I slowly stroll over the piano player double-checking to see that he has the right music.

The two female judges are too quiet for their own good. Who knows if that's a good thing or not? I guess I'm taking a blind leap of faith. The exact same way I took a leap of faith with Billy, but look what happened there. Everything turned out all right after all, so I guess I just have to trust my gut feeling once more.

"Whenever you're ready," the curly haired brunette chooses to be the brave solider out of the females to speak up.

I nod and look at the piano player. Watching intently as his fingers take their places on the keys, I take my last deep breath before the notes start.

Quickly I decide to put the piano player on pause for a second to grasp the hold of a grand idea. They think I'm going to move and be over dramatic like I belong on Broadway or something. I'll fix them all right. I won't move at all. I reach for the barstool with a giant smile. I'm gonna pull a good ol' fashion bar singing. Everyone knows what it's like when you watch those girls that sit in that one single spot and pour their soul out, making the audiences just swoon. Sure I haven't had much practice, but I know that I can totally pull that off. I mean all I need to do is play off my crowd, or better yet just pick one focal point.

Plopping the stool down right in front of the piano player I try to find my inner pinnacle of my poignant emotions. After a moment I close my eyes as I begin to remember the horrible things I've been through with Billy. I cue the piano player to start again while I recall the times Billy has let me down, hurt my feelings, or done something completely unacceptable.

Billy follows DK through the window into the pitch-black house. They entered through the very back bedroom assuming no one was home, because the back entry is the most unable spot to be seen.

DK leans over to whisper to him, "You start in here. I'm gonna try the next couple of rooms."

He nods and scans around the room at the multiple places to look in. Even though it's dark they know how to maneuver their way around. They've been getting into this sort of trouble since they were adolescents, so it's not like they don't know what their doing.

As DK disappears Billy tries to stay calm, reminding himself how many times they've done this and not got caught, reminding himself this is the last trouble he has to get mixed up with for DK, and that in just a few hours he will be in Florida far away from any sort of problems.

My eyes meet with the piano player's who remind me of Billy's in a way. Can you imagine how much easier this song would be if he was sitting right there instead? I suddenly focus my energy on picturing Billy next to him. Accidentally taking it one step further I see Billy sitting there, his hands on the keys, listening to me begin the song with my "Mms" and "Yeahs."

DK starts tossing papers around pissed that he can't find exactly where his money was put. He knows it there. It has to be there because this is house he saw it brought to. This is the exact spot he tracked them down to and won't leave until he gets his cash back in his hands.

"Every girl dreams of her prince," I let a small smile creep across my face as I watch the image of Billy I have created smile back while his fingers slide up and down the keys. "The man who came straight from her dreams. Who gives her everything, so she feels like she's supreme. Finally, she's a queen," I say proudly, sitting up a little and smiling wildly. I glance over at the female judges hoping to touch them. "He's done things she's never seen," come to think about it, Billy has done some amazing things that I didn't know were possible. Remember my birthday? Looking into the eyes of the farthest female judge I try to reach her first. "Life is now so serene …"

Billy quietly opens a few file drawers completely clueless where to look. He starts thinking about if he or DK had that money where would he hide the money if it was in this room. Shaking his head he wonders if DK will ever get it that there's more to life than money, a lot more.

"I'm that girl who's got that man," I point to my chest pleading at the same female judge. It's strange singing without a microphone. I'm not sure if I'm capturing all the right notes. That's probably the reason why they make us do this without a microphone so that we can't help ourselves, so that we have to reveal our flaws, and I guess so that they see how we handle ourselves bare. "I'm that girl whose livin' that plan, they say my life's just began, but there's some'n they don't understan'," I watch as I touch the judge I've been trying to. Her weight shifts as I reach something I didn't expect to. Maybe I'm doing better than I thought if she can connect with my song. Yay, I'm a third away from scoring one for the team. "I thought you gave me all the love I needed, but you haven't quite succeeded. You've still got a ways to go." Frustrated I point at him, "My prince isn't everything he seemed. Some how I feel as if I got schemed." You ever realize how love is sometimes like a shady deal? It feels like its bootleg of something better ya know? "This isn't my fairy tale love ..."

DK slams a drawer pissed at the fact that he can't find what he wants in the room. Aggravated, he strolls into another room convinced the money is still in the house. While DK is fiddling around in his second room, Billy is still in his first. He too decides to give up and heads to another room further down the hallway.

Reaching there, he ignores the fact there's bed in the room. He darts straight for the drawer thinking he might have struck gold but quickly starts to try to open the locked space. After fooling around with it long enough, he whips out his pocket knife to pick the lock when he hears a movement of some sort from behind him. Figuring it's probably just DK he continues to pick at it determined to get it open.

"Don't move," he hears a deep voice that is unfamiliar to him.

Telling himself it's just DK trying to mess with him he shrugs him off. He gives it another tug and grumbles, "Look nigga I've almost got this damn thing open."

The voice says in a bit of a tremble, "I'm warning you again. Don't move."

With a roll of his eyes, not in any mood for DK's games, he takes one last tug at the drawer before feeling a sharp burning pain in his arm.

"They say," I look up in a pain of misery glazed on my eyes. My attention focuses on the other female judge. She looks harder to reach than the other one. I notice the wedding ring on her finger. "I've got a good man to keep; his love for me runs deep." Any woman who's happily married feels that way, especially if all her single friends long for what she has.

Billy turns around gripping his right arm over the blood wound of where the bullet hit him. Seeing a tall Caucasian middle aged man holding a shaking gun, he drops the knife onto the carpet between his two feet. Their eyes meet and a fear suddenly takes over his body like he's never experienced before.

"Barbra," the man says trying his best to keep the gun steady. "Call the police and tell them to come right away with the paramedics," he does his best not to panic as well. Billy looks both ways wondering where DK is when he needs him.

DK hears the voices, pops open the window in the room he's in, and jumps out. Getting ready to run to save his life, it hits him that his best friend is trapped inside probably looking for his help. Torn, he takes deep breaths right outside the window determining the best thing for him to do.

"He's also hurt me bad," my eyes glance at 'Billy' playing the piano and then at the female judge I've been working on. She looks down at her ring and thinks about something for a second. Yeah that's right lady, even the good ones do bad things. "Made me more than burning mad, that's not how the story is supposed to go … Sometimes his words hurt; I've even had to watch him flirt …" I look back scornfully at the image in front of me who looks disappointed in himself. I picture the look that I saw in his eyes on Valentine's Day, "with other girls … I'm that girl who's got that man," I enforce and reach out towards her pleading like I would to a judge. "I'm that girl whose livin' that plan. They say my life's just began, but there's some'n they don't understan'."

"Move over this way," the man motions with his gun at Billy as his wife talks in terror to 911 on the phone.

Billy inches his way over still grabbing hold of his arm traumatized by the blazing feeling taking over his body. Should he run? Would it be smarter to run and try to get away from the cops and this man or be taken straight to jail and prosecuted for the crime? If he got away he could move, not be found, forgotten about even, but if they take him to jail it's over for him. As he moves closer to the doorframe he starts calculating his chances. Some friend DK is. He's not even here to have his back like he swore he always would.

DK shakes his head and starts off hearing sirens. There was no use in getting both of them nailed. If Billy was to go to jail he'd bail him out the second he got there, but he had heard gunshots and is unsure if they hit Billy or not. Each time his foot hit the ground he knew he was punking out worse than his best friend ever had. You know that sometimes it's more important to watch out for yourself than others, or at least to him it is.

The second Billy reached the doorframe and had convinced the man he wasn't going to run or do any harm; he attempted to take off the way he broke in. His freedom is just a dash away. The window, after all, is just at the end of the hall. He swore with everything in him he could reach it if he's given the chance.

Billy runs for his life towards that window, the same window that he knew he should've never came in, the same window, he some how knew he probably wouldn't ever make it back through.

The gun shot off once more, this time pegging him in the back of his calf slowing him down impeccably. He stretches his legs to keep moving through the unbearable pain ignoring the requests and then the commands of the middle aged gentleman. With his arm extended towards the window, he takes the last bullet in the back knowing the old saying of three strikes your out was finally becoming true for him.

"Whoa …" I begin with the chorus looking shamelessly at the creation in front of me. "I thought you gave me all the love I needed, but you haven't quite succeeded. So, so far to go. My prince isn't everything he seemed," closing my eyes I run my fingers through my hair. Glancing over at the judge I've been working on I belch out, "Some how I feel as if I got schemed." Lowering my head a little, I look at her out of the corner of my eye as I song whisper the next line, "Not real fairy tale love …"

DK watches as the police and the ambulance pull up with their sirens blaring loudly. Being hidden best as possible, he waits to see if Billy is being taken to jail or the hospital.

They rush into the house around the man and his scared shrieking wife straight to Billy, who's having trouble breathing as he's sprawled out on the back bedroom floor.

Trying to stay conscious, he decides the best way to go about that is to think about thoughts that have to do with me. Anything revolving around me pushes him to stay awake and away from that bright light that seems to be calling to him.

The paramedics rush him to the ambulance where they quickly begin off down the road with DK still watching, waiting for a clear coast so he can follow after Billy.

It's time I work on the iceman over there. He looks like he feels a bit out of place, almost denied the same amount of attention as the other two. The truth is that the next part I have is just for him. I want him to realize in the back of his mind that the stories he tells his children, or his nieces and nephews isn't reality. It's like he's lying to them, and I'm dying to have that guilt eat away at him.

"Cinderella had her perfect dance, the mermaid got her chance, snow white had her romance, and even sleeping beauty lived out her trance," I plead looking at 'Billy', but out of the corner of my eye seeing the judge who seems a bit questionable about something.

The EMS starts hooking Billy up to all sorts of things he couldn't recognize even if he knew what the hell was happening to him. There are three people hovering over him saying words he can't quite make out, but figure they must be important at how fast their lips appear to be moving.

"We're loosing him," one says to another.

"He's loosing lots of blood," another speaks up moving around some things.

"He's going into shock!" one screams while Billy just floats in and out of reality.

His eyes start to close picturing my face swimming around in his mind. Thoughts begin about the two of us, in our later years, married …

❧   ❧   ❧

"Do you take this woman to be your lawful wedded wife, to have and to hold, in sickness and in health?" The minister asks him as he beams into my beautiful eyes.

"I do," he smiles brightly touching the side of my face.

"Through the power invested in me and the state of Texas, I now pronounce you man and wife. You may kiss the bride," he gives us the green flag.

Billy plants his lips lightly on top of mine embracing me tightly with his arms cradling my lower back as our family and friends cheer loudly in excitement.

❦   ❦   ❦

Suddenly his thoughts drift from marriage to life with kids, in a house, happy.

❦   ❦   ❦

"Daddy!" our little girl screams at the top of her lungs. "I can't find my box of crayons!"

Billy casually strolls in with a box and her favorite coloring book, "Here you go sweetie."

"Thank you," she runs at him, her big brown curls bouncing up and down.

"You're welcome," he says with a giant smile as he sits down on the edge of her bed.

"I colored you and mommy a picture," she giggles as she picks it up off the floor by her Barbies. "Will you put it on the fridge?"

"Of course," he says taking it from her. Billy stares at the picture long and hard for a moment. It's a mom, dad, and a little girl all playing at the park.

"Can we do that tonight daddy?" She dumps the box on the floor.

"As soon as mommy gets home," he smiles, continuing to stare at the pictures.

Squealing she begins coloring rapidly, "Yay!"

❦   ❦   ❦

The hope of living out those dreams he had forgotten about since his childhood seem to be fading. As the faint burning in his chest becomes less apparent to him he notices that breathing isn't much of anything anymore. It's almost like he doesn't need to any more, his mind can live without it.

"He needs air!" one screams loudly panicking, not expecting Billy's body to respond the way it is.

"He's not gonna make it," one says in a soft bitter tone knowing nothings worse than watching someone die in front of them.

"So when does this princess get her true love?" my notes take control of their ears as I look down at the manufactured mind version of Billy, "Where's my love sent from above? When do I get everything I've dream of? I'm still waiting for my happily ever after …" I hear the music come to the few closing notes. They instruct that you can do the chorus only twice, two or three versus, but the last one leads to a closing of some sort.

Billy notices the warm feeling that's been making his chest ache is slowly vanishing much like the other places he was hit. His eyes fall for the last time as he begins to wish he would have been in Florida to cheer me on. As Billy lays there, his mind falling from actuality, he wonders was his friendship with DK really worth the bullets that he could no longer feel? Was cheating himself out of so much in life really worth a friend who wasn't even there to protect him when he needed him? The very last thoughts to cross his mind have nothing to do with DK, but with me. Would I ever forgive him for the disappointment he's created, did he love me enough while he could, but most importantly, would I still love him even once he was gone? Slipping away into peacefulness where no pain would ever be felt again he let out a whisper. In his mind quite strident, were four words he swore he hadn't said loud enough, strong enough, soon enough, and just plain enough. I love you Kie.

I take one deep breath to bring myself back to reality looking at a very surprised piano player and three very pleased judges. Wow, I didn't realize they were capable of smiles.

"Kie," the first judge I sang towards starts. "Was that an originally written, performed, and produced song?"

"Yes," I nod standing tall with my arms behind my back.

"It was beautiful," she compliments me. "Done very well."

"Thank you," I try not to smile too big.

"It was performed excellently. Predominantly females come in with a big over dramatic, over done performances that people, we more than anyone else, get tired of seeing. Seeing you take the strong, solid, grounded approach was more than invigorating," the other female judge pays me a compliment.

"Yes," the male nods slowly. Great, let me brace myself for the solid snowball comments that are going to just destroy my slightly damaged ego. "The connection you made was powerful. The only words or advice I made note of was that …" he glances down to recall like he forgot. That fool knows damn well he didn't forget, especially not that fast. "You can afford to stretch your voice and your notes. Your voice is capable of more than you're letting it experience, so I recommend that when you continue your singing career you push it."

That's it? That's all he has to say? Oh my gosh! Oh my gosh! That's amazing! Out of all the things he could say that's it. I sigh relieved.

"Thank you," he dismisses me.

"Thank you," I say back and head out towards the room.

I never thought anything in my life would be so stressful and grilling on my emotions. When I imagined being judged by my peers as the worse thing I could go through, I never once thought about how it would feel to be criticized by three single judges who literally get paid to tell people they suck. It's very rewarding in my own head that no bad comments left their mouth.

I try not to laugh, feeling a bit more secure about myself. I know that I'm not out of the hot water or in cradle of success yet, but I know that this was the make it or break it day. Today determined how far I, as an individual as well as my group, would go in this competition.

It's funny how only a few people or events can determine your fate. You always choose every action with thought and caution, because it could always be critical or in some cases lethal. Everything has its repercussions, and what I did today will have its sooner or later. My choices of today will eventually have some sort of effect, so I guess you could just say that today was judgment day.

PART V

ENDINGS

CHAPTER 17

Pain and then there's Fame

It's been four and a half days of intense training. I've never worked so hard a day in my life. All those weeks and hours of rehearsing, dieting, and preparing did not come in handy as I thought they would. I thought we were doing good, I thought we were somewhere close to what was in store here, I thought we had a chance of surviving at that state of mind, but boy I had a rude awaking.

These last few days have been absolute hell. My throat hurts, my eyelids are so heavy I feel like the sandman is ready to pay me to go bed, and worst of all I haven't had human contact besides these contest people for over ninety-six hours. Do you have any idea what it's like to drain yourself to the point where you begin to question is everything you're doing really worth it?

I'm happy it's finally Saturday. The winners are announced and everyone can finally go home. Home where three things are waiting for me, finals, my family, and Billy, who if he's lucky will still have a girlfriend.

"If our final groups will take the stage," the male judge from my room announces. Wow he looks like he's had less sleep than us. How hard is it really to weed out the bad from the good? I can tell you it's much harder trying to be the rose in the bunch than it is to try to be the picker.

Our group takes the stage on the far right. We huddle together, our bodies leaning on each other knowing we don't care anymore how we stand, because the votes are in. I look at Natalie who's lying on me, and Mia who I'm lying on. I've already decided in my head that it doesn't matter if we win or loose because these are my girls through thick and thin, no judgment can ever change that.

"This has been a very intense competition," the iceman begins. "It's been stiff, long, painful on your voices as well as your body, which is only a peek into what is in store for one of you. You all share the same dream, the same goal, the same focal point, so even if you loose this competition you will still have a good picture in mind of what the music industry brings to you," he clears his throat from behind the table.

My eyes fight my eyelids as my ears struggle to grasp his words. Tick tock buddy.

"You all came here thinking you were a group, believing you were a group, telling yourself you were going to be the group to win, which is very admirable, and helped you get as far as you four have."

Yes that's right. It's just a measly four of us, go figure our group is the biggest.

"Throughout all the dancing, music, interviews, observations, there was just one single moment that defined the winner of the competition. We knew at that point who the winner was and unfortunately for you guys it was Thursday. We as judges felt compelled to still provide each of the groups with all the preparations to make it out there. Now I know you're all wondering what exactly separated you," his eyes fall on individual faces, one of them being mine.

"We asked each leader from each group the same single question," the unmarried female judge starts. "The other questions frankly weren't important. There was only one we needed an answer for us to pick who we believed would do best in this industry."

"When the four of you each came to see us we told you that you had the best voices out of your group. We explained how we thought you were so incredible you didn't even need a group. We would still give them a deal, but you would become a solo performer leaving them to be a group alone. In the process of telling you this we analyzed facial expressions, body language, even tone of voice in your response when we asked you would you be willing to leave them and sign a solo contract," the iceman finishes up his explanation. "I'd like you four to please step forward."

"Only one of you said no," the married judge says disappointed. "Only one. Can you believe how sad and shocked we were to hear that? We picked the four best groups to only come and find out that only one of you is an actual group. A group is a team. Teams don't leave their mates behind to fend for themselves when something better suits them as an individual. Teams stick by each other through thick and thin. So to the three of you who so anxiously left your team behind, you might want to look into that and determine whether or not a group is where you belong," she leans back disgusted.

I try not to let excitement go to my head. I said I wouldn't leave my girls behind. I swore we would do this together, we would be together, succeed together, because that's what we are, homegurls for life. I denied every offer they threw at me which has to mean we won. Oh my gosh … we won. Wait. Stay calm Kie.

"We are overly content with the most sincere heart to announce the winners of this competition," the unmarried speaks again. "Kie … you and your group have won."

Now you would think instantly they would start screaming and yelling acting like a bunch of hormonal teenagers who just saw a teen idol, but they aren't. They haven't moved. Their frozen faces only reveal ultimate shock. I really wanted us to win, but I had so many doubts buried inside me we would loose, worse than theirs. Now look at us. They look anxious at the judges waiting for the green light to celebrate the way they would like.

"It's ok girls you can scream," the iceman states.

I rush over and start screaming at the top of my lungs with them. We're jumping up and down. Someone probably thinks there's an earthquake from all the screaming and shaking. I can't believe we won! I mean … wow, what do you say when your dreams finally come true?!

"The four of you have won yourself a recording contract, a year of intense training, as well as the guarantee you will be given the opportunity to tour for a touring season. You will be announced within the next couple of weeks as the winners. Congratulations," he smiles more so at me.

Back off iceman I have a boyfriend, well as far as he knows. Is it forgivable to stand your girlfriend up like he did? I'm sure after long enough time has passed and enough apologies have been made, and karma has taken effect all will be well with us.

"We'd like to thank all you for the time and effort you spent working and preparing for us. It was enjoyable to hear you sing," the married judge smiles and nods. "You can go back to your rooms and prepare to leave."

"Thank you," our group screams as the others sneer in spitefulness. Hey they can keep them dirty looks to themselves because it's not my fault that their leaders left them high and dry.

When we arrive in our hotel room we immediately begin to pack. Our flight leaves at six, and we have to be at the airport in a couple of hours. You would not believe how much we have to store away. All of our clothes are tossed around along with so much other stuff.

You know I haven't talked to my family or my boyfriend in four days? Four *long* days might I add. Throwing clothes around disregarding the simple fact I'm supposed to be packing I look for my cell phone.

"Have you seen it?" I scream at Mia who is calmly packing her stuff away.

"No," she shakes her head.

"Have you seen yours?" I ask throwing a pillow across the room.

"Mine's dead," she shrugs. "No battery."

God I pray mines not dead. The last thing I need right now is a dead phone. I'm already an exhausted and frustrated girl; the last thing I need to be is an exhausted frustrated girl with a DEAD phone.

I dig between the headboard and mattress to come to find it. Yes! Score! My prized electronic miracle to help me out in my times of need has finally been found! I scream with joy while Mia shakes her head at me. Quickly I try to turn on my phone and nothing happens. Not a single thing. I try it again thinking just maybe I accidentally hit the wrong button, but I didn't. Nothing happens again.

"Oh my gosh," I fall backwards on my bed. "My phone is dead!"

"Calm down Kie," Mia stuffs her clothes into one of her bags.

"Calm down? Calm down? I haven't talked to my family in four days, haven't heard from my boyfriend who was supposed to show up," I screech and stomp my feet on the floor. "I swear if Billy isn't hurt or something dyer didn't happen to him, I'll kill him for not being here to support me when he said he would."

"He could've tried to call, but someone's phone is dead," Mia mumbles heading to the bathroom I assume to steal soap or something else from the hotel like she's so accustomed to doing.

Honestly I'm too tired to even care about arguing with her. It doesn't matter. I could care less about anything I can't control right now. I mean all I can do now is pack like the other girls and prepare for a long flight back to Texas, which I will sleep on from the time we board until the time I arrive.

After boarding the airplane and taking our seats, I find myself closed off from the others. I'm so tired I don't want to think about anything. It takes effort to make conversation with them and frankly I've spent the last week doing that intensely, so a few moments to me are great. We're drained, a bit too thrilled for words, yet miserable in another sense.

You're probably thinking what the hell do you have to be miserable about after getting the chance to fulfill your dreams? You'd be surprised. I mean we miss our families. Sure we realize what our future has in store for us requires just that, but at least then we've secured our emotions, and come up with ways to keep in touch. This came as a total shock. We knew it was a chance, but none of us ever expected that we'd make it to that point. On top of family we're missing normal things that we took for granted like eating ice cream straight out the gallon container. Might as well say bye-bye to those days because they are no more. Poor Mia will have to find a new way to survive without food as her main energy source.

I look at her on my right to see her drooling away already. I swear the girl is like a leaky faucet. Now that I think about it, I've never seen any other human being leak out so much liquid from their mouth. Smirking, I look at the other two girls in front of me who are passed out as well. Well I guess I know where I'm headed. Looking out the window at the clouds I slowly drift off.

Some time during the flight the others girls wake up and leave me knocked out. They know better than to wake me up, especially with me being upset about Billy who, let me just add, has to be the most inconsiderate idiot to walk this earth. I just know he didn't leave me a voicemail or anything. Ya know I would walk through hell and fire to see him perform, to see his big break, and if for some reason I couldn't I would find a way for him to know at any cost.

I slowly come out of my dream like state when I hear the flight attendant offer us peanuts. See I could go right back to sleep if Mia wasn't ruffling the bag, and then smacking so loudly you wonder if her gums are just going to fall off.

"So what now?" Andrea asks leaning around the seat.

"What do you mean?" Mia munches away on her peanuts constantly licking the salt off her lips much like DK use to randomly lick his lips. What's with people and all that spit?

"What happens to us now?" she looks confused.

"We'll go home and take our finals, pack and jet off to L.A.," Mia shrugs.

"But what about our family?" Natalie pops her head over the seat. "And our friends?"

Between munches Mia responds, "What about 'em?"

"So we're going to be away from them for like the next year?" she sounds almost scared.

"Pretty much," Mia answers knowing she's already made her peace with the small fact of having to part away. "It's like college came early."

"I don't know you guys," Andrea's eyes get the same looks as Natalie's. They have to doubt us the most anyone ever has. My question is why?

"You two need to stop," I say in a groggy voice.

"Oh the dead has awakened?" Natalie giggles at me.

"Mm," I yawn as I sit up. "You two knew exactly what was going to happen if we ever got our break, and now we have it. Yeah I'm sure we'll all miss our families and friends, but remember we're doing this for us. This has been our dream for so long. We've worked hard at this. We deserve this break. We deserve all the glorious things ahead of us and you know what? This is what our friends and family want for us. It's time we grow up and realize it's our time to become independent."

The two of them nod while Mia looks at me as if she's enlightened. "She's right."

"Yeah she is," Andrea tries to find a smile in her.

"Look I know it's going to be hard on us, but we can handle it. We're all here for each other through thick and thin, good and bad," I smirk leaning forward. "We're family, and we can do this. Hands," I say putting mine in to feel it joined quickly by the three others for a small group chant.

We giggle and settle back down.

I know I probably sound like I'm too philosophical or too cliché, but either way I mean what I say. It's not to sound like I'm better than everyone because I have my faith insured in this, but to actually help them get out off the route of insecurity they drift onto so often. It took a while and a few wake up calls from Billy to instill that fear of certainty for my dream coming true.

Our arrival is a long awaited one. I know it's my dream to sing and dance while traveling the world, but that doesn't mean I can't miss home because I sure do. It will be great to see familiar faces that love and missed me.

Searching around the crowd with my eyes while waiting for the girls to get their luggage, I ponder who was supposed to pick us up. I know it was someone from my family. Was it my dad? My mom? Forgive me for forgetting it through all madness of the past few days.

"Kiara!" my sister screams six feet from me. Oh she's doing the pick up. Well rather her than my dad.

"Hey," I say a lot less excited than her.

"Why haven't you picked up your cell phone? Why haven't any of you?" her voice in a bit of a panic.

"I explained to everyone before we left that if we made it to the finals we weren't allowed our phones or anything. If there was an emergency with our immediate family, like something happening to mom, or dad, we'd be notified," I say dropping my bags knowing they're too heavy to just hold on to like this. "Besides I would've checked my messages when I got back to the hotel, but my stupid phone died because I left it on and forgot to charge it."

A sudden change of panic to extreme shock comes across her face. What's her problem? First she's all in a panic, and now she's in distress about something else. This is way too much drama to just be back in Austin for less than ten minutes.

Choking on her words she manages to get out, "So you don't know?"

"Know what?" I ask almost annoyed with her behavior.

Shaking her head at me she folds her arms, "I refuse to be the one to tell you."

"Tell me what?"

"Let's just get home, and they will tell you," she grabs the bag I put down.

"Wait we have to take the girls home," I point as they round the corner clutching their bags. "And tell me what Chenille?"

She doesn't say another word. Now I love my sister as much as I can, but she's acting a little too strange for her own good. She's defensive and hates to have to keep secrets, so for her to just shoot me down like this is a bit more on the scary side. Oh well though. I mean it can't be anything to stress myself over. After all I just got the chance of a life time; there's no bringing me down.

The car ride is pretty vigorous for four overly worked teenagers. We can't stop smiling and gushing about our possible new found fame, but for some reason my sister is trying to bring us down with the solemn look on her face the entire ride.

After we drop Andrea and Natalie off we head back to our house. Mia's going to stay with me until tomorrow night when her parents get home. It's cool though. My parents won't care; they never do.

As soon we arrive to my house a sudden feel of relief comes over me. Just being in my driveway is a sense of closure no one will ever understand. Even though I know my parents won't just let us sleep the next two days away, I'm still thankful that I'm home and can sleep in my own bed.

Mia and I drag our bags into the house where we find my parents at the kitchen table in an awful gloom mood. What's with everyone? Did it become a crime to smile while I was gone?

Shaking my head as we throw our stuff in my room I get an excited look on my face. I have the best news in the world to share and I will not stand for them to bring me down.

"Mom!" I squeal like a giddy schoolgirl. There's a sound I never thought I was capable of making.

"Hi Kie," she says not nearly as happy.

"We won!" I scream at the top of my lungs. Mia starts jumping up and down with me being just as excited hoping to liven up the mode.

"You did?" she questions, her tone raising some.

"Yes! We won! We get to go to L.A. and record and tour! The whole nine yards! Aren't you excited for us?" I say throwing my arms around her followed by Mia's who attach themselves too. She considers my mom her mom, so it's really no different than having my sister hug my mom in unison with me.

"Yes," she nods sniffling a little. Well I didn't expect to bring tears to her eyes, but a bit more joy than I'm receiving would be great.

"That's great Kie," my dad nods. "I'm proud of you girls."

"Good job," my sister sits down on the couch near us.

After we let her go she asks, "You enjoy yourself?"

"Pretty much," Mia answers for us.

"Even though …" she starts off.

"She doesn't know," Chenille quickly chimes in.

"I don't know what?" I ask looking back at her.

"Oh …" is all my mother manages to whimper out.

Ok I'm tired of being out of the loop. Nothing is more frustrating than being left out of something that has to clearly be bigger than I'm thinking. Mia and I patiently wait for a response from the silent trio. No one says anything.

"Well?" I question slipping my hands into my back pockets.

Taking a long deep breath I watch my mom's eyes begin to water a little implanting a little fear into me. "Um …" her jaw starts to shake. "While you girls were out in Florida," she folds her arms tightly, "something happened."

"What?" I immediately dart out.

"I don't know how to say this to you," my mom starts again with tears now actually leaving their quarters.

"Kie something happened to Billy," my dad clears his throat saying in a voice I've never heard him use before.

"What happened to Billy?" I repeat it back to him crossing my arms as well.

"He ..." my father's voice trails off.

My sister finishes what they couldn't even though she didn't want to be the one to tell me, "He was shot and killed."

"What?"

"He died a few days ago," my mom nods slowly.

"What?"

"Billy is gone," my dad's head drops.

"You guys are messing with me," I shake my head denying anything like that could ever happen.

"No," my mother's eyes let a few more tears slip away.

"Yeah. Look if you don't want me to date Billy this is so not the way to go about it," I roll my eyes.

"Kie," my sister stands up and touches my arm gently. Shaky she says, "It's not a joke. Billy was killed Tuesday night."

I look her dead in the eyes noticing no sign of untruthfulness. Suddenly I feel my body become less stable than it's ever been. I close my eyes, and suddenly I feel the world around me stop. I hear nothing. I see nothing. What do they mean he's dead? What do they mean he was killed? I mean just a few days ago he was on the phone wishing me good luck telling me how far I was going to go, and now they expect me to believe that he's no longer with us. No. There's been some sort of mistake.

"You're wrong," I say flatly. "You've mistaken him with someone else."

"No," my mom shakes her head, "there's no mistake Kie."

"There has to be!" I scream at her. "Billy couldn't have died. I just talked to him on Monday!"

My mom starts, "Sweetie—

"He's not gone!" I yell cutting her off again.

Chenille tries next, "Kie—

"Shut up!" I shout at her. "I don't wanna hear it." Lies. All lies.

"Kiara," my father's voice cuts through everything. He stands up in a solid manner and steps towards me. In a very cold voice he states, "Billy died on Tuesday. It's *not* a joke. It is *not* a mistake. It happened."

"When's the funeral?" Mia whimpers out tears flooding her eyes.

"It was Friday," my mom clears the tears stuck in her throat.

"We missed it?" Mia's jaw touches the floor.

"We didn't miss it because it didn't happen," I interject.

"Yes you did," my mother says in a distraught tone. Wiping away a few more tears she reaches for something from my father. Slowly she approaches me handing me a pamphlet.

With a trembling hand, I take it from her looking at Billy's face on the front with his birth date to his death date. That's my Billy. He's ... He's ... I feel a sudden rush of heat come across my body before I collapse like a house built of cards. One second I'm staring at his picture, and the next I'm passed out on my living room floor.

Hours later I wake up in my bed with my family and Mia surrounding me. What's with these people? Do I invade their space and watch them while they sleep? Yawning, I rub my head feeling a bit of a bump. Where did that come from?

"Kie ..." Mia whispers out surprised, I guess that my eyes are open.

"Yeah?"

"Are you ok?" My mother rubs my arm, staring at me with her blood shot eyes.

"I guess so. I had a bad dream though," I reach for the glass of ice-cold water my sister is trying to hand me.

Softly Mia questions, "It wasn't that Billy died was it?"

"How did you know?" I take a sip.

"That wasn't a dream Kiara," my father speaks up once more. "That happened."

I look around at each of their faces all with the same murky expression. My mother places the pamphlet I had been holding before I passed out back in my lap.

"His funeral was Friday. We tried our best to get a hold of you, but we couldn't. Big Mama wanted him buried as soon as possible, and didn't want to burry him a week before his birthday," my mom's eyes look like their going to water again. "I'm sorry honey."

I glance over at Mia who looks like she's starting up on another cycle of tears.

In a surprisingly strong voice I ask, "What happened?"

"Um," my sister leans against my bed on the opposite side of my mom. "All they said was he was shot three times while committing some sort of crime. The first bullet hit his arm, and the second one hit his leg. If that would've been all, he would've made it, but he was hit a third time in which the bullet pierced one of his lungs. He died in the ambulance."

I shudder my mom and sister off me. I don't want them touching me.

"So let me get this straight," I clear my throat. "While I'm in Florida, my boyfriend is shot, dies, has a funeral, and is buried, but I'm never informed."

"We tried to get in touch with you, but it was impossible," my mom sighs.

Silence fills the room for a moment. My eyes scan each person before Mia starts again to begin to ball. I lift my trembling hand to push a strand of hair out of my face. For some reason, I can't bring myself to cry.

Politely I ask, "Can I be left alone?"

"Yeah," my mom tugs at my father to let him know to head out. "We're sorry Kie," she turns around. I nod.

Before my sister and dad follow her out she says, "We're all here for you."

I turn and look at Mia whose eyes might be broken. "Is it dark outside?" I randomly ask. She merely nods. Looking back down at the pamphlet I trace the outline of his face. "He sure knew how to take a picture."

Blotting her eyes she takes a deep breath, "Yeah."

"Billy looks really good here," I shrug staring at his smiling face. I don't think I've ever seen him take a bad picture. "Have you seen it?" she nods almost confused. I simply open it up and scan what songs were sang at his funeral, who spoke, and what time it was. "Looks lovely."

"Kie are you ok?" she crawls into my bed next to me with a box of tissue in her hand.

I nod and close it to look at his picture again.

"You're not crying. Are you not sad? I mean it's ok to cry. I'm here for you," she places her hand on my back to offer a bit of comfort.

"I'm fine," I say pulling away from her. "Just a little tired that's all," I rub my eyes. "I'm going to bed for the night ok?"

"Sure but—

"Will you get the light?" I ask laying my head down fluffing my pillow.

Mia doesn't say another word to me. She gets up, hits the light, and turns herself back into bed to cry. I drown the sound of her sobbing out by humming a tune I create out of nowhere. I do my best to get to sleep, figuring I can't think about it if I'm sleeping.

I sleep for what feels like an eternity. I waste no time awake. It's really simple when you think about it. If I'm not conscious I can't feel pain, I don't have to think about the unlivable feelings I'll be forced to experience, and best of all I don't have to live with the reality that my boyfriend was robbed of his life.

You know I don't know if I hate it more that there's more to the story that I don't know, or the fact I know who's got the other half and not giving it up.

What do you when someone you love so much, someone who you don't know how you'll make it without them, someone you depend so much on, just passes away? What do you do when the love of your life dies? How do you get away from the pain and anguish that will be there every day of your life?

Have you ever thought about it like this, maybe just maybe if you don't subject yourself to focusing on the fact that the person is actually gone you won't have to worry about it? Maybe if you don't think about their death and force yourself not to center in on that sadness, that you can make it. Deny the pain, deny the suffering, and most of all deny that you can't make it. That's the way to get through it. The little four letter word that seems to get people out of jail sentences sometimes. Deny.

Sunday goes by pretty fast considering I sleep through almost all of it. No one bothers me figuring I'm mourning and will eventually get over whatever the sad feelings they think I'm feeling are. Too bad for them I'm spending all my time sleeping not thinking about anything.

When Monday morning arrives and Mia picks me up for school, she's still got a bit of dimness to her spirit. I'm not cheerful or anything of the sort, but I don't look nearly as bad as she does.

"Have you cried any yet?" is the first thing she asks when she sees me.

"No," I bluntly remark.

"Ya know Kie it's very unhealthy for you to keep these emotions built up in you."

"I'm fine," I fasten my seatbelt.

"You are not fine."

"Yes I am."

"No you're not. I know what you're doing. You're denying all of this figuring if you don't think about it or focus on it that it'll all go away. Well newsflash Kie, postponing the pain is only making the healing process harder."

Rolling my eyes, I look out the window ignoring her. Oh what does she know? It's not like that dog DK she cares so much about was shot to death. You know though, out of the two of them, isn't it ironic that the one with the most potential is the one to die? Not the one who degrades women, not the one who's an outstanding criminal, oh never the one who has karma coming back extremely hard on his ass. What's that about? Good is supposed to triumph over evil, yet DK is walking this earth while Billy lays six feet under. Has anyone seen DK? Funny how his best friend dies and he disappears.

At school people are looking at me differently. I didn't expect the whole entire world to fucking know. I meant he's in my private life. This has nothing to do with them, but with three loud mouths for friends what do you expect?

If only you knew how annoying it is to have someone come up to you every five minutes checking if you're ok.

I wish I didn't have to go to school this week, but I do. I don't have a choice. It's finals week. No exemptions because we missed all last week. Lucky me huh? I have to sit through every class with people staring and whispering about me. It used to be ok when it was just about something I had done or someone who they heard wanted to date me, but now it's deeper than that. I don't enjoy being the butt of jokes, the butt of a bond, and worst of all I don't enjoy being the butt of teacher conversations.

Everyone knows. I mean everyone. I have teachers and councilors come up to me every five minutes asking me if I'm alright. Do I need a few extra moments for my finals? Do I need some time by myself? No! I don't want to be in solitude with thoughts of sadness. I just want to finish my junior year, so I can start my career far away from here. Far away from Texas and all the trouble that I found here. Far away.

Every night I try to force myself to sleep I end up having haunting dreams of Billy being alive, forcing me to down a couple of sleeping pills. Sure it's not the safest way to get to bed, but I've got news for you. I don't give a damn.

Wednesday night is the hardest I've faced. Here I am lying in bed after I've taken my pills, just waiting for them to kick in and all I can picture is his face in my mind. I try to think about what's waiting for me and my girls just a couple of weeks away, but all I see again is his face. When I picture us in the studio there he is. I see him in the crowd of the tour we do. I see him reading a magazine we're featured in. It doesn't seem to matter what I try to think about he finds himself there.

Now realize the rest of the week I haven't had this problem at all. It's been pretty easy not think about it. I just set my mind back in time. I program it at the beginning of the day to creep back into that bitter shell when I didn't have a boyfriend, when I didn't need, let alone want a man. It had worked up to this point. It was almost like the good ol' days, but for some unexplainable reason tonight Billy just doesn't want to go away.

Well fine then. If he doesn't want to leave I'll talk to him.

"Go away," I whisper in my mind at him.

"No," he says in a loud firm voice.

I open my eyes to see him standing in front of my TV. Trying not to scream I cover my mouth in an instant. I don't see dead people. No ghost. Bad ghost. Go away.

"Go away," I snap at him.

"No," he folds his arms.

"Yes. This is my room and my life. Go away," I coldly whisper out at him covering up my half naked body like he's never seen it before.

"Kie I need you to face what happened and say goodbye," he moves closer to me causing chills to run up my body. I snuggle under my blanket.

"No. I'm not saying goodbye to you because there's nothing to say goodbye to. I erased you. I made you disappear. You don't exist anymore," I shake my head. "What are you doing here anyway? Shouldn't you be in heaven playing basketball with angels or something?"

Billy moves towards me once more, "I can't go Kie. Not until you say goodbye. You know how much I love you, and how much you mean to me. I can't leave without knowing you're going to be ok."

"I am ok!" I scream in the loudest whisper I can. "I'm fine."

"No you're not," he sits on the edge of my bed next to me.

"Yes I am. Everyone lounges around and tells me how I'm feeling, tells me I'm not ok, telling me it's ok to be in pain. I'm not in pain. Nothing is wrong with me! I've dealt with this issue and moved on. You are gone, and frankly I am fine."

"Really you're fine?"

"Fine and fucking dandy," I growl at him the way I use to when we first met.

Billy leans in and strokes the side of my face with his ice-cold hand. His hand touches my chin that's angled down, "Then why are seeing me right now?"

I lift my head up seeing the mere hallucination gone. Shaking my head I cover my face with one of my pillows. Stupid medicine is messing with me. I just wish he would go away and leave me alone because I am fine. I'm just as fine as a person can be.

After my last final Thursday morning I arrive home to see both of my parents home in the middle of the day. Great. More suspicious behavior. The last time they were acting funny they had just screwed up my life with the news of my boyfriend's death. I wonder what news they'll bring to me today.

"Kiara please change," my mother turns the pages in a novel.

"Why?" I ask slowing down.

"We're going out, so please change into something a bit more casual," she looks up with a soft smile.

"Where are we going?"

"Just do as your mother says," my father changes the channel.

I storm off to my room in a huff. All I wanted was a little peace and quiet now that I've said goodbye to school and the horrible tests I've been forced to take. I put on a pair of slacks and a collared brown shirt with a pair of sandals. You know the way to heal a broken heart is not bonding with your parents. I can tell you that much.

Loading myself into the car with my purse I think about how long it's going to take to pack. In a little over a week I will be off living a new life, a great life, an ideal life.

My parents give me radio dibs and let me listen to whatever I want. I must admit that ever since Billy's death they've been giving me much more attention than I've ever known them capable of.

After a good thirty minutes later we're outside of a building. It's a brown, one story building that looks like a funeral home or place for motivational speakers to speak.

"Come on," my mom says leaving her book. There's the first clue that I have to pay attention to something. If she leaves her book behind it means intense listening. Perfect. I just get out of schools and away from lectures, and here I go having to listen intently to something I probably could care less about.

I get out and adjust my shirt as I check out the cars. Why do I know some of these vehicles? Isn't it strange how no matter where you go you feel like you recognize someone?

Following them inside the dreary building I notice the creepy music playing. It's death music. Geez, I hope they don't think that because I couldn't go to Billy's funeral that another one will make up for it, because that's just sick and twisted.

When we enter a room full of people they turn their heads to face us. I know every single one of them. A good portion of them are my peers, a few are from Ft. Worth, while the rest are friends of the family. What hell is this?

"Kie," my mother loops arms with me. In a whisper she explains, "I know you didn't get to go to his funeral, so we thought we'd give you your own memorial ceremony. We thought maybe it would help with some closure."

Are these people taking crazy pills or something? Are their brains really missing that many screws? I can't believe them. How do I get out of this? Is there a back door I can slide out of?

"I don't wanna be here," I lean over and whisper to my mother as we sit next to Mia and my sister.

"It's ok Kie," she rubs my arm. "This is for the best."

Rolling my eyes I cross my legs and hang my head. Kill me now.

The service, if you have to call it that, begins. People stand and speak nice things about him, recite poems, shed tears, and try to establish a closing point for them. I don't know what everyone's trippin' on, but they need to come off it, because they're really hitting my last nerves with all this bullshit.

Just when I think that all is said and done, just when I think this hell-forsaken ceremony is about to be over someone else strolls up. As my luck has it, it's actually someone interesting, someone who probably has a guilty conscious, and someone who I haven't heard from since Billy's death.

DK takes a stance behind the microphone, slouched over looking real disheveled. Well look what Satan brought in.

"Hello," he begins slowly. Hi? That's how the moron starts? "Many of you know me. I'm Deacon Kristiansen, best known as DK. Billy had been my best friend from day one. We've been so close that people actually believe that we're blood related brothas. We were raised as if we were so in my head and his that's exactly what we are. We're brothers. No one in this world was down fo' Billy as much as I was. No one. I loved my boy like no other. I didn't get to go to his funeral," he continues.

Wow you and the rest of the world. And if you were so down why didn't you go?

"I know you're probably all thinkin', 'if that's yo' boy how could you not go to his funeral? How could you not be there to say goodbye?' Well it's simple really. A guilty conscious will do that to you. There have been many speculations on what went down that day, where Billy was, and why he was shot. Many people don't know the truth, and I believe if you care enough to be here then you deserve to know what happened that day," his focus begins its way to me.

You're damn skippy I deserve to know what the hell happened to my fiancé.

"On Monday night I asked Billy for a favor. At the time I thought it was harmless. I had asked him fo' stupid small things like this so many times I assumed he'd jus' agree and it would happen. Fo' the firs' time I can remember Billy didn't jump to say yes. Actually he said no, and I pushed fo' him to do this. I felt I needed him more than Kie did."

Of course you thought that you selfish bastard. Everything is always about you. I swear if … no. Stay calm Kie.

"Ya see, he was supposed to go see Kie in Florida, but I wanted him to do a job wit' me. Billy thought he was doin' the righ' thing, the safe thing. He decided that he would take a later flight so that he could help me out firs'," his eyes paste themselves on me. "Tuesday night Billy and I went to what appeared as an empty house. I had money stolen from me earlier in the week and wanted to rightfully claim it back. Because Billy was my boy, he was down fo' whatever to help me. Well that night we broke into a house together. We began to search it fo' my money. Billy and I separated. He ended up in a room wit' people who owned the house. They were sleepin', and he paid no mind because he was so focused on helpin' me out. When Billy got caught he tried to make a run fo' it and was shot for the first time," his eyes are meeting mine.

I begin to cringe a bit. Do not get up and beat the hell out of him. Do not do it Kie.

"He then proceeded to run away only to be shot twice more. I can only assume he was runnin' fo' one las' chance at life. Where was I? Runnin'. I was runnin' fo' my fuckin' life while my bes' friend, my brother, the one person who never gave up on me in this world needed my help, searched fo' me, was dying. I even watched the ambulance take him away. When I saw him I knew he wasn't gonna make it. Every chance he got he was graspin' fo' air, and I knew in my heart that was it. I'd fucked up fo' the las' time. I've killed my best friend. No I didn't intend to. When I woke up Tuesday morning I had no intention of anything bad happenin'. We had never run into any sort of trouble befo', and the first time we did I ran like a punk. I lef' my bes' friend out to dry, and that's a guilt I will have to live wit' fo' the res' of my life. A torment and pain I will never be able to forgive myself fo'. No one loved him like I did, and no one is to blame fo' his death, but me," he claims responsibility. "I'm so sorry. It was an accident and I'm sorry from the bottom of my heart."

The entire audience is in utter shock. No one was expecting to hear that DK was the cause of Billy's death. Well by no one I mean everyone except me. I knew that fucking coward was to blame. I just knew he had something to do with it.

Mia's jaw is on the ground once more and tears are filling her eyes like it's that much of a shocker. Come on.

"I'm sorry Billy. I wish it would have been me," he hangs his head low as do a few other people. Me too.

"Go say something," my sister whispers to me. "It'll help."

Say something? She wants me to say something? Oh I'll say something alright. I'll say every single thing that's crossed my mind.

Getting straight up I head to the microphone. I take the spot DK was just holding. As I adjust the microphone for my height I notice DK nervously lingering next to me assuming I have something to say to him, which I do.

I clear my throat before I begin, "You know I've heard a lot of nice things about Billy today. It's nice people who barely knew him looked at him in such a marvelous light."

The crowd looks in awe for a moment. Suckers.

"Not one you hold the right to stand up here today and say shit about him. You speculate on what you've heard or seen, once, maybe twice. The boy was not as perfect as you make him out to be. The boy was a genuine asshole," I say bluntly catching everyone's attention. "Sure he was sweet when he *felt* like it, but to sum it up his level of jerkiness out weighs his romantic side. For those of you who don't know, Billy was not Mr. Perfect. He got me shot at, cussed out, almost in a car accident, talked trash about getting me into bed, flipped out for no reason, nearly cheated on me, and worst of all he always, *always*, put bullshit in front of me. Exhibit A," I point to DK next to me. "He did very little good for this world and particularly me. Yes. He will be missed, but his behavior that seemed to be the general way he was will not," I make it very clear to everyone.

At the moment everyone is too busy covering their mouths and being frozen in their seats to even object.

"By the way you all are out of your damn minds. You drag me here to listen to you say things about someone none of you knew, let alone knew as well as I did. After I tell you I'm fine, I'm doing just peachy, you bring me here anyway to discuss something I tell you repeatedly I don't want to. Would it really kill you all to listen to me when I said I didn't want do this? You're all sitting in the audience thinking I'm off my rocker, that my sanity has flown out the window because I have the decency to stand up here and say the truth about him. You are a bunch of hypocrites. I've never been in a room full of people hearing them say how much someone will be missed that they know damn well they aren't going to give a second thought about. Well let me go ahead and be completely honest. I'm done with Billy. He's gone forever because when it came down to bullshit or me, he always chose bullshit."

I pause for a moment and stare out at the faces that are dying to stop my mouth from running away like it is but can't seem to find ammunition to.

"Mom and dad, you didn't love the idea of me dating a hoodrat's prince charming, so to sit and act like it's the saddest thing in the world for you is living a bit of lie don't you think?"

My mother quickly raises a hand to object, "That's not—

Ignoring her I continue, "Chenille you wanted to make him stop breathing the second you found out we were together. Well guess what he finally has, and you couldn't be any unhappier. You get your wish, and you're still unhappy? Can we say selfish?"

She begins to start to cry as I go onto my next victim, "Mia, I fucking told you it was not a good idea to get involved with them. I tried to drill into your brain like nail, and you made me do it anyway. They're worse than drugs, more addicting and clearly more harmful as you've seen in the past year. Maybe you'll learn to listen to me now that he's gone," I roll my eyes.

Through her tears all she can belt out is, "Kie I just—

"Last but never least," I turn to DK. "You're very brave for standing up here and telling the truth. It's about high time you let the world know what a dickhead you really are. You know that I've hated you from the moment I met you? I did everything I could for the sake of the people I loved to try to be nice to you, attempt to like you, give you a chance to prove you weren't just another piece of ghetto trash," I say with a smirk.

"And?" DK asks ready to take his beating.

"And you did nothing but fuck up every last opportunity given to you. And you know why? Because you're absolutely worthless. You are the biggest pussy I've ever known, and the biggest waste of great god given space," my right fist clenches. "You disgust me, and there's something I've always wanted to say to you but because of Billy I couldn't."

He looks mortified, but broken at the same time. In a whisper he asks, "What's that?"

Not expecting my fist to make contact with his jaw and a bit of his nose he falls to the ground like a tree in the woods. Frankly it would have been funny to yell timber.

"I hate you," I snarl out and lean over him as he struggles to stay conscious. "I will never forgive you for killing my heart and soul you stupid son of a bitch."

"Kiara!" My father cries out in horror.

I stand back up with a smile on my face, "Yeah?"

"You ... You ... You—

"You what? You know what? Whatever it is you can tell me when you meet me at the car." With a simple sigh I head out of the building without so much as a glance back.

Now I know that wasn't the ideal behavior of a heartbroken girlfriend, but let's face it. I don't know who I am anymore, and I honestly don't care.

CHAPTER 18

Final Goodbyes

Since when did packing become such a difficult task for me? I used to have no trouble doing it. I could pack a bag in no time without the least bit of trouble yet all of sudden I have more problems than my algebra 2 final.

You know this last week of my life has been pure bred hell? I've spent exactly one week today fighting people, being annoyed and hounded, and most importantly without Billy. I don't see what the big deal is about not crying or anything. So I don't throw a fit because the one person I ever truly loved is gone. Does that make me a bad person? Well if it does than you might as well pin me heartless because I refuse to shed a single tear. Why? Why? Isn't that obvious? I don't feel anything worth weeping about, plain and simple.

"Where's the bubble wrap?" I ask Mia looking around at the boxes surrounding me wondering if it disappeared in between them.

"I think we're all out," she says like she's confused that we could've used it so quick. What can I say? I have a lot of stuff.

"Damn," I mutter admiring the boxes.

"I'll go get some more," she bounces out of my room.

Nice to know she's made her peace with this whole situation, but more importantly she's found her focal point back where it should be.

Grabbing the masking tape to seal one of my boxes, I hear the doorbell. "Mia get that please!"

My parents are out shopping for some things they think I'll need basically living on my own in another state. I still can't believe they're letting me live away from home at the age of seventeen. That was the agreement though. If we won I was allowed to leave with the other girls in search of stardom, even if stardom is all the way in California.

"Kie it's for you!" she calls back.

If that's not thoroughly predictable, what is? It's my house, being the only young adult in the house, of course the door is for me. It's more than likely someone here to send their great apologies for Billy's death or their overly ecstatic blessing on our job opportunity in L.A.

Putting on a fake grin, knowing I have to use it either way, I approach the door avoiding boxes that have somehow already migrated their way here. Damn I've really got a lot of stuff.

Mia opens the door all the way to reveal DK's disturbing face. I thought I got rid of him at the funeral. What is it with this boy? Nearly a year of me bulling him away and he still doesn't get the hint I want nothing to do with him. What's it going to take to permanently make him stay away? A knee in the balls?

"Can I help you?" I say through the glass screen door.

"Yeah. I need to talk to you," he clears his throat adjusting his hands in his pockets.

"I'm sorry you must be looking for the psychiatrist."

"No," DK shakes his head. "I need a—

"Pharmacist? Sorry they don't prescribe pills for killing your best friend."

"Kiara," Mia hisses.

"Kie seriously," he says in tone I'm not use to. Usually when I mouth off and knock him down he responds in this complete jackass voice, but today it's so mellow I'm almost convinced he doesn't take joy in pissing me off anymore. "Can I talk to you?"

"Was the informal invitation my fist made to your jaw not enough to clarify that I don't want to ever see you again?"

"No it was crystal clear," he slumps over more. "I've got some of Billy's stuff fo' you," he fiddles around with what I assume is change in his pocket. Stuff of Billy's? Why would I want it if all I'm trying to do is get him out of my life?

"I don't want it."

"I think you should get it," Mia encourages me. Has she not learned encouragement from her does not go a long way?

"But I don't want it," I repeat myself at her.

"Come on," she shakes her head. "Don't act like this."

"Ugh, where is it?" I look around for a box or something.

"It's not here. I've gotta take you to it," his tongue grazes his lips like the good old days.

That boy has finally fried every last cell in his brain. I must say it's about time.

I try not to laugh in his face but can't seem to find a way to stop it. "No."

"I don't have to drive you. You jus' have to get there."

"No," I say again. I hate repeating myself. Would it kill them to listen to me the first time?

Mia starts at me, "Kie—

"No. I told you I didn't want the shit, and the fact that it's not here ... means I really don't want it."

"Please don't be stubborn about this. I'll take you."

"We—

"We could use a break. Besides it could help with closure."

"I am closed, but if it'll shut the both of you up then fine," I shrug. Turning toward DK I say, "We'll go. Let us get our shoes, and we'll be right out."

About thirty minutes later we're standing outside Mia's car at a graveyard. Great he brought me here to look at the grave of my dead boyfriend. Fabulous.

"Come on," he says to us heading towards where I assume Billy is buried. Reluctantly we follow behind weaving in and out of paths. We arrive in front of a solid gray rock rounded edge square tomb stone that reads his name, his birth date to his death date, and a quote.

"The minds greatest challenge is the hearts desire," Mia reads out loud. There's a moment of silence in which I assume the two of them are wallowing in the deep thoughts of how this could have been true for Billy aka wasting my time.

"Hate to interrupt the spiritualness you two must be feeling, but what the hell am I doing here?" I question.

"Thought you migh' like to see where he was buried," he shrugs innocently. "I'm supposed to be meetin' wit' someone who's bringin' the things."

"You take a moment to say goodbye Kie while DK and I will go wait over there," she points back towards the car. Figures she'd want to run away with the hoodlum. Graveyards scare her. "It'll be good for you."

She attempts to start to try to make him leave until I stop them dead in their tracks, "Wait a second. I'm not that stupid. Why else am I here?"

DK looks shamefully at the ground. I knew saying goodbye couldn't have been the entire story. I swear that boy will be a liar until the day he dies. "I thought it would be nice if I gave Billy the one birthday gift he would have wanted."

My eyes lifelessly stare at him. I was trying hard to forget it's his birthday, but everywhere you turn someone wants to remind you. As DK and Mia stroll off I stare at his pale gray tomb. Bowing my head and closing my eyes for a moment, I begin to wonder what is it going to take for people to just let this go and move on.

Opening my eyes I see Billy sitting on top of his grave. My jaw starts to drop when I realize it's probably just my mind playing with me again. "Stop stalking me."

"I'm not stalking you …"

"I'm pretty sure if you're a ghost you are."

"I'm a mind hologram," he replies with that classic smile I was accustomed too.

Rolling my eyes I shake my head. "Are you honestly telling me my mind has nothing better to do than to picture your annoying face again and again? Making you taunt and haunt me every chance you get?"

"Pretty much," he shrugs dusting off his jeans.

I let my eyes roll once more before I start off towards Mia. Do I look like I have time for this because I'm pretty sure I don't. It wouldn't matter if I had nothing to do today because there will still not be any time for this.

"You can run all you want Kie. It doesn't matter because I will follow you until you get the message," Billy adjusts the white backwards baseball cap on his head as he leans against his tomb stone.

Slowly I turn back around with a glare on my face, "I'm not running away; thank you very much."

"Yeah you are."

"No I'm not."

"But you are," he dusts off his white t-shirt too. "You're running away just like DK did."

My jaw flies open as I approach him once more, "How dare you compare me to that ignoramus," I bark. "He ran. He ran and left you to die. I'm not running from anything and damn sure am I not leaving you to die!" I yell in a whisper. DK and Mia probably already think I'm crazy, but let's give them a little less evidence by whispering.

He nods and begins to smirk, "He ran, and so are you. Ok, you aren't leaving me to die, but you sure are running."

"Go to hell," I sneer at him preparing to walk away again.

"Can't. Heaven called, hints the white," he looks down at his white shoes that match the rest of the white on his body.

I let out a deep loud sigh and step back towards him. "Damn it! What will it take for you to leave me alone for good?"

Billy pauses and looks at me for a second.

You know my minds image of him is a bit off. I remember his head use to be funnier shaped than that, he was a tad bit smaller, and his voice was totally less attractive.

"If you sit down and talk to me, so you can say your goodbyes then I'll leave you alone."

"Swear?"

"Only if you start telling the truth."

"I have been," I sit down in front of him.

"So you're fine?"

"Other than seeing and constantly being forced to talk to you, better known as my subconscious that's all sort of fucked up, I'm actually fine," I smirk back like I use to when we first met.

"Wow Kie. You know if this whole singing career doesn't work out you should totally pursue acting because you know how to put on one heck of a performance."

"Excuse me?"

"Today for instance. Sitting here telling me you're fine, but I really liked yesterday. Yesterday's was award winning," he begins chomping down on my vulnerability that is very scarce.

"Thank you," I sigh still smiling.

"I especially like that whole thing about me being a complete and total jerk. To be specific, I liked the phrase, and I quote, 'He did very little good for this world and particularly me.' It was so moving that for a second there I actually thought about believing you."

"You know what? Fuck you. I was completely sincere about that," I stand up for myself.

Chuckling to himself he rubs his chin at me, "Yeah sure Kie. Sincere? Obviously all those advanced classes you took sure didn't help you much with your honesty."

What's with him and insults? It wasn't enough to do it while he was alive now he has to do it while he's dead too? You would think my subconscious would be nicer to me, capture the sweeter more romantic side of Billy. That goes to show you I'm wrong again.

"Tone it down with the insults before I change my mind on being here."

"Sorry," he licks his lips at me.

"Better be," I mumble under my breath.

"No good for you? Is that how you really feel?" Billy dusts off his shoes again like their magically going to get dirty. Freak.

"Yup."

"No good huh? So answer me this then," he folds his hands on his bent knees. "Who rescued you that night at the club?" I look down shamefully. "Who risked his life to save yours from the gunshots?"

"Who got me in those situations?"

"Who helped you with your trust issues? Who's responsible for whoopin' the crap out that guy who tried to rape you?"

"Well—

"Explain to me who was behind you 110% about anything you did?" he leans forward as I shrug, pretending I don't know. "You don't know? He was the same guy who made you breakfast after your first date with him."

"And the same guy who made me breakfast after he basically cheated on me."

Side stepping my comment he says, "He was the same guy who you would call in the middle of the night when you had a bad dream or just couldn't sleep. He was the same guy who you called at random times of the day just to hear his voice because you missed it that much."

"He is the same guy who I will never have to let plague my life ever again."

"Yeah the same guy who wants you to say what's on your mind."

"Whatever's on my mind?"

"Whatever."

"Does it have to be nice?"

He shakes his head and waits for me to say something.

We meet eyes, and I notice something different in them. You know when he was alive and around me I brought this glow around the edges of his eyes. Literally you could see the changes in his eyes from the impact I had made on him. People use to say you could see it in mine too, but of course I always beg to differ. His glow is gone now. Maybe because mine is.

"I'm waiting …" he starts tapping his feet away. "You know I do have all day."

I don't say anything. I just look off into the faded gray sky. How come there's no sun? Where's the sunshine when I need it? This *is* Texas. It's not supposed to be this dark and gloomy.

"Ya know, you have to be the most stubborn person I've ever met."

Offended I snap back, "Said pot to kettle."

"Don't even start with me. You are the most uncompromising person ever born," he attempts to push my buttons. I won't let him get to me. "Since the moment I met you all I wanted was to prove to you something that seemed basically impossible. There's no pleasing you!"

Quickly I try to inject, "That's not—

"You're only happy when you have something to complain about," Billy begins to yell at me. When he used to yell at me in the early days he would get an ear of full fledge Kie on bitch mode. Is that what he wants? 'Cause I'll give it to him. "I did everything and anything I could for you, and you're still upset. Why? Just tell me why!"

"Because I hate you!" I explode getting up.

Standing up too he asks, "Really you hate me now?"

"Yes! I hate you! I hate everything about you!" I give in to the temptation of putting this fool in his place.

"Tell me what you hate about me Kie. Let a nigga know."

"I told you. Everything and anything," I try to calm down some. Wouldn't want DK or Mia to wander back this way or place a call to throw me in the crazy house, though I sure the hell wouldn't blame them. I'm thinking about locking myself in there.

"Examples?"

"I hate the way you tried so hard to be with me after I strictly told you time and time again no. I hate the way you use to walk through water and fire to please me. I hate the way you challenged yourself and became a better person for *my* sake. I hate the way you make me feel!" I shove him. "I hate this aching feeling you left in my heart! I hate the stupid fact every second you're gone that all it does is burn! I hate knowing that you're never going to come back and wrap your arms around me! I hate this gut wrenching pain in my stomach that knows for the rest of my life I have to live without you!" Small amounts of tears enter my eyes, "I hate you …" I shake my head looking down. "I hate the way you use to hold me like I was the most fragile thing ever. I hate the way you loved me so much. You know what I hate the most? I hate," I begin to sniffle. Another tear falls as I try again, "I hate …"

"What Kie?" I feel the cold embrace of what is supposed to be his arms. "What do you hate the most?"

Breaking away from him with tears I swore would never come in my eyes I say, "I hate loving you!" Falling to my knees I let the tears stream down my cheeks as the rain starts.

He kneels down beside me trying to protect me from the rain, "You're mad because you still love me?"

"Yes," I nod. "Nothing hurts more than loving you and knowing I can't ever be with you again," I shake my head letting it sink. "How could you do this to me? You swore you'd never hurt me again."

"I—

"You promised to always be here when I needed you and look where you are. Look what you did. You lied to me," I wrap my arms around my cramping stomach. "You lying son of a bitch."

"I—

"You never even loved me," I roll my eyes. "I was such a chump for believing you."

"Hey," he reaches out and lifts my chin up. "I don't care if I'm gone or not. I never want to here you say that. I always loved you Kiara, and you know that. Don't sit here and try to BS me like that. You know how much I did to show you that."

"Then why, if you loved me *so much*, did you choose DK over me?"

"It wasn't like that baby. I know you needed me. Why do you think I ran? I ran to try to escape, to try to give myself a chance to see you. You know I couldn't live with you seeing me locked up. DK is family—

"And what am I? A stranger? Oh my bad just your fiancé. Suddenly DK is above me on the Billy social pyramid?"

"No Kie. You are right. You are wifey," his lifeless hand runs down my face with the rain along side my tears. "You are the one I wanted to marry, to have my kids, you were my future. DK was my past. Your past will always catch up to you, sometimes for the better and sometimes for the worse," he looks off in the distance. "Ya know if I could change what I did I would, but I can't … Is that why you're not wearing the locket I gave you and the ring I proposed to you with?"

I look down in ignominy. I haven't worn either since I heard about his death a week ago. Why wear tokens of love when you don't feel that way?

"Look Kie," he crawls to be right in front of me. "You can't hold hate in your heart because you think it'll make the pain stop. It's just going to make you hurt more in the end. Trust me. I know. I tried to do it when my parents died, and it almost ruined my life. Don't make the same mistake Kie," his wet fingers touch mine.

I nod in understanding.

"Come on," he gets up to help me. I stand up with him trying to stop crying. "Now you listen to me," his wet body clings itself next to mine.

"Yeah …"

In my ear he whispers, "I'm going to love you each and every day even if I'm not there physically. You were the most important thing in my life, and I'm glad that you came to me. You were my heaven sent angel every single moment you were with me happy and unhappy, but honey it's time to say goodbye."

"I can't."

"You can. You've got to let me go, and go be who you were destined become. Don't give up on yourself just because you don't think I'm at your side. Any time you miss me wear my loving gifts and remember every word I've ever said to you about how much you mean to me is true," he kisses my forehead with his wet lips. "I love you Kiara."

Somehow I whimper, "I love you Billy."

"I'll watch out over you ok princess?" his fingers run their way through my wet hair.

I nod and try to wipe away some tears, but only more replace them. "I'll miss you."

"I'll miss you," he lifts my chin up. "Thank you for giving me so much more in life than I thought possible."

"Thanks for the same," I smile for the first time in a while.

His lips touch mine as the rain pours down on us. I linger in the last kiss I'll ever have with him. It's amazing how he can still knock me off my feet even now that he's gone.

We pull away to get lost in each others eyes one last time before I smile, "Happy birthday love."

"It is now," he slips away from me moving backwards. "Bye Kie."

"Bye Billy," I wrap my arms around myself and bow my head once more.

As I sniffle water up my nose I notice the rain only comes down harder. Ya know what? I'll be ok. I don't know when or how, but I just know that one day I will be ok. Looking back up I see Billy's grave without him there. With a small sigh I stroll away without another word towards DK and Mia who have been patiently waiting, I assume for quite some time now. The cold rain pours down on me to wipe away all the anguish that's been haunting my life. As I approach them I notice that their hiding under an umbrella.

"You ok?" Mia asks breaking away from DK's slight embrace.

"No," I shake my head and grow a smile. "But I will be."

Proudly nodding in understanding she touches my hand a little.

"Uh, Mia can you leave us alone fo' a sec?" DK grips the umbrella harder.

"Sure," she nods. "I'll be in my car."

We both nod and watch her walk out of site. Eventually our eyes meet again, and for the first time in a long time I don't feel them squint down to a glare. He attempts to cover my head as well, but I step out of the way.

Taking the hint he just covers himself. "I'm sorry."

"I know," I nod folding my arms. "I know."

"You know Kie you were the reason for him. Billy didn't die with unfinished business or unhappy. Nothin' in this world meant anything to him compared to you, not even me," he shakes his head. "I know what I did was stupid—

"Reckless …"

"And jus' plain brainless. I don't blame you fo' hatin' me more than you already did, but I thought that you should know you didn't only impact his life, but mine."

I raise my eyebrows in curiosity. I know I made his life pretty much parallel to hell, but I never saw that as of any importance.

"Sometimes I wonder and wish Billy would've never met you so that he would have always been the same ol' nigga I always knew. He changed so much in fron' of me I thought that if he kept on one day he would never want anything to do wit' me because he finally saw me fo' what I was really worth. Befo' you I was all he needed, but then you made him grow up. You made us both grow up. All the never endin' pushin' really made us both into men. If it weren't fo' you my eyes would've never opened up and saw what I needed to see. I wish it wouldn't have taken his death to make me realize how valuable you were, but God works in mysterious ways sometimes. Call me crazy fo' doin' this but," he leans down and hugs me. Without hesitation I throw my arms around him and hug back. In a low tone he says, "Thanks Kie. Fo' everything."

I whisper back, "You're welcome."

Pulling away he asks, "I know it's a long shot, but will you ever be able to forgive me?"

After a glance back at Billy's grave I smile, "Some day."

"I have his stuff fo' you," he fishes around in his pocket for something that jingles. He pulls out a set of car keys, opens the palm of my hand, and places them there. "His mos' prized possession befo' you. There's some stuff in the trunk fo' you too. You're who he would've wanted to have his belongings."

As I look down at the keys I let out a heavy sigh, "Thanks."

"No problem," he shrugs hearing the horn of his own car being honked by someone. "I've gotta go, but good luck in Cali. I'll see you 'round?" DK sticks out his hand.

I stare long and hard at it. There are millions of hands I never imagined myself shaking, and this has to be one of them. I never thought our feuding would cease for good, but if the east coast and west coast war can come to an end I guess so can ours.

Slowly I place my hand in the palm of his giving him a firm handshake, "Yeah. I'll see you around DK."

Watching our hands slip away he closes his eyes as if to say a quick prayer or something. DK waves once more to Mia who's warmly sitting in her car waiting for us to be done. I watch him disappear into his car and eventually down the road heading somewhere I might never know. Unhurriedly I stroll towards Billy's car as I begin thinking to myself.

About an hour later I wander back in the house alone. I told Mia it was ok if she went home. Finally I decided I needed some time alone to gather up some of my very own closure besides saying goodbye to him. I walk through my front door with a slightly light box under my arm.

Before I get the opportunity to pass my mother who is lounging on the couch she stops me, "Kie that company called and said they have a business meeting for you girls tomorrow. You'll be saying goodbye to us and Texas in just a few days."

"Yeah," I look down at the ground noticing I have a lot to say goodbye to.

She gets a sad motherly look in her eyes. You can tell she's going to miss me so much. I don't know how she sits and tries to be strong, knowing her baby girl is about to leave her to get a jump start on the real world sooner than expected. She doesn't have to cry or tell me for me to know that I'll be missed. I can see it.

"Are you ok honey?" my mother politely asks finding some way to tear herself away from the movie she's watching.

Thinking to myself for a second I nod. "I'm fine."

"Are you really fine, or are you still pretending?" she twirls the remote to the DVD player between her fingers.

"No. I'm really fine. I'll be in my room ok?" I continue that direction.

Stripping out of my soaking wet clothes into some that are dry and lounge worthy, I take my place on my bed next the box. Before I open it I rush to my bathroom to put on the jewelry Billy gave me. Wow now that I think about it, it did feel like something was missing on my body. I twist the diamond around on my finger and make sure the locket is settled comfortably around my neck.

I rip into the box to see just four things I wasn't expecting. Something inside of me was waiting to open this to find something as important as buried treasure not ... this. I'm looking at an envelope, a VCR tape, a hat, and small collection of photos. What is this about? Seriously? Look at this stuff. I know Billy had more stuff than this, so I wish someone would tell me why DK decided this is what he wanted me to have.

Finally noticing the note tapped to the inside of the box I read it out loud, "Some things that meant a lot to him. Enjoy, love DK," well I'm glad he uses the term love lightly like Billy hated.

After I take out the Lakers hat I place it on my head. Giggling, I remember the day I saw him wear it. I thought it looked better on me, and I still do. With a twist it's backwards like he used to wear it.

I grab for the pictures with the other hand. As I look at the old photos of Billy as a young boy, an early teenager, and a few from what I can only assume was this year, I notice something about all of them. He's smiling. Every single picture he's smiling. I always thought this boy had a smiling problem like he was a little too addicted to it for his own good, but damn. It's like his face has been programmed to stay in that position permanently. The pictures bring a warm feeling to my body I guess to tell me that I'll never have to be without his smiling face.

Placing the few photos on the outside of the box I peek in the envelope at a butt load of cash that I could care less about. Something in me has a feeling that this is money that DK felt rightfully belonged to Billy, and now wants me to invest in his biggest dream, me.

I leave it in there unsure if I will ever actually touch it or see it again, I snatch the video tape quickly popping it into my VCR.

Dangling my feet over the edge of the bed I wait for it to start. Within the next couple of seconds I see a man, a woman, and a toddler on the screen.

"Billy come on, say your first word," his mother calls to him from behind the camera. He stops crawling and rolls over onto his back to begin to laugh. Continuing to giggle for no apparent reason she begs again, "Come on. Say your first word for mama."

Damn even as a baby he was just too happy. How do people get to be that happy all the time?

The video clips to his first basketball game at the age of five I guess. He shoots his very first basket that I'm sure his parents idolized him for at least the next two weeks. Still smiling. I never really realized just how much he enjoyed smiling I guess.

It cuts off again soon after the other team gets the ball back to bring me to another clip of them at a park. The same park he brought me to that night.

"Billy tell dad what you want to do when you grow up?" his farther says pushing him on the swings.

His parents look like nice people. They look they would have really liked me.

"I don't know," he says kicking his feet.

He sounds so cute! I bet that's just what our kids would look like, well our little boy that is.

"You can do anything you want to do," she says from behind the camera. "Don't ever forget that."

"Ok," he says like any other seven year old would. "Anything?"

"Anything," she replies as the camera focuses on Billy's smiling face in the sun.

"I want to grow up and be happy," he chuckles kicking rocks as his dad slows down the swinging.

My hand covers my mouth afraid tears are going to start themselves up again.

"Just happy? Not a firefighter or a police officer like daddy?"

His dad was a cop? Ain't that ironic? He rebels against the law for as long as I can remember and his dad was a cop. A freakin' cop! Some things I will never understand.

"Just happy," he shrugs scratching his slightly curly head.

The camera focuses in on his face one last time before it cuts off for good. I look at the black and white fuzz on the screen realizing something for the first time in a while.

Life isn't just black and white. It isn't just about right and wrong. It's about a lot of the in between. The unjustified, the unspoken, and the unknown are what make life ... well life. Everyone's going to go through so many changes and experiences that will define who they are, but it's the ones you don't think about that will have the strongest shock.

Hopping off my bed to get the tape I notice the pictures from the carnival of Billy and me sitting in my mirror. Slowly reaching to hold them in my hand I study each one. People always say when life hands you lemons make lemonade and other annoying clichés like that, but what do you do when life hands you death?

As I lock eyes on the picture of our lips touching, I remember the kiss I dreamed we shared in front of his grave. When you're handed death ... embrace life.

978-0-595-40818-4
0-595-40818-4

Printed in the United States
69530LVS00005B/47